Sarah Bartrum grew up in the North of England but moved south to study Education at Exeter University. She has travelled extensively around the world and worked in a variety of locations. She now lives in Devon with her husband and two children.

www.sarahbartrum.com

KEEP THEM SAFE

Sarah Bartrum

Thou shalt not covet

1

It was the hair that did it. Flashed gold so bright that it left blue spots before Sid's eyes. A beacon against the drab cement walls; a distraction from the stench of urine. It shot straight through Sid's retina and lit up the dark corners of his brain, the parts that were better kept in shadow.

He was standing with his hands under the dryer when she flew past him. At first he thought he'd seen a vision, his heart leaping up to his head knocking him out and then falling back into his chest to bounce around his rib cage. It was him. It had to be; no one had hair like that, no one. The slam of the cubicle door told him it hadn't been a vision. That streak of shimmering sunshine had been real, it turned his hands watery, he could feel them getting hot and wet despite the warm air from the dryer. The back of his neck prickled. Behind him, there was a rustle of clothing and then the unmistakable tinkle as the child relieved herself. Of course it wasn't him - it had been a girl, there had been a blur of pink too as she whizzed past the urinals and into the toilet. It would never be Tommy, how could it?

His mother had called it liquid gold, and then with a darkening of her eyes 'Midas touch'. It wasn't until years later that Sid began to understand what she meant, but it wasn't Tommy who had the Midas touch, it never had been. He remembered running his fingers through that hair, ruffling his face into its softness. Just like my Tommy, he thought, as the vision and blue spots began to fade. But then he heard the shifting of feet and the flush of the toilet and the sweating started afresh.

She came out of the cubicle holding something yellow in her hand. She thrust it up at him.

'Axihent,' she said with a small down-turn of her lips. 'Din mean it,' she added. 'Mr Man, you dry them pleece.'

Sid stared at her hair; there were soft curls just above her ears, the fringe curving in two different directions. He could feel goose pimples racing along his arms. He shifted his gaze down to meet hers. She had brown eyes; they were staring at him expectantly. Tommy had blue eyes not brown. She frowned and waved the object at him.

Sid automatically took it, his brain rapidly trying to catch up and decipher what she had said - even her words sounded familiar. That delightful childish tone. He looked at his hand; a pair of damp yellow pants moistened his fingers. He too frowned and then at last he shook himself into the present. This wasn't Tommy. He didn't know this girl, had never met her. He understood now what she wanted, and spread the pants out between his two hands holding them under the dryer. He had to press the button again to keep the hot air going. He kept his eyes resolutely on the pants; there was a motif on the front, a grey fat character next to a three-wheeled trike. Tommy had had Winnie the Pooh. Sid smiled to himself and couldn't help looking back at the girl, at the top of her head, the curls, the warm lustre.

'Jessica! Jessica! Where are you?' the voice was loud, angry.

Jessica let out a gasp, and departed as swiftly as she had

arrived. One more flash as the sun struck her head and she was gone. Sid stood staring after her. Sudden pain in his left hand reminded him he was still holding the pants under the blasting hot air. He stuffed them into his pocket, suddenly nervous. A man approached the entrance; Sid had no choice but to march out.

Under the willow tree, a woman was bending down and pointing at Jessica, strong words rushing out of her mouth. Jessica's head was bent but she turned it towards him as he watched. Sid turned and headed in the opposite direction, not daring to look back, not wanting to be caught by that Midas touch, to be caressed by it, drugged by it. He could feel the sweat drying on his forehead as the air swept past his face. He willed himself not to run, his sights locked on the black gates ahead. There was a flutter in his chest, the unravelling had begun.

Joanie looked up from his desk at the clock on the wall, it wasn't quite straight but at least it was correct. Much like his whole office really, it was well equipped, clean, still new-looking but something about it all was slightly off. Like his desk, a smart modern curved woodchip veneer with a boxed shelf on one side. The computer screen in front was just too big so the edge ended up being hidden by the box shelf. Or the desk chair he was sitting in, comfortable, adjustable, but the arms on it prevented him getting close enough to the desk so instead he had to lean forwards to use the keyboard. Still he couldn't complain. It was a vast improvement on the old building, despite the lack of parking. The clock read 9:15; she was five minutes later than usual. But then he could see Kelly's auburn hair through the square window at the top of the door, followed by a smart knock.

'Come in.' The door opened and Kelly appeared with two steaming mugs of coffee. 'Ah, Detective Sergeant Mowbray, what a saviour.'

'Here you go sir, anything exciting to start the week?' She perched on the corner of his desk, folding over the edge of a stack of pink forms.

'I wish.' Joanie lifted his hands indicating the computer screen and the papers strewn across the wooden desk. 'Not what I would call exciting. You know it does make me wonder why we have an administration team when my desk looks like this.'

'That's what you get for being in such a senior position.'

'Well from this senior position, may I remind you that you have your butt, Kelly, on my expensive, superior pink forms?' Joanie noted the smart black skirt fall neatly back into place as Kelly stood up again.

'Sorry sir.' A smile played at the corner of her mouth.

'But you obviously have news.' Joanie sat back and steepled his fingers, 'how is the new boy?'

'You don't miss a thing do you? Well now, Constable Curtis, a little over-eager if you ask me, but it makes a nice change for my team. Some new blood will shake the senior citizens up a bit.'

'I hope you don't talk about me in that tone, aren't I even older than the rest of your team?'

'Yes, but at least you don't keep harping on about what the police used to be able to do, and all this namby-pamby policing nowadays giving the dirty bastards more rights than we have.'

'True, but if you're referring to Barry, which by that voice, I know you are, at least you've got a trustworthy experienced ally, despite his whinging.'

'It's alright, I'm not complaining.' Kelly put up her hands in defence. 'He's a good copper. Besides what I really came here to say is when do you want to meet this new kid Curtis?'

Joanie checked his watch, 'Give me another half an hour with this delightful senior person's junkbox of emails before you send him in.'

Kelly nodded and left.

True to her word, exactly half an hour later, there was another knock at the door before it opened.

'DI Johnson?'

Joanie glanced up at the expectant face.

'Great, they've sent me someone who can't even read.' Ignoring the confused look, Joanie continued ripping open the envelopes, from the morning post, that littered his desk.

'Sir?'

'Try reading the sign on the door again.' Joanie didn't bother to look up, instead he scrunched up envelopes after scanning the contents digesting any important information and disregarding the rest. He filed the papers onto various piles heaped across his desk ignoring the cascading red filing stack.

'Jo-HAN-son,' Joanie continued, 'Detective Inspector Johanson. Stop standing in the doorway Curtis and get yourself a seat.'

'Sorry sir.' The officer closed the door. Joanie stared directly at Curtis as he stood uncertainly, a mug in one hand and a doughnut in the other. Joanie moved a couple of papers aside and pointed at the small rectangle of space on his desk.

'Thanks, it's someone's birthday,' he indicated the doughnut which was already shedding sugar crystals onto the veneer. Curtis pulled himself a chair from the corner and sat on the far side of the desk. The young man's Adam's apple wiggled as he swallowed nervously under Joanie's intent gaze.

'I assume Detective Sergeant Mowbray has shown you around.'

'Er yes, she's been very helpful, I haven't...'

Joanie waited, raising his eyebrows as Curtis paused.

'I haven't worked for a woman before.'

'I see.' Joanie studied the younger man's face, wondering if that might be a problem. 'You could learn a lot from Detective Sergeant Mowbray, consider yourself lucky.'

'Yes sir.' Curtis looked down at the doughnut.

'Go ahead.' Joanie rocked back in his chair studying Curtis.

His head a mass of unruly blond curls yet his face set square, the strong jawline moving rapidly to finish the doughnut.

Joanie made a steeple with his fingers, flexing them in and out of a prayer position.

'Could I ask you something sir?' Curtis began, leaving a shower of white on one of the piles of paper.

Joanie regarded the raised eyebrows and gave a short nod of his head.

'How come they call you Joanie?'

Joanie could see the wide blue eyes behind Curtis's last piece of doughnut. He leaned forwards, his face coming uncomfortably close to Curtis.

'I won't say this again Curtis. It's Detective Inspector JoHANson to you.' He pronounced each word with great precision. Curtis stopped chewing until Joanie sat back and began steepling his hands again.

'Sorry sir.'

Curtis sipped his coffee in silence.

'What do you know about me Curtis?' He fished out the penknife from his back pocket and began scraping beneath his nails. Small white flecks fell onto his shirtfront.

'Er how do you mean sir?'

'Just tell me what you think you know.'

'OK, well you're one of the best when it comes to detection, that's what the boys said even in my last unit.'

'I'm not interested in flattery Curtis,' Joanie's icy tone cut across.

Curtis coughed self-consciously, 'You're head of the Public Protection Unit for the Eastern Unit, most commonly involved with sex crimes and family crime. Last year you were commended for your part in the Simpson case.' Curtis paused struggling to think.

Joanie stopped scraping and glanced at the certificate on the wall. The Chief Constable's commendation, and justly deserved too. However, most officers knew about it. He certainly wasn't impressed with Curtis's information so far.

'Umm, you're married,' he pointed at the ring on Joanie's left hand. 'Over forty er..'

Joanie laughed, 'That's it keep guessing.' Curtis coloured slightly and said nothing. A dark look turned his angelic face into something far more earthy. So this blondie wasn't all innocence and light Joanie noticed. Rather like seeing a Barbie doll with its head on backwards. Joanie recognised how useful that look might be in their line of work. He nodded slowly. Carefully he flicked the penknife closed and replaced it in his back pocket. He struck forward abruptly, placing his hands firmly onto the desk.

'Constable Dan Curtis.' He stated. 'Born February 22nd 1975. Married to Bella three and a half years ago, honeymooned in the Dominican Republic. You have a son, second birthday last month.' He barked these statements at Curtis without pause.

'Suspected joyriding when you were thirteen but never charged. Joined the police six years ago. Been working the beat for four, and missed promotion due to an unfortunate incident. Inquiry. And I believe your career has suffered since. You play football, not bad by all accounts, and you read Stephen King.' Joanie sat back and studied the younger man. He looked shocked, pale around his blue eyes and a purple tinge to his lips. He was breathing hard.

'Relax,' Joanie stood up, 'I like to know who I'm working with, that's all.' Joanie took two box files from one of the shelves by the door; dumped them in front of Curtis on the desk on top of his papers.

'Read these, and cross reference them on the computer,' he commanded, 'It will give you an idea what we do here.' He checked his watch, 'Give me a brief on the top three nutters you think we need to watch and why you think they should merit our time and effort. As you can see, today I'm a bloody secretary.' Joanie spread his fingers at the multi-coloured paperwork and the screen saver bouncing across the blackness. He yanked his coat from the back of his chair, hung it on the hook by the door, rolled up his sleeves and walked through the doorway.

Out in the open-plan office Kelly was on the phone, she waved Joanie over. Making her excuses she dropped the receiver back in its cradle.

'What do you think?' she nodded back at Curtis who was sitting down at his desk with the files.

Joanie smiled. 'More to the point, what do you think Detective Sergeant Mowbray, he's on your team.'

'You've read his file, he might be trouble. Feels a bit stiff to me, but then it is his first day,' she kept his gaze.

'Constable Curtis will reveal his colours given time, people always do.'

Joanie returned Kelly's suspicious look, he knew he couldn't fob her off that easily, they'd known each other too long.

'But what's your gut reaction?' she persisted.

Joanie smiled and started to walk away patting his large stomach. 'That eating the last doughnut was better for Curtis than me,' he called back. But she was right; there was an edge in that cold look he'd given Joanie. The report from personnel hinted at some problems. It might be nothing. Perhaps he'd have to shave off the sharp corners of this newbie, 'Time will tell,' he said to himself as he went to check the empty doughnut tray.

Sid strode purposefully across the park, ignoring a faint call from the woman. Out onto the street by the bus stop, he swung left along Barrack Road. The sleeves on his jumper stuck to his skin, the sun was already high and it weighed heavy on his body. The treasure in his pocket felt so enormous he was sure someone would notice. He had not received such a precious prize in a long time. At the traffic lights he waited impatiently for an old lady in a blue Micra. Across and up the snicket banked by high wooden fences. A black and white cat watched him coming down the narrow path and leapt deftly up and over into the nearest garden. Sid met no one, his sweat-streaked face unnoticed and the agitated way his legs moved not quite in rhythm but more of a stumbling hurry. Finally he reached the doorway of No.10a Compton Drive and unlocked the door.

Inside the hall he tore off his damp sweatshirt and hung it on a peg. He paused listening through the wall for his neighbours, nothing. He looked at the flight of stairs before him and slowly hauled himself up. It was only when he shut the door at the top of the stairs that he felt safe. The familiar smells of his flat relaxed him further. His T-shirt was damp under the arms but he ignored this and flicked on his computer. He needed to calm down, 'stay in control' as Dr Casey put it. He just had time to do a little browsing before work. As he sat down the bulge in his trouser pocket nudged his thigh. He tensed; slowly he withdrew the panties from his pocket and laid them on the desk next to his computer. His hand fluttered over them, touching the picture, stroking the cotton. He picked them up and held them close to his face. The stench of urine surprised him and he dropped them. His head swimming with that distinctive fug, the acid smell of fear, of failure. The trembling came from his chest and radiated outwards to his fingers. Shutting his eyes; Sid could feel Tommy's back pressed against him, he hugged him tight, whispered in his ear. The smell so strong, he didn't even know which of them had done it. They shook together, and Sid pressed his lips into Tommy's hair. They lay silent, listening, the smell, an almost living thing in the small space under the bed.

A loud thump came from downstairs. Sid's eyes flicked open, the neighbours were in. He picked up the pants and thrust them into the washing machine. Back at his desk the computer had booted up. Sid could see Jessica in his mind's eye, the top of her head, those gorgeous curls. He sighed, the hair, the innocence, the blue eyes. He knew his psychologist, Dr

Casey, would not approve, but it was she that had inadvertently set him onto these websites.

'Perhaps you should find a group that has suffered in the same way, who share your feelings. If it's too much to go for a group session, there are lots of chat-rooms on the internet these days where you can anonymously seek support.'

It had been one of the few sessions that had actually got him thinking. Finding people with the same feelings as he had. He'd upgraded his computer and got broadband, but it had still taken almost a month of surfing to find his first site. Now of course, he visited several, and they did help, she was right. They fed the craving and quieted the memories like nothing else.

He was interrupted by the bedside alarm clock bleeping irritably. 'Fuck.' Sid looked across at the clock beside his bed, 11:30am. A young boy stared at him from the computer screen, impassive to the beeping of the alarm. Sid stared back at the boy. No, not this one, but he needed to remember this website and the code word he'd been given in the chat room. Switching the alarm off he picked up the novel he'd been reading beside his bed, turned to page 100 and with a pencil wrote the code word in the margin. Back on his computer he glared at the web address, then took his pencil into the bathroom and awkwardly scrawled inside the toilet roll. Once he was satisfied, he cleared the saved files and closed down the computer.

He changed clothes and flung on a bright fluorescent jacket. He hated this uniform. On the one hand it made him utterly visible and on the other, anonymous within the huge supermarket car park. His shift started at midday and with it being Monday, he could expect it to be busy.

David was in the staffroom when Sid arrived. He nodded at the kid, and fetched himself a mug of tea. David beamed at him, his blond hair catching the sunlight from the window.

'Morning Sid.'

'Alright?' He slid into a chair opposite David.

'Have a nice weekend?' David grinned in that vacant way of

his.

Sid couldn't help but smile to himself. The funny thing was, it wouldn't matter what he said, David would still be smiling. He could tell him about the girl in the park that morning and David would keep on smiling and ask if they'd had a nice time together. Of course he wouldn't - tell him, that is. David was useful but you had to know how to play him. The boy had no concept of what a secret was. The bakery lads had taken advantage a couple of months back describing all kinds of sordid deeds that David might like to do with a woman. The problem was David then approached female customers asking them if they ever did those kinds of things. There were complaints of course and the bakery lot received official warnings. It wasn't difficult to find out who had been leading him along; all you had to do was ask David and with that big smile of his, he was happy to oblige.

They finished their tea and left the building together. At the entrance David jigged excitedly from foot to foot. Sid could count almost every tooth in that wide grin.

'OK, you take the front.' he conceded.

'Oh good, good, good. Thanks Sid.' David raced off to the nearest trolley-collecting point and began gathering the trolleys into a line. Sid headed across the black and white stripes and down the footway to the rear of the car park.

In many ways Sid was grateful for having David as his shift partner. He was simple and kind; he didn't delve into your social life and even when he did ask, it didn't really matter what you told him, anything would suffice just as long as it was believable. You didn't need to worry too much about the small details, David was unlikely to remember or notice inconsistencies. So long as Sid always treated David seriously there was never a problem; if he thought you were making fun of him, there would be trouble, and Sid liked to avoid trouble. He suspected the lad had been bullied mercilessly at school and perhaps that was why he now took great offence if he thought you were making fun of him. Like that time when that annoying woman wanted the trolley right at the end of a line that David had carefully put together.

'No not that one, the one at the end please.' A woman with a cigarette pointed.

'This one's a good one miss.' David tested the trolley rolling it up and down the ramp onto the walkway. Sid watched them as he trundled his own line of trolleys past.

'It's got a wonky wheel,' she insisted, 'I want that one.'

David again thrust the trolley in his hands forwards and backwards. 'No it hasn't,' and then suddenly his happy disposition was replaced by slit eyes and a deep frown.

'Are you taking the piss?'

The woman stepped back looking shocked.

'I most certainly am not.'

'I think you are.'

It was at that point that Sid had slid between them. The urge simply to watch and see if David would be angry enough to slug the bitch was almost overpowering but the consequences would not do Sid any favours. David couldn't hit the customers, he'd be out straight away and where would that leave Sid? With a new cunt that kept sticking his nose in Sid's business. No, Sid's ethos was to keep things always on an even keel. He took great pains to keep the equilibrium in his life. Dr Casey approved of keeping normality. It helped to contain the times when he stepped dangerously close to the edge.

'David could you help me with this lot? It's a bit awkward.' David's face changed instantly like clicking your fingers.

'Sure,' he beamed and immediately turned to help push the trolleys across to the entrance. The woman stood forgotten fuming at the faulty trolley.

David was like that; he would be Sid's best friend if Sid wanted him to be. At times David's naivety was like a drug pulling Sid in, whispering of the possibilities, of how he could use David's naive ability to his own use.

He watched him now, a young woman smiling at him as David handed out one of the special trolleys with a baby seat. He was a Day-Glo beacon of innocence that women were maternally drawn to. Sometimes, if Sid was lucky, he could stand nearby unnoticed. Of course David was a double-edged sword. On the one hand Sid could hide behind him, but he also filled him with hatred; the way people would come up and ask David for a trolley. He'd even seen a child happily hold David's hand to cross the striped pathway. They thought he was cute. Sid wasn't cute. He'd never been cute. At school the other kids had mocked his lanky hair and called him skeleton when he changed for PE. Sid had spent his whole life being avoided by beautiful people. Sid sometimes dreamed of taking over David's body, pushing out the dumb trusting brain and replacing it with his own sharp one. Imagining a child's soft hand in his own, to lift a child up and into the trolley, his large hands wrapped around the child's chest under their armpits. A life where children trusted and loved him unconditionally. Just like Tommy had.

There it was again, those memories, swimming like tadpoles just below the surface. Years ago, they'd been deeply buried in the mud at the bottom, but now it seemed they increasingly reached the surface. Was it an age thing, his memory playing tricks on him? Or maybe it was like Dr Casey said, that his past required resolution without which he wouldn't be able to 'move on' as she put it. These memories had started to grow legs, mature tadpoles popping their noses above the surface when he didn't expect it. Like this morning, that had been a fully-grown toad leaping out. He could feel his breath trembling again as he thought about the two of them under the bed. Sid scratched hard at the scars on his arms until they stung, and all he could think about was that pain.

He stopped and looked up, the trolleys were scattered across this end of the car park. Although it wasn't raining, the handles were damp from an earlier shower. Sid gathered himself and the trolleys together, increasing the length of his metallic line snaking its way across the tarmac. Sid saw a flash of David's teeth even from back here as he gave out a trolley to a woman holding a toddler's hand.

Sid took a deep breath. He would turn on the washing machine when he got home, but this simple thought made him pause as he considered the tiny item that would be swallowed up by the rest of his clothes, thrown around the drum, soaked, soaped and finally dried, and then what? He watched again, in his mind's eye, as Jessica darted out of the doorway. She had been knickerless. The thought made him tingle and a static shock from the handle of the trolley felt like the mental slap from Dr Casey. Fuck it. He didn't need her any more. He was fine, perfectly fine, nothing bad had happened. He wasn't doing anything wrong, and he certainly wasn't having a breakdown. With a frown he leant hard against the stack of trolleys and began pushing it back towards the entrance.

Joanie was deep in the middle of filing a load of the pink forms when Kelly knocked again later that day.

'Yes.'

'Something's come in,' she pointed at Joanie's computer. Curtis hovered impatiently by her left shoulder, obviously pleased to get an interruption to his study.

Joanie wished he felt the same. Although he hated paperwork and the never-ending inbox, there were times when he delved into the mountain and things began to make sense and he was able to reduce it or at least pass it on to more deserving officers.

'Go ahead.'

'Some woman claims a guy in the park stole her kid's pants. Not much to go on I'm afraid, she seemed kind of embarrassed to report it.'

'Did she see him take the pants?'

'No.' Kelly shrugged. 'In fact the statement doesn't really

point to any misdemeanour as such but I thought it was worth an interview at least. I'll take the doll with me.'

'Fine,' Joanie sighed slapping his hands on the maze of papers. He looked up at Kelly with a shrug at the work.

She smiled back. He knew she could sympathise with admin, every police officer could. With her back to Curtis, who was still looking on with interest, she gave a questioning glance over her shoulder. Joanie caught exactly what she meant. It was a good idea. He desperately wanted to make more headway through this pile today. Curtis had surprised him, diligently reading the folders he'd been given and checking things on the computer. He'd worked quietly too, not asked loads of questions, which was what Joanie had expected.

'Curtis.'

'Yep.' Curtis straightened and stepped forward immediately.

'Alright, off you go.' He pointed his biro at Curtis. 'You're there to observe, take notes from the brilliant Detective Sergeant Mowbray, got it?'

Kelly grinned and led the way out of the office. The door swung shut and a yellow sheet blew off the desk onto the floor uncovering the phone that had lain hidden and forgotten for the last hour. Joanie tapped his pen on the desk, what was it he was going to check? He glanced at the clock on the wall. Of course.

He checked the computer and noted a familiar name. Picking up the phone, he rang the Detention Officer downstairs. 'Morning Gary, anyone still in the housing block?'

'Just two, sir, Joseph Brown, he's a new one, breaching the peace. And our Mr Charles.'

'Not again. Where did they pick him up this time?'

'Displaying in St Mary's - the church that is, not the school, yesterday morning. But that's not all, I'm afraid, he attacked some guy.'

'Attacked? That doesn't sound like our Mr Charles.'

'No, that's what I thought, but we've got several witnesses.

However, I'm about to let him go; the victim has dropped the charges. He's up with PC Short at the moment.'

'Can you hang on to Mr Charles for another ten minutes?'

'Sure.'

Joanie leapt up and strode across the room and through the main office. He bounded up the stairs two at a time. Just as he rounded the banister at the top, a blond-haired man came through the door and started down. Joanie caught a brief glimpse of a bruised eye. He turned and watched the man reach the landing below. Joanie watched the figure descend in deliberate steps but he couldn't help thinking this man would rather be running down. Joanie thrust open the doors and cornered Short by the coffee machine.

'Was that him, with the black eye?'

'Mr Charles's handiwork, you mean? Yep, must have given 'im a pretty good thwack.' Short smiled. 'Not bad for an old fella.'

'So why's he not pressing charges?'

'Well, he said it didn't seem fair,' Short shrugged.

'And what exactly is that supposed to mean?' Joanie could feel his anger rising, not so much at Short's pathetic reply but at the snub of the witness.

'The guy reckoned Mr Charles must be a sad shit and suggested we get him help rather than locking him up.'

'Oh, did he?' Joanie wasn't amused. Even though it was virtually a daily occurrence when members of the public told them what they ought to be doing, it seemed at odds with such an obvious physical assault.

'So you dropped the charges?' Joanie was standing too close; he could smell the other man's coffee.

'Er, yeah, there didn't seem much point, I mean, it's not like Mr Charles has got a record for that sort of thing.'

Joanie backed off. Short was right. Although they could still use Purple-eye as a hostile witness, there didn't really seem much point. Mr Charles wasn't a danger to people; at least, he hadn't been up to now.

Joanie let Short go past and got himself a coffee and then, with second thoughts, he got another one and went down to the cells.

'Here.' Joanie walked into the interview room and proffered the plastic cup.

'Joanie! What a nice surprise.' Mr Charles accepted the coffee.

They sat together in companionable silence sipping their respective drinks.

'Gary said I could go, but when he said you'd like a word, well, I couldn't turn down an old friend could I?' Mr Charles gave him a shy look.

Joanie had to smile; of course, Mr Charles wouldn't have been given any choice.

'How's the lovely Sammy?' Mr Charles continued.

'She's fine, just fine,' which reminded him, he ought to ring her tonight, she was about to take her finals and she'd appreciate a call.

Funny, here was Mr Charles, such a sweet old man in all respects except when it came to hanging his willy out in public places. Sammy had been seventeen when she'd first seen Mr Charles in the high street, had thought him hilarious in his classic raincoat. But he'd never been known to be violent, quite the opposite in fact.

'Listen,' Joanie looked directly at Mr Charles' face. 'About this incident yesterday,' Joanie shrugged as if to show he needed an explanation.

'I'm sorry.' Mr Charles looked genuinely upset; his white moustache drooped down at the corners. 'There was nobody in the park, you see, and the high street was full of yobbos. Can't see why everybody shops on Sundays nowadays anyway.' He wiped a drop of coffee from the edge of his lip. 'It was one of those impulsive moments going in the church. I haven't been in a church for years. Are you religious, Joanie?'

'No, no, not really, I used to go as a kid. Carry on.'

'Well, it was just all a bit peculiar really. Getting Mr John Thomas out in the church and all that, and that man, well, he was in the way, sort of. It was all wrong, all wrong.' Mr Charles began to wring his hands, shaking them at the empty coffee cup.

Joanie let his hand rest gently on one of the fluttering limbs. 'But why did you hit him?'

'I won't do it again, don't know why, got angry at God or something, I don't know, it just was all wrong, all wrong. I won't do it in there again, I promise Joanie, really I do.' Tears rolled down Mr Charles' face, wetting his moustache that made it droop even further. It was almost comical watching Mr Charles if it wasn't so sad. Joanie patted his hand; this was the gentle soul he was used to.

'OK, sure, but you know it's illegal to do it anywhere, Mr Charles. We will be charging you for the indecent exposure. Aren't you still on probation from last time? You can't keep flashing anywhere you please.'

'I know, I know, I'm sorry.'

'And what exactly is this?' Joanie held up a strange contraption of leather straps and buckles Gary had given him at the desk.

'Ooh good, can I have it back? It's a lovely device, I sent off for it from the Netherlands.' He sniffed and wiped his eyes. Leaning forward, he whispered confidentially. 'It holds it up, you see. It gets more difficult at my age, you must know, Joanie, you're not so young.'

Joanie blinked but otherwise remained impassive, ignoring the slight against his virility.

'I could show you if you like.' Mr Charles picked up the straps, his eyes alight with amusement.

Joanie snatched it back and stood up.

'Forget it. This is confiscated. Don't let me see you back here, Mr Charles. Much as we like you, we don't want another visit OK?'

'Sure, Joanie.'

Joanie opened the door to leave.

'Hey,' Mr Charles stood up. 'Make sure you say hi to Sammy for me.'

Joanie shook his head and left.

2

The sky had begun to darken when Sid finished his shift. The evening air had a balmy feel to it, as if the sun hadn't quite let go of its hold on the sky. Sid scribbled quickly on his time sheet and left the building at a trot. Hurrying along the main street, he swung into a lit doorway and ordered fish and chips. Sid snatched the offered bag of grease and headed home. Upstairs he opened the bundle on the small desk by the window. With his hands he stuffed the food into his wet mouth. Fat smeared his lips, which he wiped away with the back of his hand. When he finished he scrunched up the paper and chucked it towards the bin, it missed. Throwing off his clothes, he opened the cubicle door of the shower in the corner of his tiny bathroom and stepped into the hot dribble of water. The shower gel was almost finished but he eked it out with some extra water. It was important to be clean. Dripping on the bare floor, Sid pushed his wet hair aside searching for his towel. It was bunched up on the floor beside his bed. He grabbed it and rubbed vigorously at his white skin. It left him red and blotchy. Next he threw all his clothes in the washing machine, ignoring the yellow item at the bottom; he grabbed a few more from the laundry basket and switched it on. No one could call him dirty now; not since school had he had people complain about him being the smelly kid, the dirty kid, skanky lanky. He didn't care what Dr Casey had said about that, it was better to be clean than smelly and if that meant washing his penis ten times in the shower then so be it. What did Dr Casey know anyway? All she had was a slimy cunt.

After dressing again, he went to his desk, pausing only briefly, Dr Casey's voice wittering on in his head about other hobbies and keeping his time focused. He stopped her. If she'd seen Jessica's hair, she would have understood and known how important it was. Sid licked his lips and began reviewing the pictures on the screen. At times his hand clenched tightly on the mouse, at others he had to turn away reminding himself why he was doing this, his member hot and hard straining against his trousers. Sid bit his lip. The scars on his arms tightening white, the urge to scratch them, to break them was undeniable but he kept his right hand on the mouse and his left on the keyboard.

At eleven Sid stopped, the picture on the screen had not changed for the last ten minutes, beads of sweat stood out prominently on Sid's forehead and his penis ached. He turned from the computer and threw himself onto the bed, his right hand moving rapidly as he sobbed into the pillow.

Afterwards he felt purged, light headed and bright. He hung the wet washing around the room taking the yellow panties into the bathroom where he placed them delicately on the tiny radiator behind the door. Back at his desk, Sid moved the keyboard and mouse to one side, the screen was already dark. And out of the drawer he withdrew his drawing materials; lining them up carefully onto the flat surface. A pencil, sharpened to a fine point, his rubber, a clean sheet of paper, a second pencil, this one darker, softer. A sense of calm settled over him as he picked up the pencil and began to draw. Dr Casey approved of his drawing, a 'healthy hobby' she called it, but then she'd never seen his work.

The light was on in the hall when Joanie got home. He hung his jacket in the cupboard. Pausing in the hall mirror, he looked at his face. A dark shadow across his chin and a couple of saddlebags under his eyes. He used his forefingers to smooth them away but as soon as his fingers left his face, they settled back like old friends. Then it occurred to Joanie that something was different, he checked his watch; it was five past six. Normal time. Then he sniffed the air expectantly and listened. There was a gentle clink but nothing more. No smells of cooking or the clang of pan lids that he was used to. Joanie walked down the hall and pushed open the door into the kitchen. Margret was stood leaning over the kitchen table. In front of her was a vase of carnations, a large piece of paper with some tentative brush strokes and a jar of murky water.

'What are you doing?' Joanie cocked his head around his wife's shoulder and could make out the green stems and the start of a flower.

'What does it look like?' Margret kissed his cheek as he dropped his chin onto her shoulder.

'I see. Any dinner?'

There was an almost imperceptible sigh that Joanie felt under his chin rather than heard.

'You can have salad, there's some ham in the fridge.'

'Have you eaten?'

'No,' Margret was staring at the pink marks she had made on the paper. She swirled the brush in the jam jar, 'I'm not hungry.'

'Oh.' Joanie decided it was probably best not to pursue this further and busied himself putting a plate of cold ham, lettuce, tomato and cucumber together. He pulled out a strange looking pot.

'What's this?'

Margret barely glanced at him, 'I think you can read.'

Joanie took the lid off, sniffed, stuck his finger in and licked it, bit strange he thought. He put it back and instead he went in search of something more traditional; finding a fresh loaf in the bread bin, he carved off a thick slice.

'Are you sure you don't want anything?'

'No I'm fine.' Margret added a couple more pink strokes and stood back closing one eye.

'Don't sit there!' she shouted.

'What?' Joanie had pushed the paint palette aside to give just enough room for his plate at the table.

'I don't want all your crumbs and mess getting on my painting. Take it into the lounge can't you?'

Joanie stiffened seeing how quickly this might degenerate into an argument. They seemed to be getting more common these days, flaring out of nowhere and leaving him feeling weak and confused. He picked up his plate and left the kitchen. In the lounge he found the coffee table was clear with not a magazine or newspaper in sight, now where had she put those? Instead he picked up the telephone handset from the windowsill.

'Hello pumpkin,' Joanie spoke into the receiver clasped to his ear.

'Hi Dad, what's up?'

'Nothing much, thought I'd see how your studying's going. Had your first exam yet?'

'No, this Friday. Jemma's been helping me with the genetics module.'

'Genetics? Isn't that for medical degrees?'

'It's all part of biology, not my favourite part that's for sure, but I'm getting there. Dad... are you eating?'

'Mmmm,' Joanie swallowed his mouthful and cleared his throat. 'Your mother banished me from the kitchen. I think she might have given up cooking.'

'What? She loves cooking, what have you done this time?'

Joanie paused for a second, this was a fair question, there had been times in the past when Margret had stopped doing certain chores, like washing the clothes when he'd accidentally sprayed them, hanging on the washing line, with garden fertiliser. Another time she had refused to vacuum for three weeks when Samantha and four of her friends walked mud through the entire house.

'She's painting,' Joanie replied popping a cherry tomato into his mouth.

'Mum doesn't paint. Why on earth would she be redecorating the kitchen?'

Joanie nearly spat the tomato across the room. 'No, no,' even the very idea of Margret taking up any of the 'man's' jobs around the house was farcical. 'She's painting a bunch of flowers in a bowl.'

Joanie could hear his daughter's giggles down the phone, and once she'd started he couldn't help but spray some breadcrumbs back onto his plate and snuffle into his hanky.

'Sammy stop it, she's in the kitchen. You'll get me into trouble and then I won't be allowed to eat for a month.'

'Dad, look, I've got to go, I'm meeting Matt at eight. You could always try those meals for one from Tesco's.'

'Thanks for that. Oh, and do you remember a Mr Charles?'

'Who?' her voice sounded faint for a moment and Joanie wondered if he'd lost her attention already.

'You know, the flasher, when you were seventeen.'

'Oh him. God is he still around?' he heard her giggle into the phone. 'He was the one with that little pink woolly thing on his dick.' She hooted with laughter down the phone. 'It's about time you put him away somewhere Dad for his own sake.' It was good to hear her laugh; he missed it round the house.

'Got to go Dad, see ya.' She hung up and Joanie forked up the remains on his plate.

Sid was on the early shift next day, sweating under a cloudless sky as the tarmac baked beneath his feet. It was almost time to stop; he scanned the car park but couldn't see David anywhere. Then he spotted the manager standing at the entrance frowning, with his hands on his hips. Sid followed his line of sight and spotted David who'd stripped his top off standing bare-chested probably in response to several semi-naked customers that had gone into the store. No wonder Sid hadn't spotted him, he rushed across.

'Put your shirt on,' he hissed grabbing the T-shirt from David's belt where he'd tucked it into the back of trousers.

'What's up Sid?'

'Put your shirt on now!' Sid thrust the T-shirt at David.

'But it's too hot.' David sulked pulling it down over his head.

Just then the manager arrived.

Sid put a protective hand on David's shoulder. 'It's fine, everything's fine, it's his first hot day,' gabbled Sid.

The manager looked from Sid to David and back again. Without a word, he nodded his head and turned back to the store.

'What did he want Sid?'

'It's alright. You mustn't take your shirt off David, you're at work, remember?'

'But everybody else has'

'Those are the customers. You have to look decent.' Sid paused trying to decide how to explain. 'It's the right thing to do.'

'OK.' David smiled. 'Thanks for being my friend Sid.'

Sid realised he still had hold of David's shoulder. He gave it a little squeeze and then dropped his hand. A funny feeling tickled his chest. Was that the feeling of friendship? Did Sid the loner actually have a friend? Sid looked at David's innocent beam. He wasn't sure he was ready for that.

'Time's up, let's get this back.' Sid nodded at David's stack of trolleys and together they pushed it into the lines by the entrance.

'Will you have ice-cream today?' David bobbed along beside

him as they made their way down the vegetables.

'I don't know, maybe.'

'I'll have ice-cream on Saturday, when me and Roddy go to the arcade in Bournemouth.'

Sid nodded; it seemed to be a monthly event for David, meeting up with his friend in Bournemouth.

'We're going to play the racing car game, and the money slides thing, you know where it knocks the coins off. Roddy won two pounds last time and he said it's my turn to win this time. Do you think I will?'

Sid looked at David's wide hopeful face. 'Maybe.'

'I'm playing football this afternoon. I've got me some football friends.'

This was new; Sid glanced at David out of the corner of his eye.

'Do you know the football field?'

'No.' Sid shoved open the swing doors at the end by the cheese stack.

'Down by the river, near the back of the church.' David jiggered about excitedly. Sid tried not to let himself get irritated by this overgrown child.

'Do you want to come? I'm sure they'd let you play too. It's the boys that live on my street, they're fun, and they let me be goalie. Will you come?'

Sid collected his things from the locker. 'No.' he said.

'They're really nice; they don't take the piss or anything.' David kept trying.

'I don't play football,' Sid watched David's face fall, 'but I'm sure you'll have fun.'

As he strode back down the aisle past the potatoes, he stopped and remembered the shower gel. He selected a green tube and grabbed some more milk on his way.

It was only when Sid was back in his flat changing out of his uniform that he thought about what David had said. Playing football; with children. Now where did he say it was? Sid stared out of the window; the sky had gathered a few fluffs of cotton but remained otherwise blue. Sid tried to picture the path by the river. It had been a while since he'd walked that way, and maybe he'd take a look. Dr Casey came into his head, warning him to avoid situations of temptation. But it was hot, the flat stifling even with the windows open, he was just going for a walk that was all. He pulled on a T-shirt and a sweatshirt, he knew he'd be too hot, but he hated to let people see his arms. In fact he hated anybody seeing any part of him, which was why he kept his dark hair long and never, wore shorts. Being beautiful with brown skin was for other people, not him. Pale and sickly, his skin white and often flaky where the edges of his socks rubbed his ankles. Too many taunts at school had taught him to stay covered. It made him more invisible. Imagine if he went out today with bare arms. The whiteness of his skin would reflect the sun so brightly that people would stop in the street and stare. They'd probably even start pointing their bony self-righteous fingers at him. They'd start talking about him and shouting rude things at him. Sid clenched his fists, fucking people and their fucking ideas, always trying to fuck him up. He could hear them screaming in his head, 'Fucking pervert, fucking whitey, take it up the arse do you?' Sid stood trembling, his arms wrapped around his head. For a second he wasn't sure where he was, a red haze had filled him so that when he looked up and saw his reflection in the cracked mirror it was a surprise to see he was at home. Breathing deeply he went over to the chest of drawers and put his hands on the little clothes. The new pants lay on top, pride of place. He stood quite still, concentrating on each breath allowing the feel of the children's clothes and the exquisite pleasure of where they'd come from to calm his mind.

He found the river path easily enough and turned towards the church. A little further along a mowed field opened up on the left with a single white goal post. There were no children playing but two mothers had laid down a rug and were sitting with a baby between them and another in its pram. Sid wished he had a dog. If you had a dog, people expected you to be wandering along and pausing now and then. You could go in and out of parks as often as you wished. Sid had tried with a Jack Russell puppy. It had been brilliant at first, luring children over and giving him a great excuse to hang around the playground. But at home, it peed on his towel on the floor and the neighbours complained about it barking while he was at work. White hairs stuck to his clothes and Sid discovered he didn't actually like stroking it; skin was so much smoother than the short coarse fur. One weekend Sid decided to go to Norfolk, he couldn't take the dog so he left it behind. It chewed up the bedspread and was lying ill and panting on the floor when he got back. The next day people in the park wanted to know what was wrong with it and kept coming up to him to ask questions. Sid was quite particular about smells, and the little Jack Russell just didn't smell right. The kitchen rubbish bin was one thing, but damp dog and doggy poo under the bed was quite another. Then the landlord sent a rude letter about him not being allowed to have pets. After one particularly annoying evening when the dog had impatiently fussed at his feet and caused him to waste two sheets of drawing paper, he took it to the industrial estate and bashed its head with a brick.

Sid continued along the path, averting his eyes from the women. A little way ahead a bench stood looking over the river encouraging you to 'Rest with George and Mary 1997'. Sid did so and wondered what time the kids might be about. A couple of ducks swam over to him and hopped out waiting on the riverbank. Sid ignored them and closed his eyes for a minute. The sun was hot on his eyelids, making blooms of gold and red across his eyeballs.

When Joanie arrived the following morning, the office was already stuffy. He cranked open the window. The double-glazing moved slowly on the complicated fixings, opening only 3 inches at most, a safety feature to prevent him hurling himself out the window. Not that he had any intention of doing so, at least not down onto the bike park below. Joanie noted there were two bicycles in a rack made for twenty. Another ingenious improvement that didn't quite fit; very few were brave enough to cycle in to work given the surrounding dual carriageway and commuter roads. Another valuable parking space lost. Temperature controlled using the latest state-of-the-art thermo-something or other they'd been told. Joanie believed there was some expensive system that magnified the outside temperature and brought it inside. Thus in winter, his office was a fridge, and now that spring had arrived, it would soon be time to wear his swimming trunks at work. Joanie leaned a little harder on the window hoping to force it open a little more.

'Morning sir,' Curtis bumped his way into the room and put a mug down on Joanie's desk. 'Kelly told me how you like it.'

Joanie looked at the mug calculating the hue, he looked up at Curtis. 'More milk next time.'

The muscles in Curtis' jaw clenched. 'Yes sir.'

Joanie merely nodded. 'I don't suppose she could have supplied you with a fan too could she? Prop open the door will you?'

Curtis wedged a Styrofoam cup from the bin under the door letting in the general hubbub of the main office. Phones trilled and voices wavered up and down.

'Tell me,' Joanie sat himself at the desk, 'how did you get on yesterday?'

'OK, there was nothing much the woman could say.'

'Not that.' Joanie pointed with his mug to Curtis' desk beyond the door. 'I've already read the report Kelly entered about the interview yesterday.' Joanie picked up a sheet of paper from the desk. 'You were creating a report for me Curtis about the cases you thought seemed important.'

'Sure.' Curtis looked worried.

'Do you need more time?' Joanie watched him. Curtis shuffled his feet, shook his head and stepped out of the door to grab some papers.

'Er.' Curtis returned with a sheet of hand-written scrawls and pulled a chair closer. 'Ok,' he began.

Joanie leaned back and listened. He watched the way Curtis moved his mouth, how often his eyes came to rest on Joanie and on the paper. The boy stopped often, running his finger down the page looking for something. A thin line of sweat twinkled from his smooth upper lip. Joanie said nothing, occasionally nodding and sipping his coffee. Despite the hesitancy, Curtis spoke clearly and Joanie was pleased with the analysis so far.

'Is that it?' Joanie finally asked after a long silence.

'Er, yeah, it's as far as I've got,' Curtis stared back.

'What about John Duncombe, Peter Nevis and Marisa Rovira?'

'I haven't got to those cases yet.' At least he was honest Joanie mused.

He took the sheet of paper from Curtis and scanned it. The handwriting was almost illegible, the words leaning down across the page, cutting across the lines and sometimes running into each other.

'Can you read this?'

Curtis laughed nervously, 'not always.'

Standing up, Joanie turned his back on Curtis and scanned the bookshelf on the wall behind the desk. He ran his finger along the titles then pulled one out and tossed it at Curtis.

'What's this?' Curtis turned it over in his hands.

'Speed reading,' Joanie explained. 'I need you to be fast but effective. What you've told me is passable, your reasoning shows promise although you might wish to review what you've written about the Bob Grindhead case. However, the biggest nut of the lot of them is Peter Nevis, and you haven't even glanced at that case yet.'

Curtis lowered his gaze.

'Another thing,' Joanie tossed the sheet of paper back at him. 'Learn to type. This isn't going to get you anywhere, you'd have to rewrite it for anyone else to understand and that amounts to double time on the same piece of work. Short's team have got a CD Rom that'll teach you to type. See if you can borrow it.' Joanie could see he'd said enough. Curtis was looking pink and moody.

'Finish the other cases, read up yesterday's interview on the computer and any spare moments you have, improve your skills,' Joanie pointed at the book still in Curtis' hands. 'I don't need someone who can just get by.'

'Sir.'

Curtis glared at him and sloped back to his desk. He banged the book down and opened one of the files. Joanie hadn't expected thanks but he knew how difficult it had been for himself and if the kid could learn the easy skills first, it would make a huge difference. There were many skills that Joanie thought should be included in basic training. Most of the fine-tuning he had taught himself. Body language was invaluable, and things like speed reading and typing just made the whole ogre of files, forms and computer work that much faster. It was a technique he'd learned when Sammy was little. The only way to get home and spend any time with her, was if he could get his work done faster so he could finish on time. That had prompted him into all kinds of self-improvement. Unfortunately rather than enable him to have more time, instead it made him a better copper and thus more in demand.

Joanie took a deep breath and ran through his latest report; he had a meeting with the chief at ten.

On the small grassy field three young boys were playing football. Sid's eyes widened with glee as he came back along the river path. The two women had already packed up and were walking ahead of him back towards town. The boys appeared to be alone, roughly aged eight to twelve he reckoned. There was nowhere to stop, no bench and Sid wasn't foolish enough to sit on the grass to watch. Instead he continued slowly past the field, glancing slyly left until the hedge grew up again. Once behind it, Sid paused and looked up and down the river path. The mothers were disappearing around the bend and there was no one coming from either direction. Sid shuffled about a bit until with a slight crouch he was able to get a clear view at the boys.

The youngest boy wrestled his T-shirt off and flung it on the ground beside the goal post. His young body was swift and shiny with sweat. Small pointed nipples leapt across the field, danced circles in the air and rolled across the ground. Sid breathed deeply stroking his hand down his thigh; he glanced briefly left and right but stayed where he was. The ball was kicked high; it rose into the air over the goal post, bounced and rolled towards the river.

'Go and get it!' one of the boys yelled. The semi-naked boy chased after it, dashing down the field towards the water. Sid kept very still watching the lightly tanned skin glisten in the sunlight. Already damp under his arms from the heat of the day, Sid felt his collar moisten and drips form across his brow. The ball rolled right onto the path and Sid could see the beautiful child coming closer. The urge to reach out and touch made Sid tremble. He could see his hand running down the boy's spine, slippery with sweat and then drawing it to his lips to lick the salty wetness.

'Sid!'

Sid was bumped roughly into the path of the boy who looked up surprised and then smiled at the person behind Sid.

'Hey Kieren,' David had hold of Sid's arm; he thrust him towards the boy. 'This is my friend Sid.'

Sid felt himself propelled forwards. He tried to smile at the boy who gave him a funny look in return. Grabbing the ball he ran back into the field.

'Have you come to play Sid? Come on.' David still had a firm grip on Sid's arm and made to drag him up the field.

'No. Get off.' Sid could feel himself trembling no longer with pleasure but something far worse.

David looked confused and backed off. The boy named Kieren booted the ball to his friends and called back at David, 'Come on, you're goalie.'

David switched his attention, grinned broadly and trotted up the field. Sid stood breathing hard, his hands were locked at his sides, he was staring at the river, which seemed to be changing colour, glowing pink at the edges as if a mist of red fog was blurring his vision. A dog sniffed at his trousers and Sid struck out with a foot, the dog yelped and disappeared.

A hand materialised out of the fog and punched Sid full in the chest; he toppled backwards and sat down hard on the grassy edge of the field.

'Fucking bastard, that'll teach you to kick my dog. Are you drunk or something?'

Sid shook his head blinking furiously; he could feel tears rolling down his cheeks. He wiped them away feverishly which seemed to help get rid of the red fog. With more blinking he could detect a man in jeans and bare back walking away down the path, a small white terrier trotting along by his feet. Distant jingling wafted down to his ears and he looked across the field to see David and the boys disappearing through the top gate towards the sound of an ice-cream van. Sid stood up and rubbed his chest. There was no one else in sight. The discarded T-shirt lay in a crumpled heap by the goal post. Sid hurried across the field, snatched it up into his fist and set off towards the gateway where the boys had disappeared.

3

When Joanie arrived home on Tuesday night, not only was there no dinner but Margret wasn't even there. She'd left a note on the kitchen table:

Gone to painting class, back at 9pm, M.

Joanie scrunched up the note and shoved it in his pocket. The fridge contained some cheese, broccoli, Cauldron foods (whatever that was) and some odd jars of sauces. The freezer wasn't much use either not if he wanted something other than frozen peas and croquette potatoes. Retrieving his wallet from the hall Joanie decided he'd better get a takeaway. There was a good Indian in town that he and Margret used to go to; he tried to remember the last time they'd eaten out. The drive took ten minutes and during that brief journey, Joanie realised they hadn't been out since they went to visit Sammy almost six months ago in Manchester and before that there'd been a Sunday with Margret's sister and their family. Maybe that was the problem, Joanie tried to concentrate on the menu in the window. Maybe he hadn't taken her out enough. There had been a time in their marriage when they went out at least once a week; meeting each other after work for a drink and then a meal before walking home back to their flat. The arrival of Sammy warranted more space and they'd moved out to the suburbs. It had suited them at the time, but now with Sammy gone, maybe Margret was feeling isolated. Joanie thanked the young Indian man and took the curry back to his car.

The answer phone light was flashing when he got back; he waited until he had his curry all laid out with a beer before switching it on.

'Inspector Johanson, sorry to call you at home sir. We've got a missing kid, thought you should know.' Joanie paused with the fork just before his lips. The answer phone clicked off and the room fell into silence. Joanie chewed, kids going missing were not unusual, but for someone at the station to give him a call meant they thought it might be serious. Joanie kept eating; there was no point in spoiling a good curry.

'What's going on Dave?'

'Hello Sir, we've got a missing child from the Harding Estate, hasn't been seen since four. Got a few officers out asking questions door to door, nothing yet.'

'How old's the kid?' Joanie was sitting on the sofa, a large pad of paper on his knee.

'Seven.'

'Damn, that's young.' Joanie glanced at his watch, it was eight thirty, another half an hour and it would be dark.

'How many men have you got out?'

'Six. I can get hold of another three if necessary unless we're going the whole caboodle.'

'No, not yet. Keep it tight, kid's friends, neighbours, you know the drill. If you've still got nothing by ten, call me.'

Joanie tapped the biro on the pad, wrote the number seven and drew a ring around it. It was a statistical thing, twelve years and up, most of the time you could expect them to return or be found kipping at a friend's house. Occasionally they'd be gone for longer, something going on at home, that kind of thing. But seven wasn't good, not good at all. It had been three years since they'd lost Martin Hempstead. Joanie wrote that on his pad too and added the number six. It had taken a month before his body had turned up, mutilated and dumped in a skip at a building site. Joanie thought about the report that Kelly had given him, and then the later one that Curtis had presented that afternoon. A child called Jessica, just three years old. Possibly touched by someone in the toilets at the park, stolen her pants. Or, as Kelly pointed out, maybe Jessica had taken her pants off at some other time during the day and was trying not to get in trouble for losing them. It was damn hot after all, and the mother admitted that her daughter was prone to preferring nudity when the chance arose. Joanie smiled to himself, he'd had the same problem with Sammy when she'd turned two and learned how to undress herself. She was forever taking off her clothes and folding them up. He remembered one time in the supermarket when Margret had been ill. The two of them had gone off to get the weekly shop, he and little Sammy. Absorbed at the cheese counter, he hadn't seen Sammy wander down towards the tinned vegetables. Laughter from another customer made him turn around to see her standing only in her pants, carefully hanging her dress over a can of baked beans.

A key turned in the lock and Joanie listened to his wife slip off her shoes and walk down the hall.

'Oh? You are in. It was so quiet, I thought you must be working late.'

He smiled, 'Nope, just had a takeaway.'

'Any left?' she arched her dark eyebrows hopefully.

'Sorry,' Joanie scooped up the empty cartons and pushed them back into the paper carry bag. They walked through into the kitchen.

'Good class?'

'Yes thank you, I took my flowers in and James was very encouraging. We're having a nude next week.'

'What a male?'

Margret laughed and took a carton of juice from the fridge. 'I don't expect so, Pamela thinks it's old Mrs Parry.'

'Mrs Parry is going to sit nude for you?' Joanie leaned past her and took a beer then changed his mind and got another glass for the juice.

'Well I think so, why we can't have some beautiful lithe young man, I don't know, I'm sure I won't want to paint Mrs Parry's varicose veins.'

Joanie couldn't help smiling; this was the Margret he knew, dry humour said with such a straight face. He wrapped an arm around her waist and kissed her on the cheek.

'What was that for? The fantastic Indian I cooked you?' she turned away, heading towards the lounge.

'Hmm, can we talk about food for a minute?' Joanie wanted to know if this was it from now on, no dinner, no food in the fridge; at least not that he could eat.

'No.'

'What? We can't even talk about it?'

'No.' She patted the sofa beside her and Joanie went to sit down.

'Never?'

'Never.' She stroked the few strands of hair that were sticking out at the side of his head.

'Maybe tomorrow then?' Joanie settled himself comfortably against her.

'Maybe.'

The phone rang and for a second neither of them moved.

'It's for me, I'll take it upstairs.' Joanie ran up the stairs and sat on the double bed in their room. As expected it was Dave again.

'I was hoping not to hear from you.'

'Me too,' Dave agreed. Joanie could hear him sigh. 'No change, we've found nothing and no one's seen anything. He was last seen playing football with his two friends.'

'What then?'

'They split up at the ice-cream van; apparently he didn't have any money and went home to get some.'

'How far?'

'About three streets away, but he never made it.'

Joanie told him to hold on, and ran back down for his pad of paper. Margret, frowning, had it in her hand; she glanced up and gave it to him. Her look was both pained yet hopeful. Joanie shrugged and ran back upstairs. Dave told him all he could and when Joanie was satisfied that he had all the details he tapped his biro on the pad again.

'Sir?'

'Right. Leave someone with the family; anyone on duty should be combing the area. Pay particular attention to anywhere that a kid might hide on the estate. At six tomorrow we'll start the show. Does the chief know?'

'Yes sir, he said the same as you. Full works tomorrow morning.'

Joanie nodded, despite their differences, the chief superintendent and he were usually in accordance when it came down to operational procedures. On a more personal level, things were quite different. Where Joanie was calm and thoughtful, the chief was agitated and aggressive. You could argue it both ways, they both got results, but Joanie wondered how many enemies the chief had accumulated over the years.

'I'll be in at six.'

When Margret came upstairs, Joanie was still sitting on the edge of the bed looking at the pad of paper.

'Is it bad?' she leaned against the doorjamb.

Joanie tried to smile, 'It's not looking good, we'll have to wait until tomorrow.'

'I'll cook dinner,' she slid away from the door and down the hall to the bathroom, 'tomorrow,' she added.

When Sid got to work, David was nowhere to be seen. He put his things in the locker and sat with a glass of water. At five minutes past twelve, he went down to the car park. As he walked out into the sunshine David came running up to him.

'Look, look,' he jabbed a finger at a badge on his chest; Sid had to squint against the sun to read it.

'It's my birthday.' David squealed and held aloft a bag. 'I got me lots of cakes; Mum said I should bring them to work to share with my friends. You can have some Sid.'

'You're late David. We'll have them at break time OK?'

David nodded his head and darted into the store. Sid sighed with relief, for a moment he thought something must have happened. Feeling lighter, Sid stepped across the car park. It was too hot to go shopping and the car park was only half full. Sid took the pick-up arm and went to gather litter instead as most of the trolleys were stacked neatly by the entrance. Sid couldn't remember the last time he'd celebrated his own birthday, each year passed as a blur punctuated only by the lights at Christmas in the High Street. It would be nice to receive a present. He imagined the postman handing him a package and then sitting on his bed opening it. What would it be? In his mind's eye, he cut the sellotape and undid the wrapping paper. Inside was some pink tissue paper and as he pulled it back, there were Jessica's panties and a lock of her golden hair. Sid sighed.

David came out of the store and trotted over to Sid with a single trolley.

'Do you know how old I am?'

Sid had read it emblazoned on his badge but staring at the kid's excitement, he shook his head. 'No.'

'Quarter sentry,' David nodded with his hands on his hips. 'That means I'm twenty five that does.' He nodded again.

Sid bent down and picked up an empty crisp packet.

'How old are you Sid?'

Sid had to think for a minute; half a century and a bit, old enough to be this kid's Dad. 'Fifty three,' he said.

'Wow,' exclaimed David and then he paused, 'Is that more or less?'

'More,' Sid groaned, 'a lot more.'

'Oh that's not fair, that means you get first pick at the cakes.' David gave him a sullen look and walked away with his trolley back to the entrance. Sid watched him go, his eyes widening as he saw two police officers climbing out of a car. They stood and waited for David to approach. Sid searched the ground frantically for more litter; his fingers began to tremble. Marching quickly towards the furthest hedge he reached up for a plastic bag that was snagged on the thorns. He busied himself with the rubbish behind the trolley stand for a few minutes and when he looked up he couldn't see either the policemen or David.

'Excuse me,' a car rolled up beside him.

Sid almost fell over the bag of rubbish in his fright; the policeman was leaning out of the window.

'Are you Sid?'

Sid pulled the rubbish bag in front of himself for protection and nodded.

'David's a bit nervous and he asked for you. You don't mind sitting in on a few questions do you? It's too hot to walk. Here.' The passenger door swung open.

Sid stood very still; he was trying to grasp what the man had said amidst the panic that fluttered around his mind like butterflies caught in a net. But the open door was an obvious signal. Sid walked around the front of the car and got in. He pulled the bag of rubbish up in front of him and laid the pick-up arm on top.

The driver cruised across the car park and stopped in the disabled bay. They got out and Sid waited for the officer's lead.

They walked into the store and through the staff doors into the common room. David was sitting at the table looking worried, a large glass of water and the remains of some chocolate cake smeared across his lips. Sid pulled out a chair and sat down.

'Sid?' David visibly relaxed, then looked guilty. 'I'm sorry Sid, I know you should have first choice but he said it wouldn't matter.' David pointed at the officer who was sitting at the end of the table. Sid nodded his head at the policeman.

'It's alright, I don't like chocolate anyway.'

'There's apple cake,' David thrust the bag towards Sid.

Sid opened it and peered inside. Cake was the last thing on his mind but with two uniforms staring at him, the best he could do was act normally. Carefully he broke off a small piece.

'So David, tell us about Kieren.' The officer who was sitting down asked.

Sid clenched the cake in his hand inadvertently; glancing up he saw the policeman was watching him. He opened his palm and deliberately rolled the cake into a tight ball and popped it into his mouth. Grimacing, he started to chew. He knew that name, David had said it. For a second Sid stopped chewing as he thought about the semi-naked boy in the park.

David was frowning at the police officer and Sid realised he wanted confirmation; Sid nodded at him and added 'Answer the questions David. They're not taking the piss.'

'Kieren's my friend. We play football.' The officer nodded and noted something down on a small pad. Gaining confidence, David continued, 'I'm goalie. I'm the best goalie they said cos I'm big and strong see.' David puffed up his chest to show them.

'Did you play football yesterday?'

'Yes.' David wiped his nose on the back of his hand and smiled at Sid.

'Was there anybody else there?' the policeman continued.

'You don't play football do you Sid?' David ignored the question.

Sid coughed suddenly on the ball of compressed sponge in his mouth. He swallowed with difficulty. The last thing he wanted was to be included in this conversation. Sid merely shook his head. The policemen didn't seem interested in Sid as they continued to ask questions about when and where, the ice-cream van and what David bought. Whether he knew where Kieren lived and so on. At one point they made the mistake of asking the same question twice.

'Sid,' David leaned across the desk conspiratorially, 'they asked me that already.'

'It's OK, maybe they forgot.' Sid reassured him. The sooner David got through these questions, the sooner they could leave.

'I had strawberry flavour and went home.' David stated.

At last the policemen seemed satisfied and stood up to leave.

'Can I go now?' David jumped up holding himself and shuffling his feet.

'Sure, but if you think of anybody else who knows Kieren, let us know.'

'Sid knows Kieren.' David smiled back at Sid and dashed off to the toilet. Sid had half risen with his empty cup, his body almost froze but he forced it to keep going towards the sink. He felt rather than heard the policemen change position and stare at his back.

'You didn't say anything,' one of the policemen accused.

'You weren't asking ME questions.' Sid kept his back to them while he rinsed his cup. He was blinking furiously, trying to calm the twitching he could feel across his face.

'So how do you know Kieren?'

Sid grabbed the tea towel and concentrated on drying the mug thoroughly, 'I don't, I mean I only met him briefly, David introduced him.' Sid shrugged and hung up the towel. It was hard trying to sound relaxed when all he wanted to do was scream at them to fucking well leave him alone.

He turned to see the two policemen looking at each other.

'I was on the river path, the ball rolled down, and David appeared and said this is Kieren and then they went to play football and I carried on into town,' Sid could feel himself gabbling. He picked up the remains of the cakes and tied them up in the bag. 'I've never seen him before; don't know if I'd recognise him again.' What did they know? Sid turned his back on them again and stood in front of the lockers, he hadn't meant to take the rest of David's cakes but now he had them in his hand he'd better do something with them. He unlocked the door and thrust them in on top of his umbrella.

'You didn't see anything else? Anyone else?'

Sid thought about mentioning the tattooed man and his dog but the memory was painful and he didn't see any point in humiliating himself further. 'No.'

They asked him to sit down and went through the questions again, this time taking careful notes. Sid kept to his story, stated it again, agreeing to come to the station and sign a statement later. They wanted his address too.

Finally they left and Sid hurried gratefully into the car park. David, deep in concentration, was sorting a bunch of abandoned trolleys as they had become entangled with each other. Sid ignored him and raced down to the end of the car park. Above him, the sky had grown suddenly dark and large drops began to pattern the tarmac. Sid felt the plastic smoothness of the trolley handles and the rain on his head cooled his troubled mind. There was a part of yesterday afternoon that he didn't quite remember, and that was more frightening than anything else. So much for tadpoles near the surface, something heavy had sunk to the bottom. Sure he remembered staring at Kieren through the bushes, and he remembered how the bruise he'd seen this morning in the mirror had appeared in the middle of his chest. He even remembered arriving home, his body drenched with sweat but which way he had walked or whom he had seen, he couldn't say. Thunder rolled overhead, and Sid closed his eyes, it was OK, the police were gone, they had been more interested in David not him. Water ran down his face washing him, soothing him, telling him everything was fine, nothing had changed. Opening his eyes, Sid welcomed the sight of trolleys discarded across the car park and more in the stand. Everything was just as it should be.

'Do you want to get a bite to eat?' Kelly leaned around the door of the incident room. Joanie was sitting at one of the tables; a large map of the Harding Estate lay before him with a red dotted line to mark the boy's route. At various points lines branched out to bits of paper stuck on, names of people, places, possibilities. Joanie was tired; he hadn't stopped since six and his stomach growled in response.

'Sure.'

They went down to the canteen and with trays in hand settled at a small round table. Joanie ate quickly, his mind never stopping to look at the food but running over and over the details that had come in so far.

'How's Margret?'

'What?' Joanie was thrown. He tried to push through the jumbled data and back into his own life.

'Ummm painting, why do you ask?'

'It's what you taught me,' Kelly drank a mouthful of coke, 'to think about something completely different when you're too snowed under.'

She was right; Joanie shook his head. He could see Margret in the kitchen with her paintbrushes, which reminded him he ought to ring her. There was no chance he'd be home for dinner, he might not even get home tonight full stop.

'Yes, give your brain a rest.' He sat back in his chair and pushed the plate to one side. 'I've often thought that swimming would be good. You know up and down, watching the clock to see how fast you can do a length.'

'So why don't you? An hour at the pool might help.'

Joanie gave her a quizzical look, 'I'm sure the chief would be thrilled to discover I'd started working off my waist in the middle of a damn murder hunt.'

'You don't have a body,' Kelly challenged.

'No, but do you think the boy's still alive?'

Kelly looked away making Joanie feel guilty for bringing it up. Sure they both knew the likely reality but he didn't need to rub it in her face.

'Coffee?' he indicated the counter and she nodded. He returned with a couple of cappuccinos. Kelly rolled a cigarette between her fingers but didn't light it. Low murmurs from the other tables eased the tension.

'What's your theory then?' he asked her. Joanie liked to hear Kelly's take on things; it helped him to get out of his own head. Often she would mention something that would get him thinking along a different tack and thinking as laterally as possible was what it was all about. Sex offenders and child murders were rarely straightforward.

'Opportunity, maybe. Kid on his own, no one around. Car comes by, two seconds and he's gone. Or, if you want to go back to the Hempstead kid, then maybe we've got ourselves a serial. Same age, both boys, but this was daylight. The family seem really nice not that Hempstead's were bad but I got the impression Hempstead probably wasn't the happiest of kids. More prone to grooming than this one.'

Joanie noted how she didn't mention Kieren by name. Neither did he, it was a tactic, a method of self-preservation. By not stating the child's name, he became less of a child and more of a case. A missing person case officially, at least at present. If you started saying Kieren all the time, then you got a picture of the boy in your head, the things he liked to do, the sort of shirt he wore and then it became more difficult. Harder to stop that ugly pull at your heart, harder to pretend this was just a job.

By eleven that night the river had been dragged, the local dump and garages searched with a fine toothcomb. The parents and some twenty odd associated adults interviewed and still they knew nothing. That wasn't strictly true, there were always a million possible threads and in a case like this one, it would take a lot more than twenty-four hours to follow them all. A plastic bag and an old penknife had been found in the undergrowth at the edge of the football field. Forensics would let him know in the morning but they hadn't looked like much. Probably just rubbish. Joanie was leaning back in his chair, his fingers steepled together. Curtis was asleep on his arms; his golden hair had fallen over his face. There were voices from the outer office from the night shift.

Joanie picked up the thick wodge of information already gathered. He leafed through them one by one, pausing at David Jones. He pulled it out and the sheet behind came with it. Joanie pulled them apart and put Sidney White back in the pile. From the information they had, David was the last adult to see Kieren. Joanie tapped the sheet with his pen. He'd like to meet this guy, ask some more questions. He got up and gently shook Curtis' shoulder.

'Go home. I'll see you in the morning.'

4

It was just before midnight when Joanie opened his front door. As soon as the key was in the lock, he realised his mistake. The faint smell of cooked food depressed him further. The hall light was on, but the rest of the house lay in dark stillness. Joanie slipped off his shoes and padded into the kitchen. The table was bare, no plate in the fridge either, then his foot crunched on something by the sink. He went back to the doorway and switched on the light. Bits of plate and food were scattered across the floor. Big mistake, he thought. As he bent down to clear up, he worked out it had been sausages, mash and broccoli with onion gravy just how he liked it. The bottom of his sock had picked up some of the gravy already. He used the dustpan and brush from under the sink and then a damp cloth to collect the congealed mess. It wasn't that Margret didn't usually get angry, or that it was rare for her to break anything, the fact the results of her violence had been simply abandoned worried Joanie far more. There was something chilling about it, rather like walking into the scene of a bloody fight after it's over. All the rage and noise spent and only a body and some blood painted in the silence. She must be in bed already. Joanie boiled a pan of milk and made himself a hot chocolate; he also grabbed one of the sleeping pills he kept in the cabinet. Despite being dog-tired, he knew sleep would be hard to come by. It always was with a case like this.

Sliding into bed next to Margret, she felt warm and snug and was snoring ever so slightly. The moon was bright tonight, and it shone through the curtains bathing the room in a pale blue. Joanie closed his eyes, the incident room and the faces of his staff crossing his mind. Suspect faces. A photograph of Kieren Matthews. He sighed and turned over onto his side. Margret stopped snoring and turned away too. He should have rung her, but then why didn't she ring him? She normally would. Shame about the plate, no doubt she would blame him next time they needed the full complement and came up one short. Then he thought about the plate at the Matthews' house - blackberries around the edge of a plate of chocolate digestives, which became only crumbs by the time they left. Better to be only a plate short than a son short. The look of despair and confusion on their faces. Why us? It was always why us? And sometimes Joanie wondered, and why me?

'He's a mongol.' Curtis was standing in front of the interview room looking through the little window. He looked questioningly at Joanie.

Joanie couldn't believe what he'd just heard; he rolled his eyes. 'For Christ's sake, were you asleep on your diversity course? Don't ever come out with language like that. You should have read the details; he has Down Syndrome to be more accurate.'

'I,' Curtis looked embarrassed, 'I didn't realise what that meant.'

Joanie's eyes widened. 'Let's see what he's got to say.'

They went in and David stood up immediately. Tear streaks

had stained his face.

'Can I go now?'

Joanie smiled warmly at him and sat down at the table. 'Where would you like to go?'

'I've got to get to work. Sid'll be angry and the boss'll give me a black mark.'

'It's alright, we've spoken to your boss, and he's given you the day off, if that's alright with you.' Joanie pulled a packet of maltesers out of his pocket and casually opened them on the table.

'Oh.' David said and sat back down. He took one of the sweets without being offered. Curtis sat down too, moving his chair back slightly from the table as Joanie had instructed before they came in.

'I hear you're good at football,' Joanie ate a malteser. 'Do you like football?'

David nodded his head and took two more of the chocolate balls. Joanie carefully covered the packet with his hand and rolled one out keeping it gently under his finger.

'What position do you play?' he moved his finger towards David but kept the malteser trapped.

David made to reach for the sweet but when he realised Joanie wasn't going to let go, he retracted his hand and looked him in the face. Joanie allowed his muscles to relax, letting the lines smooth out; he turned up the corners of his mouth and knew that his eyes would be twinkling. It was a look he had used on Sammy often and she would shriek with laughter and tell him to stop tweeking at her.

'Goalie.' The chocolate ball was released and David grabbed it before it rolled. A big grin broke across his face, as he understood the game. He nodded his head excitedly. So simple Joanie thought, wouldn't it be nice if all suspects responded so easily. He continued with a few more easy questions. David was looking genuinely pleased with himself. Joanie decided he could take things on a different tack.

'What would you most like to have?'

'A brother,' the answer fired back immediately taking Joanie by surprise. He let another malteser go and paused. This was interesting.

'Would Kieren make a good brother?'

'No, he's too small,' David gave Joanie the kind of look that meant 'Don't be stupid'.

'Why's that?' Joanie kept the malteser rolling gently under his finger.

'It's no good, when I sit on him he cries and the other boys hit me. It doesn't hurt when they sit on me. They said I need someone big like me. I need a big brother, then we can play all the time and he won't cry.'

Joanie could see Curtis biting his lip to keep a straight face.

'Did you make Kieren cry the other day?'

'No. After that time, they said I wasn't allowed to sit on him, that they'd tell their Mums. I don't want to get into trouble. Kieren's my friend.'

Joanie gave out the penultimate malteser and watched David pop it into his mouth, crunch down and swallow all in what appeared to be one motion.

'Thanks David, you've been a great help.' Joanie stood up watching David's face carefully.

'But you've got one left.' David pointed at the last malteser that Joanie now had lying in his palm.

'Ah, but that's for Curtis for being so patient.' He placed the chocolate gently on the table on the corner closest to Curtis. Joanie's eyes never left David's face. Watching the way the young man's gaze followed his hand and stared at the sweet. He could see disappointment registered on his wide face, his shoulders sagged and he made a humphing noise in his seat.

Curtis picked up the chocolate and put it in his mouth. David's bottom lip poked out and he crossed his arms but made no aggressive move. Joanie was pleased. They left the room and Joanie went to speak to David's mother waiting in the relatives' room.

By that afternoon, it was broadcast across the networks, and the evening papers were emblazoned with slogans like; 'Innocent child abducted', 'Who's Kidnapped Kieren?' and another paper that had obviously done its homework read: 'Will Kieren be the next Martin Hempstead?' Officially the Hempstead case was still open, but Joanie hadn't seen the final report on that one, it hadn't been his baby back then.

Joanie was sitting in his office with Curtis; they had a list of all the people interviewed on the board. Joanie put a line through David's name.

'You seem pretty sure about that. Couldn't he have done something by accident, these Mo.. err I mean, well those kind of people can get quite physical, not know their own strength,' Curtis argued.

Joanie turned and studied the young officer for a moment.

'People with Learning Difficulties is the correct term.' Joanie paused, 'What do your instincts tell you?'

'Instincts? I thought we were supposed to look at the facts, take all the evidence.'

Joanie nodded, 'We are, but what do your instincts tell you?'

'Well, that he's innocent but that's not the point, he's certainly got the strength to do it.'

Joanie was pleased Curtis was still trying, he approved of officers that kept asking questions when it mattered.

'OK, in your terms, look at it this way. What motive does he have? Do you think he's capable of lying? If he accidentally killed Kieren, is he likely to hide the body so well? Wouldn't he let something slip? He's been questioned by four different people now, and none of his answers contradict each other. Sure there's a little elasticity in timings but most people don't know the time they do things.'

Curtis shrugged but said nothing.

'His emotions are all over his face, did you see how his whole body gets involved when he's upset? It's like watching a five year old, they don't hide anything.'

Curtis shoved his hands into his pockets; 'I just thought it was a bit early to cross him off already.'

'The only thing I can see David being useful for, is to lead us to someone else, which reminds me, I'd like to meet his colleague, what was his name?'

'Sidney White,' Curtis replied promptly.

Joanie hadn't needed to ask of course, but he wanted to make sure Curtis was on the ball. The more details you could keep in your head, the easier it became to make the links when new information came along.

'Have you got an address for him?' Joanie drained the last of his cold coffee.

'Er, yeah,' Curtis shuffled briefly through some papers and followed Joanie out of the door. 'But he might be at work at the supermarket.'

Sid raced across the car park like a fevered demon, without David there today; the trolleys were all over the place. The work, although hard, helped to stop Sid's mind racing away with that boy Kieren. He was sure David's absence had something to do with it. Last night he'd had nightmares about the boy. They started innocently enough with that beautiful tanned skin rippling in the sunshine but then as he got closer and saw the beads of sweat down his back, the spine had turned into a dark red line and had split open. Out came huge tentacles that wrapped around Sid's neck, his body, his cock, pulling him into the open cavern of red gore. Sid woke himself up shouting, his bed damp beneath him. He got up and took the boy's T-shirt out of the drawer. There was something cursed about it, and he knew he should get rid of it, but in the light of the electric lamp it seemed so innocuous. He climbed into bed and pulled the T-shirt close, he could smell Kieren on it.

At break time, Sid hurried up to the staff room. A large photo of Kieren in a school uniform stared back at Sid, as he stood rooted to the spot in the doorway. It was as if someone had struck him with a sledgehammer. His bruise from the other day throbbed painfully and Sid wondered if he was having a heart attack. The picture was on the front of a newspaper folded open as another member of staff was sitting reading it. Sid turned and fled to the toilet, his stomach churned and he had to sit for some time before the feeling passed. When he returned, the staff room was empty. Sid scrunched up the newspaper and thrust it in his locker; he found another one on a chair by the door, this one with a different title but the same picture. He tore it into thin strips and carried them down to the outside bin.

Back in the car park it was raining lightly again. He swore angrily at a woman before he could stop himself and then hurried into one of the trolley stands. The rain pattered on the roof making it hard to concentrate. Something was wrong, so very wrong. Sid lifted up his hands and sniffed the ends of his fingers, he didn't smell right. If David wasn't here, then that meant the police had him, and that meant they'd soon have Sid. A trolley rolled gently into him and he swung around to confront an old lady.

'Ooh, sorry love,' she backed away.

Sid blinked over and over, breathing deeply, keep calm, keep control. Everything was fine, he had nothing, had done nothing, had he? The T-shirt. He should get rid of it, tonight. And then he remembered that he had had to give his address when he signed the statement yesterday. Would they come for him at home? He had to get back and quickly. Darting out of the trolley stand, he ran back into the store and grabbed his things from the locker. Sid almost knocked the manager over as he left the staff room.

'Whoa, take it easy. I thought you were on till eight Sid?'

Sid kept breathing, think, think.

'I've got a doctor's appointment,' he wheezed. 'I forgot, I'm late.'

The manager leaned a bit closer, 'You do look a bit peaky,' he said. 'Let me know in advance next time,' he admonished and stood to one side.

Sid wasn't used to running, by the time he reached the end of the car park and was heading along the pavement, he had to slow down and walk. His throat hurt and his chest felt uncomfortable under the bruise. A police car drove past and Sid tried to shrink his head into his neck. It turned into the supermarket without stopping and Sid crossed the road and half stumbling, half running, made his way home. The hall was empty and quiet, nobody hanging around outside. Sid pulled himself up the stairs using the banister. He'd been so careful, everything had been going so smoothly and now look at it. One T-shirt and he was on the edge of oblivion. A burst of energy sent him ripping at the graphic drawings that adorned the walls of his bedroom. Most of the blu-tack came off with the pictures but here and there it took a bit of paper with it and stayed firmly on the wall. Sid couldn't help crying out when one drawing ripped completely in half. He shoved them under his mattress and then yanked open his favourite drawer. He couldn't destroy them all, what to do? There were Jessica's pants lying on the top. Sid heard a car pull up outside. He ran into the kitchenette and then back again, and then finally Dr Casey came in useful.

'Breathe' she had always told him, 'breathe, nice and deep, let the air calm your nerves, see it lifting the fear, dissolving the anger'. And so Sid sat on the edge of his bed and practised the technique for the first time since they'd finished their sessions together.

The doorbell rang. Sid stood up, smoothed the quilt behind

him and let out a long slow breath. Sliding his hands over his hair he slowly walked down the stairs.

A young man with blond curly hair stood on the doorstep with an older man in the shadows behind. Sid didn't say anything.

'Sidney White?' the blond one said.

'Yes.' There was nothing else to say really, it would be foolish to deny it.

'I wonder if we could come in and ask you some more questions.' He flashed some ID at Sid.

Sid opened the door wider and the blond man started to move in but there was only the narrow hall and the stairs leading straight up.

'Why don't you go on up, and we'll follow,' the man advised.

Sid walked slowly up the stairs, he had to hold onto the banister and concentrate on his feet. He was feeling sick and light-headed, so long as he kept breathing, it would be alright. He went into the main room and stood by the desk, his eyes searching along the surface and across to the chest of drawers looking for anything that the officer's might think was suspicious.

'I'm Detective Constable Curtis, and this is Detective Inspector Johanson, we understand you were by the river on Tuesday.'

Sid stared at the young man, and then noticed the older one was absorbed in looking around his room. What was he looking for? Sid focused back on the blond-haired man and started to answer the question.

'I made a statement yesterday,' he stumbled, 'your colleagues, they must have it.'

'Yes, we know, in fact I have a copy of it here, but we wanted to check a few details with you.' The police officer paused as if reading the statement. 'I understand you were by the river on Tuesday.'

'Yes,' he paused, 'I went for a walk.' There was no need for long explanations, so long as he answered what they asked, it would be safe. Yes and No were easy and this guy asked a lot of those sort of questions. Then the older one stood forward and Sid blinked, there was something familiar about him, about the eyes. Sid pulled out his desk chair and sat down, the officers remained standing. He could feel goose bumps under the fabric of his sweatshirt and prickling where the collar touched his neck.

Then the other police officer spoke, 'Would you like to touch Kieren?' the voice was flat. Its effect on Sid however wasn't. His foot twitched, his skin became alive crawling with invisible ants, his mouth flooded with saliva and Sid was suddenly frightened that he might vomit there and then right onto the man's brown leather shoes. Sid shook his head violently.

'No, no,' and he would have said it a third time if he hadn't bitten his tongue to hold it back. Too many no's, was he stupid? The blond-haired man's face had changed, as Sid looked up again he could see disgust written on his face, small dark flames glittered in his eyes. Sid clenched his hands together to stop them trembling. The older man stood quite calmly though, no change on his face, maybe it would be OK; he was obviously the one in charge.

'Is there anything you'd like to show us?' Again that perfectly expressionless voice. Sid's eyes flicked uncontrollably to the chest of drawers and back to the older man's leather shoes. There was a scraping sound and Sid leapt to his feet, the younger man had opened the middle drawer.

'What are you doing?' Sid shouted.

Silence fell and the police officers said nothing. Curtis picked up a large pair of wide-fronts, grimaced and replaced them.

'You need a warrant, that's my underwear.' Sid appealed to the older man who nodded ever so slightly at his colleague. The drawer was closed and now the older man asked more questions, the same ones, but somehow they were more difficult to answer. How many times would he have to tell this story before they left him alone? At last the men made their excuses and left.

Sid watched the car start up and disappear along the road. He laid his head on his arms and sobbed. What had gone wrong? Three years he'd been here, going about his business, working with David. It was good; things had been under control, normal and now look. Sid smeared snot and tears across his sleeve. His sweatshirt was aggravating him under the armpits. He stripped off his top and dropped it onto the desk, if only Jessica had never come into the toilets, he'd been fine before then, and now look, he was a mess. And yet that wasn't quite true, it wasn't Jessica that had led him to Kieren. Sid wished he'd never set eyes on that beautiful skin, on the way it moved and shimmered in the sunshine. Damn Kieren, damn David for putting him in this situation. If it hadn't been for David, Kieren and the other boys would never have seen him. Fucking dumb, stupid, numbskull David.

'We can't just drive away,' Curtis was agitated.

'Pull over here,' Joanie instructed after they turned the corner. He got on the mike and called for back-up.

'We'll put a watch on him for now,' Joanie explained.

'But the bastard's guilty, you could see it on his face as soon as you said about touching the kid, he went weird. How come we don't just take him in now?'

'On what evidence? If he's killed the boy and hidden the body, chances are that someone that nervous will go back to check he hasn't left anything. If the boy's alive, I certainly don't think he's in that flat. It was tiny, there's no basement, a flat below and another flat above his on the top floor. Where would he put a kid? Having said that, I want a full plan of the whole building.'

'What about getting a warrant to search it? Jesus even you think he's guilty, I don't get it. I hate fuckers like that.' Curtis spoke so vehemently that Joanie noticed specks of saliva appear on the windscreen.

'I didn't say I think he's guilty, I think he deserves analysis.'

Joanie took out his penknife and started to clean his nails.

'Analysis? You sound like some kind of psychologist who gets a kick out of understanding these bastards. They need fucking shooting.'

Joanie paused; Curtis was certainly wound up about this, almost as if it was personal. Maybe that was what having a little kid made you feel like, but then he hadn't remembered feeling like that when Sammy was little. Somehow work and home were two separate things. Home was safe; it was where Margret held him close in the dead of night, it was where Sammy watched TV and jumped loudly down the stairs. Not the place for people like Sidney White. There had been something though that had made Joanie uncomfortable, not about the case, something about Sidney, there was a gesture he'd made scratching his fingers along his sleeve. It was almost familiar. And for a sudden scary moment Joanie wondered if this man had crossed over into his own personal life. Joanie brought his attention back into the car and realised there was an uncomfortable silence, Curtis was staring away from him out of the window.

'I try not to jump to conclusions,' Joanie explained. 'Yes I think the man was acting guilty but guilty of what I'm not sure.' Another car swung into the road and Joanie jumped out and flagged the officers down. They left them under strict instructions to follow Sidney's exact movements and keep the station posted. Joanie drove the two of them back to headquarters and sent Curtis home. An angry mind was no use when looking for subtleties in a case. It was late, but Joanie wanted to check up any records he could on Sidney White before getting home himself for a few hours kip.

Margret was still up, watching some film or other on the box. She looked up as he came in but said nothing.

'Sorry,' he said.

'For what?'

'The dinner, last night.'

'You didn't even say goodbye this morning when you left,' she accused crossing her arms tightly.

'I didn't want to wake you, it was quarter to six.'

'Sneaking in and out, I have to read the papers to find out what my own husband's doing.' She switched the TV off.

Joanie silently swallowed, this looked like a big one.

'I even told you I was going to cook the day before. The least you could do is call if you can't make it. It's all very well for you absorbed at work but what about me here home all day long.' She crossed her legs and sat huddled and stony on the sofa.

Maybe that was it, the change from working to being at home; it had only been two months after all since Margret had agreed to her company's offer of early retirement. Joanie wasn't sure if he could risk sitting next to her or not, she might reject him, or she might welcome an apologetic hug. God knows he could do with a bit of comfort himself. Joanie sat down cautiously.

'I'm sorry, you know how I get wrapped up in these cases. It's not an excuse, it's just I thought you'd know by now.'

'What? Know not to expect any common courtesies, that your home life gets put on hold because somebody else's child has gone missing? Does that mean I need to be kidnapped, murdered or raped for you to take any notice?' Her breath was hot on his face and he could see tears welling in her eyes.

Joanie bowed his head, 'I'm truly sorry love. I'm just trying to do the best I can.' He softly laid a hand on her leg but she brushed it off and stood up.

'Sometimes I think you understand your villains better than you do your own wife.' She slammed the door and stomped up the stairs. Joanie sat quietly. She might be right about that. Certainly at the moment, time was, when Margret would have rung him to find out why he was late, and then been sympathetic about the case, asking him questions about it. He didn't understand her at all at the moment and the uncertainty in his heart worried him. Was he uncertain of their future together? Surely there couldn't be a life without Margret? He could barely remember a time when she hadn't been around, sharing his triumphs, soothing his failures. Was this how it started when people separated? A change in the old habits, a realisation that perhaps this wasn't the life they had wanted? Perhaps Margret had confided in Sammy, he could ask her. Damn he'd meant to send a Good Luck card for her first exam.

Upstairs, Margret was cleaning her teeth.

'I was going to send a card for Sammy,' he turned on the taps to run a bath.

Margret rinsed her mouth, 'I've done it.'

'Oh, thank you.'

'So you haven't completely forgotten about her too?'

Joanie decided not to reply to the snide remark, it wasn't worth it, he was tired. They'd end up saying things they didn't mean or maybe they'd say things they did mean but had never dared voice before? Joanie pushed the uncomfortable thought away, steam was rising from the bath and beckoning him in.

5

Sid looked at the clothes in his special drawer. An odd mixture, each with its own story. Thank god they hadn't opened this drawer. A part of him knew it would be risky to keep them, especially now the police were involved, but another part couldn't bear to give them up. Maybe he could hide them somewhere at work for a few days, until they'd sorted this whole Kieren thing out. There was that space behind the big freezers in the storeroom which might work. He folded them up carefully and placed them into an old plastic bag. He checked the time and decided he ought to get going, get in early to hide his secrets.

Pouring himself a strong coffee, Sid felt almost cleansed. With the clothes now safely stashed, he was free. No evidence. No crime.

David strode in beaming at Sid.

'Morning Sid.' He continued to his locker to put his lunch carefully away. Sid hadn't been able to eat any breakfast that morning and opening his own locker, realised he still had the remnants of David's cakes.

'Here,' Sid dropped the bag on the table. David looked across with wide eyes making it necessary for Sid to explain.

'Your birthday cakes, I kept them for you, when the police came remember?'

'Oh yeah, thanks Sid.' David brightened and tore into the bag. There was a small piece of the chocolate cake left and most of the apple one.

'Want some?' David muffled through a mouthful. Sid shook his head but sat down anyway. This felt almost normal, at least for a minute. Sid could feel tears welling up in his eyes, if only it could be normal again. Him and David stacking the trolleys, no police, no Kieren splashed across the newspapers. Sid wished he'd never gone to the riverbank that day. It was David's fault, telling him about football, about his young friends. Sid watched him munch through the entire cake, maybe he should help him, stuff that cake in so far and so deep until David couldn't breathe. Sid jerked his eyes away, no, no, no. David was Sid's friend, his only friend, he didn't know any better. It was Sid who had fucked up; he must try to remember what had happened that afternoon. He'd spent most of the night thinking about it, forcing himself to remember so hard that he made up all sorts of different scenarios to see if anything triggered off what really happened. Most of them ended with Sid lying on the grass stroking Kieren's body in the sunshine, like two lovers in each other's arms.

'My Mum says Kieren's gone missing and that's why the police wanted to speak to me.' David had finished the cake; crumbs dotted his lips and cheeks.

Sid merely nodded.

'One policeman gave me maltesers, he was nice. I bet they'd give you some if you went. I could ask them if you like.'

Maltesers. The police gave him maltesers? So far they'd given him the fright of his life and left him with stomachache and a pain in his head.

'Mum says someone's taken Kieren. Where have they taken

him Sid? Do you think he went on holiday? Mum and me are going on holiday this year to.. ,' David frowned.

'Majorca,' Sid added.

'Yeah, how did you know?'

'You told me before.' Sid sighed. 'I don't think Kieren's on holiday.'

'Where did he go then? He hasn't been to play football, nobody came to play football yesterday, maybe they've all gone away. Maybe they've moved house. People do sometimes.'

Sid couldn't help smiling, yes maybe they'd all moved away, that would be so nice, so easy. Maybe there really was nothing to worry about, Kieren had simply moved house. Sid dug his nail into his hand. Stop being stupid he told himself, the police don't go round asking awkward questions when someone moves house. It was tempting to get lost in David's simple happy world. Sid looked at him across the table; he was staring at the clock on the wall trying to work out if it was time to go. Sid was jealous, not only for David's ability to get close to children but now even for his mind, so easily pleased, so innocent and trusting. Wouldn't it be nice to crawl inside David's head and stay there nice and safe?

'Come on Sid.' David was up and heading for the door.

The afternoon passed swiftly enough. Judging by the contents of trolleys leaving the store, it was barbecue night for the whole town. Sid couldn't remember ever having a barbecue, which was something happy families did or groups of friends gathered in a smoky garden. He didn't have a garden. Sid tried not to think about the other things he didn't have. David seemed his usual self that afternoon; it was obvious his experience with the police hadn't affected him. Sid wished he felt the same.

By the time they knocked off, heavy thunderclouds had gathered and Sid grinned at the prospect of washed-out barbecues. Serves them right for being so damn happy. Before he left, he bought a few provisions and stomped home but as he neared the flat he became nervous. Perhaps the police were back; maybe they were in there now searching through his drawers, ripping up his pictures that still lay tucked under the mattress. Sid was sweating when he put the key in the lock but the flat was silent save for a dull thudding of music from downstairs. He grilled some cheese on toast and then ate most of a cherry cake washed down with a can of Boddingtons.

His room looked different now, the walls uniformly blank with a few marks where the blu-tack had been. The drab curtains did nothing to lighten the mood and looking at the rumpled bed, Sid realised he hadn't washed the sheets for some time. The scene depressed him, rubbish spilling out onto the floor. Rather than dwell on the mess, he flicked on the TV switching between channels until turning it off in disgust. He was desperate to turn on the computer, but didn't dare. What if they were watching, had tapped his broadband connection. Was that possible? He wasn't sure, and it would be too risky to try, instead he pulled out paper and pencils. Sid tried to remember the silky thighs of a small boy on the swings in the park. He'd passed it on his way home, had paused for a few seconds but then hurried along when he thought about the police visit. Sid let the pencil glide across the page but the line he had made looked like Kieren's spine, ready to break open and let the tentacles out. He chose a thicker, darker pencil and holding it tight in his fist he scratched great black lines across the paper, tearing it, ripping apart that spine, obliterating any likeness to the boy with the glistening skin.

Pulling on his navy sweatshirt, he left the flat walking swiftly through town and down towards the river. As he neared the path, his footsteps slowed, golden light reflected off the river. The earlier clouds had passed over but the air still felt heavy and threatening. Smoke trailed up from the back of someone's garden and voices carried across the water. At the bottom of the football field Sid stopped, the grass lay dark green, the posts turning yellow with the dying sun. A crisp packet tottered briefly towards the goal then lay still. Sid remembered sitting on the grass, but not facing the boys, instead he had faced the water, why was that? Then he remembered the tattooed man and that made him clench his fists even now. But then what? Where had Kieren been? Sid stared at the football field, at the spot he remembered the T-shirt lying in the grass. Frustrated he moved on, there was nothing to see, he continued past along the narrowing path until a large oak tree spread its roots across the earth. Sid stopped and stared dismally at the water. Beneath the tree it seemed particularly dark as if the sun had already left the sky. He turned and walked back the way he'd come. Ahead he saw a figure pause briefly then continue briskly towards him. It was a young man neatly dressed.

'Evening sir.' The man nodded never slowing his pace.

Sid said nothing, followed the path back to Wembury Road and cut through the alley towards the kid's park. The light was failing now and only a few teenagers on bikes stood near the slide. It was too late for the little ones. Sid checked his watch. They would be tucked up in bed. It would be nice to tuck a child into bed. Snuggling the covers around their naked form. One of the teenagers shouted something obscene and Sid hurried away back towards home.

Joanie called a meeting first thing Friday, he would have to report to the chief later and so far Joanie had nothing to tell him. He surveyed the faces in the room; Curtis was sitting near the front, papers in hand whispering to Officer Short. The air barely moved despite two fans, one on each side. The large windows along the west wall were open but it seemed to make little difference. The officers looked sweaty and bored. Joanie caught a smile from Kelly standing near the back.

'Right.' Joanie projected his voice, the murmurs stopped instantly. 'We've got a suspect currently under surveillance but this does not mean we've got our man, far from it. Brian and Tony will do some enquiries in that area, the rest of us are going to interview every damn adult that kid knew.' He nodded at Curtis who started to hand out sheets.

'I know there's a lot of them, this kid seems to be involved with the whole damn neighbourhood. If you get anything, anything at all, copy it straight back to the station. If there's any chance this kid is still alive, we need to move rapidly.'

Joanie paused; despite the heat, he had everyone's attention.

'Do not, whatever you do, get slapdash, you need to be thorough. Don't miss anything; pick up on any possible leads no matter how outlandish. You will miss nothing! Is that clear?'

There were a few nods and a general murmur. It was a good team, the chief had been generous and Joanie had chosen carefully.

'I want a result.' He cast a stony look across the room. 'Today!'

With that, chairs scraped back, and a louder hubbub than before filled the still air. Joanie watched as they left the room. As Kelly drew level, he stopped her and motioned her into his office.

'I'm going to swap with you,' he said. 'I'll take Curtis with me at least for the morning. I'd like you to stay here and keep tabs on it all.'

Kelly stared at him, 'Is this an early promotion or something?'

'Don't you think you're up to the job?' he kept her gaze.

Kelly swallowed. 'Sure. I'm just curious.'

'So am I.' Joanie said with a glimmer of a smile.

Curtis was waiting outside; he stood up as Joanie appeared.

'You're coming with me, let's go.'

Curtis grabbed his jacket and fell into step behind Joanie.

'We'll go for the swimming teacher first,' Joanie tapped the sheet in Curtis' hand.

'Do you want me to drive?' Curtis was eager to get going. They were heading across the car park to one of the standard

Vauxhalls.

'No.' Joanie had the keys in his hand. 'I'll drive.' He didn't add that it made him feel nervous to be the passenger. Ever since Thompson died. Joanie could feel his heart squeeze, and wondered if that feeling would ever go, or was it something you lived with for the rest of your life. Like a tumour that lives inside, although this one not getting bigger, simply taking up residence in his chest and giving him a nasty nudge now and then when a memory hit. Margret had expected him to get over it, the accident, and he had really. Getting over the death of a good friend and colleague was one thing, trusting someone else at the wheel was quite another. Joanie always drove.

'I assume we're headed to the leisure centre,' Joanie asked glancing briefly at the sheet in Curtis' hand while they waited for the lights.

'Yeah, there isn't another pool is there?' he looked up.

'There's the private health club behind the carpet factory, they have a pool, and then of course there's Lady Bartholomew.'

Curtis laughed. Two months ago there had been a spate of cat deaths, all drowned in her private pool. It had caused quite a scandal at the time with the press hinting at witchcraft at the old manor house, and no end of puns and jokey posters round the station.

'Shame it's not about dead pussy cats this time.' Joanie watched the smile fade from Curtis' face and then the lights changed and he pulled away down Forest Street.

Mr Evans was a huge man towering over his charges by the pool's edge. They'd arrived in the middle of a lesson, watching through the glass as the man barked orders at the line of shivering children. Mr Evans walked behind each child, laying a hand on every shoulder giving them a number. Only one child shied under his hand, a smaller boy wearing shorts that hung to his knees. Joanie watched curiously as the boy cowered and rolled his shoulders in an attempt not to receive the firm grip. Difficult to tell who had the problem there, he thought, child or adult. The other kids didn't seem bothered.

'Bit touchy feely isn't he,' Curtis grimaced.

Joanie said nothing leading the way to the poolside. The manager said they could use his office and the three of them crowded into the tiny fishbowl. Through the glazing Joanie could see the children break ranks and splash into the pool under the disinterested gaze of the lifeguard.

'It's about Kieren isn't it?' Mr Evans began. 'I saw his picture in the paper.'

Joanie nodded watching the slump of his massive shoulders. He let Curtis ask the questions. Mr Evans had a perfect alibi; he'd been teaching 'tadpoles', which apparently stood for intermediate kids club, at the time of the disappearance on Tuesday, and later had been for drinks with other members of staff. Joanie flicked through the manager's file on the desk to see Mr Evans' name sketched into the Tuesday slot. He peered a little closer, it was in pencil, in fact most of the entries were in pencil, and some obviously had been rubbed out and re-written. Maybe they swapped staff around often, he looked carefully at the Tuesday 4pm slot. Difficult to tell if it had been written more than once.

'So how long have you been teaching Kieren?'

'Oh, almost a year I guess, he's very good, in my top group.' Mr Evans stood relaxed, his hands clasped gently in front of him, his back against the pin board.

Curtis scribbled on a notepad.

'Reception will be able to tell you exactly how long he's been coming.'

'Have you ever seen Kieren outside of the swimming club?' Joanie watched a vein throbbing in his large neck. He was ex-services, a tattoo stood out on his forearm. This guy obviously worked out, the kind of figure that earned a certain respect.

Mr Evans shrugged, 'Maybe,' he paused, 'sometimes I bump

into some of the kids at the supermarket or in town. I can't remember seeing Kieren specifically.'

Joanie nodded, the shrieks from the poolside were getting louder and he could see Mr Evans following his gaze and frowning.

'One more thing; who normally has access to the schedule, to change it I mean.' He pointed at the sheet.

'We all do,' Mr Evans shrugged. 'Sometimes we need to swap a lesson between ourselves, or fill in for someone on holiday.'

'Hmm' Joanie frowned. 'Well thanks for your help, we'll leave you to it.' They all shook hands and Joanie opened the door to let Mr Evans pass. As Mr Evans left, he gave Curtis a hearty slap on the back.

'I sure hope you find him, he's a good kid.'

Joanie was surprised to see how Curtis winced under the guy's hand and afterwards attempted to scratch his back where Mr Evans had slapped it. Joanie sent Curtis to check the rotas and attendance sheets at reception while he stared through the glass again as Mr Evans resumed strict control of the screaming children. Once they were lined up he blew a whistle and six children jumped in and started swimming furiously. Mr Evans had grabbed hold of one of the standing children amidst screams of protest from his team. When the others had almost reached the far side, he pushed the child in.

'What did he do that for?' Curtis stood beside him frowning.

They watched as the child became a blur of foam. By the time the others had got back to the side, he had caught them up and the second kids were leaping in.

Joanie slid his hands into his pockets, sometimes it felt like you wanted to see someone doing something inappropriate, just so you could prove you were doing your job. It was difficult not to read into every action or mannerism. The boundaries between what was acceptable touching with kids and what wasn't was such a fine one, and one that in the hands of different people, meant different things.

'He didn't have to do that,' Curtis grumbled, 'just cos the kid's fast.'

'Let's go.' Joanie pushed open the swing doors.

'Mind you,' he caught him up by the car, 'he has got a water-tight alibi.' He grinned, pleased with himself. 'Get it? Water-tight.' Curtis let out a guffaw as Joanie slid into the driver's seat.

Their next interview was across town in one of the smart new homes on Dalton Drive. They pulled up in front of a pale blue door. A red car was sitting in the drive looking like it had been recently washed. As they approached the front door, they could hear the sound of scales being played up and down a piano. Joanie stepped over the flowerbed and looked in the front window. Net curtains distorted the view of a young girl of about eight or nine sitting very erect at the piano. Beside her, with his back to Joanie, was a blond-haired man also sitting incredibly straight. Joanie tapped on the window. The man spun round and Joanie could tell by his posture that he wasn't amused at being interrupted. Joanie stepped back across the flowerbed and waited by the blue door. When the door opened, Joanie blinked and realised he was looking at purple-eye except the purple eye had faded to just a green smudge by the edge of his brow. It was the man who'd rushed past him down the stairs at the station a couple of days ago.

'Officers?' His voice clipped. So purple-eye remembered him too. 'Is this about the flasher?' he asked.

'No. We've come to ask you about one of your pupils, Kieren Matthews.' Joanie deliberately stood rather too close to the open doorway. Ross Thorpe moved back a step.

'Of course,' he conceded but then looked annoyed. 'You do realise I'm in the middle of a private paid lesson.' Mr Thorpe pursed his lips. Joanie didn't move.

Checking his watch, Mr Thorpe added, 'Penelope will be finished in ten minutes, you'd better come in and wait.'

Curtis raised his eyebrows at Joanie. They followed him down the hall and into the lounge; they were guided to a sofa covered with a bedspread opposite the piano. They sat and waited. Mr Thorpe resumed the lesson with his student.

'Now Penelope raise those wrists and lets here G again.' He picked up a ruler from the top of the piano and slid it under Penelope's wrists ensuring she didn't let them drop.

Joanie stared around the room, three pictures on the wall evenly spaced showed landscape scenes of Yorkshire. A vase of carnations stood on the windowsill. The piano itself was a grand, highly polished in a dark wood. Good enough for a concert hall by the looks of it. To their left, an open archway led through to the main sitting room with a cream sofa and armchair and another piano, this one an upright, against the wall.

Curtis looked bored and started to tap his pen in time with Penelope's fingers on the keys. Joanie took out his penknife and began to clean his nails.

'Good Penelope, now I've written down your homework.' He closed her exercise book and folded up the music. 'Remember fifteen minutes a day and keep those wrists off the edge of the piano. You're not an elephant, lightly, gently, tap, and tap with those fingertips.'

'Yes Mr Thorpe,' the girl slid off the stool and turned around to stare at the two strangers.

Mr Thorpe stood up and frowned at the gawping child. 'Thank you Penelope,' he said firmly. The girl looked up, took her books and ran into the hall. Joanie watched Mr Thorpe follow; through the window he could see Penelope trotting down the drive to a waiting vehicle.

Mr Thorpe re-entered the room and carefully turned his chair to face them.

'How may I be of assistance?' He composed his hands in his lap and looked with disgust at Joanie's penknife. Joanie brushed the bits from his front and leaned forwards.

'I presume you know that Kieren has disappeared,' Joanie began.

Mr Thorpe's face remained impassive, 'Indeed, I am not a complete ostrich, I assume you have some leads and will find the boy soon.' His eyebrows moved upwards, Joanie noted they seemed rather darker than his hair colour.

'Well perhaps you can help us with that.'

'Me?' Mr Thorpe put a hand across his chest, 'I don't see how a mere music teacher is going to help you find a murderer.'

'Nobody said Kieren was murdered.' Joanie studied him carefully, but Mr Thorpe's face didn't even flicker.

'Well it's what everybody thinks, isn't it?'

'We haven't spoken to everybody Mr Thorpe. Was there somebody in particular you meant?'

'No of course not, don't take me for a fool sergeant, even the papers have mentioned a link to the Hempstead case. I suspect most people in this town expect this boy is dead.'

'What do you think?'

'It would appear likely, don't you think?'

'I deal in facts Mr Thorpe not coincidences, like the fact that I'm an Inspector, not a sergeant and the fact that we need to know where you were 3 days ago.' Joanie nodded at Curtis to start asking the questions.

Throughout the interview, Mr Thorpe remained incredibly composed. On Tuesday afternoon he'd given two lessons and then gone to the supermarket for a salmon steak, potatoes and green beans, the fine sliced ones. Joanie had to interrupt him before Curtis' notepad filled up with the entire contents of Mr Thorpe's trolley.

'When did you last see Kieren?'

'Last Monday at seven minutes past four' his lips thinned slightly 'for his four o'clock lesson.'

'I see, did you notice anything unusual?'

'No. He was his normal incompetent self - I am yet to be

convinced that the Matthews family owns a piano let alone that Kieren ever touches it.' Mr Thorpe's lips pressed together tighter. 'And he left my piano keys sticky.'

Joanie noted his long fingers, the disapproving face. 'You don't seem upset by Kieren's disappearance.'

'I see, so now I'm supposed to have a deep emotional attachment to all my pupils am I? It's music I love Inspector, not grubby creatures that wouldn't know a Mozart from a Chopin. What happens to my pupils outside these walls is none of my business, so long as they practise what I've taught them, and quite frankly, Kieren didn't, or not that I could detect.'

'A little harsh considering Kieren might have been murdered.'

'It's simply the truth, isn't that what you came to seek?'

God, this guy was cold. Talk about an ice heart. Sweeping his eyes around the lounge one last time, he had to admit the room certainly didn't look like a child friendly room, no toys, or books, nothing out of place. The carpet looked immaculate and he assumed the bedspread over the sofa was to protect it from those 'grubby little fingers'.

'Perhaps we could ask your wife a few questions?'

There was the briefest pause, 'I'm not married Inspector, and no, before you ask, there is no 'significant' other.' Mr Thorpe's lips had thinned so much that they now appeared almost white. Satisfied that they wouldn't learn any more, Joanie and Curtis left.

'Jesus Christ, what was his problem?' They were in the car heading for a Mrs Barnes, the Cub Scout leader. Curtis looked genuinely pissed off. 'I'm surprised he even lets the kids in the door, let alone allows them to touch his beloved piano.'

'He has to make a living somehow,' Joanie replied.

'And tell me what single blokes do you know buy fresh flowers?'

Joanie nodded, he'd wondered the same thing himself. Maybe the guy was gay; did gay men like flowers and tidy houses?

It sounded like a stereotype but then Joanie fully admitted to himself that he was very naive when it came to gay culture.

'Mind you, Bella would sympathise with the covers on the sofa,' Curtis continued. 'Our Tim has sticky fingers all the time, it drives her bonkers.'

Mrs Barnes wasn't in so they returned to the station and Joanie sent Curtis to follow up the interviews with as much verifiable data as possible. Kelly looked relieved to see him.

'How's it going?' he asked, passing her a tea he'd brought from the machine.

'Better now you've arrived. The chief's been in.' She took the tea gratefully and vacated his chair.

'He wants to see you at one.' They both looked up at the clock. It was quarter past twelve. 'I don't think he was too pleased to find you out. I did explain you were doing some of the interviews yourself.'

Joanie nodded, it wasn't Kelly's fault; he probably should have checked it with the chief first.

'Things have been a bit manic; the press have virtually been banging down the door. And Short called in saying one of his had a dodgy alibi with a prostitute he didn't trust. 'Give her a tenner and she'd swear your mother was the queen' was the way he put it.'

Joanie nodded, 'Shirley Thompson.'

'Yeah, I think that's the name,' she held up a sheet.

'Anything else?' Joanie sighed.

'Nope. Surveillance called in, Sidney White went to work as normal and is still there.' Kelly shrugged.

'Great. I'm gonna have to kiss the chief's butt to stay on this one.'

'We'll get something,' Kelly assured closing the door behind her.

Joanie's desk was a riot of post-it notes and phone messages. He glanced at some of them recognising a few of the local journalists. He stacked them up and chucked them in the bin. If Kelly didn't think they were worth mentioning, then he wouldn't waste his time.

Saturday was not often Sid's day off but today it was. He awoke early and spent some time showering and choosing what to wear. If the internet was out of bounds for a while, then he'd have to start looking elsewhere. His nerves were taut; he needed to do something special, something relaxing. He dressed carefully. The weather looked warm again so he chose his thin yet smart pair of trousers, a light fawn colour he'd bought in Debenhams a couple of years ago. A long-sleeved checked shirt on top and perhaps he'd carry his umbrella. He made sure he had his library card just in case.

By nine o'clock he was gazing up and down the adult fiction, picking books out at random and reading the occasional sentence. By twenty past, mothers had started arriving with their little ones. Sid took up residence on a chair at the edge of the children's section with a couple of the paperbacks. Opening one of the books, he stared at a page for almost five minutes. The noise of the children was getting louder. Eventually a lady from the check-in desk went over and gathered the children into the story corner, very close to Sid's chair. Sid lowered his head so as not to catch the young lady's eye, frowning at the words in his lap. The story was soon underway, a modern version of the classic Hansel and Gretel. As the children became absorbed, mothers drifted away to the adult sections. Sid sighed contentedly allowing his eyes to roam across the children's heads. Fluffy shiny hair in a mixture of colours, all of it clean as if the children had been freshly brushed before their outing. One boy turned and glanced at Sid, his cheeks rosy. Sid watched him fiddle with the lace on his shoe, and then he picked something out of his pocket, a small plastic car and drove it along the carpet. The car climbed over the hill of his leg and then vertically up his red T-shirt, under his chin and came to rest by his lips. A pink tongue flicked out and made the front wheels spin. Sid was fascinated, the lady's voice lilted along in the background. Again out came the pink tongue and flicked at the car wheels. Sid thought how perfectly formed that tongue was. The colour of a sunset blush neatly curved at the end. Saliva made it glisten as it withdrew behind the lips. Sid imagined playing a game, flicking out his own tongue, maybe they'd flick tongues together, have a sword fight with tongues. The boy's was a short quick one whereas Sid knew his to be fat and slow. He imagined the feel of the boy's tongue on his own, gentle, probing. They'd laugh and make a game of it. The boy stopped flicking the wheels of the car and turned his head once more to look at Sid. His eyes widened and he shoved the car back in his pocket, accidentally knocking the child next to him who let out an angry cry.

'What's the matter Aiden?' The lady spoke at the startled boy. Sid jerked his head away, shutting his mouth quickly, he realised he had been rubbing his own tongue across his lips. The boy looked fearfully at the lady then back at Sid. It was time to leave; Sid didn't look at the woman. He stood quickly and strode across to the history section as far away from the boy with the tongue as possible.

6

Driving home later, Joanie decided to swing by the youth club. He parked across the road and watched a handful of small boys running around in shorts and T-shirts. Inside the noise was deafening, as some kind of riotous game ensued. A guy with lanky hair seemed to be scoring in some obscure way as kids kept giving him strands of coloured card.

'Beryl?' Joanie recognised the buxom woman by the door.

'Brian.' They shook hands. 'What an unexpected surprise.'

'I didn't realise you were the Mrs Barnes, how long have you been doing this?'

'About two and a bit years now.' she smiled.

She looked more relaxed than the last time they'd met. She'd lost that pinched look he remembered when her son had been in and out of trouble with the police. Alcohol, soft drugs, thieving, that kind of thing, in the same year as Sammy at school, Joanie remembered feeling relieved that it was someone else's kid in trouble and not his own.

'So how's Michael?' Joanie hadn't seen him for a while.

'He's fine, getting it together. He's got a girlfriend and a flat in Southampton.' Beryl looked relieved.

'That's good.' Joanie nodded.

'Is this business or pleasure?' Beryl tried to laugh, but it came out a little too high and trembled.

'Business, I'm afraid. Kieren Matthews.'

'Of course.' Beryl pulled a hanky from her pocket and clenched it in her fist. 'First Martin Hempstead and now Kieren.'

Joanie remained silent. The game before them seemed to have degenerated into attacking the lanky youth. About twenty children were trying to pull him to the floor.

'You know that's why I took this on.' She looked at Joanie with wide wet eyes.

Joanie didn't understand.

'Chrissie, the lady before me, she was here when Martin disappeared. She couldn't carry on, all the children so upset. I think she felt it was like losing one of your own.'

Joanie breathed deeply, sometimes he forgot the ripples that were created with some crimes. It wasn't just the parents that suffered; there was a knock on effect in a town like this. Not everyone had Joanie's ability to put it aside and move on. He suddenly felt guilty.

'Kieren hasn't been with us long,' Beryl explained. 'Still finding his feet with the older boys I think.'

'Who's he?' Joanie nodded at the lanky youth who was now on his knees.

'Tim Ripley. He's new, one of our helpers. We had him checked by your people though. We have to these days.' They watched him finally give in and flop to the floor, the boys leapt off cheering.

'Can I give you a call tomorrow?' Joanie decided that perhaps this wasn't the right time or place to be questioning Beryl.

'I'll be at home in the morning. Do you want my number?' She suddenly looked embarrassed realising that Joanie was bound to have her number.

'Great. Speak to you then.' Joanie glanced back at the youth named Tim; he'd check him out on the computer tomorrow.

Interesting smells wafted from the kitchen as Joanie stepped into the hall. It immediately brought a sense of peace. This must be the first time in two weeks that he'd come home to find Margret cooking dinner. He wished he'd brought flowers, he'd noticed them at the garage when he filled up. Too late now. In the kitchen Margret was serving up salmon, new potatoes and salad. It looked divine.

'That looks great,' he complimented turning on the taps to wash his hands.

'It's just fish.' She plonked the pans by the sink and sat down.

Joanie joined her and couldn't help smiling at the plates.

'What are you looking so pleased about? Solved your case then?'

Joanie took a mouthful and shook his head. 'If I left Curtis to it, then yes, but actually I don't think so.'

'Am I supposed to understand that?'

'Sorry, Curtis thinks we've got our man, but I'm not so sure.'

'I see, doesn't he fit your psychological profile?'

Joanie smiled, she would often tease him about his theories.

'No, I guess he doesn't.' For a moment he frowned as he remembered that gesture Sidney made the other night that had suddenly made him uncomfortable. It tugged at a distant memory.

'Samantha had her first exam today.' Margret interrupted his thoughts.

'How'd it go?' Joanie took a large mouthful.

'Ring her and she'll tell you, I've spoken to her already.'

Joanie felt suitably chastised for not keeping in touch with what was going on. 'This dinner's great by the way. Thanks sweetheart.'

Margret raised her eyebrows at him. 'That's not what you usually call me.'

'I used to.'

'I know.' They sat in silence as they finished the meal. Joanie was confused, he wasn't sure if that meant he should be calling her sweetheart or not. Why had Margret become so hard to read?

After dinner, Joanie sat in the large armchair, moved the footstool so he could recline fully and picked up the phone by his elbow. After the fifth ring, just as Joanie decided she must be out, it was answered.

'Madhouse here,' her voice was instantly recognisable.

'Hi pumpkin.'

'Hey Dad, how's it going, solved the case yet?'

Joanie smiled, Margret must have mentioned it. 'Not yet, but I'm working on it.'

'You'll get him, you always do.'

'I only wish that was true. So how are things with you, first exam and all?'

'I don't know,' she sighed, 'when I came out, I felt really good about it but since I spoke to the others, I'm not so sure. Their answers didn't sound anything like mine.'

'Don't dwell on it honey, what's done is done, you have to keep looking forward. When's the next one?' Joanie flicked through his diary.

'Monday, then a two-week break before the last three.'

Joanie jotted them down. 'Do you want to come home for a few days?'

'Erm, I think it's probably best if I study here thanks. Besides I don't want to get in the way.' He could hear the awkwardness in her voice.

'What do you mean?'

'Well I don't know, you're the one that said Mum was going a bit potty, what with painting and stuff. I just thought that maybe you two had something to sort out.'

Now it was Joanie's turn to sigh, she was right of course but he wondered what Margret had said. Was it him? Had he done something?

'You'll work something out Dad.'

Joanie wasn't so sure. Of course they'd had ups and downs before but this was different, it felt like they had slipped onto different wavelengths.

'Good luck for next week love, I'll speak to you soon.'

'Sure, bye Dad.'

Margret walked in then with a mug of tea and sat on the sofa; she raised her eyes at Joanie and nodded at the phone.

'Sammy,' he acknowledged.

Margret nodded again and picked up the remote. Joanie wondered if he should say anything else, try and tackle what was bothering his wife. Instead the news caught his attention as a picture of Kieren filled the screen. Kieren's mother came on; all tears, pleading for whoever had abducted him, to give him back unharmed. Fat chance, thought Joanie but you couldn't voice that sort of thing. Even Kelly, the eternal optimist, had said as much to him earlier. He watched the screen, Kelly standing sympathetically in the background. The chief appeared and in a suitably solemn voice assured the public that everything possible was being done and urged anyone with information to come forward. He looked a lot calmer than he'd been only ten minutes before the press conference with Joanie in his office.

'So who the hell is this guy you've been tailing?' he'd demanded. Surveillance was expensive and Joanie believed the chief might be being squeezed from higher up. 'Well don't just stand there, I need answers, the press are all over this trying to link it to the Hempstead case.'

'Sidney White acted suspiciously during a routine interview with Curtis and myself, he is also one of the last adults to have seen Kieren.' Joanie folded his arms.

'Is that it, is that all you have on him? Have you searched his house, brought him in for further questioning?'

'No sir.'

'Why the hell not? This isn't a game of hide and seek goddamit.'

'We don't have reasonable evidence to warrant a search at this time.' Joanie quoted the book at him.

'Jeez!' Fortunately for Joanie, the chief played by the rules too, but it didn't stop him from hating Joanie for it.

'Damn well find some evidence then. What are you going to tell the press?'

Joanie had seen them gathering outside the building and understood a statement would be made at two o'clock. He hadn't called the conference and he was damned if he'd be the mug to stand in front of them.

'Nothing.' Joanie paused. 'Sir.'

'Somebody has to go down there and show their face.'

Joanie stared straight back, his eyes cold and hard. There would be questions about the Hempstead case, they both knew that and Joanie hadn't even touched that case.

'Get out!'

Joanie smiled to himself as he watched the interviewer on the TV badgering the chief but the chief refused to be drawn. Joanie was glad it hadn't been him today. He hated seeing himself on the television. He concentrated on Sidney's face in his mind's eye. He was sure it wasn't the first time he had met Sidney White but the name meant nothing.

'I've arranged to have lunch with the Quintons on Sunday.' Margret interrupted his thoughts.

'Oh.'

'You're not working are you?' Her voice was accusing.

'Officially no, but with this case..' He could see she wasn't impressed. 'I'll go in tomorrow and do what I can to leave Sunday free, OK?'

'I'll take that as a yes then,' she frowned at him. Joanie knew he couldn't promise, not with the chief breathing down his neck but he wanted to keep her happy.

'Sure.' Joanie tried to smile. 'Dinner with the Quintons.' At least they didn't live far away, a twenty-minute drive at most and if this weather held, it would be nice to sit in their garden.

At lunchtime on Saturday, Joanie could feel his stress levels rising. He stared at the wall, his mind ticking quickly over the people, places, questions, nothing was jumping out, nothing and everything could be a lead. What a bloody mess, no body, no evidence, no sight or sound of where Kieren went after he left his friends at the ice-cream van. If Joanie believed in such things, he'd entertain the idea that the child had been whisked away by aliens.

'Daydreaming isn't going to get you very far.' The chief stood in the office doorway scowling at Joanie. He stepped in and closed the door behind him.

'Well, what have we got, please don't tell me nothing, I can't justify all these salaries if all you can keep giving me is nothing.'

Joanie could feel the anger wafting off the man in heat waves.

He had an urge to give him a long spiel listing all the interviews they had undertaken, the physical search which covered 2 square miles in acute detail, the number of officers who had knocked door to door, in fact the number of doors they'd knocked on, but at the end of the day, Joanie had nothing. He'd known the chief long enough to realise that spouting the statistics of the operation to him wouldn't cut the ice. Instead he spread his hands, shaking his head gently.

'Fuck!' he exploded. His palm slamming down on Joanie's desk. He turned away to stare at the board - now covered with papers, pictures, pins, threads, you name it.

Then the chief spoke through his teeth 'the department can't afford to have another Hempstead outcome.'

'Yes sir, we're all under pressure.'

The chief swung around and leant forwards across the desk, his face bearing down on Joanie. 'Don't you tell me about pressure. The only thing I need from your lips Johanson is results.' The chief strode out of the office without another glance.

Joanie sighed; he added a couple of notes to the answers Mrs Barnes had given him on the phone. He'd already checked out the youth Tim. Nothing much there. All he wanted was a shred, a hint, anything that could lead somewhere. But all he had was a mass of loose ends, none of them inviting. He rubbed his temples.

They'd known the Quintons since Sammy was small. Their children Lin and Peter had gone to the same school and they'd shared lifts together for years. The tall Victorian house lay on the edge of town with a garden that sloped down to the river Test. It was an impressive view of the river valley with the Hampshire fields rolling into the distance. They sat outside on the decking built on stilts leading out of the french windows. There was less heat than there'd been earlier in the week but it was still incredibly bright and in their sheltered position, Joanie could feel himself getting sticky.

'Another glass of wine?' Bob offered. He filled Margret's glass but Joanie shook his head. He was already feeling far too sleepy.

'I hadn't realised it was your case,' Bob pointed at a newspaper on the table.

'I avoided the TV cameras.'

Bob laughed, 'You never were one for the photos, Karen was saying only yesterday how rarely you appear in any of our old albums with the kids. I would have thought you cut quite a good figure on the television. Solid, stable bloke like yourself.' He was of course referring to Joanie's expanded middle, which hadn't been helped by a huge meal of lamb kebabs followed by bucket loads of strawberries and cream.

Joanie patted his stomach; 'I blame this on Karen's cooking.'

'Ha,' Margret laughed cruelly, 'you certainly couldn't blame it on mine.'

The Quintons noticed the odd exchange and there was an uncomfortable silence.

'Coffee anyone?' Karen bounced up.

A cloud now shaded the garden, it would pass but the sudden chill led to three raised hands. Joanie could do with something to keep him awake. Although it would be nice to doze off this afternoon and not have to think about work.

'So how's the investigation going?'

Joanie gave him a tired look.

Bob raised his hands, 'OK, OK, don't talk shop. How about the fishing then. Been out recently?' Joanie hadn't but they discussed this season's catch at least for Bob and where they might go. In fact Joanie reckoned he hadn't touched his rod since last year. Bob had found a new spot out near Cheriton but the licence was expensive.

'You should come with me next time I go, you always catch the bigger ones.'

It was a running joke between them. On the few occasions when they had fished together, Joanie had done surprisingly well, easily catching the heaviest fish.

Karen brought the coffees out just as Joanie's mobile burred angrily in his pocket. He got up, excused himself and walked down the couple of steps onto the lawn.

'Johanson here.'

'Officer Short sir. I'm afraid it looks like we've got a body sir.'

Joanie was instantly wide-awake, the trees above his head thrashed suddenly in the breeze. Joanie had expected this, had been waiting for the last few days, yet the cold hard truth still clutched at his chest.

'Where?'

'Out at Falbrook farm on the way to Linksfield.'

'Is it him?' superfluous really, of course it was Kieren.

'That's the current reasoning, yeah. Not easy to recognise though.'

Joanie could detect the distress in the young man's voice.

'I'll come straight over.' Joanie flicked off the mobile and leapt up two steps at a time back onto the decking.

'My, the old man's got life in him yet.' Bob grinned.

'I have to go. I'm sorry,' Joanie leant over and gave Karen a kiss thanking her for the fabulous meal; he took a quick slurp at the coffee. Bob stood up and they shook hands promising to go fishing together sometime soon. Margret merely waved him away refusing to meet his eye.

The body had been found by the farmer in a remote barn five miles away. Unfortunately it had been badly eaten by rats but they could use the dental records to be sure. There were shreds of clothing and a small pair of trainers still tied to the body's feet. Joanie stood covering his mouth and nose with his hanky staring at those neatly tied trainers. They were tied with a double bow and the fact that they were still firmly knotted hinted that the boy's mother had tied them. To stop him tripping up Joanie thought, such an innocent, thoughtful act by a mother not knowing that something far worse could befall her son. Joanie turned away and looked across the fields. There was a stony track that led uphill towards the tarmac road. The barn itself was simple, four corner posts and a roof half-filled with hay bales. The farmer had moved about five bales out of the way to reveal the body.

'It was the smell,' the farmer responded, 'well that and the fact I saw at least three rats run out made me suspicious. I mean you always get rats but you don't tend to see them much, and certainly not three at once.' He was smoking a cigarette with a trembling hand beside a rusty tractor. 'Lost a cow in the ditch this winter, same kind of smell, thought maybe it was another one.' Officer Short was taking notes; they were standing away from the body allowing the forensics team to do their job. The hot days had dried the track to cracking point and although it had rained yesterday, the body had been here longer. Joanie suspected whatever vehicle the killer had used would not have left any marks on the hard surface.

Joanie left Short to take a statement from the farmer and went over to speak to Bob Davis. He was standing in a white boiler suit, having removed his hood, and writing on a pad.

'Afternoon Bob,' they shook hands.

'Ah, Joanie, your case then is it?'

'I wish it weren't.'

'Specially this one,' Bob indicated the body with his pen, 'Not pretty I'm afraid, and no clear indication of how he died before you ask. I expect the boy didn't die here, more likely was dumped later. Several days I would think, can't give you anything more than that.'

'OK, thanks. We're really stumped at the moment, so assuming this is Kieren Matthews, the faster you can give us something the better.'

'Can you tell me a time when you lot didn't want answers yesterday?'

Joanie smiled. 'You're right, sorry Bob.'

'Sheesh, you lot think I'm a magician, which of course I am, but even magicians need time to set things up before we can show you the magic. I'll keep you informed Joanie.' He pulled his hood up again and stepped over a bale and back towards the body.

Joanie turned away. There wasn't much he could do here anyway; it was up to the lab boys now. He went back to the office briefly, informed the chief on the phone and went home. Unless there was some clear evidence, he would have to wait for the 'magic' as Bob called it.

Joanie was in the office by seven on Monday, sitting in a room with both of the surveillance pairs. He was leaning forwards, a stack of reports in his hand.

'Listen, I don't have time to read through all this, so I need you guys to tell me straight up if anything you saw was even slightly suspicious.'

'We would have called in, if we'd thought that.' The guy with the beard looked annoyed.

'I know,' Joanie sighed, 'OK let me put it another way, anything that Sidney did that you thought was even slightly odd, or maybe it's just something you saw that has stuck in your mind for no particular reason.'

There was dead silence; Joanie thought he might be wasting his time, when one of them spoke up.

'He was carrying that bag,' he turned to his partner, 'on Thursday, took it to work with him,' he nudged his partner, 'you remember, the plastic one.'

'What, his sandwiches?'

'He didn't come out with it again at the end of the day.'

'Yeah, like I said, his sandwiches.'

Joanie interrupted them, 'What did you actually see.'

The first man continued, 'he was carrying a plastic bag with something in it, not very big really, walked to work with it, but didn't go home with it.'

'That's cos he ate them stupid.'

'How do you know they were sandwiches?' Joanie insisted.

The second officer shrugged, 'stands to reason, that sort of size, take it to work, don't bring it home.'

Joanie looked at the first officer again.

'It could of been, nothing obvious that's for sure. He didn't take a bag any other day.'

'OK, it's probably nothing, but this is good, give me something else,' he pressed, 'anything at all.'

Painstakingly, Joanie managed to glean only a couple more

things; Sidney had been to the library, nothing special there although Joanie was annoyed to discover that although one of the officers had followed him inside, he'd nipped into the toilet while he was there. 'Guy was in the history section when I came out.' Neither books that the officer mentioned meant anything to Joanie or seemed to provide any clues.

Back in his office, he briefed Kelly and Curtis, 'Kelly you follow up on those library books, and if possible see what other books our Sidney White has been borrowing lately. Curtis I want you to see if you can locate this plastic bag; talk to Dave and Tom if you need more details, perhaps you can do something low key at the supermarket. We don't have warrants at this point.'

'Anything from the lab?'

Joanie shook his head. 'In fact we don't have confirmation that it's Kieren Matthews yet.'

Curtis looked surprised. 'It is though, isn't it?'

'Likely, but not a foregone conclusion. Now go.' Joanie waited until they'd shut the door before leaning back in his chair and taking out his penknife. He cleaned his nails methodically. His mind clicking and linking, looking, turning and twisting. This case was like trying to solve a Rubik's cube.

It was a fresh Monday morning, there had been some rain in the night and the temperature had cooled considerably. Sid didn't mind doing the Monday morning shift today, although one of the busiest days of the week, it meant he was occupied, less time to think and worry. Maybe life was returning to normal, no nightmares about Kieren last night, and no more visits from the police. The repetitive trolley pushing and stacking was therapeutic. David was working diligently, picking up litter that had blown over in the change of weather. Sid wondered if it would be safe to use his computer again, maybe he could take the bag of clothes home with him tonight. The more he thought about it, the more sensible it seemed, that would certainly bring his life back to normality.

'Let's go Sid, lunch time.' David was stood by his side, a full black bag and the grabber in his hands.

'OK,' he smiled.

'Are you feeling better today?' David asked

'Much, thank you. What did your mother put in your sandwiches today?'

'Egg I think, egg and lettuce,' he grimaced. 'I hate lettuce, feels all funny in your mouth, do you hate lettuce?'

Sid smiled some more, no he didn't hate lettuce, he hated the police, but of course he didn't say this to David. Together they walked into the store and through the back to the staff room.

At eleven o'clock Bob Davis confirmed the identity of the body and gave a clearer approximation to the time of death; late Thursday evening by asphyxiation, they had found some bruises on the body's neck despite the damage done by the rats. That meant the boy had been held some place for two days before he died. Joanie hated to think what those two days might have been like.

'I know you want the 'who did it' bit,' Bob continued on the phone, 'we're testing some skin found under one of his fingernails and also some hair samples.'

Curtis burst into the room. 'I got it!' he shouted triumphantly brandishing a blue plastic bag.

Joanie frowned and looked down at the phone, 'OK Bob, got to go, keep working your magic'

He sat back and folded his arms. 'Alright big shot, what is it.'

'The bag, the one that Dave and Tom saw Sidney White take into the supermarket.'

'You've got your hands all over it!' Joanie stood up, his cheeks blooming.

'It's OK, I've already removed the original bag and sent that in to the lab.'

Joanie relaxed a little and sat down motioning for Curtis to take a seat. There was a knock at the open door and Kelly peered round.

'Can I join in?'

Joanie nodded and the three of them crowded round the desk as Curtis laid out several clear evidence bags, each with an item of clothing inside. There was a small blue jumper, with an orange stain near the neck, a T-shirt with a Thomas the Tank Engine picture on the front, two odd shoes, a small hanky with the letter P embroidered on it, and a pair of yellow pants.

'This is it.' Joanie pointed at the T-shirt, the other two nodded.

'Wait, that's Makka Pakka,' Kelly said

'What?'

'Makka Pakka,' Kelly picked up the yellow pants bag and pointed to a small printed picture.

'Yep, Timmy prefers Iggle Piggle.'

'Can one of you please tell me what on earth you're talking about?' Joanie could feel his voice rising.

'Sorry sir,' Kelly explained, 'They're characters from a little kid's TV program called 'In the Night Garden'. And, these are the pants that Jessica's mother described.'

'The dirty old man in the park?'

'That's the one.'

'Curtis, tell me exactly where you got these.' Joanie sat back again and steepled his fingers.

Curtis explained about finding out that Tom had followed Sidney into the supermarket and into the back area, how Sidney had turned right and at that point, Tom had been spotted by an employee and told to leave.

'But you see, the staff room is to the left, and Tom said Sidney was disappearing towards the cold store when he got told to leave. So I had a little nosy about. There's a gap between one of the big freezer compartments and the rear wall, shone my torch in and hey bingo. The bag matched the one Tom said.'

'Hmmm, do we have anyone who saw him put it there?'

Curtis shook his head.

'This is very tenuous, Kieren Matthew's T-shirt, and Jessica's pants both of which we think Sidney White stashed behind the freezer.' Joanie sighed. 'This won't be enough, but it's a start.'

'Let's bring the bastard in.' Curtis stated.

They were interrupted by the shrill phone on Joanie's desk. He answered it straightaway; it was the front desk.

'We've got a walk-in sir, claims to have seen someone by the river the day Kieren Matthews disappeared.'

'What? Is he willing to give a statement?'

'Looks like it, unless his wife makes it for him.' There was a snigger down the phone, which Joanie ignored.

'We'll be right down.' Joanie turned to his officers.

'Kelly, follow up on the pants, see if we can do an ID on Sidney White, and push a bit harder about what the mother thinks he did to Jessica, if you can get anything from the child herself, even better.'

'Curtis, come with me, we've got a new witness apparently.'

'But what about Sidney White?' Curtis' voice sounded almost panicky.

'I'll send someone to bring him in, we'll let him stew before we speak to him.'

7

A burly man, by the name of Dylan Griffiths, with several tattoos greeted them grudgingly in the interview room. Fluttering beside him was a slight woman in stilettos.

'I'm Inspector Johansen, this is officer Curtis, I understand you have some information for us?'

'That's right, in't it Dylan, tell 'im everythin' you told me. Bout that bloke and everthin'.' The woman leaned on the table and nodded 'saw it on the TV last week, 'bout that poor kid,' she stood up and nodded at Dylan 'go on then!'

'Shut up woman. I'll tell it in my own time.' He threw a dirty look at her and then faced Joanie.

'I were walking my dog down by the river. Tuesday like it says in the papers, about the same time I reckon. Anyway there was a geezer by the football field that's all. I didn't know him.' The man shrugged and folded his arms leaning back in his chair.

'That's not all Dyl, tell these nice gentlemen wot you told me.'

'Will you just shut yer trap. Were you there were you?' The man stood up, aggression singing from his biceps. Joanie rubbed a hand across his forehead.

'Don't you threaten me yer big bully.' The woman attacked him with her handbag slapping him with her free hand. Joanie nodded at Curtis who easily restrained the woman and took her out of the room. Left alone Dylan sat down again and eyed Joanie suspiciously. Joanie waited for Curtis to return before asking questions.

'So tell us.'

Dylan explained about his dog, sniffing at the guy's trousers and how the stupid cunt had kicked Rambo his Jack Russell.

'Why didn't you tell us this before? This has been in the newspapers since Wednesday.' Joanie asked.

'I've been away, on site in Wales, tarmacking a new bypass. You can check if you want. It was the wife that mentioned it. Look I reckon the guy was just a drunk, he seemed too fucking dazed to take a kid.'

'Not too dazed to kick your dog though,' Joanie pointed out.

'Yeah, stupid bastard.'

Joanie and Curtis left the room to confer briefly in the corridor.

'His description matches Sidney White, we must be on the right track.' Curtis concluded.

'Sidney admitted to being by the river, it's not like this guy saw him do anything.'

'Then how come Sidney never mentioned kicking a dog?'

Joanie said nothing, something wasn't quite right he admitted but it didn't feel like the breakthrough they so desperately needed.

'See if we've got a photo of White from the surveillance guys and some random photos of similar men, we'll see if our labourer can identify him.' Joanie sent Curtis upstairs, he looked through the small window of the interview door. Gary tapped Joanie on the shoulder and handed him a sheet of paper; it was about Dylan Griffiths.

'His wife's nipped out for a fag if you were wondering,' Gary added.

'Thanks', he scanned the sheet quickly, not your most law-abiding citizen with various traffic offences, some violent conduct including a recent charge relating to a violent incident at a night club in town. Looking back through the window in the door, Dylan had lit a cigarette despite the obvious no smoking sign on the wall. His foot was drumming on the floor and his free hand was picking at the plastic edge of the table. Joanie leaned back on the wall of the corridor, taking out his penknife. He imagined himself in the witness' situation. Walking down the riverbank and someone kicks your dog. Given the temperament of this guy, he'd have kicked White in the teeth, but Dylan hadn't mentioned anything like that. And why on earth would Sidney White kick the dog, had it bitten him?

Curtis appeared with a handful of photos, and they went back in.

The witness picked out White immediately and Curtis grinned triumphantly at Joanie.

'Did you hit this man?' Joanie leaned forwards.

'What?' An angry red glow appeared on the man's cheeks, 'who said that? Did he tell you that?'

Joanie waited saying nothing.

'Look, I told you what happened. I don't have to be here you know, I'm trying to be helpful.' The man gripped the edge of the table with his hands, his feet firmly on the floor and his knees wide apart.

Joanie stood up, 'Thank you Mr Griffiths, we appreciate you coming in, would you be willing to do a positive identification at some point?'

The man's shoulders relaxed, he stood up too but ignored Joanie's offered hand. 'Guess so,' he reluctantly agreed.

'My colleague here will create a written statement for you to sign.'

'Oh fuck! You mean I got to wait around?'

Joanie smiled and left.

Curtis badgered him all the way back up the stairs to the office. There was a mismatch in statements obviously, Sidney White hadn't mentioned meeting this man or his dog but what did that prove? Curtis seemed desperate though.

'Sidney White was lying, it's obvious he's got something to hide.'

'And what makes you so sure Dylan Griffiths isn't the liar?'

'He didn't need to come in and tell us, why would he bother if it didn't really happen.'

'Personal vendetta?' Joanie didn't believe this any more than Curtis but neither did he think this recent information was very useful. 'Besides if what Mr Griffiths says is true, that makes him a possible suspect who was down on the river bank around the time Kieren disappeared. He's certainly strong and aggressive enough.'

'Are we going to question Sidney White about meeting Dylan and kicking his dog, see what he's got to say about it?'

'Stop getting so excited, if Sidney White is our man, we need to take things very carefully and in the right order because the only piece of evidence we really have is that T-shirt.'

'Which I found.' Curtis gloated.

'If you want a medal kid, you'll have to work a lot harder than that, I don't have anything yet that gives me confidence in charging this guy with murder. You come chasing in like you've found the golden chalice. You haven't, not anywhere close, so stop boasting and get back down there to take Dylan's formal statement. If you think Sidney's our man, prove it to me.'

Curtis scowled in response, shoving the door hard as he left.

Sid was walking a long line of trolleys back to the entrance when two men got out of a blue Vauxhall and approached him. They looked like movie gangsters in dark suits but without the sunglasses. One of them flicked out his ID and flashed it in front of Sid's face. Sid's world crumbled before his eyes, something had gone wrong, terribly wrong. And now here it was, he felt himself grow cold and tremble, biting his lip. He followed the men to the car and climbed in the back.

David appeared at the window tapping on the glass, he had a worried frown on his face. 'Where are you going Sid?'

Sid dropped his eyes, clutching his hands together in his lap.

'Wait!' The car started to pull away, but had to stop as a lady crossed the black and white stripes with a trolley full of shopping. David ran around the car to the open window of the driver. 'Don't take him away,' David pleaded.

'Take your hands off the car son.' The driver spoke quietly.

'You can't take him as well.' The car moved forwards.

'They're taking all my friends.' David yelled behind them. Sid couldn't help twisting around in his seat. David was standing in the middle of the road, tears running down his face, people had stopped to stare at him and then at the car.

They gathered speed and swung out onto the main road, driving in silence along the slick streets. Sid felt sick; he'd let him down. There was something distinctly final about David standing there crying, Sid was certain that things would never be the same again.

At the station he had to remove everything from his pockets and sat in a room with a table and two chairs. An officer stood motionless in the corner. And so the nightmare had begun.

Sid sipped the tea carefully, he wasn't sure if they'd put something in it. Nobody made tea for Sid except Sid. He swallowed.

'The tea isn't up to much I know, out of the machine I'm afraid.' It was the woman who spoke, the one called Sergeant Mowbray. Sid looked up at her brown eyes; the overhead light reflected a sheen from her clean hair. She didn't smile; instead her lips pressed together, small movements allowing her to introduce the interview, date and time into the humming machine. When they'd asked him if he wanted a solicitor present, he hadn't known what to say, he didn't know any solicitors and even if he did, the less people that knew stuff about him the better. And besides weren't solicitors even worse than the police, crafty buggers that could turn what you said into something completely different. No he'd be better off alone, it was what he was used to. It would be bad enough having to talk to these two without doing it all over again with a lawyer.

The other person in the room was that blond-haired bastard who'd come to see him earlier in the week. The one with the nasty sneer who had opened one of his drawers. Sid refused to look at him, even when it was he who posed a question. Instead he spoke to Sergeant Mowbray.

Sid studied the map laid in front of him on the table. Sergeant Mowbray had drawn a pencil line across the map showing his route from home to the river as he had described it.

'And which way did you go then?'

He tried to recount which way he had gone home. Putting his finger on the map, he noticed it was trembling slightly. Beads of sweat bubbled up on his top lip. The burr of the overhead light gained intensity until it felt like Sid had a large wasp right by his ear. The air had grown stale and he could smell old smoke wafting out of Curtis' uniform. He couldn't read the road names clearly, the words blurring at the edges. The pencil line beckoned, the only clear mark on the paper. Sid pushed his finger across the map, back down from the football field and onto that pencil line. Carefully he followed it home.

'So you went home the same way?' Kelly confirmed. 'The suspect nodded,' she added for the benefit of the machine.

'And did you meet anyone, either on your way there or back again?'

'I met David, like I said. He introduced me to a boy called Kieren. There were two other boys in the field.'

'Nobody else?'

'There were the mothers with their babies, I've told you about them too.'

'Yes. Anybody else?'

'No.' Sid folded his hands in his lap and stared at the cold tea on the table. They'd asked these same questions so many times now, that he had begun to doubt himself, did they know something he didn't? He closed his eyes for a second trying to soothe the buzzing in his head by opening his drawer of clothes. An image of Tommy popped into his head. His beautiful face, framed by those soft curls. He grinned suddenly and opened his eyes to see Curtis almost growling at him. Sid stopped smiling and stared back at the map. He wondered, if left alone with Curtis, he might never get home.

'What did you just remember?' Sergeant Mowbray asked.

Sid shook his head rapidly, 'Nothing.'

They sat in silence for a minute and then the two of them left, another officer coming in to stand in the corner, moments later they were back.

It was Sergeant Mowbray who spoke.

'The scars on your arms,' she spoke quietly and Sid wasn't sure he'd heard her right. Alarm bells were ringing loudly in his head.

'Are you seeing anyone about them, I mean talking to anyone about a problem?'

'There's nothing wrong with my arms, I'm fine, I've stopped seeing her anyway.' He felt flustered, suddenly out of control.

'Who have you stopped seeing?'

'The doctor,' Sid paused biting his lips and gripping each of his forearms 'why am I here?'

'As you know, we are investigating the disappearance of Kieren Matthews, you were one of the last people to have seen Kieren. There's also another matter you may be able to help us with. Excuse me a minute.' She left the room.

Sid sat still but couldn't help nervously scratching at his forearms; he studied the edge of the table to avoid looking at the blond-haired policeman who was still sitting opposite.

'I know you did it,' he whispered like a snake. Sid didn't even see his lips move, but he was sure that was what he said.

Sid averted his eyes, clasping his hands together under the table. He looked at the door, wishing for someone else to come in. It opened and in walked another policeman, Inspector Johansen, the older, stocky, almost portly man who'd been to his flat.

'Afternoon.' Joanie sat down. He leaned his body back in the chair opposite Sid, steepling his fingers across his chest.

'Sidney White.'

Now he didn't know which of them to look at, Barbie head or the Inspector. It was clear they knew something, but what?

Sergeant Mowbray returned to the room and placed a plastic bag on the table. The inspector leaned forwards and opened it. Slowly he pulled out the contents and laid them on the desk.

Sid almost shrieked, his breath became short; he glanced quickly at the Inspector to see him staring at him.

'Do you recognise these items?'

'Er, no,' crikey what on earth should he say, where had they got them?

'Are you sure?'

'Yes, no, I mean....' his arms were burning, his chest hurt and the buzzing in his head had reached fever pitch. He suddenly stood up from the table and shouted.

'NO!'

There was silence, Joanie watched the man sweat, standing and shaking. Kelly had stepped back and Curtis had jumped up from the table as soon as Sidney had moved. Everybody stood in their new positions and waited.

A puff of air escaped Sidney's mouth and he collapsed back into his chair.

'I'd like to speak to a lawyer please.' His voice barely above a whisper.

Sid sat in the dim cell listening to the drip of the toilet in the corner. There was a blanket on the bed beside him but he didn't feel like climbing underneath it. There weren't any windows except the small crosshatched hole in the top of the door. The walls were bare echoing back the tiniest of sounds as he shifted his foot across the concrete floor. He was used to being on his own, it didn't bother him, but the room did, and the knowledge of where he was and why. He'd cried a lot since they'd brought him in, never in front of anyone of course but left alone in this cell. There was a dark patch between his feet where the tears had fallen.

A loud clanging made Sid draw back in horror, he clutched at the blanket as if it might hold some kind of protection. It was too much like that other locked room and despite knowing full well he was a grown man, Sid couldn't resist the automatic response as someone came stomping towards the door.

'Supper.' The slot at the bottom slid open and a tray was pushed through. 'Don't look so worried, it's only shepherds pie. You're not vegetarian are you?' A face appeared behind the bars; Sid released the blanket and tried to look normal. The face waited. Sid averted his eyes and then reached for the tray.

It was dark now and Sid was tired, his nerves raw from the constant tightening in his chest. He wanted to get out, wanted to just turn the handle and walk out. He knew he couldn't and he also knew that no one was likely to come in, at least not until morning but that didn't stop the terror that growled away churning up the shepherds' pie deep in his stomach. If he slept, he would have nightmares, that was certain, yet if he didn't he'd be tired and ragged by tomorrow and when they questioned him again, he didn't want something stupid to slip out. Couldn't let his guard down not even for a second especially if that Barbie man was there. Sid smiled as he imagined Officer Curtis to be a pathetic plastic doll that he could mutilate, pulling out its arms and legs and spinning the head round and round.

Sid awoke lying in what felt like a bath; he sat up suddenly.

There was a loud clanging and a jangle of keys, lights went on behind the door. He found his clothes were soaked and he was trembling.

'What's wrong with you? Waking the whole damn corridor up with your yelling.' A face appeared angrily at the grill and a light sprang on. Sid blinked in the harsh fluorescent beam. 'What do you want?' The voice demanded an answer. Sid shrank back against the wall beside the bed.

'Nightmare,' he spoke quietly staring at the edge of the toilet bowl.

There was silence for a minute and then the officer said, 'I'm not bloody surprised.' The light went off and steps receded back down the corridor. Sid's damp clothes cooled rapidly leaving him shivering. He wouldn't sleep again tonight. Hugging his knees to his chest, he rocked gently wishing he could simply cross the room and open the chest of drawers. Put his hands inside and like a lucky dip, pull out a special prize, maybe a white shoe, or perhaps the pink cardigan, even better would be Jessica's panties. Jessica's panties. Sid's eyes sprang open again, that had been the start, the start of the unravelling. He sobbed and started to rock again.

'You look rough.' Kelly handed Joanie his favourite mug full of steaming coffee. 'Did you go home or have you been here all night?'

Joanie grimaced. He took a sip and set the coffee on the only clear space left on his desk.

'All night then,' she confirmed.

Joanie scratched at the stubble on his chin. 'This case is like a maze, too many goddamn dead ends.'

'I'm afraid I've got more bad news.' Kelly dropped three different newspapers onto his desk. Each one had a front-page story about Sidney White complete with photos. Joanie could feel his pulse pick up, he was furious. Kelly backed out of the room as Joanie scrunched the papers into a pile and thrust them under his arm. He closed his office door behind him and surveyed his colleagues appearing to work diligently behind their desks.

'If one of you is behind this leak, then god help you!' he roared. Pale faces looked up, shrinking into uniform collars and behind stacks of paperwork. One face didn't look up Joanie noted, and that was Curtis. Ignoring the silence, Joanie strode across the open office and up the stairs to the chief.

'Bit previous isn't it?' The chief stood looking out of his window onto the car park. A copy of the Daily Telegraph was in the middle of his desk. 'I thought you said you didn't have much on this guy? You'd better get a whole lot more to make this stick. I don't want the public thinking we're complete idiots.'

Joanie was worried. Despite arresting Sidney white, they were a long way from having hard evidence to pin the murder on him. If the public thought they had their man and later were forced to let him go, the fall-out would be serious.

'What are you going to do about it?' The chief had turned around and was staring at Joanie, his hands locked behind his back.

'If Sidney White is the murderer, we'll get the evidence I'm sure. The judge should be signing the search warrant for Sidney's flat about now.' Joanie tried to relax his shoulders.

'If.' The chief repeated. 'If you haven't got your man, Inspector Johansen, what are the press going to say then? Who the hell leaked this anyway?' Words lashed out and rebounded around the small room.

Joanie wasn't about to share his suspicions with the boss, if he was right about Curtis, the truth would come out in due course, he would make sure of that. 'I'm looking into it sir.'

The chief dropped his hands onto the desk and leaned over into Joanie's face.

'Is Sidney White our man?'

'I don't know, sir.'

'Damn!' The chief turned away, his hands clenched again behind his back making the knuckles turn white. As nothing else was said, Joanie took this as a dismissal, but before he could close the door, the chief stopped him.

'Joanie.'

'Sir?'

There was a pause and then the chief looked at Joanie and said quietly, 'Sort yourself out, you look dreadful.'

Back in his office, Joanie pulled open his cupboard door; he had a mirror on the back, which he looked in now. His hair straggled at the sides, his pate smooth and shiny, stubble across his chin and cheeks, the bags under his eyes hanging low and dark. He reached inside for a clean shirt but realised he'd run out. He yawned and stretched feeling his back pop uncomfortably. At least he had his shaving kit. He'd ask Kelly to gather everyone together while he freshened up.

The hubbub disappeared into a tense stillness as Joanie walked in. He surveyed the officers, took a deep breath and began. They were going back to basics, he wanted new teams, splitting up pairs and re-arranging the teams. They would re-instigate both Kieren's parents and David the Down's syndrome man as suspects. He wanted the top ten list of adults closest to Kieren to be re-interviewed by different teams. A photocopy of the forensic report was passed around.

'See if you can get voluntary DNA samples from those listed on the sheet. We have positive clear results from the body, but at present nothing matches in the database.'

'Fat chance,' someone called out.

Joanie looked up from his papers. It was Gary, he stood up and continued.

'The media fest last month will have put most people off, I doubt anyone is going to happily hand back swabs to us.'

Joanie nodded, he was right, bad timing for them as public opinion seemed against the whole DNA database and especially against the government's debate on whether to automatically hold everyone's DNA details.

'We can at least try, sell it to them as a way to prove their innocence.'

'Guilty until proven innocent' someone else quipped.

Joanie ignored it and carried on. 'The DNA evidence we have does not match Sidney White.' This last statement caused a stir.

'So he's not our man?' One of the officers dared to voice what everyone was thinking.

'I can neither confirm nor refute that statement, what I can say is that the DNA that has been collected from the body including under the fingernails does NOT match Sidney White. Also corroboration from both Kieren's friends and the ice-cream seller indicate that Kieren wasn't wearing his T-shirt when he got to the road. Coupled with this forensic report you can make your own conclusions.' Joanie looked hard at Curtis, but he was avoiding his eye. If that bastard was the leak to the press, he should feel suitably foolish by now.

'Questions?'

One exasperated officer put up his hand, 'But sir, why are we doing all this again?'

'Because you idiots didn't get it right the first time.' Joanie realised he needed to lower his tone. 'Because we need more leads, because somebody, somewhere is guilty and we're going to find them. Four days ago, a boy aged seven was murdered. A boy that liked to play football, a boy that wasn't very good at his piano practice but loved swimming. A kid,' Joanie wanted to say 'like yours' but he couldn't bring himself to make it that personal.

'A kid,' he continued, 'who was held for 2 days before being killed.' Joanie could feel the mood in the room shift. 'That's why.'

Sid was relieved when daylight finally filtered into the cubicle.

His eyes felt heavy from lack of sleep and his ankles had swollen due to sitting up most of the night. A tray of toast, bacon and tea slid in across the floor and this time Joanie grabbed it gratefully. He wolfed it down and then found himself automatically checking his watch to see if it was time to go to work yet. David would be asking questions about where Sid had gone. Tuesdays were fairly busy; there'd be a lot of trolleys for him to stack up. Sid felt a lurch in his chest as he thought about David rushing around the car park trying to keep everything in order, on his own. That face, tears running down watching Sid as he was driven away. Guilt, that's what this feeling was, guilt. He needed to speak to that solicitor they'd got him. Tell him the facts.

Joanie considered Sidney's face that morning, drawn, his lips almost blue, sweat on his brow, it was true he was obviously highly stressed but was he guilty? His body odour that morning had hit a new height, so that he smelled like some of the drunks they pulled in off the street. Apparently he'd screamed out in the night, had some kind of nightmare. About what, he hadn't said, couldn't remember.

A team of forensics was at Sidney White's flat now. He wanted to pop over to the flat, have a look for himself.

There were several cars and a blue van parked outside. Joanie walked through the open door, just as he was walking up the stairs, a suited figure was on his way down. 'Here,' he handed Joanie a plastic bag of drawings. 'You can go up,' he glanced at the plastic covers on Joanie's shoes and nodded.

Joanie slid the drawings out of the bag and studied the top one, it showed the curve of a naked bottom, one side obscured by fabric, probably clothing although it wasn't clear. It was drawn in a brown pencil crayon, the thin lines sketched over and over to bring the form to life from the flat paper. This was good, Joanie realised, and the guy had talent even if the subject matter was all wrong. He marvelled at how it was possible to draw a bottom and for it to be so obviously that of a young child's, and not only that, but he believed it might be male. The next picture showed a full frontal, a naked boy, probably about 5 years old. This one more of a sketch, brief lines without a lot of detail and yet perfectly drawn. The next was somebody's back, the knobbles of the spine and the shading around the shoulder blades giving it a 3d perspective. There were several more, many of them showing random parts of a body, more drawings of a young boy, one of them badly ripped. The last picture was a penis, flaccid, small, hanging downwards in front of what looked like rather large distended balls. Joanie held it at arm's length, no, not distended, this was a view of a young boy's penis, different in proportion to that of a man's. He popped the pictures back into the bag and went through the top door into the flat. At least he had something to detain Sidney with for further questioning; maybe this would be the step forward they needed.

Discarded rubbish, mold in the shower, congealed food in the kitchenette and a stinking fridge. Somehow the uncleanliness clashed with the drawings, and he had to concede, they were beautiful drawings. He couldn't help looking again through the plastic; he'd left the naked boy on the top. Rather than focusing on the penis, your eye was drawn to the boy's chest and arms, the skin looking soft and white. Joanie was no art lover, but these pictures held something of the artist's emotion, and if Joanie wasn't mistaken, it was love. But then love could be twisted and moulded into something unrecognisable. Yet the few pictures that showed a child's face were either passive or smiling. Joanie couldn't detect any malice in these drawings. Perhaps he should get them looked at by a specialist. Rather like one of those graphologists that can work out a personality from someone's handwriting, maybe he could find an expert for pictures.

'I think we're almost there, we're going to move the bed out and lift the carpet.' A man Joanie didn't recognise in a white boiler suit came to the top of the stairs.

'Right OK,' Joanie checked his watch, it was nearly twelve O'clock. 'I'll leave you to it.'

Out in the street, Joanie phoned Margret and told her he'd be home late. He called Kelly and asked her to meet him at the Matthews' house. However, before he reached his car, the chief was on the line.

'We don't have a confession, yet you've sent me the paperwork to extend his detention,' he admonished. 'Put more pressure on the bastard. And where are you?'

'I'm at Sidney White's flat.'

'And?'

'I've got some pictures, drawings actually, pornographic,' as soon as he'd said the word Joanie wanted to retract it, 'well not exactly..' but the chief had already jumped on it.

'Great, get them here, that should make the blighter talk. I'll sign these papers.'

Joanie sighed, maybe it would, maybe it wouldn't, none of the faces looked like Kieren Matthews.

Joanie climbed the stairs and swung open the door to the main office. It was almost empty, apart from the stacks of paperwork and desks that littered the room which was why the angry voices carried so well. Kelly and Curtis were sitting at one of the larger desks in the corner. Even from here Joanie could see a red flush on Kelly's cheeks. Joanie strode across the room, it took a lot to rile Kelly and he wondered what was going on between his colleagues. Kelly nodded as he approached and Curtis spun round in his chair, a thunderous expression on his face that barely changed as he greeted Joanie.

'In my office,' Joanie barked.

Kelly slid into the spare chair, her cheeks already looking a little paler. Curtis stayed by the door, his body stiff.

'Kelly?'

'Nothing sir.'

'Nothing about what? Nothing about your interview with Sidney White or nothing about your argument with Curtis?' Joanie shot an angry look at Curtis who seemed about to speak.

Colour bloomed again on Kelly's cheeks. 'Nothing on Sidney White sir, although I'm trying to trace his doctor.'

'Nothing? That's crap,' Curtis exploded stepping forwards into the room, 'it's obvious he's lying, the creep keeps shaking, sweating, even his solicitor looks worried.' Joanie waited for him to finish.

'We still haven't asked him about Kieren's body, what he did to him, nothing. The bastard's guilty and all she asks him is which way he went to the scene and back and the fucking T-shirt.'

'Curtis?' Joanie's voice was quiet, almost a whisper in the aftermath. 'Did I ask you a question?'

Curtis gritted his teeth, Joanie could see the muscles in his jaw tighten. 'No sir.'

'Then shut the fuck up!' Joanie yelled suddenly making them both jump. He continued in a much calmer voice. 'Kelly was following my orders, I asked her not to mention we had discovered the body, not to lead him on in any way, merely to verify his story. I don't want you fucking up this case with leading questions that won't be admissible in court as evidence. Got it? Have you any idea how little we have on this guy?'

Joanie watched Curtis, his face a mask of hatred, this guy really didn't like being wrong but Joanie was damned if he'd let him run amok on his case. He needed to be reined in and if that meant Curtis hated his guts for it, so be it.

'Now get out both of you, and see what you can dig up on Sidney White. Friends, relatives, anyone that knows him. Get me that doctor. We need a history and a character profile.'

Joanie sat back down in his office chair and pulled out the drawings from his briefcase, why hadn't he shown these to Kelly and Curtis? But he wanted something more from them, something definite linking Sidney to Kieren's death. These drawings weren't it, he was sure. Joanie tapped his fingers on the desk, slid his drawer open and locked the pictures inside.

8

Margret was sitting on the sofa, a novel in one hand and a glass of wine in the other. Joanie could see she had already drunk most of the Chablis on the table. She didn't look up, deliberately ignoring his appearance. He stomped into the kitchen and made himself a cup of tea. If Margret was in a foul mood, at least he could talk to another member of the family. He took the phone upstairs.

'Hello?' This time, Joanie didn't recognise the voice. 'Is Samantha there?'

'Sure, is that her Dad?' Joanie wondered how the girl could recognise him so easily. He'd only spoken to Sammy's flatmates a couple of times, had met Jenny once when they'd been down to visit. Sammy came on the line.

'Hi.'

'Two down, three to go.'

'Well remembered Dad. Yeah, it's going OK. But the whole campus is talking about Brad. He got caught this morning for cheating. What a dick.'

'Who's Brad?'

'Dad! We went out for three months.' She sounded annoyed.

'The one before Matt?' he asked, uncertain if he would be able to pick the kid out in a crowd.

'Don't say it like that, it's not like I'm a serial lover Dad.'

'Sorry pumpkin, I couldn't remember, that was all. Would you like Mum to come and visit you during your break?'

'Why aren't you coming?'

'Work.' He didn't need to say more; she had grown up with his unreliable hours and short-notice changes.

'How is she?'

'She's drinking wine, I think she might finish the whole bottle.' As soon as he said it, he realised his mistake. There was rather a long pause.

'Dad. Can't you do something?'

Like what? He wanted to say. His work had always involved times when long hours were a must so he didn't see why Margret should berate him for it now. She had always been very understanding, supportive. Why should he be concerned if she wanted to sit and drink a bottle of wine now and then? But he was. It wasn't normal, not for Margret. Sure she enjoyed a glass of wine, usually with dinner and sometimes another glass in the evening, but a whole bottle?

After the phone call Joanie decided he ought to at least say something so he carried his empty mug back downstairs and sat in the armchair. Joanie picked up the green bottle and read the label, a French wine 'with a smooth, crisp taste'.

'There isn't any left.' Margret had lowered her book. 'And there's no need to look at me like that, if I want to drink a bottle of wine, I will.'

'So it would seem.' Joanie replaced the empty bottle.

'I'm surprised you even notice. You don't notice anything else do you? Not the spring-clean in the kitchen, the new vegetable plot in the garden. Nothing. All you do is work and expect to get fed. Well cooey, this is your wife.'

Joanie watched her wiggle her fingers in a mock wave. She

was right, he hadn't noticed the garden, he remembered her talking about her plans for a vegetable plot a couple of months ago.

'Here I am at home all bloody day and for what? It doesn't make an iota of difference to you does it? I bet you haven't noticed the new picture at the top of the stairs.' He hadn't. 'A painting, that I, yes me, your wife has created. No bloody thanks or well done is there? What do you want from me?' she threw the book on the floor.

What a strange question to ask, and yet he did want something from her, he wanted the old Margret, not this crazy woman who'd drunk too much wine. He wanted the Margret who created delicious meals, who asked him about his day and helped him talk about his difficulties at work. He wanted the Margret who put on her sexy pink nightdress and gave him that little smile that made him glow all over. When was the last time she had rolled across the bed into his arms and murmured her wishes in his ear? The Margret that was practical and kept the house running like clockwork, reminding him to renew the insurance or get the car MOT.

She swung her legs off the sofa. 'I thought as much, nothing.' She brushed past him and he reached for her hand.

'Wait.'

She flung his hand aside. 'You don't even know me.'

Joanie sat alone in the lounge, it was getting dark outside but he didn't bother to close the curtains or turn on a light. He had thinking to do; there wasn't enough room in his brain for all the thoughts that were clanging around. Maybe he should go fishing, it had been months since he'd gone for a night fish. Maybe it was what he needed, the solitude by the riverbank, strange noises from the night creatures and the waiting with the rod. It was after ten but that didn't matter, he wouldn't be able to sleep now anyway.

Joanie took a torch from the kitchen drawer and went down

to the garden shed. All his things were there, at the back under the gardening items that Joanie could see had been used recently, the damp earth still clinging to a trowel and spreading a pleasant peaty smell around the shed. His rod and fishing box were covered in cobwebs and strange dried up insects. Back in the house, Joanie couldn't face going upstairs so instead he shouted up the banister. There was no response and Joanie decided either she was already sleeping it off or she didn't give a damn.

The moon hung low in the sky over beyond the by-pass that crossed the river a mile or two further down. As he expected, there was no one else around. He settled himself on the stool and pulled his thick jacket around him. It was a mild evening but sitting this close to the water added a certain chill. The gentle plop of the float made Joanie smile as he watched it sitting on the black water. The moon afforded enough light to see the oily surface and the outlines of the trees and shrubs opposite. Margret had never seen the point in fishing, although she'd enjoyed a day fly-fishing with him once when they were on holiday in Devon. They'd paid for tuition and were allowed to keep what they caught to be cooked in the restaurant at the end of the day. She quickly grasped the knack and the flick of the wrist, but sitting for hours by a dingy river was something else. Joanie himself hadn't really got into fishing until he was well into his forties. It was at a particularly stressful time in his career and had proved invaluable in keeping him sane. He hoped it could still cast that particular miracle. The float ducked under the water and popped up again. Joanie wound in the reel to find an empty hook. Bit like fishing for the murderer really, he thought. Curtis certainly thought they'd landed the big one, but Joanie wasn't sure why Curtis was so positive that Sidney White was their man. Maybe he'd been doing this too long, had become prejudiced in the way he expected a suspect to act or look. Sidney White was obviously not a complete innocent judging by the drawings barely hidden under the mattress but what exactly did that prove? It was not illegal to draw pornographic images.

Joanie pictured the grimy little flat in his head, the dishevelled bed and the black mold eking out of the edges of the shower cubicle. Sidney's hair was dark and lank, and there was a smell in the flat that told of someone who wasn't apt to do the weekly clean. That gesture, Joanie tried to replay it in his mind, a nervous movement scratching his left arm. It still niggled him, a thought floating at the peripheries of his brain, one that was so ethereal; he couldn't quite get hold of it.

The float popped under again and there was a distinct tug this time. Joanie reeled in carefully but the line felt loose. Crafty little bugger he whispered into the silence. The rushes murmured a response. A shushing sound that made him think of Margret's lips, black in the semi-darkness of their bedroom, close enough to touch. A distant tingling made him aware of his hunched position on the stool. He shifted himself to make it more comfortable. He did still love her, he was sure of it. But he wasn't certain what she felt about him, he didn't know what she felt about anything. He needed to try and understand, he must talk to her, openly, put aside some time to be together. It must all be linked in with her redundancy, wasn't it? Sometimes there weren't any answers; he'd learnt that in his job. Parents crying on his shoulder saying, 'Why was it our son?' He prayed there would be answers for him and Margret. Ripples appeared and sped towards the far bank leaving a trail that widened and dissipated into the flat surface. The rod was yanked from Joanie's unsuspecting hands and landed with a splash in the water. Thrusting one welly over the edge, he reached for the rod. Cold water swirled above his boot and poured in causing him to moan aloud. He gripped the end of the rod and yanked it, finding no resistance; he fell back against the bank.

'Shit' he shouted at the stars. And that was it; finally his thoughts found a slot that fitted perfectly. Like those little hand toys with a plastic maze and a couple of silver balls that you had to shake and tilt to try and get them into the right slots. Staring at the stars, bright now and the moon low and large. A night many years ago, with just such a sky scape, cool and damp. He'd been walking, his bike by his side with a flat tyre. Muddy football boots on his feet and his bag slung across his back. There had been someone at a window, something that had made him shiver. Joanie closed his eyes and remembered the face at the window, dark hair, the boy from his class staring out. Joanie lifted his hand in recognition but dropped it almost immediately as a large figure appeared behind the boy and snatched the curtains closed. He'd quickened his pace then, staring ahead towards the moon, the bright stars twinkling and calming his sudden fear. That boy, the one with the dank hair that smelled slightly. It was Sidney White. Sitting up, Joanie hauled his feet out adding slimy mud to his soaked trousers. He reached back into the water and hauled one sunken welly out, water cascading across the stool and into his fishing bag. He cursed some more, winding in the reel as fast as he could. The hook had been ripped clean off. He shoved everything together and limped back to the car.

The house was silent when he arrived, he left the fishing gear in the car, it could wait, and instead he went up the stairs and pulled down the loft ladder.

'What the hell are you doing?' Margret had poked her head up the ladder; she was shading her eyes from the bright bulb swinging above her head. 'There's water everywhere, what the hell are you up to? Two o'clock in the morning is not the time to be doing a spring bloody clean!'

Joanie was sweating, his torso deep in a cardboard box, cobwebs stuck to his back and tangled in his hair.

'Brian!'

Joanie lifted his head and smiled at his wife triumphantly. He held aloft a black and white framed photograph. Three lines of children carefully arranged in their best uniforms.

'Have you gone utterly mad?' Margret groaned and held her

head for a moment. 'Oh dear, I don't feel very well.'

Joanie followed her back down the ladder and noted the damp marks on the landing and the stairs. His trousers were still dripping. Margret had disappeared back into the bedroom. At least he now knew. Had netted that flighty memory and pinned it to the photograph gripped in his fingers.

Joanie used directory enquiries to try and get hold of St James Primary School in Sussex. There wasn't a number listed. After various dead ends, he finally discovered from the education authority that the school had closed over a decade ago. It was possible that some paperwork could be retrieved from a central archive but it would take time. Joanie made his official request and put down the phone. He wanted a class list from when the photo had been taken. As he remembered, the skinny boy with the smelly clothes had only been there for a year or two. Long enough to become the butt of class jokes and someone for the bullies to push around. Joanie still couldn't remember his name though, it was certainly not Sidney White but he was positive the boy in the photo and the man having nightmares in the cells were one and the same.

The pictures lay spread across the table before them.

'So these are just from your mind?' Joanie asked.

'Yes.' Sid licked his lips, he had faith now in the solicitor; this was becoming easier. Apparently they hadn't charged him because they didn't have enough evidence. This was news to Sid, who assumed that if you were arrested, it was all the same thing. His solicitor had explained that they were looking for evidence about Kieren, and if what Sid had said was true, the only link was the T-shirt and he hadn't committed a crime to get that.

Sid felt himself growing in confidence. 'They're mine, I drew them, they're mine.'

Joanie pushed his chair back and stood up. This wasn't

getting them anywhere.

'Are you going to charge my client Inspector Johansen because I believe you are running out of time.'

'Thank you Mr Briggs, I am well aware of procedure and in fact if necessary Sidney White will remain in custody for another forty nine hours and,' Joanie checked his watch and did a quick calculation, 'nineteen minutes.'

'Assuming you have suitable evidence to hold him with, at least something more than artistic drawings.'

Joanie clenched his fists and walked out of the interview room. In his office, he leaned back in his chair and steepled his fingers. As he suspected, Sidney was not their man. He felt certain of that. The trouble was, they didn't have any other suspects. Joanie pulled out the photo from his desk drawer and looked at the smiling children. There he was, aged ten sitting on one of the chairs at the front. He had a grin ear-to-ear and large sticky out ears. Joanie smiled at himself. As his eyes roved across the picture, names trickled out, Jacqueline, Susan with her bows, Alex the class fool with one finger stuck in the side of his mouth and there was Sidney White, on the end next to Mrs Hatherwaite, a giant of a woman with a chest to match. Except he wasn't Sidney White back then, he was this scruffy little smelly kid. Joanie brought the photo closer to his face, Sidney appeared to be peeking out at the camera from under a long fringe, unlike the other children, he wasn't smiling. His hands were shoved deep into his pockets and there was a rip on his trousers at knee height. Sidney White didn't have a fringe but Joanie was sure the boy in the picture matched the man in the cells.

There was a knock at the door and Joanie dropped the photo back into the drawer.

'Yes?'

Curtis came in with some papers. 'We've found the doctor, apparently she's a psychotherapist. Shall we go and speak to her?'

Joanie held out his hand for the papers. 'Is he still seeing her?'

'Don't know, his GP sent him to this psycho lady about eighteen months ago. Dr Sascha Casey'

Joanie nodded. 'Leave it with me.' But Curtis didn't move. 'Something else?'

'You're going to let him go aren't you?' Curtis' face accusing.

'What choice do I have?' Joanie snatched the papers from him. 'You tell me, we're banging our heads against a brick wall. No DNA matches, no incriminating evidence in his flat, no mismatch in statements except some bloody stupid argument over a dog. Everything sums up to a big fat nothing. You tell me how a man with no car and not even a driving licence gets a body weighing roughly 4 stone across 5 miles of suburbia and countryside without being seen? Not only that but manages not to leave any shred of DNA evidence on the body or back at his flat.' Joanie pointed the end of his biro at Curtis; he'd damn well make sure this upstart pulled his finger out. 'Get me those kind of answers and I might take your personal vendetta against Sidney White a little more sympathetically.'

Curtis' eyes stopped flashing and his gaze tore away from Joanie and back to the papers on the desk.

'It's not,' he began.

Joanie stared at him, willing him to say more, to dig himself out or protest. There was silence as each man fumed within his own convictions. Curtis left closing the door a little too hard. That was something else Joanie needed to think about, all these little threads running around inside his head. Sometimes it felt like spaghetti junction. There was something about this case that meant something to Curtis. It was more than the common disgust at child molesters that he had seen displayed by other officers. He wondered if Curtis too had met Sidney White before.

Joanie studied the papers; the doctor's address was on this side of town. Perhaps a face-to-face meeting might reveal more than a phone call.

'You know I'm not obliged to give you any information at all.' Dr Sascha Casey was sitting in a tall chair behind her desk. Her hair was scraped back into a tight bun, a high-collared blouse buttoned close to her neck. The desk was an old leather one, a case notes file sitting squarely in the middle. One pen and one pencil and that was it. Probably one of the barest desks Joanie had ever seen. Certainly a long way from any at the station. Joanie was perched awkwardly on the dark leather couch.

'Yes, I realise that, but you've probably heard in the media about Kieren Matthews.'

'The murdered boy?' Thin eyebrows arched upwards. 'You think my client might be involved?'

'Possibly, we're following all leads. It is your ethical duty to provide anything you think Sidney White has said that might connect him to the murder.'

'I too know my rights and obligations Inspector.' She pursed her lips and thumbed through the file.

Joanie tried not to fidget; he couldn't seem to get comfy on the edge and didn't want to end up lying in a prone position on it. The doctor took her time.

'Sidney White didn't finish his treatment with me. He was suffering from a past trauma which was impacting his current life.'

'What kind of trauma?'

The doctor glanced disapprovingly at Joanie.

'As I said, Sidney White didn't finish his treatment. There is nothing that would lead me to expect violence towards others. He was suffering an internal torment.' She paused as if deciding whether to say anything else, then shut the case notes file, placing her hands on top.

'Well couldn't this inner torment compel him to do something?'

'Possibly, but to whom? His trauma relates to his childhood, and Sidney White is fifty six years old.'

'Has he ever mentioned any names? Jessica perhaps, or maybe Martin?' Joanie knew he was clutching at straws.

'The only name that has cropped up is Tommy. And I'm afraid that is all I'm willing to divulge. Unless your suspect goes to court, this conversation must remain in utmost confidence Inspector. Now if there's nothing else.' She rose and gestured to the door.

Joanie got up awkwardly, his back growling with pain. He looked at the file on her desk, if only he could read it for himself, make his own decision about whether there was anything important to divulge or not. Why was every turn a dead end?

'Thank you doctor.' They shook hands formally, and just as the doctor was about to let go, Joanie held on.

'Why didn't he finish the treatment?'

She glanced at their hands and pulled slightly. Joanie let go.

'Some people don't.' She frowned. Joanie waited. 'It can be too painful or they may still be in denial about what happened. Sometimes people are just not ready to deal with what has gone before, not realising of course that if they don't, it will continue to affect them.'

They were in an Italian restaurant behind the High Street. It was new; at least it hadn't been there ten years ago. Joanie thought he remembered a small cafe in its place, one that did extremely good steak and kidney pies. Steak and Kidney didn't feature on this menu.

'My birthday isn't until next month.' Margret lowered her menu.

'I know.' Joanie watched her frown and then the menu came up again to hide her face. They ordered, including a bottle of red that Joanie desperately needed. It had been hard enough convincing her to come out and now they had to fill a whole evening with conversation. This wasn't going to be easy. Joanie rubbed a hand across his eyes, he was dog-tired and the warm hubbub of the restaurant and the glass at his fingertips were only increasing his need for sleep. Joanie tried to sit up straighter in his chair and blinked a few times; he had to at least try. It was Sammy that had brought them to this. She'd burst into tears on the phone and suddenly Joanie realised how far things had gone with his wife. He had made a promise to Sammy. Twenty-eight years was worth fighting for wasn't it?

Joanie smiled at his wife and put his hand on the table hoping she'd do the same. She didn't.

'I thought we should talk.'

'We can do that at home, or do you prefer public speaking now?' Joanie winced at the reference to his recent appearance on television; the murder of Kieren Matthews was like a chain around his neck.

'Look, I know things have been difficult recently, and I'm sorry for not noticing the vegetable plot in the garden. I can see now that you've been really busy, the roses round the front looked lovely today. And I have to say your tomatoes tasted a lot nicer than the supermarket ones.'

Margret crossed her arms and bit her lip.

'The painting at the top of the stairs, it's good. I know I didn't notice it immediately, I'm not very good with things like that, but it's really very good. Well done.' Joanie paused, knowing he sounded patronising. 'Are you enjoying being at home?'

There was a silence as both of them gulped at the loaded question; this was the crux after all wasn't it? Joanie had pinpointed the start of the troubles to Margret's redundancy two months ago. In fact she had agreed to early retirement when it became clear they needed to make cutbacks. A secretary at Gregson and Gregson's solicitors for the past eleven years, it was a lot to give up. The silence between them was broken by the waiter arriving with their starters. The question could be safely ignored while they discussed the crispness of the brioche and the garlic on the mushrooms. Safe talk that relaxed them both if only for a few minutes. They could carry on in this vane, avoiding the dangerous truths; maybe they'd even start talking about the weather. They finished their plates and Joanie watched Margret staring at the other customers. Any minute now and she would come out with some comment about so and so's dress or such and such's dish.

'Margret.'

'What?'

'Please talk to me.'

'What about?' she wiped the edge of her mouth with the napkin and thrust it back onto her lap, then took a swig of wine.

'You're not sleeping well,' he pointed out. Lately she'd been waking up a couple of times a night and disappearing off to the bathroom, occasionally he'd heard the shower too and wondered if she was having nightmares.

'I'm surprised you notice, you're hardly there most of the time.'

Joanie looked down apologetically, it was true, of course. 'Is that why you're not sleeping?'

'What would you know? You're just a man!' she spat the words out but was immediately sorry as Joanie watched her eyes begin to glisten.

The waiter came and swept their plates away without a word. He returned seconds later with the main course but sensed something was wrong and merely smiled politely.

Joanie could feel his jaw clenching, 'Well perhaps you could explain to this man?' he could feel the words getting louder.

'You wouldn't understand. Stop getting at me.' Tears were now running down her face and Joanie felt worse than ever. The lady at the next table gave him an accusing look.

'I'm sorry sweetheart.' He tried again for her hand but she had picked up her knife and fork.

Later over ice-cream for him and profiteroles for her, he made one last attempt.

'Margret, if there's anything you want to tell me, or anything you want me to do, just say, OK? I'm sorry about work. I'm sorry about everything.' Her eyes were looking at him now. 'I do love you Margret.' And for that moment he truly did, a huge welling of warmth filled him up. Her eyes, as green as when they'd met, crinkles around the edges that he had watched develop over the years, the thinning of her lips and the smile lines at the edges of her mouth. Parts of her that rather than repelling him with their shout of old age only endeared her more. He really didn't want to lose her. She was the only one who understood him.

Her face crumpled, 'Don't you start as well,' she admonished, 'one of us blubbing all over the place is quite enough.'

Lying in bed, she let him spoon his body around hers. Joanie was surprised to notice how far his stomach prevented his face from nuzzling into her neck. It was a warmth of sorts. Margret felt a little stiff in his arms as if she wasn't exactly comfortable with the position. They weren't going to have sex, that was clear but Joanie didn't mind, it was the coldness that bothered him, the boneness of her shoulder and the unyielding cross of her arm. As he drifted off she murmured something, Joanie had to struggle with his consciousness to unravel what she'd said. 'It's not you.' And once he'd done so, sleep deserted him. If it wasn't him then who was it? Was Margret having an affair? Cold dread twanged across his rib cage. There had never been anyone else between them. When Sammy became a teenager, for a while, Joanie had wondered if he and Karen Quinton might have slipped into an illicit affair but the moment had passed and they had each turned back to their own families and partners. Joanie stared at his wife's dark hair on the pillow and wondered if there might come a time when he would see only the white cotton of the pillowcase.

They were letting him go. Sid could feel his chest swelling, his shoulders relaxing downwards, he lifted his head a little higher, the euphoria was trying to burst out of his chest. Finally, his solicitor had been right, by keeping to the truth and limiting his answers strictly to the questions asked, he was free. He signed some paperwork and was given back his things. He shoved his keys and money into his pocket. He felt like shouting.

Out on the street, he walked quickly away, not caring which direction just walking, and walking fast. The sun was out and within seconds he felt hot and sweaty, but what a good feeling. He wanted to whoop and shout, instead he let out a nervous giggle; there was no one about to hear. Despite the heat and the sweat, Sid hurried through the town and headed home, stopping briefly to get some chips. It was only as he opened the door and looked up the stairs that the wonderful feeling of freedom dissolved into the stillness. There was no one to share his glory, no one to go for a drink with, or even to tell. A picture of David's face through the rear window of the police car came into Sid's mind.

Deflated he climbed the stairs and opened the door at the top. He stopped and surveyed the room. It looked different, altered somehow. Cautiously Sid went from room to room, the kitchen bin was empty and there was 'evidence' tape wrapped around the body of his computer, the wires at the back hanging loose. Of course, he knew they'd been in his flat, because they'd shown him the drawings, the ones he'd put under the mattress, he stared at his bed, the sheet was tucked neatly in, all around the edge.

Sid sat down at the desk and looked at his computer, slowly he pulled off the tape, nervously he plugged the leads in at the back and switched it on. It looked normal enough, he tried the internet and that too worked. Sid frowned to himself. They'd set him free, that meant there was nothing criminal, at least nothing they'd found was criminal. Tentatively he tried a few searches, then stopped, got up and looked out of the window.

There was no one on the street, a couple of cars parked opposite but nobody was in them. Perhaps not yet, he thought, he should probably leave it a day or two. He switched the computer off again and instead turned to the television.

Sid awoke early, he waited outside the hardware store for it to open then rushed home with the new lock and awkwardly managed to dismantle the old one and fit the new. Once the door was working to his satisfaction he tucked the new key safely in his pocket. That would prevent any unexpected visitors; he didn't trust the police for a minute. He hurried off to work, he was late of course but he didn't expect it would make a lot of difference to the three days he had already been forced to miss. As he walked through the store, Valerie on the cigarette counter stared at him and picked up the phone by the cash register. Barry was putting out some apples, and he too stopped as Sid walked past. Fortunately the staff room was empty, he checked the rota, it was David's day off. He looked again and realised his name wasn't on it. He clenched his fingers and then consoled himself; they weren't to know he was coming back today. It was hardly a planned holiday. Sid opened his locker and stopped. A pink umbrella and a pair of sandals stared back at him. From the hook hung a white handbag. Behind him someone coughed.

'Er, Sidney.'

Sid spun around and stared at the store manager.

'Perhaps you'd like to come to my office?'

Sid turned back to the locker; his hand had begun to tremble. He tightened his grip on the key, shut the door and locked it. Mr Foster was holding out his hand. Sid dropped the locker key into it. They walked down the corridor and swung left into Mr Foster's comfortable office. There were three easy chairs and a small coffee table behind which stood a large corner desk filled with papers and an enormous monitor.

'Take a seat,' Mr Foster gestured at the soft chairs. For a

moment it looked like he was going to join Sid but then thought better of it and went to sit behind his desk.

'We weren't sure you'd be coming back,' Mr Foster attempted a smile.

Sid stared at his feet. 'They made a mistake,' he said simply.

'I see, right.' There was a pause as Mr Foster shuffled some papers. 'Well obviously there's no reason why you can't continue to work with us, errm if you wish to but we'd quite understand if you didn't under the circumstances. In which case we're willing to be very generous and offer you two months' pay as severance and you won't have to work your notice period.'

Sid looked up, his eyes blinked involuntarily. They were trying to pay him off. He could feel colour rising to his cheeks. They were trying to get rid of him. After all the hours he'd put in, his reliability, his loyalty. He'd never missed a day, never taken a sicky except when he'd caught the flu. And what about David, Sid had been the one to show him the ropes and been patient when he'd got it wrong. He'd never done anything indecent here, never touched anybody, he'd even handed in a small teddy once although it had taken him two days with it in his locker before he finally succumbed and gave it to lost property. If he didn't come to work, what would he do? How would he stay sane? The last time he'd been unemployed had been dangerous, he'd found himself drawn to the local schools, the library at children's story time and following the young women with their charges from the crèche. Things might get out of hand.

'Is there anything else you need?' Mr Foster prompted.

'NO!' Sid stood up. 'I'm going to work, I'm not leaving.'

Mr Foster leaned back in his chair, fear played across his face.

'Oh.'

Sid watched his adam's apple rise and fall.

'Right, I'd better sort the rota then, and you'll need a new locker.' He fiddled with the key on his desk drawer and drew out a bundle of clinking metal keys. He passed over number 33.

'I'll start right away,' stated Sid. 'The car park's a mess.'

'Umm, right, but, well, there's a new young man, Liam, he's on this shift.'

Sid frowned but there wasn't much he could do. He opened the door and left without any further comment. He'd be damned if they'd push him out, he'd had enough of other people taking over his life.

Storming out into the car park, he could see a longhaired youth with a cigarette dangling from his fingertips, leaning against a trolley. Sid strode over to him and puffed up his chest.

'Move your fucking arse!' He hissed, fighting the urge to lash out at this pathetic bundle of humanity. The youth gawped, the cigarette dropping from his fingers. Sid wrenched the trolley from his hip. Startled, the youth loped back to the store and disappeared inside. Sid grinned to himself.

By mid-afternoon, Sid had stopped grinning; in fact he'd stopped grinning shortly after the youth had fled. Customers kept staring at him, one lady had even gasped and thrust her child back into the car leaving skid marks on the tarmac. People were avoiding him, one man had sworn openly at him. The youth hadn't come back and Sid assumed Mr Foster had found something else for him to do. Keeping his head low, Sid tried to continue as if nothing was wrong. He stayed at the back of the car park for much of the time, shrinking behind the trolleys when he had to push a load of them back to the entrance. It would be better tomorrow, when David was back. Sid tried to console himself with the thought of sharing chocolate cake with him at break time.

9

Before Sid left the store, he bought one of the Fine Foods chocolate cakes and put it in his locker. He also bought a newspaper and found the reason for his awful day on page 3. He glanced through it quickly, rolled it up, tucked it under his arm and hurried straight home.

Laying the newspaper on his desk, he read about the Kieren Matthews case, the fact that the boy had been murdered and that the main suspect had been released. His name appeared in clear script. Sid could feel his heart squeezing tight in his chest; no wonder people had been staring at him. But surely, if the newspaper said he'd been released then that was a good thing, it meant he was innocent, didn't it? Sid squinted at the paper trying to read it again for a third time, but his hands were now trembling so much that he couldn't focus on the print. He threw the paper across the desk and went to open the middle drawer - it was empty, of course.

Sid groaned and wiped the sweat from his forehead, sitting back at his desk, he turned on the computer. Remembering suddenly the new site he'd found, he hurried to the bathroom and for a brief second was shocked to find the toilet roll holder empty. He'd finished it that morning and hadn't got another from under the sink. Hurrying to the kitchen bin he fished out the old cardboard roll and peered inside. There it was, the website address. He smiled to himself and took it back to the computer. The code was where he'd left it in his book beside the bed. Sid paused, impatience and worry struggling against each other. Would the police be watching? They hadn't found anything on his computer before, so did that make it safe? He felt like shit and deserved a treat. Sid closed his eyes and decided he had nothing to lose. Lucky for him, the site was still operating and he breathed a sigh of relief as the pictures came up. They stilled the trembling and a familiar warmth overtook his body.

The Kieren Matthews case had lost momentum. There was no avoiding it. The parents knew it too; they'd been into the office as soon as the papers detailed Sidney White's release. It had fallen to Joanie to speak to them. The mother incoherent with grief and the father ranting like a man possessed.

'What the hell do you think you're doing letting Kieren's murderer go free? What fucking kind of joke shop are you running here?'

Joanie sat down on one of the soft chairs; an example of calmness that he hoped would transmit itself to Mr Matthews. 'Sidney White is still a suspect in your son's death but unfortunately we cannot bring a case against him. We too have to abide by the law Mr Matthews. There is not sufficient evidence to convict anyone at this stage.'

'Why the hell not? It was obvious he was murdered for god's sake. What about all that forensics shit you guys do these days? There must be something. Don't tell me, it's been bungled or contaminated or something by your imbecile efforts.' He stood above Joanie; his two veins throbbed vividly across the man's temple.

'There has been no contamination of evidence, I assure you. We are doing our utmost to bring your son's killer to justice.'

'Justice? Some fucking justice when that pervert is walking around free. What if he takes someone else's kid, then you'll be sorry.'

'Tom!' Mrs Matthews tugged at his sleeve. The air puffed out of Mr Matthews and he sat down next to his wife. 'I'm sorry love, we'll get through this.' The woman cried openly on his shoulder, Joanie felt uncomfortable as he watched Mr Matthews stroke her hair. The man's face was beginning to crumble. The anger spent and only the grief to fill the void.

Joanie felt sick, his stomach tightened into a twisted knot. He could deal with people's anger, their questions and demands; it was this open display of grief and hopelessness that hurt. He watched Mr Matthews put a protective arm around his wife and guide her out of the room. He didn't look back at Joanie but then he hadn't expected any thanks. What exactly had he done for this couple? They'd lost their only son to some clever bastard that left not a trace, at least nothing so far, no sperm despite the medical signs of abuse, no fingerprints, fuck all. A picture of the boys trainers tied with a double bow entered Joanie's mind. Trainers that should have been running across a playing field kicking a ball on a day such as this. Joanie stood up trying to shake off the weight of failure that clung to his arms and legs.

Back in his office, there was a message from the Sussex education authority. Joanie dialled them back immediately.

'We have five possible names for you that match the class and years that you spoke of,' the lady's voice was crisp and efficient.

Joanie pulled his pad towards him and started to write. She listed them slowly, spelling each in turn but Joanie stopped writing after the third one. That was it, George Boswell.

Sid was too early for work, but he didn't mind. There was barely anybody in the car park although the store was open. Sid picked up a few stray crisp packets. He noticed that his hand was firm, gripping the pick-up stick without even a hint of a tremor, he must be feeling better. The cool of the morning was refreshing giving him the sense that he'd secured himself a peaceful bubble. Safe within the confines of the car park and the time of day. The first time since this whole Kieren thing started that Sid could feel his shoulders drop. There was an acute stiffness around his neck that began to loosen.

Sid saw David arrive, dropped off by his mother. He waved but David didn't see, heading straight indoors. Sid wasn't concerned; he'd be outside soon enough. He was coming back across the car park with a few of the larger trolleys when Sid saw David staring at him. Sid smiled and pushed the trolleys towards him. David looked alarmed, and hurried across the entrance towards the recycling bins. Sid felt his shoulders rise up defensively, he changed course and headed for the main trolley stand. It was because he'd been away, Sid thought that must be it. He hadn't told David and he was probably angry at having been left to work on his own. David liked company. It would be fine, Sid reassured himself, they'd have chocolate cake together at break time and Sid would explain. Explain what? Explain that he'd been called away suddenly to help the police with some important investigations about their friend Kieren. David would understand.

At eleven o'clock Sid surveyed the car park but couldn't see David anywhere, he must have already gone inside. Sid hurried back to the entrance and through the store. David was sitting at the table with a plastic cup of water.

'I've got chocolate cake,' Sid blurted out. He fumbled with his locker key and pulled open the metal door. Unwrapping the cake feverishly he almost dropped it onto the table in front of David. David said nothing; instead he wrapped both hands around the tiny cup and drained it.

'You love chocolate cake.' Sid confirmed in desperation.

David looked up, his face embarrassed. 'I'm not allowed to talk to you Sid. My mother said I mustn't. She said you were wicked and even when I told her you were my friend she said that didn't matter any more.'

Sid had drawn back against the lockers. The words stung like little needle points thrust into him in a million different places.

'I'm sorry Sid.'

Sid stared at the swirls of curled chocolate that decorated the top of the cake. How dare David's mum judge him like that? How dare she interfere with his life? What did she know the old witch? Sid's fingers clenched the key in his pocket, if she'd been here now he'd gouge her fucking eyes out with it. A member of staff opened the door, saw Sid with his back to the lockers and immediately retreated. Sid closed his eyes, this wasn't happening. He needed to breathe, keep breathing, his shoulders were singing in torment as if someone had nailed them to the lockers behind.

'She didn't say you couldn't eat my chocolate cake though.'

David frowned; Sid could see him trying to digest this piece of information. Sid waited in silence, praying that David would pick up on the simple logic of his statement.

'No.' David said simply and then smiled fetching a knife from the drawer and cutting himself a huge chunk.

Sid peeled his back away from the lockers and sank down into the chair opposite. Sweat poured down his face, he felt like he'd just run a marathon. He mustn't stop now though.

'She didn't say we couldn't use sign language did she?'

David looked up, chocolate smeared across his lips; he shook his head uncertainly.

'Well there we are then, and we can still be friends, we'll just make signs instead.' Sid searched around for something to show what he meant. He pointed at David's cup and motioned drinking then pointed at the tap. David nodded slowly. Sid jumped up and refilled the cup and placed it back in front of

David.

'Like that see? You didn't talk to me did you?'

David shook his head and a slow smile crept across his face. He took a gulp and then pointed to his cup, at Sid and then at the sink. Sid swallowed his irritation, got up and refilled the cup for the second time.

David giggled and nodded. 'It's like a g.. oooh.' He clamped a hand across his mouth.

'That's right; it's a game, a game that friends play. It'll be our secret game OK?'

David nodded and took another large slice of chocolate cake. When he'd wolfed that piece down as well he glanced at the clock and tapped Sid's arm pointing at his watch. Sid gathered up the remains of the chocolate cake and replaced it in his locker. For a second he rested his forehead against the cold metal. It was a success of sorts he supposed. Thinking back to previous times in the staff room with David, it had always been David who'd started the conversations, rambling on to an almost irritating degree. What would they 'talk' about now?

There had been a brief shower while they'd been indoors, leaving the tarmac dark and shiny. Sid automatically moved down to the end of the car park, away from the majority of the customers. It was busier now; car doors slammed and loaded trolleys trundled across the lines. Sid wasn't sure if this made it better or worse, there was more to do to keep his mind off things but more people to recognise him and throw their insults. An old Ford Fiesta swung into the car park, its tyres screeching on the wet tarmac. It shot down to the end, did a fast U-turn and coasted down the aisle across from Sid. Three lads jeered out at him, a tomato splashed against his foot. Sid backed away, he swivelled the trolleys around and headed for the end of the car park. Something thumped against his back but Sid kept walking. He heard the car screech again at the bottom and come roaring up his lane. Sid was now nearing the empty end of the parking slots. An object slapped against his head, Sid could feel some strange goo sliding down the side of his face. He put his hand up, long strands of egg yolk clinging to his fingers. A bottle hit him on the arm, dropped to the floor and smashed. They were out of the car now. Other people had stopped to stare. Sid tried ducking behind his trolleys but two of them moved around to his side and pelted him with beer cans. Sid stared through the cage of the trolleys and could see the security guard from the entrance walking slowly towards him; he was talking into his radio. A hand grabbed his collar and wrenched him upright, his face popped above the trolleys facing an audience of fascinated onlookers. Sid's arms were yanked behind him and another youth threw his fist into Sid's face. It was like walking into a door, not quite clear where exactly the punch had landed but feeling like a large metal object had halted all forward momentum. Sid sagged and the youth let him drop to the ground. There was more goo; Sid could see red paint dripping on the ground. A boot connected with his stomach rendering a great cry.

'Sid,' it was David's voice. Another kick brought Sid around to face the crowd; David seemed to be struggling with the security guard. Pulling himself free, David ran towards one of Sid's attackers and shoved hard. The young man went down sprawling.

'What the fuck?'

'NO!' bellowed David.

'Chaz! The pigs.' Sid could hear their feet drumming across the ground, car doors slammed and the car screeched away. Sid stared at a small ant making its tiresome journey around a can. Wavering unsteadily on its back was a large crumb. He closed his eyes again but the pain in his stomach made him want to be sick; he coughed a couple of times and felt a fresh spurt of warmth slither out of his mouth. Eventually a man in uniform helped him to his feet. Sid didn't recognise the policeman. Another uniform was talking to the crowd that had gathered.

Sid allowed himself to be led back towards the store. They took him up to the staff room and left him alone with a brown-haired lady Sid recognised from the Bakery section. She was pulling on rubber gloves and had a first aid kit open on the table. She took a fresh lint cloth and wet it under the tap then passed it to him.

'Here.' Her eyes narrowed as she watched him dab at the blood around his nose. She snatched it back again, gave it a further rinse and this time wiped his face herself. There was nothing gentle about her actions but Sid was grateful all the same. No one had wiped his face since he'd been, Sid gulped, since his mother had hugged him that time, after he'd fallen and grazed his knees. It was the last hug he remembered. Tears rolled down his face as Sid wished he could just let go and be wrapped up in her arms, his sore head held gently to her chest. Wished so hard that he could be six again and that maybe he could start his life over.

'Jesus, are you crying?' she backed away. 'That's disgusting, stop it, there's no point in crying is there? If you haven't done what they say you've done then there ain't no need for crying. And if you have then I don't want to know.' Despite her angry words, her fingers became lighter as she removed the egg from the side of his face; it was partly matted in his hair. Someone came in the room behind him; it was the policeman from earlier.

'Thanks Irene, perhaps you'd like to come into the manager's room for a moment Mr White?'

Sid followed the black uniform down the corridor.

'You can come back with us to the station if you want to make a statement,' the policeman paused and turned to stare at Sid, 'or pop in when you're feeling better.' Sid had no intention of going to that god awful station again, not unless they dragged him.

They continued into Mr Foster's office and Sid sat on the same blue easy chair. He wiped the back of his hand across his nose, wincing at the pain; Sid didn't want to look up.

'We've suggested to Mr Foster that he might move you to a different department, somewhere where you won't come into so much contact with the customers.'

'That is unless you'd like to take us up on my previous offer?' Mr Foster interrupted hopefully. Sid looked at his face. His skin was smooth, pale, probably didn't even have to shave thought Sid. The policeman stood next to the desk waiting for a response. Sid didn't know what to say, there was something so surreal about today. He'd never been attacked, never so much as had his wallet stolen. And here they were more concerned about the company's image than him. Bastards. Sid wiped a hand across his top lip. If they moved him off trolleys, what about David? Would they move David too? Sid looked up and was about to open his mouth when he realised how childish it would sound. He couldn't ask a question like that.

'Fine.'

They both frowned.

'You're going to leave?' Mr Foster clasped his hands and leaned forward expectantly.

'No.' Sid stared back. 'I'll move.'

'Right, of course, OK then.'

'I'll leave you to it Mr Foster. You might want to get your nose checked out at the hospital before you go home Mr White. It looks broken to me.' The policeman walked out and left Sid and Mr Foster alone.

'Erm, I could probably place you in the docking bay. The unloading, its rather heavy work though. If you want to take a couple of days off, I'm sure that would be fine, considering.'

Considering what, Sid wanted to know. It certainly wasn't considering Sid. It felt like he was in the grasp of some humungous black cloud that rained down bad things on his head in a constant torrent.

He was drowning.

A cold plate sat in the fridge awaiting Joanie's stomach. He pulled it out and plonked it on the table. Aside from the salad and corned beef, there was a large pale creamy mound that he didn't recognise. Almost like mashed potato but grainy. He dipped his finger, and nibbled a bit. Tasted of nothing very much. A noise outside alerted him to Margret by the window, she had a pair of secateurs in one hand and a couple of roses in the other.

'Hi.' Joanie smiled as she came in the back door.

'You found it then,' she nodded at his plate.

'Yes thanks, what's this bit?'

Margret looked at the plate and then at Joanie. 'It's couscous, you've had it before. You don't have to eat it if you'd prefer to go out and gorge yourself on a takeaway curry. That's just fine with me.'

'I didn't mean,' Joanie stopped and sighed, he took out a knife and fork from the drawer and sat down at the table.

Margret rolled the roses up in some newspaper and replaced her gardening gloves and the secateurs under the sink. He heard her footsteps mounting the stairs. So far, he hadn't dared to approach the comment she'd made the other night. Didn't think he even wanted to, but he'd promised Sammy. Damn. He ate slowly waiting for her to reappear. She did so a few minutes later searching for her keys. She had make-up on Joanie noted.

'Who is he?' he asked her back as she pulled a drawer open.

'Who's who?' she shut the drawer and pulled open the next.

'The one that's not me.'

'What are you talking about? Have you seen my keys?' she disappeared into the lounge. Joanie followed.

'You said the other night, it's not me.' She was glancing around the room barely listening and then made to walk past him. He grabbed her shoulders.

'Margret.' She stared at him surprised. 'I want to know his name.' It was a lie, he didn't want to know at all, didn't want to ask her this question or any other questions, just wanted to eat his dinner and watch television.

'The painting teacher? James, James Stewart.' She shrugged him off, 'Where are my keys?' she sounded angry.

How could she say it like that, say it like it didn't matter? Was she really having an affair with the painting teacher, with James? The purple eye shadow marked her face, a flag to his growing unease.

'Are you going to see James?'

'Yes, of course I'm going to see James and I'm going to be late.' She thumped back upstairs.

Joanie stood in the hallway; something was so far askew that he wondered if perhaps he was in the wrong house. Surely Margret wouldn't be so blasé about her affair, at least not if she thought it mattered.

She came trotting back downstairs and into the kitchen. Joanie was drawn like a sheep. She tipped up her handbag, letting the contents cascade onto the table, a lipstick bounced and landed in the uneaten couscous.

'You're having an affair with James Stewart?' Joanie faced her across the table.

'What?' Her face jolted up, the keys gripped in her hand. There was silence as the world that was now completely upside down began to right itself. Joanie felt almost dizzy. The clock in the hall ticked loudly.

'Are you mad?'

He had hold of her arm now, the one with the keys. 'You said the other night, that it wasn't me. So is it James Stewart?'

Margret yanked her arm back, her face contorted with confusion. And then slowly as if the dawn light was making its steady progress across the kitchen floor, she understood.

'You stupid, stupid idiot.' She scooped the scattered items back into her handbag. He was still looking at her. 'You bloody imbecile. I can't believe you can be so damn short sighted. It's not you, you blundering buffoon, because it's me! How the hell did I ever end up with you? You have absolutely no idea about women do you? Let alone understanding your own wife, for Christ's sake. No, no, let's blame it on another man shall we? Make it all much simpler wouldn't it if I was having an affair. Wrap it up as a neat explanation for my behaviour. Bloody hell!' She slammed the kitchen door, and seconds later the front door. Joanie stood beside the couscous; the lipstick perched on top gently leaned and rolled off the plate. Sheer Berry he read as the label turned towards him. He waited for the world to drop neatly back into alignment and then let out a deep sigh. Maybe he was in the right house after all. She wasn't having an affair with James.

Joanie wiped the lipstick with the dishcloth and emptied the couscous into the bin. She was right, how could he be such a good detective and completely useless when it came to understanding his own wife? They hadn't been spending enough time together recently, maybe that's why he was getting the wrong end of things, and maybe also why she was so touchy.

Joanie was still feeling hungry and after routing through some cupboards found an unopened packet of chocolate digestives. It was some time later when the phone rang, it was Sammy. Joanie put the television on mute and looked guiltily at the now half empty packet of biscuits.

'Hi pumpkin. When are you coming home?'

'Dad. Don't say it like that, kids are meant to leave home, you know, grow up and all that.'

'I know.'

'Look, I've got some news, me and Matt have decided to go travelling around Europe for the summer. We're going to take his car and a tent and stuff and just see where we get to.' She sounded excited.

'What about jobs? Aren't you meant to be going to job fairs or something?'

'We've done all that, I'm not going to start until after the summer anyway, you know that. Surely I can have one last summer before I get stuck behind a desk for the rest of my life? It'll just be a couple of months Dad.'

'What do Matt's parents say?'

'Dad, we're not kids.'

Joanie looked across at the photo on the sideboard; it showed Sammy when she was ten on the swings in the park.

'And yet, you're ringing me to get permission right?' He knew her too well.

'No.' There was a pause. 'We're going to go anyway,' she added defiantly.

'I see. Your mother and I will no doubt muddle through.'

'Oh God, don't be silly Dad, how is she?'

'I'm trying pumpkin, I'm trying, it would be easier with you here though.' Joanie knew it wasn't fair to involve Sammy but he couldn't help himself, if he couldn't talk to Margret, at least he should be allowed to talk to his only daughter.

'We'll come and spend the night on our way to the ferry.'

'Ah, so you are coming home.' Joanie smiled.

10

Sid stared into the mirror; he used the grubby towel to wipe away the smears so he could see more clearly. The bruising was almost gone but he could see there was a subtle difference in his appearance. He ran a finger down the length of his nose. There was a definite tilt off to the left and the funny knuckle bit at the top of his nose was slightly more pronounced on one side than the other. Not that it mattered, Sid was no picture. He hadn't even bothered to go to the hospital or his doctor. The humiliation was too raw, the number of faces over which a sour kind of recognition flickered were too numerous. Blubbing into Irene's shoulder had left him feeling naked and vulnerable; he didn't want to repeat the episode at the hospital. So here he was with a different face, he turned to the left and then the right. He had allowed his stubble to grow and a week's worth made him look rougher than ever. He needed to have patience. With a beard, people would no longer recognise him. Bit by bit he realised, he could move away from his photo in the papers and maybe even dissolve back into society. Sid scratched his chin, today was his day off and he was toying with the idea of taking a stroll. It would be the first time he had walked anywhere other than to work and back.

There was a thump as something landed on the mat downstairs; Sid paused sniffing the air cautiously. Last week a stink bomb was dropped through the letterbox. He peered down the stairwell and saw a brown envelope.

There wasn't a postmark, just his name in block capitals printed across the front. MR. SIDNEY WHITE. Sid flipped up the letterbox and peeked out at the pavement, nothing. He ran back upstairs to the kitchen window. The street appeared empty. Sid sat down and ripped open the flap, across his desk spilled several photographs. Sid frowned and pulled away as if he'd been bitten. There was something wrong with them. That strange metallic smell of new photos made him wrinkle his nose. Without touching them, he let his eyes rest on the nearest one, it was twisted round the wrong way but there was no mistaking the colour of skin. Sid grabbed his shirt from the bed and covered the photos with it, stepping away from his desk. He hadn't seen anything, he told himself. It was a mistake; they weren't his. He wiped a hand across his eyes and paced to and from the kitchen, wringing his hands. His eyes constantly flickered to the blue shirt. He would go for a walk. Fresh air, he was having a nightmare that was all. When he came back it would all be normal. Sid picked up his wallet and headed for the stairs and then stopped. What if whoever had delivered the pictures was waiting for him? Sid scratched at his arms and then went to sit on the bed. His forearms smarted under the fresh scabs; he had probably made them bleed again. Perhaps he should go and visit Dr Casey. At the thought of her neat office and tidy hair, Sid began to breathe a little deeper, taking slow breaths and stilling his nervousness.

After a few moments he was able to return to the desk. Slowly he lifted the shirt and stared at the two photos that faced up. One showed someone's back, a body stretched out; a deep red line ran across the shoulder blades. Sid shivered. It was a child. The second showed the boy naked lying on a bed, a rope tied around his wrists to something beyond the edge of the picture. About four inches below the left nipple was a dark spot. Sid leaned closer, it was a black mole.

'No,' he moaned softly. A flash of sunlight leapt across Sid's mind lighting up his memory of that skin running across the football field. Feverishly Sid turned all the photos up the right way and laid them in a line across the desk. In one, the boy appeared to be eating something very large, Sid let out a sob, further down his body he could feel his groin stirring.

'NO.' He threw open the drawer, rifling through the pens and pencils until he drew out the orange-handled scissors. With shaking hands he started to cut the pictures. Long slashing cuts in every direction. But it was too slow. Sid dropped the scissors on the desk and grasped his stiff member through his trousers. He was breathing in short gasps. The pictures before him were disgusting, evil and sick. Suddenly he grabbed the scissors with his left hand and started to stab the desk, the points of the scissors driving through the photos into the soft wood of the desk beneath. His right hand was soothing his throbbing penis, but then the scissors veered off the desk and he was cutting flesh. He whipped his right hand back onto the table, swung open the scissors with his left hand and made deep slashes across the black hairs of his arm.

'No, no, no, no,' he sobbed over and over as the blood welled up and trickled onto the glossy photographs.

Something banged loudly from beneath him and a distant voice yelled, 'Shut the fuck up.' Sid stopped. Blood smeared across the photographs. The scissors clattered to the floor and Sid dropped his head onto the desk, his body shuddering with the strength of his sobs.

It was like waking up when Sid eventually lifted his head, but he knew he hadn't been sleeping. The blood and tears had dried and he could feel a piece of photo film stuck to his cheek. He clawed it off and went to the sink. The wounds weren't deep;

he washed his arm carefully wincing at the sting and then bandaged it as best he could manage with one arm. The few photos that were still intact, he turned over and cut into small pieces, slipping the whole sorry lot back into the envelope and then into a plastic bag. The marks on the desk he could do nothing about. Deep dents that would torment him whenever he tried to draw anything, the pencil scooting off into an unexpected dip leaving annoying marks on the page.

For a while Sid slept. Dreams slaked across his mind, one causing his arm to fly up and protect his head. When he awoke, it was to an afternoon sun, bright and warm burnishing the desk. Sid sat up and tried to think about things logically. His arm was throbbing and he cradled it with his left. The only person who really scared Sid was that Barbie man at the station. Curtis. The one that had whispered in his ear after one of the many interviews. Sid remembered the acrid smell of his breath, the stale smoke on his shirt and that damp hiss in his ear.

'I'll get you, you bastard.' Those ice blue eyes would like nothing better than to string Sid up and leave him to rot. No one else had heard the threat, Sid was sure of that. Back in his cell, he had used the cup of water they'd given him to wash his ear. Wash out that serpent's tongue. If anyone wanted to screw him up, it was Curtis. Was that who had sent him the photos?

The file for Annette Dorking was open on Joanie's computer; she'd been raped three days ago in the city park. There was a report missing that Curtis was supposed to have completed. Joanie sighed and went into the main office. He opened a drawer and flicked half-heartedly through the mess of papers. Curtis didn't seem to have a filing system from what he could see, although he was pleased to note that a lot of the paperwork was now printed rather than Curtis' illegible scrawl. Joanie didn't expect to find what he needed; he would have to wait until the young officer returned. As he closed the drawer, something caught his eye, a piece of clear plastic with some white on the corner. It looked familiar. Joanie grabbed it and yanked it out of the drawer. Inside were the drawings that had been confiscated from Sidney's flat.

'That's my drawer sir.'

Joanie spun round and stared at Curtis.

'Wrong. This drawer is the property of the police authority and anything inside it will remain so unless proved otherwise. This,' he shook the bag in Curtis' face 'is evidence that by law should have been returned to Mr White.'

Curtis' cheeks reddened, 'But the case isn't closed yet sir.'

'We have copies of these in the main file, as you well know. These should not be here.'

Curtis lowered his eyes; other officers were watching the exchange from nearby desks. 'I just want to make sure the murderer goes down sir.' Curtis stared up defiantly. There was a murmur of consent from around them.

Joanie addressed the room at large, the bag hanging from his fingertips for all to see.

'And I want to make sure we nail the right man!'

Joanie strode back to his office slamming the door behind him. He was beginning to feel like a pariah in his own department. Public opinion had a lot to answer for. Not only had the local residents homed in on Sidney White, but even his own team seemed to blame him for Sid's release. Doubts slipped across his mind, he needed to find out more about George Boswell.

There were three Boswells in the criminal database. A young man up in Liverpool with several counts of burglary, another Boswell down in London about the right age but the photo showed a weedy looking man with buckteeth. The other Boswell was Henry Robert Boswell. Released in 1985 after a twenty-year stint. Joanie scrolled through the information, child abuser caught in 1965, charged with 5 counts of gross indecency and 3 counts of abuse. Convicted of all charges. There was no mention of a George but it seemed too coincidental to mean nothing. The address listed was for a nursing home in Scunthorpe.

The home didn't have any records for a Mr Boswell but they suggested he try the local registrar for deaths. Joanie paused before making the next phone call, just exactly what was he doing? Did this investigation really have anything at all to do with the murder of Kieren Matthews? Was it helping him to reach the killer? Joanie decided he would continue out of hours, he should get on with the file in hand. Annette Dorking had suffered a serious attack, which was one thing he could do something about. George Boswell would have to wait.

Joanie had the pictures on the passenger seat. He tried to kid himself that he was only doing what was right. Returning pictures that by law were not considered pornographic despite their content. He had a moral duty to return them to their owner now that Sidney White had been released. Joanie pulled up opposite the flat. If he wasn't in, he could simply post the pictures through the letterbox, but Joanie knew he wouldn't do that; he wanted the excuse to see Sidney again. To say a few words. Besides, if he wasn't there, Joanie shouldn't risk letting the pictures get into the wrong hands. It was only right that he hand them over in person.

There didn't seem to be a bell any more, a rough rectangle stood bare on the doorframe. Joanie knocked loudly. He could hear a television but it might be coming from the downstairs flat.

No response, it looked like there was a light on at the top, Joanie rapped his knuckles again several times on the wooden door. He flicked up the letterbox and put his mouth to the slot.

'Mr White, it's Inspector Johansen. I have some property of yours.' The flap clicked shut again.

Finally, the door opened a fraction and Sidney White peered round, suspicion etched across his face. Joanie was surprised; the beard or at least the start of a beard aged Sidney considerably. His nose too, Joanie noted from the incident in the car park, looked a little swollen at the top.

'Here.' Joanie held out the clear plastic.

Sidney's eyes flicked to the bag and then back at Joanie; he made no move to take them.

'Your pictures, Mr White. You're a good artist, I have to say. Studied did you?'

Sid shook his head slowly.

'Bet it was your best subject at school,' Joanie continued. A strange burnt smell reached his nostrils coming from the flat. 'Are you cooking?'

Sidney's eyes widened, he reached for the pictures and was about to shut the door when Joanie stuck his foot in the way.

'They call me Joanie,' he said, removing his foot. Sidney stared at him but there was no blinding light of recognition, perhaps Joanie had been wrong. Maybe his school photo was of someone else completely. His hints certainly hadn't triggered anything. Joanie paused wondering what else he could say, what other string he might pull to see if this was the George Boswell he remembered at school. They looked at each other, each searching for something they couldn't find.

'Well goodnight then,' finally Joanie turned and left, the door closing behind him.

Upstairs Sidney watched the Inspector get in his car, start up and drive away. He had the pictures clutched to his chest like a talisman. Sid put the pictures beside his chips and continued to eat. As he did so, he stared at the uppermost drawing through the plastic. It showed the back of a toddler sitting on a blanket. Sid had drawn it last year after a day trip to the beach. A gloriously hot day in the school holidays, the beach teaming with children. A slow smile leaked across Sid's face. He finished the chips, washed his hands and took out the drawings. They were all there from what he could remember. Rather than putting them back on the walls, he tucked them safely into the desk drawer. But why had they been returned? Sidney's ease slid away as he wiped the grease from his mouth. Were they setting him a trap? His arm throbbed and he could feel the tension tightening in his chest. Good job he'd burnt those photos under the grill. At least they couldn't trap him with those. Tomorrow he would make an appointment to see Dr Casey. She had helped him last time, maybe she could help him again, help him get back to a normal life, help him think clearly.

Margret had cooked. A Thai green curry with rice was bubbling on the stove when the doorbell rang. Joanie had come home early and now leapt out of his chair. He met Margret at the front door as she came hurrying through from the kitchen. They shared a brief smile; at least this was one thing they could agree on. Joanie opened the door to a tall youth with shaggy hair. Joanie's face dropped at the beaming young man.

'Hi Brian, Sammy's just getting our bags.' Joanie looked past him to see his daughter bending over the boot of a small rusty Peugeot.

'Come on in, it's lovely to see you both.' Margret took over elbowing Joanie to the side to allow the young man entry. Joanie stepped outside and caught Sammy in a bear hug as she shut the boot.

She hugged him back, hard. It felt good. A young woman who's head no longer pressed into his stomach but tilted and rested on his shoulder. It always amazed him how their quirky little eight-year-old had turned into this.

'Welcome home.'

'Thanks Dad, here.' She passed him a duffel bag and they went back into the house.

'What's that?' Samantha laughed. They were standing in Sammy's old room.

'It's the zed bed from the loft.'

'I can see that. I'm not sure we'll be using it though; Matt and I can share the single bed. We're used to it.'

Joanie looked across at Margret but she was smiling to herself. They'd argued about the sleeping arrangements, Margret surprising him with her offhand comment, 'Oh I'm sure they've had loads of sex.' That may be true but Joanie wasn't happy about simply letting them share a bed. At least the extra camp bed showed a modicum of morality. When Sammy was young, he'd never have thought it would be him to be the prig echoing his own parents with their 'not in our house' mentality.

Over supper, Joanie questioned the longhaired hippy about his future. Lawyer he said but Joanie would believe it when he saw it. He couldn't imagine anyone employing this shaggy baggy-trousered youth. He looked more suited to a charity shop or a fast food takeaway. Samantha bubbled away chatting about the exams and their plans for Europe. It was nice when she did this, filling the house with sound and laughter.

'So what about you two?' Samantha looked at her parents.

Startled, Joanie avoided Margret's eye, 'Oh you know, ticking along, thought we might take a week in Portugal in September.'

'First I've heard,' Margret muttered.

'So Matt, got all your car insurance sorted? I presume you've got breakdown cover for that vehicle.' And they were off again, the difficult moment averted, or at least postponed.

In the lounge, Joanie sat alone with a glass of port. He had hoped Sammy would have one too, stay up and talk for a bit but she'd gone to bed with Matt.

'I'm going up, are you coming?' It was Margret at the door; she'd finished the dishes in the kitchen.

'I'll just drink this,' he held up the glass.

'Maybe I'll join you.' She walked across to the cabinet and poured herself a small measure of the deep red liquid.

'She looks happy with him,' Margret spoke after taking a sip.

'With who?'

Margret sighed settling herself into the sofa. 'With Matt, what do you think?'

Joanie thought. 'His hair's too long, his trousers look like they're about to fall off and his palm was sweaty.'

'I didn't ask what you thought about him, that's obvious. I wondered if you thought Sam was happy?'

Joanie creased his brow, he hadn't really been trying to gage that sort of thing but now Margret had said it, he supposed Samantha had looked happy. But maybe that was to do with being excited about her trip.

'Did you notice how much she touched him?' Margret smiled. 'His hands, a squeeze on his shoulder. Little things, it reminded me of us.'

Joanie hadn't noticed and quite frankly he wasn't at all certain what Margret was talking about. Of course they'd touched when they'd been dating. In fact they'd touched for most of their marriage, more or less, at least in bed, until recently that is.

'Do you remember you used to do that silly thing with your palm on my nose? Rubbing it in a circular motion as if you were making it shine.'

Joanie looked across at his wife.

'Like this.' She rubbed the flat of her hand on the end of her nose.

Joanie nodded and took another sip. Sure he remembered. It had been their special sign of affection. Another of those things that had fallen by the wayside. How is it that these things happened? All the little gestures and statements of love, repeated over and over, begin to fade, the distances between each recurrence growing ever longer until those little events simply didn't happen any more. Was that what she wanted, Joanie thought, to be rubbed on the nose and called sweetheart? Would that fix the great rift that had opened between them?

Margret drained her glass and stood up. 'Are you coming?'

Joanie looked at his empty glass, 'In a minute.'

She left the room leaving Joanie to feel like a failure, that he'd failed to maintain those special little love signs and even now when she had so clearly asked him to bed, he had declined. Why was that? But a part of him knew. A part of him felt that he could no longer make the grade. That no matter what he did, it wouldn't be enough. He was failing at work, and he certainly wasn't winning at home. Maybe it was time to accept his lot. Joanie switched on the television and turned the sound on low. Blade runner was on, a favourite despite having seen it umpteen times before. He got up and poured himself another port.

Sid rarely saw David these days. Work had become a monotony; lifting and shifting boxes and dragging the great big pallet trolleys across the warehouse at the back. Nobody talked to him; even the line manager was as brief as possible. The shift patterns were different so that he didn't even coincide with David's tea or lunch break. Now the work merely provided a structure for the week, paying the rent and filling the hours. Sid dragged the empty trailer back to the docking bays. Trevor, one of the younger men was leaning by the open door smoking. They both knew that smoking on the job wasn't allowed.

'Truck's late, caught in an accident on the M3,' Trevor stated as if by way of explanation for the damp roll-up pressed to his lips. Sid turned away and glanced at his watch, it was eleven. David's break time, if he was working today that is. Sid decided to take a chance and disappeared up to the staff room. There were a couple of women putting away their coats in the lockers, someone by the sink and David hunched over at the table.

'David.' Sid couldn't contain his pleasure. A smile erupted across his face as he slid into a chair opposite.

'Sid.' David looked up in surprise but then his face clouded and a scowl replaced it as he looked down at the table.

'It's OK, I'll do the talking. Sign language remember?'

The man at the sink turned around to stare at them; it was the ugly youth Sid remembered meeting in the car park on his first day back.

'Oh great.' The youth cocked his head at them, his hair sliding across his face. 'The pervert and the fucking dimwit. Right couple you make!'

The two women bustled out ignoring the confrontation.

'Fuck off!' Sid snarled under his breath.

The youth put a proprietorial arm on David's shoulder, leaning down to his ear. 'The only thing you'll get from him is children to eat.' He slapped David on the shoulder turning to pull open the door. David swivelled round in his seat and sent a large gob of spittle flying across the room. It splatted against the closing door, the youth shoving one finger in the air through the window at the top.

Sid blinked; it had been a long time since he had seen David spit at anyone. This was bad news. He remembered when David had first arrived; his instant reaction to anything he didn't like was to spit. A bad habit he had picked up from the last years of school. Management of course wouldn't stand for it and Sid had often averted David's attention from situations that he knew would make him angry. Gradually as David settled into the routine and begun to take a liking to Sid, the spitting had stopped. That bastard youth was obviously a thorn in David's side. Sid knew it was his fault, if he was still working the trolleys with David they'd both be happy.

'Does he work the car park with you?' Sid asked.

David nodded, his face pouting in a sulk.

'Don't you let him get to you; he's just a stupid boy, not like you. You've been doing this job far longer than him, you're the boss.' Sid wondered what else he could say to try and change the expression on David's face. It was depressing; he had come up hoping to hear David chatter to him, forgetting of course that David wasn't allowed to speak to him any more.

'Do you want a coffee?' Sid sure did.

David shook his head.

'Chocolate cake? I could go down and buy one, it'll only take a minute. You wait here.' Sid hurried out of the staff room and down the stairs. Unfortunately the basket-only queue was long and despite being an employee, it didn't secure him faster service. By the time he was back upstairs David had gone. Sid locked the cake in his locker and went back down to the warehouse. Mr Bradley the storeroom manager was waiting for him.

'And where the hell have you been?' The truck had arrived and was half empty already, his colleagues scurrying past. Sid shrugged and looked at his shoes.

'You might have been able to scoot off any time you please when you were working the trolleys, but that doesn't happen here. Got it?'

'Sorry.' Sid muttered and stepped around him to the back of the truck.

It was actually a relief to walk into the doctor's familiar office. In an odd kind of a way he liked Dr Casey, not in a womanly way. She was far too officious in her buttoned up shirts and tight skirts, but somehow she had shown him how to relax, how to get to some kind of peace in his head. She'd made him feel safe. After recent events, this was just what he needed. He lay back into the leather couch smiling up at the rose fitting on the ceiling and the large ornate lamp that hung down into the room.

'It's nice to see you again Sidney.' She spoke like a Radio 4 presenter.

Sidney wondered what it must be like for her to have a client like him. He doubted she liked him, was certain that it wasn't 'nice' to see him again. Did she think him strange, but then she must see loads of strange people, at least he wasn't crazy.

'Is this a one-off visit or do you intend to resume your sessions?'

Sidney frowned at a small cobweb caught in the intricate detail of the lamp. He hadn't expected to be questioned about his motives for coming. She normally started with 'so how are you feeling today?'

'I had a bad day,' he started, knowing he wasn't answering her question.

'I see,' she paused, she did a lot of that, silences, which in the beginning had made Sidney feel very uncomfortable but later he'd found them calming, almost comforting.

'I've let someone down, a friend.'

'Umm mmm'

'I didn't want to let him down, I couldn't help it, I mean, it wasn't my fault they've moved me into the storeroom.' She did one of those silent things again, so Sidney continued.

'They arrested me.' Sidney detected a shift, perhaps she'd only moved her pad but it felt as if she had stiffened, come to attention.

'How did that make you feel?'

'Bad, really bad, I cut my arm.' Sid automatically covered his right forearm with his left hand as if protecting it from further damage.

'How long has it been since you last cut yourself?'

'I'm not sure, six months, a year maybe.'

'And what do you think triggered it this time?'

'The police, they're trying to get me, trying to say I've done things, nasty things, things I hate, things that are wrong, evil, disgusting.' Sidney could feel his palms sweating.

'Why would they do that?'

Sid was startled, what did she mean? Was she insinuating that they should?

'I haven't done those things, I don't like those things, it's not fair, I just want to..' and suddenly he stopped and swallowed. He couldn't speak.

'What is it you want to do?' her voice was sweet, cajoling.

Tears welled in Sid's eyes and trickled down into his hair at his temples. He stared hard at the lamp, trying to bring his mind into the room, focusing on the cobweb that waved gently. Sid swallowed again, a hard lump forced down his throat.

'Yes?' a seductress whispering in his ear.

'Save....Tommy' he whispered. Tears streamed down his face, he gripped his forearm, pressing on the fresh scabs, willing the pain to make his tears stop. Why did this always happen, why did it always lead back to Tommy? Whenever he felt extreme sadness or love, it was Tommy, always Tommy. He sniffed loudly and drew his sleeve across his face. A tissue appeared above his head and he snatched it from her manicured fingers. The tears stopped, and he blew his nose loudly, the sound bouncing off the large mirror above the fireplace. The tick of the carriage clock filled the room. Sid listened, each tick a year of his life, going on and on, each tock a reminder that Tommy wasn't there.

They veered away from Tommy, onto emotions and control, what was happening at work. Sid could feel himself relaxing again, his emotions receding. They reviewed the techniques he could use when he got stressed; he even had a practice and felt his limbs go all light.

'Your mind is like a closet. At the back you have pushed away an important event in your life that was very upsetting. However, the door to your closet is faulty and keeps swinging open. I would suggest that we carefully go into that closet and pull out what you have pushed away. It can be very healing to gently go back to the event that caused you so much pain, to talk it through and see it in the light of day so to speak.'

Sidney listened to her clearing her throat.

'That way you can accept and forgive what happened.'

Sidney stiffened, there would be no forgiving, not ever, he could feel his face twisting into a grimace.

'There is another way,' she spoke quietly. Sid thought he heard her sigh ever so slightly.

'Some clients find it helpful to re-remember the event but to change the outcome,' she waited for a response but Sidney remained silent.

'Let me give you a simple example, imagine you were

running a race as a child, a really important race that you
wanted to win, your parents were watching, now in your
memory you know that you lost, but you can replay your
memory and change the picture to that of you winning. You
can visualise the race, visualise yourself winning, how
wonderful it felt, how great your parents praise. When you do
this enough times you can overlay the bad memory with a
better one and this may help you to move on.'

Sid sat up and turned to face Dr Casey. 'I can't change the
past!'

She looked back at him, calm, her face flat, 'No, but it is your
perception of the past that is haunting you, and it is that
perception that you can change.'

Sid frowned trying to make sense of what she'd said.

'Imagine a play,' she continued, 'many plays are stories of real
events in history. However, often they are not an exact portrayal
but changed slightly maybe to make them more dramatic or
have a happy ending. If you've ever seen a book made into an
American film, they nearly always change a sad ending into a
good one for the film because that's what people want to
watch.'

Sid could feel a flutter of hope, he barely noticed the
handshake, the promise that he would return and resume their
sessions. He paid the secretary in cash and walked home. In his
head he was thinking about all those films he'd watched that
had had happy endings. He felt like a child believing in Father
Christmas. It felt good.

11

Joanie was watching the sport when Sammy and Matt finally came downstairs. He didn't want to think what they might have been doing until this time. It was ten o'clock after all and Margret had insisted he wait until everyone was up before having breakfast. The result was he felt famished and grumpy.

'Mum, you didn't have to go to this much trouble.' Sammy surveyed the grapefruit halves in bowls; bacon lay spitting under the grill sending out a delicious aroma.

'No,' Joanie agreed. 'Dry toast would have been fine, I'm sure it's what they're used to.'

'Dad.' She gave him a funny look.

'Let's get started then.' Joanie dug into the grapefruit, which spurted across the table and hit Matt's T-shirt. He couldn't have aimed any better if he'd tried. Matt was too busy reaching for the cereal to notice. By the amount he poured into his bowl, you'd have thought they hadn't had dinner last night.

When Margret dished out the eggs and bacon, Joanie was surprised to see his serving was the smallest. He frowned at his plate and looked at Margret.

'You don't need a big fry-up,' she said, pointing the spatula at his large girth, 'you're not about to go gallivanting off across the continent.'

'No, that's true but fighting crime is no easy job.'

'I thought you weren't going in today.'

'I'm not, just building up for tomorrow.' Joanie smuggled an extra piece of bacon from Margret's plate while her back was turned. He winked across at Sammy but she gave him a warning look.

'So how is fighting crime these days? Had any exciting murders or terrorist activities?' Matt ducked his head as if avoiding bullets from the doorway in a smooth James Bond like motion. His wet hair was tied back this morning, which gave him a cleaner, smarter look. He grinned across at Joanie, munching on the cornflakes.

The family fell silent; Joanie noted with satisfaction the appalled look on Sammy's face. Margret stood frozen by the sink, the frying pan hovering above the bowl. Matt stopped crunching his cereal and looked at the others.

'Murders are not exciting.' Joanie spoke into the stillness. 'Somebody losing their wife, boyfriend, child or relative is never exciting, it's bloody awful.' Joanie looked directly at Matt ensuring his meaning was clear.

'Sorry Mr Johansen, I didn't mean, well you know.'

Samantha touched Matt's shoulder. 'Dad deals with some quite horrific cases.' She smiled an apology at Joanie.

'Right.' Matt looked embarrassed. 'I guess not a good subject for breakfast then.'

'At least it looks like it will be nice for your crossing,' Margret gestured out of the kitchen window. 'You could have a walk before lunch.'

'Oh we won't be staying that long. We want to buy some things in Portsmouth before we get on the ferry. We need a tent for a start.' Sammy shrugged her shoulders and scooped up the rest of the egg yolk with her toast.

'Cutting it a bit fine aren't you?'

'We know the one we want, checked it out on the web, we can get it in Blacks.' Matt added obviously feeling grateful for the change in conversation.

They left shortly after. Joanie hugged his daughter goodbye and shook Matt's hand which he was pleasantly surprised to find was dry this morning. Margret became a little tearful and Joanie put his arm around her.

'They'll be fine,' he said watching them reverse down the drive.

'I know. It's just that I miss her, all grown up and everything.' Margret wiped her eyes with a tissue.

Joanie waved, nodding to himself. He missed her too. This would be the first summer without her.

A brown envelope was sitting on the mat, just like the last one. Sid stared at it in horror. He glanced guiltily behind him up and down the street, no one. Shutting the door, Sid carefully stepped over the envelope and hurried upstairs. He fixed himself some dinner and sat there eating with the television on. It didn't help; his mind was on the envelope, a part of him eager to open it. Graham Norton chattered on, the studio audience laughing but Sid couldn't concentrate. Eventually he switched it off and sat in the silent room, he couldn't just leave it there, neither could he put it in the outside bin; someone might find it. Perhaps he should burn it without opening it. Sid jumped up and ran down the stairs. He grabbed the envelope and took it straight into the kitchenette. Firing up the grill, he touched the corner of the envelope to the flame; it started to smoke. The brown paper blackened and curled and a flame sprouted from the corner.

'Shit.' Sid threw the envelope in the sink and turned on the tap. Gently he tore open the flap and pulled out a sodden sheet of paper. The part of him that had been so full of expectation now slumped; there were no photos. Laying it on the counter he attempted to unfold the paper but it ripped and a damp piece came away in his fingers. He would have to let it dry. For a while he paced around feeling restless knowing the paper would take longer than a few minutes. He was tempted to speed up the process under the grill but he might lose it entirely if he did that. Finally he went to his desk and sat down. Sid took out a sheet of clean paper and his pencils and set to work. He wanted to capture the dirty knees of a small boy he'd seen walking with his mother on his way home. Short stubby legs with mud and green stains smeared across the milky skin. The child needed a bath and it was this desire that aroused Sid's imagination. Dirty knees meant needing to get clean. To get clean, you had to take off your clothes and someone would have to wash you. Wouldn't it be lovely if that someone was Sid? Gently sliding the wet, soapy sponge over those knees and upwards. Tommy's smiling face met Sid's and he continued to draw. He had tried to draw a child in the bath before but he found it almost impossible to draw solely from his imagination. It had to be something he'd seen, witnessed in reality. The pencil twisted into one of the dents in the desk and Sid cursed moving the paper slightly and going over the detail again. Beautiful chubby knees marred by grime that were crying out for a delicate touch. Maybe the mud hid a painful graze that would require extra tenderness.

The picture consumed Sid for over an hour until his mind switched back to the envelope. He dropped the pencil and went back into the kitchen. The paper had stiffened slightly but was still damp in the middle. Gently Sid peeled it open and spread it flat. The writing had blurred but was still legible. Although printed, the lettering had a looping style as if to mimic perfect handwriting. It read:

You and I have much in common my friend. I know what it is you crave in the darkest corners of your mind. When the lights are out and there's nothing but the dreams.

I know those dreams.

We are alike, you and I, different from the rest. Those dark desires that make you sweat and hide guiltily from others. They are good dreams, beautiful dreams that shouldn't be denied. I can help you. Together we can make our dreams come true.

Your friend

Sid could feel goose pimples rise on his neck, he looked behind him and listened intently to the noises, a slight murmur from the television downstairs, a dog barking a couple of streets away. Was somebody watching him? Sid pulled the curtains and re-read the letter. Was somebody inside his head? How could they know these things? Sid's hands felt clammy, they smelt of old garlic; he didn't even like garlic. It had to be the same person that had sent the photos. Maybe that bastard Curtis had used some kind of drug on him when he'd been in the cell, slipped something into the food that he didn't remember. How could anyone know what his darkest desires were? Sid scrunched up the paper and threw it across the room; it bounced off a cupboard and rolled across the floor. He shut his eyes panting, when he reopened them, the ball of paper stared up at him. He picked it up and tried to flatten it out again, reading the words over and over as if there was some kind of clue as to who the 'friend' was. Sid didn't have friends, only David. He didn't receive letters only bills and junk. Would Curtis have sent it, to follow up the photos?

Sid slept badly that night tossing and turning under the quilt; twice he got up and went to the kitchen to read the letter. In the morning he grilled it along with his toast until there was nothing left but ash.

It was almost dark outside, Joanie stood up to switch the light on; he stretched and left the office to find a coffee. A couple of officers who'd arrived for the night shift nodded his way as he walked past. The machine had run out of milk so Joanie had it black with two sugars to counteract the bitter taste. As he waited for the little plastic cup to fill he thought about George

Boswell. This morning he had discovered that the convicted Henry Robert Boswell was George's uncle. Joanie knew how common it was for family abuse to repeat itself. Which put George Boswell aka Sidney White squarely back under suspicion. Although none of the reported victims were named George Boswell in the criminal case, he knew that trials of this type rarely managed to represent all the victims. As was common, some victims would never come forwards. What Joanie had yet to prove was his certainty that George Boswell, the kid he'd known briefly at school was also Sidney White. Somewhere along the line, he had changed his name, maybe to get away from the abusive Boswell family. Joanie pulled out the plastic cup and took a sip. He grimaced; even the sweetness wasn't enough to disguise the peculiar machine taste. He trudged back to his office and started looking through successive years of the electoral roll for both Sidney White and George Boswell. Joanie's eyes, which had been glued to the screen, glazed over; his mind plucking the name George Boswell like a broken string.

'George! Stand back. It isn't polite to stand so close.' Joanie watched the teacher's face as she grimaced at George, others in the class sniggered. George reluctantly stopped leaning his body against Ms Felsham's side. Everybody knew he smelt, called him Georgie Pongie in the playground. Joanie had seen George do that before, rubbing up against a teacher or one of the dinner ladies like he was some kind of dog waiting to be patted. Yesterday they'd encircled him dancing around with hands on their noses, playing an adjusted game of Ring a Ring of Roses, this one was the pong of Georgie that made them all fall down dead. By the time the bell went, George stood alone, tears running down his face as the other kids disappeared inside. Joanie felt guilty then, he knew what it was like to be taunted. His nickname was a constant source of amusement, the funny thing was, he seemed to tread a fine line between being bullied and respected. Joanie's hair was longer than the other boys' and it was this that had started his name. He didn't know then, that it would stay with him throughout his life. Long hair meant he looked like a girl and by simply twisting his surname, the name Joanie was born. However, the big boys, those that hung around the senior school and smoked had long hair and it was this that saved Joanie.

'Oooh, Joanie, going to put your curlers in tonight?' Barry yanked and Joanie's head tipped backwards.

'You're just jealous,' Joanie shouted back, he lifted his chest, determined not to lose. 'You're still a baby and so your mummy won't let you have long hair.'

'I wouldn't want to look like a girl.'

'Oh, so Tommy Simpson looks like a girl does he?' Tommy was a notorious bully at the senior school and often in trouble with the police. Tommy's hair reached his shoulders.

Barry gave Joanie a kick and raced off across the playground. Joanie took up the chase and cornered him by the bike rack. Joanie wasn't sure what to do now, he had his fists clenched ready to hit out, but he knew he was slow, that Barry would probably dodge him and get him back worse.

'You'd better watch out, or I'll tell Tommy you said he was a girl.'

'No I didn't.' Barry looked nervous.

'Yes you did.'

'Anyway I didn't mean it,' Barry shrugged acting like everything was fine. Which it was really, so long as the other kids believed that Joanie had some kind of link with Tommy Simpson. The fact that Joanie had never spoken to the boy in his life and never intended to wasn't something anyone else needed to know. And so it went, the other boys taunting him about his hair but never quite getting the upper hand.

Joanie stared at Georgie; the tears had left clean streaks down his face. He was snivelling into the sleeve of his ragged jumper. Mrs Dawes, one of the dinner ladies was yelling across the playground at them.

'My mum says I have to have a bath twice a week.' Joanie blurted out suddenly, then he spun on his heel and ran across the tarmac, straight past Mrs Dawes angry face and down the corridor to room 3B. He'd meant it as advice for George, an act of kindness to stop the kids making fun of him. But as the weeks went by, Joanie began to wonder if perhaps George Boswell didn't have a bath at home.

Joanie rubbed his eyes; the glare from the screen was giving him a headache. He stood up and crossed to the window, looking out on the dark wet streets. A cyclist complete with lights, reflective strips and a helmet whizzed past sending up a spray from the big puddle by the Police Station sign. They'd never bothered with lights and helmets when he was young, everyone had a bike then, or so it seemed. It was the only way to get around, unless of course you were going up to town in which case you took the bus. It was a wet night like this when he cycled past George's house that time. Joanie paused, his hand on the pane of glass, his face caught in a frown.

He'd stayed late at school, a rugby game with the boys from Priory Lane. Just outside the school gates, he'd run over a broken bottle hidden in the leaves by the side of the road. Normally it only took him ten minutes to cycle home but the wheel was as flat as Mickey's baseball cap after they'd chucked it in front of that lorry. His kit bag slung over a shoulder, he plodded down past the terraced houses. There was a light on in an upstairs window and as Joanie drew closer his eyes flicked up. A boy stood staring out into the dark, behind him a large man came close to the window and the boy spun round. The light caught the boy's face as he turned and Joanie recognised George Boswell. The curtains were yanked shut and Joanie looked back at the pavement. He couldn't explain why, but he picked up his pace, the pedal from his bike crashing into his calf as he dragged the bike through the narrow streets, staring at the moon and stars, willing them to shed more light. Panting on his doorstep, his mother looked surprised and then worried.

But there was nothing to tell. Just a bad feeling and a decision that he wouldn't use that route home again.

Joanie dropped his head and sighed. He shivered involuntarily despite the humid warmth in the office. He was too young to know, he reassured himself, that man might not even have been Henry Boswell, but a part of him knew it was, knew that even then he had sensed evil in that house. This was getting him nowhere, his shoulders were stiff and he was getting emotionally involved. Remembering George Boswell, a boy of eleven, was not the same as dealing with Sidney White, a man of fifty-six. There was no telling what had happened in the intervening years. Joanie tidied his desk, shut down the computer and headed home.

He noticed it straight away, a postcard pinned to the notice board in the kitchen. Joanie pulled it off and read the back. It was from Sammy. They'd driven down through France and were on their way to Switzerland. The photo on the front showed the Eiffel Tower lit up at night. Joanie let his fingers run over the words. She'd made dents in the cardboard with the biro, two small kisses at the bottom under her signature. He raised them to his lips but stopped when he saw an M for Matt scrawled just beneath Sammy's. Joanie stuck the picture back on the board and went over to the fridge. The house was silent although he knew Margret was still awake, he'd seen the bedroom light on from the driveway. Peering inside he pulled out some cheese and hunted for crackers in the cupboards. He didn't bother going through to the lounge, instead he scattered crumbs on the kitchen table smearing the stilton onto the dry biscuits. Upstairs he heard the toilet flush but she didn't come down.

It was later than he'd realised, after dumping his plate in the sink, he mounted the stairs with wooden feet. Margret lay on her side, a book open in her hand; she turned towards him as he came in.

'I did phone remember?' He couldn't prevent the plaintive note in his voice.

'I know.' She looked at his trousers. Joanie followed her gaze and brushed crumbs onto the carpet.

'Why are you looking at me like that then?'

'Can't I even look at my husband any more?' she turned back to her book huffing loudly.

Joanie took off his trousers and laid them over a hanger. Then padded through to the bathroom and began to clean his teeth. He paused as he heard Margret shout out.

'I just want to know what is so fascinating at work that means you don't want to spend any time at home?'

He hated it when she did this, shouting out from the bedroom when she knew perfectly well he was busy cleaning his teeth. Why on earth didn't she wait till he was back in the bedroom?

'Well?' she yelled.

'I'm cleaning my teeth,' toothpaste and spit sprayed the mirror. Joanie shook his head and continued with his task.

She was reading her book again, or at least appeared to be. Joanie threw his shirt, pants and socks into the laundry basket and slid under the duvet. Margret turned towards him.

'No answer then?'

'Answer to what?' he was beginning to feel annoyed, his head was throbbing and he was dog-tired.

'You're never home, I hardly see you, it's as if you were back at training or something. Is it still the Kieren Matthews case that you're so overwhelmed by, or is it something top secret, or maybe you're just fed up with me?' her breath was hot on his face and smelled slightly fishy.

'It's the case, it's complicated. I don't know myself really.' How could he explain his feelings? A conviction that Sidney White was innocent despite flimsy circumstantial evidence and his desperate desire to protect Sidney in some way, but from what, Joanie wasn't sure. He hadn't even been able to speak to

Kelly about it. This thought struck him with surprise, he and Kelly worked well together, had done for a couple of years now, but since Curtis had come on the scene, he realised he had withdrawn from their usual one to one chats. Why was that? Had Curtis upset the balance of their professional relationship? Perhaps. And then of course the case, there were so many unknowns, he was used to having gut feelings about suspects, a curious insight to probabilities and events but this case had touched him and he thought maybe it had thrown his reasoning out of kilter. Without Kelly as his sounding board, no wonder he felt out of sorts. Not only was he failing as a husband, but at the moment he was beginning to think he was failing as a police officer too.

'Or you don't want to tell me.' Margret surmised. She switched the light out and plunged them into blessed silence. There was Sammy too, travelling across Europe with Matt. Was he a man to be trusted? The thought scared Joanie. Now he was being silly, the guy was fine, a bit daft maybe and could do with a haircut, but he wasn't a threat. Would he look after Sammy? Make sure she wasn't alone at night in a strange foreign city where Sammy couldn't speak the language. Joanie turned over and pulled the quilt up under his chin. It was George Boswell that had got him all spooked. George and the man in the window.

Sid lay on his back watching a large spider make its way across the ceiling, it paused at the light fitting, circled around it and continued to the far corner. Underneath, Sid lay naked on the fresh sheets, the window open to allow the sound of the warm rain to fill the space around him. It was soothing, a light patter onto the conservatory below and the shushing as an occasional car went by on the street outside. His hands rested on his chest, covering the thick black hairs that sprouted from between his nipples. His penis pointing up at the spider. On the desk lay a sheet of paper, this one had neither been burnt nor soaked, but lay crisp and new. It was an invitation. An invitation to meet the friend.

Sid was thinking, weighing up all the possibilities. If he went to the meeting point and discovered it was a trap set by Curtis, he would have the letter as proof that he had been coerced into something. Surely it wasn't possible to arrest someone for agreeing to meet with a stranger. And that was all the letter said really. Maybe Curtis wasn't out to get him; maybe he too felt like Sid did, after all there were always bent coppers. Maybe Curtis' aggressive behaviour at the police station had been a deliberate act to throw off the other officers. Or maybe it was someone else entirely, then there was no telling where it might lead. This excited him still further; it seemed to Sid that someone had opened a door. After weeks of abuse and unhappiness at work, someone wanted to be his friend. Sid had managed to block out the horrific photos that he'd first received and now that his arm had healed, there was nothing to remind him of the possible intent of the so-called friend. They had a common link, this friend and Sid, they both wanted to love children and that was fine, his friend had said so.

Sid tried to remember exactly what the previous letter had said. It was difficult, he'd been upset, frightened but now that he was calm, he was sure he remembered it correctly, how it talked about the need for children to have loving adults in their lives, that together they could help those little children and give them all the tender care they needed. This was his dream and he knew the letter had said that they both had the same dream. Films with happy endings. That was what he needed to make, a film with a happy ending. His mind leapt and grabbed the thought, how utterly magical, just like Dr Casey said, he needed to re-enact his past but create a beautiful outcome, a happy ending, and maybe he could do it, with this new friend, maybe together they could re-live that love.

Alone at work, he could think of little else, the meeting would be next week and Sid decided he should go. He couldn't lose; his life had become nothing but a number of hours that filled each day. All the children's clothes that he had so painstakingly gathered over the past two years were lost, only the internet and his drawings remained. His job monotonous, his colleagues abusive and the cake he had bought for David had gone mouldy in Sid's locker. He despised his existence, but here was a new opportunity. A chance to hold his dream.

'I've got some new information,' Curtis burst through the door into Joanie's office.

'It's been a while since I had to remind you to knock Curtis.'

'It's important.'

'So it would seem,' Joanie assessed Curtis' wide eyes and the sheaf of papers gripped in his right hand. 'You'd better take a seat then.'

Curtis started talking immediately while he dragged the spare chair close to Joanie's desk.

'I've been doing some background work on Sidney White. You're gonna like this. Look, here, in 1978 he changed his name to Sidney White when he was twenty. He used to be George Boswell AND his uncle was the infamous Henry Boswell put away for child molesting for umpteen years. Now I reckon Henry probably used George or Sidney, as we know him, as his accomplice, maybe even trained him into his disgusting hobby. That puts Sidney squarely under suspicion. He was never questioned in Henry's trial so he may have been hiding all sorts of information.'

Joanie watched Curtis' animated face, he was clearly pleased with what he had unearthed; Joanie was not. Pressing on the paper, Joanie could feel his right hand gripping his pencil hard.

'And is there any criminal evidence held against George Boswell?' Joanie knew the answer but he wanted to find out just how far Curtis had gone with this line of investigation.

'He was caught for joyriding when he was nineteen. Crashed into a tree, and that means he can drive, so he could have used a stolen car to take Kieren to the barn.' Curtis paused for breath.

'Did George Boswell have a driving licence?' Joanie cut in.

'No.'

'And exactly how far did he manage to drive the stolen car?'

'Erm,' Curtis looked through his notes. 'From Stanley Drive to an Oak tree on the corner of Watling Street.'

'Perhaps you'd better look it up on a map.' Joanie knew for a fact that it was all of 500 yards.

'Do you know this already?' Curtis was looking suspiciously at Joanie.

What could he say, of course he knew about it. But he couldn't say so to Curtis; new information about any of the suspects was always shared amongst the team. But so far Joanie hadn't shared any of the background work he had been doing himself. If Curtis dug too deep he might discover they were in the same primary school together and then there would be questions that Joanie wanted to avoid.

'It's quite common for joy riders to crash very close to where they stole the vehicle usually because they don't actually know how to drive, or are so high on drugs or drink that they can't control the vehicle.' The lie sounded plausible at least.

Curtis changed tack, 'But his background has got to be a major factor in this.' Joanie could see that Curtis was willing him to say he was right. But Joanie wasn't ready to give Sidney up.

'What if Sidney was abused by Henry Boswell rather than being an apprentice as you put it,' Joanie leaned across the desk accusingly. 'What if he changed his name to get away from the horror he experienced as a kid?'

'He wasn't one of the victims according to all the evidence, he didn't testify in court.' A red flush was creeping up Curtis' neck.

'You're telling me that every one of Henry Boswell's victims came forward, you and I both know that's bullshit, you never find all the victims in a case like that.'

Joanie watched Curtis drop his eyes, there was the slightest of tremors in his hand and when he looked up again, a peculiar look spread across his features, one that Joanie couldn't read.

'Some people can't come forward.' Curtis added quietly.

'Exactly. So we have no way of knowing if Henry abused him or not. Unless of course you want to go and ask him?' Joanie could see that Curtis was getting angry again.

'OK if he was a victim, then it's a known fact that some victims go on to become abusers themselves.'

'Correct.'

The two of them were sitting in silence staring at each other. Joanie got the distinct impression that Curtis had said more than he wanted to. He was also astute to realise that Curtis had expected a pat on the back for his research. Not an argument about his hypothesis.

Joanie sighed, this was the officer he had badgered to improve, and now had done some thorough research and all Joanie wanted to do was to tell him to get the hell out of his office. Why did he feel so threatened? It wasn't him on the line, it was Sidney White, or George Boswell, take your pick. In actual fact, now that Curtis had this information, it would be added to the file, so Joanie would no longer feel like he was hiding evidence. Ok they didn't know about the school history but was that really important?

'You've done well, I can see you've spent time on this and I'm pleased, but quite frankly where does it lead?'

'Sidney White is guilty!' Curtis thumped his fist onto the table.

Joanie felt like grabbing him by the collar.

'You don't have any evidence, only a hypothesis based on a supposed association with his uncle thirty odd years ago. Get me some hard evidence that will stand up in court.'

'Fuck.' Curtis stood up waving the papers at Joanie. 'I don't think you want this bastard put away at all.'

Joanie could feel himself trembling with suppressed rage. His voice came out cold and hard. 'When we put whoever killed Kieren away, it will be the right person, backed up with solid evidence. Now get out and bloody well knock next time you want to spoil my day.'

12

Joanie was sitting in the canteen mulling over what he needed to cover in his update with the chief later that afternoon, biting into a tuna sandwich, he dropped mayonnaise onto his trousers. Attempting to mop it up with the scrappy tissue that passed as a serviette, Joanie watched the paper dissolve onto the fabric leaving a flurry of white flakes.

'Mind if I join you?'

It was Kelly, paper bag in hand, and a half smile tilting up the left corner of her mouth. Joanie immediately moved his coffee to one side and motioned to the spare seat.

'These damn serviettes are nothing but blinking toilet paper,' he fumed picking ineffectually at the white fluff spread across his crotch.

'I get mine from the sandwich bar across the road. How can you stand those disgusting wet sandwiches they make here? What flavour is that supposed to be?'

'Tuna.' Joanie laughed and shook his head. He looked up at Kelly and could see her face looked serious. He knew that look.

'Spill it.'

Kelly looked behind Joanie briefly and started in a quiet voice. 'It's about the Kieren Matthews case,' she paused gathering a breath, 'I was wondering what your current take on it is. It's not like you to give up on a case like this.'

Joanie took one of Kelly's more formidable napkins and wiped his mouth.

'What makes you think I've given up? Just because I kicked Curtis out with a flea in his ear, what's he been saying?'

'It's not so much Curtis, although that's part of it, others have started talking too. Barry said you've been putting in some late nights, but I haven't noticed any new information in our current files.' Her look was accusing but she dropped it quickly and took a bite of her baguette.

'I see, checking up on your own boss now are you,' Joanie could feel the heat rising at his neck. Kelly couldn't reply, her mouth chomping rapidly. So maybe that was why he hadn't had his normal chats with Kelly, she'd turned against him too.

'Since when do I have to answer to you Sergeant Mowbray? Not only do I have Curtis thinking he's the greatest investigator that ever lived but now you seem to think that one day in the hot seat gives you the authority to tell me what I should be doing.' A general hush had descended on the surrounding officers. Joanie realised his voice had risen.

Kelly's face turned a deep pink. She stood up, picked up her half eaten baguette and made to leave. But something in her was stronger than that, she turned and hissed at him.

'That wasn't what I meant, and you know it.' She left him, disappearing through the swing doors.

'Get on with your lunch you lazy bunch of earwiggers.' Joanie cast a cold stare across the room, jerked his chair back and stormed out. When he got upstairs, Kelly wasn't at her desk, Curtis didn't know where she was and Joanie wasn't about to start searching the building. Maybe she'd gone to the ladies. He slammed the office door behind him and was confronted by the chief sitting at his desk. It was like a kick in the stomach,

Joanie stopped and took a breath.

'I thought our meeting wasn't until three,' said Joanie quietly, controlling his breathing to calm his racing pulse.

'Just popped in on the off chance,' the chief smiled, 'you seem a little agitated, anything I should know about?'

'No, just ensuring discipline amongst my team, sir.'

The chief raised his eyebrows and waited for Joanie to continue, but he wouldn't give him the satisfaction. What did he want anyway?

'I thought perhaps you might like to bring me up to date on Kieren Matthews' killer, it seems to have slid into the undergrowth don't you think?'

Joanie stood stiffly, 'Of course. I'll bring it with the other case information at three.'

'Ah, yes, I mustn't disturb you in your work, I'm sure you have appointments and things to do.' The chief stood up from Joanie's chair and walked to the door. Joanie stood aside. 'See you at three.' The door opened and closed with barely a sound.

Joanie puffed out a rush of air. Damn, he thought. This was nuts, how come he'd been so easily riled by Kelly, he couldn't believe he'd lost his temper in the canteen; it was so unprofessional. There was a time and place to get angry, and normally Joanie used his anger in a calculating and careful way to get the results he wanted. Not splashing it around like some hormonal teenager. And what exactly was the chief doing in his office? It didn't look like anything had been disturbed, besides Joanie wasn't hiding anything was he? Well maybe that old school photo in the bottom drawer. It should be taken home again, stuffed back in the attic box where it had come from. Hadn't he told Curtis only the other week that everything on or in Curtis' desk was presumed Police property so he could hardly be upset about the chief in his own office. Glancing at the clock on the wall, Joanie knew he didn't have time to worry over it; he needed those reports ready in an hour and a half. It wouldn't do to turn up late to see the chief.

'What you looking so cheerful about?' Trevor nodded his head at Sid. 'Didn't think you could smile.' Trevor chuckled to himself dragging the empty pallet back down to the drop point. Sid scowled, he hadn't meant to smile, didn't realise that the pure excitement he was feeling had registered on his face. It wouldn't do to seem out of character. Sid lowered his head and continued with the cereals across to the dry store area. Inside, his organs were jumping around like baby frogs. It was today at six that he was due to meet his friend. He'd barely slept and yet this morning he was full of energy, had unloaded almost twice as many pallets as he usually did. He should slow down; he didn't want anyone else to notice. But the quicker he did his work, the quicker the end of the day would come and he could go home, shower, change and get ready for the meeting.

Sid had now decided that his friend had a child of his own, that he was looking for someone else to share in his care. Not like those gay people you saw on television, no. More like a surrogate granddad maybe, he was old enough certainly. In fact he was sure the man was married, was happy and normal and had somehow discovered how much Sid longed to be part of a happy family. Maybe they'd go to the park together and Sid would lift the child up and put him into one of those swings. Nobody would stare, and nobody would call the police because it would be perfectly normal. A grandfather with his grandson. The fantasy whirled around Sid's head, the colours ever brighter and the feelings ever stronger. The love he felt for this child was overwhelming, as if they'd known each other forever. Sid caught himself smiling again and glanced nervously about him. He checked his watch for the hundredth time that day, the hands showed quarter past three. A whole ten minutes had passed, ten minutes closer to his dream. Maybe he should get a bag of sweets before he left work, or perhaps a nice present; there were a few kids' toys in aisle eight. A gift from granddad.

'Yes' sprung from his lips, loud in the still dank air of the storeroom. The sound frightened him; he clamped his mouth shut and headed back to the waiting truck. Trevor gave him a strange look as he passed but said nothing.

Sid was out the door like a shot when the long hand on his watch touched twelve and the short hand rested resolutely on five. He ran up the stairs but had to stop at the top gasping for breath before continuing into the staff room to his locker. He snatched his jacket out and slammed the door shut with a clang. Outside he had to count his steps in an effort to stop trotting along the pavement. He breathed in time with his feet, slowing the whole rhythm down, concentrating only on getting home without anyone noticing him. The breathing was difficult. He felt like he wanted to pant like a dog but he held each breath in and let it out in a slow sigh. Two steps for a breath in and two steps for a breath out, nice and easy.

Sid turned the corner into Compton Drive at a steady gait. However, one glance down the street towards home and his breathing stopped completely. Sid froze, rooted to the spot beside a laurel bush. There was a police car parked about half way down. Panic shot up Sid's throat and he felt himself gag. There were no pedestrians, and at this moment, no cars moving along the street. Sid tried to see into the blind windows of the houses nearest and then turned around and walked stiffly back the way he'd come. His heart thumped so hard, he wondered if it was trying to batter its way out of the cage of his ribs. His mind fluttered madly, jumping in and out of horrific scenarios, for a second the terrible photos flashed across his mind and Sid thought he might be sick. What was that? Something he'd seen on TV? Sid assured himself that he didn't recognise the gruesome pictures in his head.

Turning left down the parallel road, he couldn't stop his feet gathering speed towards the snicket that cut through to the close behind, he could then bear left again, and pick up another alleyway that would lead to the opposite end of Compton Drive. In the safety of the snicket, Sid slowed down, checked both ways and stood still. He needed to think. What was a police car doing there? Dread plucked at his chest as he wondered if maybe it had been Curtis all along. But wait, the car hadn't been outside his front door; it had been closer, more towards the middle of the street. A beam of hope set his feet moving again as he cut left once more and walked ever slower up the alley towards the bottom end of Compton Drive. The police car was still there, a silent Panda waiting to pounce. Sweat tickled the side of Sid's face and he wiped it away unconsciously. Despite the summer afternoon, the alley was gloomy, large bushes and trees overhung from gardens, full with ripe green leaves that served as a heavy blanket blocking the sun's rays. Sid clung to the shadow of an oak and waited. Seconds ticked by, he swore he could hear them on his watch. Then minutes. His left leg started to ache and Sid shifted his weight. He checked his watch; it was half past five.

At quarter to six, Sid's shirt was soaked through, the only action had been a couple of cars arriving, pulling into driveways and a woman with her dog had appeared and fortunately turned away from him in the other direction. If Sid waited much longer, he would be late for his friend and that wasn't in his plan, not part of the dream by a long shot. What if his friend didn't wait, what if he thought Sid wasn't worth it. Trembling slightly, Sid pulled himself from the shadows and walked hurriedly out of the alley, his eyes squinting against the sudden brightness, his legs gathered momentum. Fiddling in his trouser pocket, he had his front door key ready. The police car was just two doors up from Sid's. He thrust the key at the lock, missed and scratched paint off. He stabbed again and then realised he had the wrong key in his hand, this was his locker key. In his haste the keys slid from his grasp and jangled loudly onto the pavement.

'Hello sir.'

Sid's head jerked up almost giving himself whiplash, a young police officer with red hair bent down and gave Sid his keys.

'Thought you should know, as you're here, your neighbour was burgled this morning. I recommend you..' and the officer stopped.

Sid watched his green eyes narrow, something clicked into place and the eyes flashed dangerously. Sid knew, yet again, that someone he'd never met before recognised his face. It didn't matter that several weeks had passed since then, that his beard had grown considerably. In the queue at the supermarket on Monday, somebody had looked at him twice and then stared so he'd changed queues. On Thursday a woman dragged her whining child out of the newsagent's after a studied look at Sid's face.

Sid turned away, anger replacing the fear that had kept him rooted to the spot. He unlocked the door, went inside and closed it behind him. The officer remained standing in the street saying nothing. Sid waited in the hall, his eyes felt wet and his chest seemed to be trying to hiccup. It was several seconds before the officer's shadow moved away from Sid's front door and he could hear an engine start and disappear down the street. Sid wiped at his eyes and sat with a thump on the bottom step. A few gasps and he swallowed several times, the desire to sob loudly passed and he was able to stand up a little shakily at first and go upstairs.

The invitation was waiting for him, crisp and white in the middle of his desk. Sid picked it up and sat on the bed. An urge born of the panic and fear he'd felt outside made him want to rip that perfect white paper into tiny shreds. Instead he read the words again, slowly.

They were sitting at a small table in the corner near the door. The Royal Oak served real ale and Joanie sighed with pleasure as he took a generous sip.

'Looks like you needed that.' Kelly indicated his glass and sipped at her own white wine.

Joanie nodded, it was the best thing that had happened all

day. The meeting with the chief had been awkward, the Kieren Matthews case being the crunch of course, but Joanie had prepared for that in the hour between finding the chief in his office and their official meeting. Joanie had spoken again to Curtis and was able to place the notes before his superior. It wasn't really getting them anywhere but it was a bluff to show they were at least trying. Well, that Curtis was trying.

And then of course Kelly hadn't been easy to persuade, and Joanie, not used to giving apologies had finally sat down and admitted defeat.

'I wanted to say sorry,' Joanie paused waiting for Kelly to meet his gaze. 'About lunch time, sounding off at you like that. It wasn't..' Joanie searched around for what he meant to say.

'I know it wasn't me.' Kelly stated. Her mouth set grimly.

'That's right, exactly, it wasn't you. It's this damned case.' Joanie took another refreshing gulp, using his tongue to lick his creamy moustache. He tried a smile and shrugged his shoulders hoping his apology would be enough.

'You and Curtis are both touchy on this case, I don't get it, what makes this one stand out so much. I feel like I'm dancing between a cauldron and a fire with barely room to breathe.'

Joanie frowned, 'What do you mean?'

Kelly put her glass on the table. 'Curtis is determined to get Sidney White arrested and convicted. It's like he's obsessed with him, that there couldn't possibly be anybody else. He thinks it's only a matter of time before he gathers what we need in evidence to put him away.' She paused to sip the cool wine. 'And then there's you at the opposite end, getting touchy when anyone even mentions Sidney White's name and giving out looks that could kill if anyone presumes to know anything at all about Sidney's possible guilt.' Kelly shook her head.

'I didn't know Curtis was that sure.' Joanie frowned into the pint glass and wondered how much had been going on that he didn't know about. 'And what about you? What do you think?'

Kelly sighed, her right hand twisting a wedding ring on her

left. 'I don't know what to think. With you two dropping off the ends, I feel like I need to stay in the middle and try and look at this objectively. You know it's not Curtis that worries me, it's you.'

Joanie appreciated her frankness; he had been concerned that his outburst earlier would have put up a wall between them. They had shared much in the past, both about work and their private lives. Kelly confiding in him when she was going through a trial separation from her husband Tony, and Joanie sharing his fears for his job three years back when he'd been set up as the fall guy.

She hadn't finished, 'You're normally so sane, so thoughtful, you get an instinct and then you meticulously gather data without letting your instincts alter the truth of the evidence. Sure, normally you're right, but it never stops you from looking at other possibilities. This case seems different though, you don't talk about it and it seems that you've already made up your mind.'

God she knew him well. It was a shock to be sitting here in a pub having a meaningful conversation with a woman who wasn't his wife. With someone who perhaps knew him better than his wife. This thought only served to increase the sadness in his chest.

'I hate to say it, but I think you're right.'

Kelly's face looked surprised. 'I know, but I didn't think you'd admit it so easily.'

'Oh thanks. Do I never admit to being wrong?'

Kelly smiled. 'Kind of, but then you're normally so right.'

A man in jeans brushed against their table making the glasses jiggle, if it had been earlier, they would have spilt, but as it was, Joanie had nearly finished his and Kelly wasn't far off either.

'If it's not Sidney White, does that mean you're protecting someone else?' Kelly's voice was quiet, their heads automatically leaning into the middle of the table.

Joanie sat back, his eyes hard, watching the way her hair

brushed the top of her shoulders. 'I'm not completely deranged. No, I don't know who the murderer is, and if I did, I wouldn't be protecting the sick son-of-a-bitch. But it's not Sidney White, that's all I can tell you.'

Kelly sighed again, Joanie knew he wasn't giving much away, he couldn't; it made no sense why he felt this way. But she was right about one thing, if it really wasn't Sidney White then why the hell wasn't he busting a gut trying to find out who it was?

'What did the chief say?' Kelly changed tack.

'Same as you really, that I'm slipping.'

'No you're not, the mugging on Clarence Road has been passed back to Hampshire and we're definitely moving on the rape case. Will you be interviewing the husband tomorrow?'

Joanie nodded and they continued to chat about the current caseload. It was true; he hadn't neglected the other important issues, his faulty brainwork or whatever it was that was going wrong seemed to be confined to the Kieren Matthews case. And perhaps Margret.

'Kelly, I wonder if I could ask you something.'

'Sure, whatever.'

'You and Tony, I know you've had your tough times, but I was wondering, what were the signs that Tony was having an affair?'

Kelly frowned at him, and he could see anger cross her face.

'Why do you want to know?' her voice took on a harsher tone, but then her eyebrows rose, 'not Margret surely. You don't suspect Margret of having an affair?'

Joanie felt embarrassed. He had suspected, and a part of him still did.

'Oh Joanie, but Margret....' she paused, 'I'll get us another drink.'

Once she'd returned, Kelly appeared more composed. 'I think it's different for men and women, I mean if they're having an affair. Some things are the same. Like denying they're even having an affair.'

Joanie looked up from his pint.

Kelly sighed and continued. 'A change in their normal routine, working later, longer. Perhaps a new hobby that takes them out of the house a lot. A heightened interest in sex,' she blushed, 'or less sex than normal.'

Joanie gripped his glass and thought about Margret's painting, about her redundancy, their reduced sex life. But couldn't all of those things simply be what they were, a new hobby, a change in working routine.

'Do you really think she could be having an affair? Margret's so....'

'Reliable?' Joanie offered.

'Hmmmm. But you know it's different for each person, she might just be going through the menopause that's all?'

'The menopause?' Joanie looked up thoughtfully, now that had never crossed his mind, what would the menopause entail?

Loud radio music greeted Joanie when he got home. He heard it even before he reached the front door. For a moment his spirits soared as he thought maybe Sammy had decided to come home. It certainly sounded like Sammy's music. When he entered the kitchen Margret jumped away from the table, startled.

'God,' she grasped her jumper with one hand, 'You don't have to sneak up on me.'

'The music's too loud.' Joanie went back through to the lounge and turned it down. 'What song is it anyway?'

'I don't know, one of Sammy's.' Margret was dabbing a deep green onto a landscape. Joanie cocked his head to see what it was, a bush maybe in front of a sweeping hill. Margret caught him staring and tensed her lips.

'How was your drink with Kelly?' she asked rinsing the brush in an old marmalade jar.

'What makes you think I was drinking with Kelly?' A flutter of guilt twittered somewhere deep in his gut, swilling the beer he'd drunk earlier. On the phone he hadn't mentioned which of his colleagues was going to the pub, in fact he remembered insinuating that it was a group of them. Margret raised her eyebrows at him, her brush poised in the air.

'Yes, it was Kelly, but nothing's going on. I mean there's nothing between us, just work. This difficult case that I've been working on.' There was some leftover Bolognese on the stove that Joanie helped himself to, sticking it in the microwave.

'You don't need to explain. I know there's nothing going on,' she paused, filling the brush with a lighter green, 'There's nothing going on between you and me either.'

'What's that supposed to mean?'

She shrugged but wouldn't look at him.

'What do you want me to do? Come singing through the door, sweep you off your feet and call you sweetheart every time I come home?'

'That sounds nice.' Margret dabbed over the darker splodge she'd made earlier. The microwave pinged and Joanie clenched the fork in his hand.

'That's stupid, I never did that, not even when we were newly-weds. Besides it's just not me, you're cold and frosty, always painting. I took you out to dinner the other day and that was all wrong too.'

'It was three weeks ago.'

'I've been busy.' Joanie knew he couldn't win the argument, he didn't know why he tried really. They were just going round in circles the last couple of weeks, blaming each other for the lack of love in their lives. Just at the moment, Joanie wasn't sure he had the energy to tackle why his marriage was on the rocks. It was so much easier to lose himself in work, and yet that wasn't any less complicated, but at least he knew there were truths and answers to be found. What truth was there in a marriage? Just two individual's subjective feelings and they could hardly be relied on to be fact. If there was an answer to all the difficulties with marriage, then there wouldn't be so many divorces would there? No, truth and answers were inconceivable; all they had was a melee of mixed emotions and misinterpreted meanings.

Joanie fought the urge to retreat to the lounge.

'Margret, I need to be honest with you.' He put his dinner plate down on the table. Margret added another brush stroke to the paper.

'Margret look at me,' he felt like shaking her.

'I'm listening.' She glanced at him, dropped the paintbrush in the water jar, turned towards him and folded her arms. 'Right, well honesty is usually a good thing. Fire away.'

Her confidence took Joanie by surprise.

'I..well, I wanted to ask you some questions.'

She raised her eyebrows. 'I thought you said you were going to be honest, not start an interrogation.'

Joanie paused, she was right, why should he be asking her questions, he could simply tell her what he'd been thinking. That would be far less confrontational, she was right, they weren't in the police station now.

'I'm sorry,' he began, unsure of how to proceed. 'I think I may have made a mistake, you see, I thought, well think, you're having an affair.'

Margret dropped her arms, her eyes darkened considerably.

'Wait, let me finish,' Joanie continued. 'You've been different, and I think it's because of ..... the redundancy isn't it?' And now as he thought about it, Joanie realised how lost he would feel without his work as an Inspector. 'It's a huge change and I don't think I've been supportive enough, so I want to say sorry, and ask you what you need.'

'I see. Anything else?' her voice was soft; a smile tickled the corner of her mouth.

Joanie watched that tickle, wanted to put his finger on that twitch, a sparkle had come back into her eyes.

'We've had twenty seven long winters that I wouldn't have wanted to spend with anyone else.'

'You silly oaf.' She pulled his hand, dragging him towards her. 'I'm not having an affair. And yes, you've been a selfish lump these past few weeks.'

Joanie felt his shoulders relax just a little.

She sighed. 'Oh Brian, how can you be so blind sometimes. You give so much to your work, that you forget that I might need some too.'

Joanie slid his arms behind her. 'And not just that.' She wriggled free and picked up the paintbrush once more.

'Your dinner's getting cold, and I need to finish this painting before it dries out.'

Sid was in such a hurry he didn't notice the man until they collided.

'Oof,' said Sid as the air expelled from his chest.

'Sorry,' said a polite voice, 'You should look up instead of at your feet.' A man with blond hair and a strong nose spoke politely, nodded his head, turned away and headed down the street. For a sudden second, Sid thought it was Curtis with the blond hair and blue eyes but the man was taller and strode away on long legs. The park gates were only steps away and Sid rushed in to the park.

Strangely enough he was five minutes early despite the contretemps with the police officer. Waiting on the bench half way between the tennis court and the children's playground, he knew his watch was right, he'd checked it on Ceefax before he left. At quarter past six a line of little boys came past in green sweatshirts. Cub scouts on their way to play rounders on the large grassy area deeper in the park. Sid had stood up, nodded shyly and tried to smile. Maybe his friend had a son who was in the cub scouts; perhaps one of these boys could be his grandson. A cute one at the back with blond hair smiled back. Sid almost followed them but he knew that without his friend, he wouldn't know which boy was his.

By half past six, Sid was agitated; he had waited patiently

sitting upright on the bench nodding as members of the public went by. For some strange reason, he felt he had a right to be sitting there in the park, something he'd never done before. Usually he walked quickly with his head down. But this evening, his friend had made him feel like a responsible member of society, waiting to meet his grandchild. Nobody spoke to him and Sid began to wonder if somehow he had missed him, if that gentleman, who'd tipped his hat at Sid, had meant him to follow, but he was too old, a grandfather himself. He didn't know what the friend looked like, hadn't envisioned him at all, not like his grandson although now he'd seen the Cub scouts, he was convinced it was one of them. Sid began to doubt that he'd read the invitation properly, maybe he was meant to be at a different bench. The one overlooking the tennis court, or the mothers' one by the swings. He thought there was one near the toilets too. None of this helped of course, if he got up and moved, he might be wrong and miss the friend. But judging by the time, he had missed him already. That couldn't be true, he was here on time, early! Something clicked in Sid's brain and he swivelled on the bench, stood up and peered at a small plaque on the seat. 'In memory of Betsy'. Yes. That was right, he remembered that from the invitation. Although maybe Betsy had more than one, maybe Betsy had benches all over the park. Perhaps it had been Betty not Betsy, or Brenda or something. Sid left the bench and marched across the grass to the one by the tennis court, he kept turning around to make sure he didn't lose sight of Betsy's bench. There was no inscription on this one, at least none that he could see. As he turned back he saw a figure approaching down the path, Sid hurried back to the original bench and sat down. The man ignored him, strolling straight past.

It was getting dark, and with it the air had lost its warmth. Sid shivered briefly in his sweatshirt. The heat of summer had faded, a few more weeks and the leaves would be falling. He thrust his hands in his pockets and decided to make a circuit of the park. He didn't want to look at his watch again but he couldn't help himself. Over an hour. Sixty long, lonely minutes waiting. Sid kicked at a crisp packet and trudged down past the tennis court towards the road.

And so it had gone on for another hour and a half until Sid felt utterly dejected. He'd failed; a simple meeting and he couldn't even get that right. The road was busy and Sid decided it would be pointless to circumnavigate the park. His friend wasn't there; he was tired and hungry plus a little chilled. On the way home, he made a detour to the Fish and Chip shop on the roundabout.

Standing in front of his door, warm paper package in one hand, Sid routed in his pocket for his keys. They weren't there. He patted his pockets, searched in them again, but still no keys. He never lost his keys. Never. Sid turned around and looked back the way he'd come, surely if he'd dropped them he would have heard a noise. Panic began to rise up from his gut, what if someone else had them, what if someone was in his flat even now? Sid put his hand on the door, it didn't move. He turned the handle and the door swung back. Saliva filled his mouth. He could feel his fingers digging into the warm chips through the paper wrapping. There were no lights on, just the silence of the hall and his coat on the peg. A shiver ran down Sid's spine. Now what? Burglary? Wasn't that what the police officer had said? Had he been burgled? A drop of sweat tickled down across his temple and onto his cheek. Standing here all night wouldn't solve anything. He switched on the light and waited, his ears pricked forwards. There was no other way out, unless you climbed out the kitchen window and down onto the conservatory. Nothing, just muffled laughing from the neighbour's TV. Sid wiped the back of his hand across his brow.

'Hello?' his voice was quiet; he took a breath and tried again, louder, 'Hello!'

Cautiously he walked up the stairs, the mushy package in his hand wasn't going to make much of a weapon but he held it high as if ready to chuck it at the intruder. Upstairs, Sid turned more lights on and there on his desk were his keys. Sid sighed deeply, lowered his arm and put the damp chips next to the keys. Turning slowly around he walked through to the bathroom and then the kitchen. So he'd forgotten his keys, there was always a first time wasn't there?

Sid ate slowly squashing the already mushed chips against his teeth mulling over the evening. He had the invitation in front of him, had re-read it again five times. Six o'clock at the bench on the path between the tennis court and the playground. Betsy's bench. He'd been right all along, so how come his friend hadn't shown up? Sid crunched on some fish batter, the grease leaking onto his tongue, his mind trying to work out an explanation for the disastrous evening. There was no explanation; the bastard had played a trick on him. The sly conniving bastard had probably been watching from the trees, laughing at him wasting his time sitting on some old biddy's bench. Sid slammed his fist onto the greasy paper.

'Bastard,' Hh said out loud, both fists crashing repeatedly onto the desk. He must have been so wound up what with seeing the police man by his house and wanting to be on time for the friend that he'd left his keys behind, causing even more aggravation. Everything he'd hoped for lay in tatters. He squeezed his fists tighter until the short sharp nails dug into his palms. A bead of blood welled up and slid down to the desk. Sid opened his hands and stared at the red streak. He was so fucking stupid to have believed that bastard. It was what he deserved, believing in fairy tales, happy endings. That wasn't life, not at all.

13

As was typical, the trucks arrived together. Trevor was standing at bay 2 and Sid at bay 1. As the trucks pulled up and the drivers opened the rear doors, Trevor let out a groan. He was confronted by Cote de Rhone.

'Here Sid, you do this one, I'll do yours.' Trevor shouted across.

Sid looked back and his eyes picked out the wine boxes. His own lorry revealed larger boxes of cereals. A lighter load and certainly a lot easier. Trevor came sauntering over.

'Off you go then,' he added assuming a cocky tilt of authority.

'No.' Sid hissed through his teeth not meeting Trevor's eye but starting to remove the boxes.

'What's up with you? I said we'd swap, I'm bay 1 and you're bay 2.'

Sid knew that Trevor had no authority whatsoever in the matter. They both knew which was the easier truck. Sid wasn't about to be walked over again. Not like yesterday evening.

'This is my bay,' Sid fixed him with a stare. Although he

found he couldn't see Trevor that clearly, there seemed to be an opaque curtain in the way. One that burnished red at the edges.

'Jeez, alright boy, I was only asking.' Trevor backed away staring at Sid's hands. Sid looked and as the fog cleared he noticed his fingers had dug right through the cardboard into the packaging beneath. He ignored the other packers and got on with unloading.

The morning had started badly, spilling his cup of coffee across his desk over two of his new drawings. It dribbled through to the pencil drawer and dripped into a puddle by the wall. On his way to work, a car had splashed through a puddle soaking his trousers from the knee down. He hadn't been able to shake the thought that he'd been set up, made a laughing stock by his so-called friend. If he ever showed up, Sid would give him what he deserved. The other packers gave him a wide birth as Sid dragged the pallet trolley across to the shelves. He could see Trevor sweating on the other side with the heavy bottles. It gave him a moment of silent glee. A small triumph in a turbulent sea. His life had never been an easy one. It was a shame really; the last five years had lulled him into a sense of calm. Working with David, visiting the park and the library to gather what he could. A glove here, a cardigan there. That moment with Jessica had been a step too far, he realised that now. In fact maybe it was Jessica that had upset the balance, not Kieren at all. Maybe it was the panties that had brought about all his bad luck. He had to admit, that it seemed to start around the same time. The throb from his arm reminded him of how dangerous life could be if you let it get it to you.

Sid finished unloading the pallet, ignored Trevor's sour look as he passed and headed up to the staff room. He needed to buy some food before he left today. Feeling hungry made him grumpy, a plate of sausages and mash would go down well tonight.

Sid put down one of the bags he was carrying. The milk slid sideways and dropped onto the pavement. He cursed as he unlocked the front door and shoved it open. Reaching down to retrieve the escaping milk he noticed a brown envelope lying on the mat. Sid stopped, let go of the bag and picked it up. 'Mr Sidney White' in neat printed letters. He couldn't believe it; he looked behind him, gathered up the shopping and slammed the door. He wrestled up the stairs and dumped the bags in the kitchenette. Sitting at his desk, Sid tore open the envelope, his lips set in an angry line.

> Dear Sidney
> I am so sorry I missed our meeting yesterday.
> Unfortunately Alfie has caught a cold and so he
> had to stay at home. I've told him all about you
> and he's very excited to meet you. I'll let you
> know when we can get together again.
> Your friend.

Relief flooded through Sid like sliding into a warm bath. He let out a little whoop of joy. After reading it for the third time, he started to whistle while he put away the shopping. How silly he'd been, of course he should have thought that something might have happened. Something to prevent his friend from coming. So now he knew it was a boy, Alfie. Maybe he went to the Cub scouts and that was why they were going to meet in the park. Of course if he was sick, he wouldn't go. And Sid didn't have a phone, not any more so his friend wouldn't be able to call. There had been a time when Sid had used the phone a lot but unfortunately it sent his bill sky high. The phone had been cut off and cut Sid off from his addiction to those titillating voices. He didn't trust himself to get it reconnected; besides there was still an outstanding bill of a couple of hundred pounds. Sid smiled to himself. Alfie. It was a nice name, a perfect name for his new grandson. He tried to imagine his hair, the way he smiled and moved.

All through making and eating his dinner, Sid had a raging

hard on. By the time he switched on the TV it had lessened but he still felt euphoric. Everything was going to be great. Better than he'd ever had it before. Imagine him, Sidney White; being a grandfather to Alfie, it would be like heaven. It was only when Sid was undressing getting ready for bed that his mood dissipated. He had a small cabinet beside his bed on which stood a lamp, a couple of screwed up tissues, a book, and a blond hair. Sid froze, it was the light from the lamp making it gleam just so, he leaned over and picked it up with his finger and thumb. Definitely blond, definitely not Sid's. He thought about his keys and the open door when he had returned last night. Curtis had blond hair. Was he following him, trying to set him up? Sid thought about Alfie, about his new friend, there was nothing he had done wrong, nothing the police could pin on him. It was a bona fide friendship. In fact maybe this hair didn't belong to Curtis at all, maybe it was Alfie's, maybe it had fallen out of the recent letter. That was possible; in fact more than possible, it was likely. Nobody had been in his flat, not since he'd been locked up. And this hair, well it made sense didn't it, perhaps Alfie had helped to fold the letter and put it in the envelope. Sid smiled, what a clever boy.

The line was so clear that Sammy could have been calling from the student house in Manchester. She wasn't of course.

'It's really beautiful Dad, you and Mum should come here. A wedding anniversary or something, you know like a second honeymoon. It's so romantic with the lights on the water. Mind you, the pigeons aren't much fun in St Stephen's square. I don't understand why they encourage them, shitting all over the place and flying up in to your face. The Japanese love it, buying seed and having them land on their shoulders and in their hair. Yuck.'

'You're not selling it very well. How's Matt?' Joanie surprised himself at the question.

'Fine. We're heading further down into Italy tomorrow. I

expect I'll be doing most of the driving again.' She sounded pissed off.

'Why's that?'

'Matt seems to think it's important to drink his way from city to city. Which generally means I have to do the driving the next day because he's either still drunk or got a hangover. He's not an alcoholic or anything, but I've had enough of bloody beer and pizza.'

Joanie was somehow pleased that Sammy was having arguments too. But then he chided himself for being selfish. Just because he and Margret were having a rough time, didn't mean he should wish it on his daughter, especially as she was miles from home and friends.

'I'm sorry love. It's a bit different when you spend twenty four hours a day with someone.'

'Tell me about it.'

Later as they were sitting watching a film, Joanie looked across at Margret and thought about Portugal. He'd made that offhand comment when Sammy and Matt were having breakfast with them. Maybe he should book it, a week in a pretty villa somewhere might be just what they needed. He already had the week booked off work. The first week in September.

'Would Portugal be alright?' he asked.

'What? What on earth has Portugal got to do with the stolen Monet?' Margret was annoyed at the distraction.

'I wasn't talking about the film. I was talking about going on holiday, you and me, the first week of September.'

She looked at him, her eyes drawn away from the film, 'I'm afraid you're too late.' There was an angry twist to her mouth. 'I'm going on a painting week to the north of Spain.'

'What? You never said anything; you knew that was the week I'd booked off. We talked about going to Portugal.' Joanie spat the words out.

'We never talked about Portugal; you mentioned it out of the blue in front of Sammy nearly a month ago. And seeming as you haven't mentioned it since, I decided to sort my own holiday out. If it wasn't for me all these years, you would have spent your holidays stuck in that bloody armchair. Well for once, I thought you were going to organise something, and when you didn't.' She paused catching her breath. 'A few of the people from class are going.' She added almost apologetically.

Joanie wasn't sure who he was most angry with, Margret for leaving him out of her holiday plans or himself for not getting off his butt and booking something. 'And exactly when were you intending to tell me?'

'When you bothered to discuss your holiday plans with me. In all these years, I can't remember once when you've bothered to book us a holiday. You always come up with some plan and then expect me to execute it. Well, this year I've got my own plan and you can do as you please.'

'Right.' Joanie crossed his arms tightly and stared resolutely at the television.

'I'm just sick of always having to organise everything.' He could tell she was feeling guilty now, 'I haven't done it out of spite, in fact the painting group sold it to me. It sounds really lovely, very tranquil with fabulous scenery. I thought it might make a change.' She sighed heavily. 'I could find out if there are any spare places.'

'I hardly think I'm going to fit in with your painting friends.'

'No.' Her lips pursed. 'You're probably right. But it wouldn't hurt to explore your creative side you know.'

His creative side? He didn't even know he had one. Creative in what? What was he supposed to create? Painting was out, he could barely hold a brush correctly, let alone make dabs of colour that looked like something other than dabs of colour. His mind wasn't like that. He created scenarios in his head. Possibilities in the cases that he investigated. That was his creativity, not moulding some hunk of clay into a blobby shape that described how he felt. In fact he didn't know how he felt, other than angry of course. They fell into silence, the missing Monet being chased across New York in the trunk of a Cadillac.

As he turned the light out, Joanie wondered about the week in September. Sammy would still be away and if he stayed at home, it would feel empty especially without Margret. He had never been at home without Margret, sure a few hours or the occasional night but not a week. He could smell her hair on the pillow beside him. His fingers reached out and he stroked it, she turned to face him, trying to read his eyes in the dim light from outside. Stroking her cheek, he softly kissed her lips. She responded, warm and gentle. Their lips moist, exploring each other in the silence. Joanie slipped his hand from her cheek to the hollow between her neck and shoulder. She shivered slightly at his touch. A deep yearning locked them together in a fervent embrace. She asked him to take his pyjamas off and he did so. Revelling in the smell and taste of her as her silky nightdress slid between them. Neither of them spoke other than the sexual murmurings of shared pleasure. It was gentle and satisfying. It felt like an apology, sorry for not being a better husband, hers an apology for planning a holiday without him. They were both at fault; both wanted to be salved by this act.

Joanie felt strangely sad when it was over. He clung to her back as she turned onto her side ready for sleep. Surely this meant they still loved each other. An intimacy that had seemed impossible only a couple of hours earlier. Did it change anything or was it just a brief reprieve in their downward spiral. Joanie clung to Margret as his mind clung to the hope that this was a step towards bridging the gulf that hung between them.

Alfie brought a certain sparkle to Sid's life. He'd experienced this sense of excitement and joy when he'd been six. Before Uncle Henry had come to stay with them, his mother had given him a brand new bicycle. Much better than all the other kids had. Bright red with silver handlebars and a shiny bell that clanged all the way down the street. It was special beyond comparison. And it was his. This was how Sid felt about Alfie. It didn't matter that he'd never met him. The fact that there was a little boy out there who was eager to meet him, who needed a grandfather figure like Sid was enough. He was an angel, perfect in every way, and he was Sid's. He cleaned the flat, clearing out years of grime from along the skirting board and the back of the cutlery drawer. He even bought some window cleaner and rubbed hard at the glass. Actually the window cleaning didn't work that well, no matter how hard he rubbed, it always seemed to end up with a smear somewhere. He trimmed his beard to a neater shape and got his hair cut in the barber's down town. Fortunately the barber was so old and squinted so much that Sid didn't think he read the papers. He certainly didn't seem to recognise Sid. In fact he was beginning to feel invisible again, the odd looks were fewer now. Sometimes people frowned as if they might have known him once but on the whole people ignored him. Sid walked around town a little more freely. Buying himself new trousers to replace the ones that had ripped at work caught on the edge of a pallet. This state of intense activity and expectation sustained Sid for two whole weeks. He even offered Trevor a jam doughnut on Tuesday although he wouldn't do so again. The ugly man had grasped it hungrily, didn't even say thanks just nodded his head at Sid as if it were his due.

On Sunday Sid walked through the park, an old lady on the bench by the road smiled at him and tapped the seat beside her. Sid thought it might seem rude not to oblige. He sat down, staring back the way he'd come past the swings.

'Good to see them outside don't you think?' she began. 'Too many computer games I say, making them all white and lazy. No wonder there's so much crime, all that energy and nothing to do with it. Have you got grandchildren?'

Sid turned and looked startled into her milky blue eyes. The veins around the edges stood out starkly from her pale skin.

'Yes,' Sid looked at his hands, 'His name's Alfie.'

'That's a lovely name. How old is he?' the woman was smiling at him, a full set of dentures splitting her face.

'Umm, five, he's five yes. Had his birthday last week.'

'Oh that's nice. I bet that was fun, not for the adults of course.' She chuckled. 'God they make such a mess don't they? Food everywhere, toys all over. I remember when my two were small. Damn noisy they were too.'

Sid didn't like this. Alfie wasn't messy or noisy. He ate perfectly putting small round cookies into his lovely little mouth. He wouldn't drop crumbs everywhere or throw his toys around. Alfie was a perfect child. Sid was about to tell her so, but she had silently risen.

'Can't sit around too long, my joints stiffen up, and then I'll never get home.' She waved her stick at him and hobbled down the road towards the pedestrian crossing. Sid frowned, she'd never met Alfie, she wasn't to know that Alfie was different. The fact that Sid hadn't either never crossed his mind. He got up, tempted to walk down by the river but decided against it. Instead he took the long route home, past the fire station and the old city wall.

Waiting for him on the mat was another brown envelope. Sid smiled, what a perfect day. He tapped it on his palm and went upstairs, taking his time to remove his thin jacket and make himself a cup of coffee. He sat like a proper gentleman at the desk and slid a nail bitten finger under the flap.

Joanie made a decision. Enough of Sidney White, Kelly was right; he needed to be looking for the killer. So far he had avoided links with the Martin Hempstead case after advice from above. Now though, Joanie wanted facts. If the two cases were linked, he wanted to know about it. Something about Martin Hempstead might tally with the current case. It was possible that one might shed light on the other. Joanie put together a strategy and called a team meeting. There were only four of them, but it was better than one. He had two weeks before his leave, and he wanted some leads by then.

'Don't just look for similarities, look for factors that are blaringly different, even opposite between the cases. Sometimes killers are deliberate in attempting to throw us off. I want more detail on these seven people.' He pointed to the board where seven of the original adults that were interviewed were printed. They included the piano teacher, swimming instructor, the young man at the youth club, a neighbour, a brother-in-law that lived in Manchester and an unidentified man that had been seen around town on the day of Kieren's disappearance. An odd one out, thought Joanie, possibly just a vagrant passing through. He'd been seen by several people at the train station and later hanging by the school gates but not by the river or in the housing estate. They had a pretty good description. And finally at the bottom of the list he had written Sidney White. Not what he wanted to put up, but he knew there would be talk if he didn't. Besides, if he was true to himself, the small amount of evidence they did have, pointed to Sidney White and he couldn't ignore it.

Curtis stuck his hand up. 'Shouldn't Sidney White be at the top?'

Joanie could see a nod of agreement from Barry. Kelly merely stared at the carpet.

'I haven't ranked them in order of priority,' well except for the last one Joanie thought to himself. 'They all need further investigation. Try friends, neighbours, and colleagues of these men. But keep it low profile. I don't want angry phone calls accusing us of intimidating anyone. Got it?'

They nodded at him. Joanie shut the lights off and clicked the mouse to show the first picture projected onto the wall. They'd seen them before but it wouldn't harm to refresh their memories. Mostly it was shots of the murder scene with Joanie commentating on the evidence found at the scene and the nature of Kieren's disappearance. A close up of Kieren's laces tied in a double bow struck Joanie once again. For a kid who'd been playing football the afternoon he went missing, it seemed just a little too damn neat.

The slides of Martin Hempstead were more distressing. His body had lain undiscovered for two months and that made the evidence that much more difficult to pin down. Still he went through the case, pointing out the main facts.

After the meeting, Joanie sat in his office fingering the picture of Kieren's feet. From this angle, all that could be seen was a hay bale, with two trainers sticking out. They were white Nikes, fairly clean with a few dark scuffs. One foot was twisted slightly towards the camera and that was where you could see the double bow.

Joanie leaned back in his chair and steepled his fingers. A minute later and he was on the phone to Mrs Hempstead. Not an easy conversation by any means, but it confirmed his suspicions. Kieren hadn't tied those laces into a double bow, a single bow, maybe, but like his mother said, they were always coming undone. Which meant that someone else had tied them. A boy playing football, and then later ends up with double bows. Would one of his friends have tied them? Unlikely, laces weren't something kids thought about, let alone did for each other. No, the most likely possibility was that the killer had tied them.

Joanie pulled the list of the seven men towards him and ran his eye down the names. Only two struck him. Teachers always picked up on things like that, runny noses, muddy hands, undone laces. Mr Evans and Mr Thorpe were the only teachers. And Mr Thorpe kept a very tidy house.

Standing in the chief's office the following afternoon, Joanie knew there was something wrong. The chief was sitting in his chair staring at the door when Joanie entered, as if he'd been waiting all day for him to come in.

'Afternoon sir.' Joanie attempted politeness.

'Sit.' The chief could have been speaking to a dog but Joanie was used to his blunt manner. He held a pen in his right hand, twisting the lid on and off a couple of times before he began. 'As I remember it, you were told to steer clear of the Martin Hempstead case, am I right?'

'Yes sir. But..' he wasn't allowed to finish.

'And yet, from what I hear you have now started an investigation into that very case in attempts to link it to Kieren Matthews.'

'Well sir, as I understand it' again Joanie was cut off.

'No. Inspector Johansen, you don't understand at all. You were under specific instructions not to start messing with that case. There is no reason to suspect the two are related. Should the public hear of your rummaging, they will be shouting about serial killers and then where will we be?'

'I can't ignore it sir, there may be significant similarities in which case we must consider the possibility of them being linked. If Inspector Morgan was still with us, I would ask him to assist but as he isn't, I'm afraid my officers will have to do their best with the files we have.' Inspector Morgan had been in charge of the Martin Hempstead case. He left shortly after. The case wasn't closed as such, more shelved. Now Joanie was beginning to wonder what those files were hiding.

The chief was quiet, obviously calculating his next move. From where Joanie was sitting, it was stinking like a huge cover-up.

'Don't get me wrong Inspector, I encourage my officers to be thorough,' so he was backing down, can't be too big a scandal then Joanie thought. 'But the Martin Hempstead case is a sensitive one and I trust that whoever you are sharing this with will treat it with the respect it deserves. There may be some who won't take too kindly to you opening this particular can.'

'Perhaps you could save me the time chief. What exactly is

the problem?'

'There isn't a problem. That'll be all.' The chief dismissed him with a wave of his hand and immediately picked up the phone.

Back in his office Joanie pondered the peculiar meeting. Why on earth would the chief warn him off and then back down the very next second. Was he trying to help Joanie? What was there in the Hempstead case that might cause problems? Was there something more to Inspector Morgan's early retirement?

Joanie pulled the nearest file towards him and began to study it in more depth. He had given the team the bones of the Hempstead case but there was plenty of detail to plough through. For a start he wanted to cross-reference all the adults with the Kieren Matthews case.

Sid stood in the phone box trembling. In his left hand he held the letter with the phone number on it. It took him three tries to punch in the numbers correctly and then when he heard it ring, he slammed the phone down. What was he going to say? Ask him about school, that was what he could say. Find out if he'd had a good day at school. No, that was stupid, it was the summer holidays. The kids didn't go back until next week. He could ask him about Cub scouts, about what he was wearing and what he had had for tea. That would do. Sid wiped away the line of sweat that hung on his top lip.

A distant phone rang four times and then it was answered. Silence echoed back at Sid and then a child's voice, a little boy, Alfie's voice said 'Hello.'

Sid's eyes grew so large that anyone walking past the phone box at that moment might have thought he was having some kind of attack. Sid mouthed the word Alfie but no sound came out.

The voice giggled at him, then through the giggles said 'Come on let's play googers.' The giggling continued and then there was a click, followed by a second one. The line went dead and Sid put the receiver down. He stood quite still for almost five minutes. That had been Alfie, he'd said hello and wanted him to play googers. What was googers? Sid had done absolutely nothing but listen dry-mouthed. Alfie hadn't seemed to mind though, what with all that giggling. The phone trilled suddenly and loudly. Sid grabbed the receiver and almost shouted into it.

'Alfie?'

There was a click and the phone went dead again. Had he called him back? Surely he would have said something. Sid stared at the black handle; there were white scratches by the mouthpiece. He placed it back down and for the first time noticed the graffiti scrawled across the plastic behind which an informative poster explained the workings of the public telephone. A wrong number surely? Nobody called up phone boxes on purpose, except in those silly spy films.

Sid walked home in a kind of daze. Those few seconds listening to Alfie lengthened in his mind to at least minutes and yet he couldn't remember what they had said to each other. One thing he did know, he needed to find out how to play googers.

The morning was cool, a misty rain swirling in the breeze down Compton Drive. Sid thought about taking his umbrella but decided his light jacket would do. It was still summer after all. A couple of leaves patted the arm of his coat, curled brown at the edges. On the corner of Market Street, there was a sudden blast and Sid felt his hair ruffle and the edge of his coat flap against a lamppost. He pulled it back and continued on. He was the first of his shift, early by almost twenty minutes. Sitting with a coffee in the staff room, Sid watched other members of staff come and go. It was difficult to tell who would be the right person thought Sid. It wasn't exactly etched across people's foreheads. If you filled a room with people, it might be impossible to tell which of them were parents and which weren't. He would have to make an educated guess depending on age and manner. Irene walked in and Sid seized his chance. She was maybe too old but he was pretty sure she had kids even if they were mostly grown up.

'Irene. Do you know googers?'

'What?' she spun round, a wet umbrella dripping onto the floor. She frowned at him and Sid suddenly realised she was the last person he should ask. In fact he couldn't really ask anyone here. Everybody knew he'd been arrested by the police for something to do with Kieren. If he started asking them about children's games, they were sure to call the authorities.

'What's that? Some word in one of them cryptic crosswords? I can't do them to save my life, prefer the word searches myself.'

'Erm yes.' Sid struggled, 'Do you have a dictionary.'

She looked at him incredulously, 'Here? Don't be daft. You should look it up on the internet, that's where Don finds all his peculiar words.' She shut the locker door, turned the key and left.

Sid's shoulders dropped. Thank god he hadn't given the game away. How could he have been so stupid, thinking he could walk in here and start discussing children's games? The old Sid mocked him, of course nothing had changed. He was still Sidney White, a pathetic old pervert. Who had called him that, he wondered for a brief second, but it didn't matter. He was a fool to think things had changed.

Sid rinsed his mug and went down to the storeroom. The manager was checking his clipboard and saw Sid approaching.

'I need you to do some shelf stacking in the store. This lot here for aisle eight.' He moved off to speak to Trevor. Sid didn't get a chance to say anything, hadn't he realised that Sid wasn't meant to be seen by the public? Surely the man hadn't forgotten why Sid was put here in the first place. He looked at the pallet; it held what the supermarket described as 'seasonal goods'. Orange and black were the predominant colours for various sweets, toys, masks, even pumpkin chocolates. Maybe he'd find something among this lot that said Googers. Sid picked up the handle and dragged the heavy pallet out through the swing doors. Carefully he manoeuvred the load along to aisle eight where about half way down, a wide area of blank shelves were waiting. Someone else was there putting out plastic monster fingers.

'You can line the chocolate stuff up here, and then we'll put the masks and other stuff on the top.' The young man explained to Sid. This was somebody new, Sid thought, not a face he recognised. When he'd been working the trolleys, he'd got to recognise most of the workers going in and out of the supermarket. But that was two months ago now. Sid put a box of scary chocolate faces onto the shelf, lined it up neatly and put another in front. The man might be too young to have kids thought Sid. His hair was short, very short, the fashion these days according to what the barber had said last week. His face was clean-shaven but not so smooth that he didn't need to shave. Also his confident authority in telling Sid what to do added a few years. Mid-twenties Sid decided, old enough to have a child but perhaps not yet. Sid studied the packaging of a plastic game that involved flying bats. No mention of Googers. The chocolate pumpkins had truffle centres and Sid thought he might buy some when he finished.

The young man was staring at him. Sid put the packet on the shelves and started to work a little faster. His first time out of the storeroom, it wouldn't do to fuck it up. An hour later and Sid was flattening the empty boxes back onto the pallet. The shelves looked rather pretty now he'd finished. He wished the young man would come back and look but he'd moved on to another aisle. Sid pushed the pallet back through to the storeroom. He thought about how to find out about Googers. Irene was right; he could look it up on the internet when he got home.

14

There were at least forty something statements held in the file, some just a couple of pages; others were transcripts from an hour's interview. The easiest thing to do was to speak to Morgan. He would remember the case and be able to highlight problem areas, or leads they had followed without tracking it all by online documents. This way was tedious and Joanie was running short on patience this morning. He wasn't sure Morgan would help; he was certainly under no obligation to do so now he was retired. In fact they may not even have a valid address or phone number for the ex-Inspector. Then there was the chief's comment; so far Joanie hadn't spotted anything suspicious or any malpractice. There didn't appear to be any missing reports, at least not that he'd discovered so far. But would Morgan be willing to talk about the case? Joanie decided he should know more before bringing Morgan into it. He didn't want to appear like a blind fool in front of Morgan.

They had a team meeting at eleven. Kelly had been looking at the forensic evidence and stated how both sites seemed extremely clean although the Hempstead case was difficult because of the time lapse in finding the body. A lot of evidence may have been lost simply to the weather and decay. DNA evidence was thin, the strongest and most frequent samples being that of the father. The Matthews body, although a lot fresher, provided little. There was no DNA to link Sidney with Kieren. Whoever had killed and subsequently dumped Kieren's body had used gloves and probably a wig judging by the synthetic hairs found. However, under one of Kieren's fingernails was some skin. This provided a DNA sample that Bob Davis had mapped out. It didn't link to any current samples they had, or to the database.

Curtis had perhaps the most interesting find.

'Remember Evans the swimming instructor?'

Joanie nodded. 'I thought the Hempstead kid had a woman coach, Harris, or Hunt or something.'

'Yes,' Curtis looked surprised at Joanie, 'Well for 3 weeks in June before Martin went missing, Miss Hunter was off having surgery on her knee and Evans took that class instead.'

Joanie pulled out his penknife and slipped the edge under his thumbnail. 'OK, any other adults you've found knew both boys?'

'The lollipop lady on Carswell Road, although the boys went to different schools, all the kids tend to cross over there. Oh, and you might like to know that I discovered Martin's route to school often took him along the alley at the bottom of Compton Drive.'

'What's significant about that?' Barry was looking non-plussed.

Joanie stopped scraping his nails. 'It's where Sidney White lives,' he added. He could see the confident smile on Curtis' face. 'Yet Kieren lived on the other side of town from Sidney White, in fact, from what we know, Kieren and Sidney had never met until the day he disappeared.'

'So he says.' Curtis muttered disconsolately.

'Right. Let's give Mr Evans another visit. Was the lollipop

lady ever interviewed?'

Curtis shook his head.

'Kelly, you can take Curtis with you later to find out if she can give us anything useful, first we'll head off to the leisure centre. Barry, I need you to do some checking on the schools. Find out any teachers, or kids that went to both, or maybe swapped schools. Also supply teachers that serviced both schools during the run up to either of the boys disappearing.'

Before Joanie left the office, he took the interview notes Curtis had made on their previous visit. For speed he ought to let Curtis drive while he refreshed his memory, but instead Joanie drove and then they sat in the leisure centre car park while Joanie flicked through the papers.

'What is it about other people's driving you don't like?' Curtis was bored, staring out at a blue Vauxhall trying to park.

'Don't take it personally.'

Curtis looked at him. 'So what happened?'

Joanie looked up from the interview notes, studying the furrow that creased Curtis' brow. He wasn't a bad kid, Joanie thought. He'd pulled up this bit on Evans that was unexpected. Maybe he deserved a little trust.

'A colleague of mine, he was driving. It was late, on a Friday night.' Joanie sighed and began to explain.

The road had been dark, one of those country roads with sudden corners and various side roads. One that Sergeant Thompson knew well. They were heading back to the station after a reported firearm incident. It turned out to be a farmer shooting a fox too close to his neighbour's front window for comfort. The Ford Fiesta came up behind them, hanging close on their tail. Joanie could see the bright glare reflecting in Thompson's face as his eyes flicked to the rear-view mirror.

'Tosser,' Thompson said. It was clear the other vehicle wanted to pass. Sergeant Thompson drove faster, taking the corners wide and then cutting in tight as the bend sharpened. He knew his car and although Joanie wasn't entirely comfortable, he had no reason to think Thompson couldn't handle it. As they summited a rise the car behind revved loudly and pulled out. The two officers looked across at three jeering lads hanging out the window with music blasting. When the boys recognised the two men were wearing uniforms, their faces dropped. It was like a switch, abusive wild-eyed cheek to nervous surprise.

'Watch out!' Joanie saw it first; a car on the other side of the road waiting to turn right. The lad in the Fiesta mouthed the word 'Fuck,' his hands rigid on the steering wheel. Thompson braked hard, pulling the steering wheel left to allow the car beside them to pull in past the stationary car. The car in front started to turn, in slow motion, the metal body twisting sideways. Thompson pulled even harder left, bounced over the grassy verge, across the side road and blackness. Before the seat belt tried to cut Joanie in half, he saw the Fiesta connect with the back of the turning car, sending both vehicles into a spin. If only they had pulled left into the space provided by Thompson, they could have sailed straight through unharmed. As it was the lads careered straight on hitting the rear corner of the turning car spinning it and them into a war zone.

Joanie himself was severely concussed and his leg broken in two places. Thompson took the full brunt of the engine shoved forwards by the oak tree. He didn't stand a chance. The front seat passenger of the other car died and so did the elderly driver of the turning vehicle. If Thompson hadn't gone so fast, if the lads hadn't egged them on, if they'd overtaken earlier or later. If they hadn't been wearing their uniforms, the driver might have kept his head. So many ifs that Joanie went quite crazy lying in a hospital bed with his leg in plaster. His final conclusion was that if such a situation happened again, he wanted to be the one to make the decisions. That if it was the wrong one, he would only have himself to blame.

Joanie spared Curtis the self-analysis but told him the rest.

'Ouch, that's tough. So now no one drives but you huh?'

'You got it.'

Joanie sprung open the door, he needed some air. Suddenly it felt stifling in the car, and yet his hands felt cold. Joanie focused on the big windows of the leisure centre behind which they could make out some kids splashing in the pool.

'You know, I think this is a dead end.'

Curtis followed his gaze to the steamy glass. 'Touchy feely remember.' Curtis glanced at Joanie. 'But actually, I think you're right.'

That was the first time he had ever heard Curtis openly agree with him. Maybe his thinking was back on track at last. They crossed the car park and entered the shrieking interior. Mr Evans was taking a break, drinking coffee behind the front desk. They ended up in the same goldfish bowl office; a couple of young kids barely out of school were on lifeguard duty.

'So what now?' Evans didn't appear as accommodating as the first time they'd met.

'Three years ago, you taught a young lad by the name of Martin Hempstead.'

'Three years ago? Are you kidding me? Hey, wait on, wasn't he...' The big man paused nodding. 'I see what you're doing. Kieren and Martin. You think they were done by the same person. Look, I hardly knew Martin, taught him maybe once possibly twice. If he walked in that door now, I wouldn't recognise him.'

'That's unlikely to happen sir.' Curtis' blue eyes glinted.

'You taught him three times to be exact, when Miss Hunter was away.' Joanie was sitting at the desk, his hands clasped across his chest.

'I don't know what you want me to say, I didn't know him, don't remember even what colour hair he had, well not his eyes anyway. This is crazy, I teach loads of kids, how am I supposed to remember one kid from three years ago that I only taught twice, OK three times? If you've got something else, fine. But this is shit. I can't help you with this.'

Beads of sweat twinkled on his brow under the electric light. Joanie watched his eyes shift between Curtis and Joanie.

'Fuck. I didn't do anything. I'm just a bloody swimming teacher.' His cheeks had two high dots of pink. Joanie wondered if they'd caught him on a bad day. This was certainly a more stressed individual than the concerned man they had met last time.

'If you remember anything, anyone hanging around. What the adult looked like that picked him up, anything.'

'I don't even see the kids get changed. They wait for their parents in reception, I stay by the pool. It's only if the parents come and sit by the pool that I ever see them. I don't remember Martin Hempstead or anyone with him.'

Curtis pulled out a photograph of Martin Hempstead. Evans barely glanced at it.

'That could be anyone. He wasn't a kid that stood out, at least not for me.'

Joanie nodded and slipped a card from his inside pocket.

'I'm sure we don't have to say this, but it's important that if you remember anything,' Joanie held out the card. 'Call me.'

They left him and went back to the car. Joanie tapped the steering wheel with his fingernail. Sometimes it was difficult to judge if someone was just highly strung or they were hiding something. It was the summer holidays, the pool was busy. He turned to Curtis and raised his eyebrows.

Curtis shrugged in response, 'Bit dodgy. Wasn't too happy to see us again, makes me wonder if he was prepared last time, but this time we caught him off-guard.'

'Hmmm, I'd like to know what he's so ruffled about. See if you can do some digging. Maybe he's just overworked.'

'Aren't we all?'

On Friday morning Joanie said goodbye to Margret. She had two suitcases and a flat picture case that held her paper for painting. She was standing in the hallway, waiting for her pick up.

'Make sure you empty the rubbish out, I don't want to come home to a stinking house. And the fridge, throw away anything you don't eat by the time you leave.' Her face was strained. Pale skin etched with lines that made her look particularly old this morning. Early mornings didn't suit her any more he noticed, she'd been up at six.

'I promise.' Joanie felt like a teenager being left in the house for the first time.

She pressed a piece of paper into his hand. 'This is where I'm staying and the phone number, in case of emergencies. Are you taking your mobile?'

Joanie hadn't thought about it, of course he should. He had no idea what the name of the hotel would be; it was one of those that you only found out when you arrived. It all seemed decidedly dodgy booking it over the internet like that on Tuesday. But Kelly had advised him which websites to look at, said she did it all the time.

'Yes, I'll take the mobile.'

'Good.' She seemed relieved. They were standing by the front door waiting for her friend Iris. The two of them would drive to someone else's house he couldn't remember the name of and then get a taxi to the airport.

'I'm sure you'll paint some great pictures, we could do with something new in the lounge,' Joanie encouraged. He didn't feel very jovial but judging by Margret's anxious face, he thought he should make an effort. 'Sunshine, friends, great scenery. You'll have a wonderful time.' Joanie put his arm around Margret's shoulders and she gave him a wan smile in return.

They stood in silence for a minute and then Margret checked the tickets in her purse for the fifth time and Joanie went to put the kettle on, he hadn't had breakfast yet and time was moving on. While he was in the kitchen, there was a beep from outside.

'That's me.' Margret's voice wavered slightly.

He came to give her a hug and they walked down the drive together. Joanie placed the suitcases in the boot.

'Bye sweetheart.'

Margret said nothing but turned swiftly and got into the car. He raised a hand as the car lurched off, stalled and then shot off round the corner. A terrible knot filled his stomach, this was all so wrong. What was he doing waving his wife off on holiday? Wives were supposed to have holidays with their husbands. Not separate ones like they were single. He wished he hadn't put her bags in the boot; it was as if he was getting rid of her. Putting his seal of approval on her departure. But then what could he do? Beg her to stay? It was only a week after all. Joanie turned back to the house. He had his own holiday to look forward to, he hoped.

At work Joanie had amassed more information but at present he couldn't say he had any good leads. Nothing that he could really get his teeth into. Against his better judgement, Joanie decided to photocopy much of the stuff he hadn't yet read to take on holiday with him. Of course he shouldn't, but without Margret, it would give him something to focus on, and so long as he kept the paperwork in his hand luggage, there shouldn't be a problem. He'd booked himself a week's stay in a three star hotel in Portugal for a bargain price of £357. He hoped it wouldn't be a disaster. The only evidence that he was actually going on holiday was a one-sheet printout of a confirmation email. It seemed somehow too flimsy compared to the usual bunch of papers and tickets that Margret normally gathered. It was four o'clock, time he should be gone. There was still his packing to be done and he wanted to reconfirm the morning's taxi. He was also hoping Sammy might ring tonight before he left. They'd had a couple more postcards from her and a phone call in the middle of last week but they hadn't told her about their separate holidays. There hadn't been a suitable moment, and Joanie didn't know what to say. It was all so strange.

He shuffled the papers on his desk, the team had been briefed and he'd spoken to the chief that morning. Everything was as tidy as it could be when you were in the middle of a serial killer investigation. Joanie shook his head, this wasn't really the best timing for a holiday but maybe it would refresh him. Help him see the wood from the trees so to speak. He packed the photocopies into his brief case, gave his office a cursory glance and shut the door.

Joanie could have sworn they had reduced the size of the seats. There was a young girl on his left staring out of the window and a large woman on his right whose fluffy cardigan bloomed over the armrest along with her hidden flesh. It wasn't a case of making oneself comfortable, more of finding a position that was the least uncomfortable. He had his briefcase under the chair with great ideas of doing some reading during the flight. Kids were back at school and he'd expected a quiet flight. Not so. He wouldn't be surprised if some poor sod had been given the toilet to sit on, it was so crowded.

'Are you travelling on your own?' the lady turned her head, all powder and lipstick.

'Yes.' Joanie felt their faces would be too close if he turned as well so he faced forwards and simply glanced in acknowledgement to his right.

'Me too, going to visit my Ramiro. We only met in May and this will be the third time I've been over. He's a lovely fellow, so charming not like English men. Present company excepted.' She let out a chuckle and tapped Joanie's arm.

'I'm Wendy,' she offered swollen fingers with bright pink nail varnish.

'Brian.' Joanie awkwardly clasped her hand.

'It's not easy though, a long distance relationship. We talk a lot on the phone of course but it's not the same. Who are you going to see?'

'It's just a holiday.'

'Oh. Well don't worry you might get lucky like me; I was on my own last May. That's how I met Ramiro; he runs a restaurant in the old town. Which resort are you going to?'

'Erm, I'm not sure, it's a last minute thing.' Joanie thought he should at least get his papers out. That might deter her.

'How exciting, you know sometimes they upgrade you if it's full. The hotels I mean. I used to do that, book late and get a bargain. I just buy the flight now because Ramiro can get me a deal in the Anstal Hotel. It's just around the corner from his restaurant.'

Fortunately for Joanie the safety video came on and the woman stopped talking to watch. Joanie fished under the seat, decided it was too awkward and closed his eyes instead. Three hours, that was all. He tried to think what he and Margret normally did on a flight. She tended to have a couple of paperbacks with her and he inevitably ended up reading one of them. More often than not, they'd talk about Sammy or work or what needed doing on the house. Big plans for when they got back. Margret had usually done some research too and would start showing him places she wanted to see and telling him about the history of it. Nothing too exacting but he enjoyed her telling him these things, her voice rising and falling as she read a bit out from one of the tourist magazines. Like the Colosseum when they were on their way to Rome.

'Wow, listen to this, it says that in the time of the gladiators, the underground chambers provided all kinds of intricate devices to provide special effects during the games. Lifts that would rise up or disappear down taking a gladiator with it.'

And when they'd actually been to the ruin, Joanie remembered looking down and thinking about the moving floors and lifts just as Margret had described it. Without that, it would have been just a pile of old stones. Margret and her research turned a boring holiday into a historical fantasy. She unleashed a latent imagination in him.

'Ramiro's restaurant is actually Moroccan. Gorgeous food,

the most fantastic lamb and apricot stew. Not that he's Moroccan but his chef is and it does very well. Bit of a change from the Portuguese stuff.'

The video had obviously finished and they were now taxiing onto the runway.

Joanie opened his eyes, 'Do you know any of the history of Portugal?'

The woman called Wendy looked surprised. Joanie wondered if she'd thought he hadn't been listening.

'History? Goodness me, I haven't done history since I was at school. It was so boring. I don't mind the odd church here and there but I can't stand it when they have all those boards and displays around a lump in the ground and it goes on about some amazing city that used to be there. If it was that amazing, it wouldn't be a lump in the ground, would it?'

Joanie closed his eyes again. He knew nothing about the region he was going to, he wished Margret would pop up and give him a few pointers. What was he going to do all day? Sit on the beach and read murder investigation reports?

The following Monday after the Googers phone call, Sid received a picture. It was drawn in crayon and showed two people. One larger than the other joined by stick hands. The heads were bigger than the bodies and both were smiling. The envelope had a postmark on it and this worried Sid. All the previous ones didn't have a stamp, not even an address, just his name printed clearly. He hadn't really thought about it before, but that meant someone had been coming to his door each time, and it wasn't the postman. Sid couldn't believe he hadn't thought about this before. His friend had been to the house loads of times without Sid realising. Not loads but four possibly five and this was the first letter that had come through the post. What did it signify? Besides the picture, there was a printed letter too, explaining the drawing was from Alfie and that he was very busy now that school was back. Sid's heart plummeted. Did that mean he would have to wait until half term before he could see him? At the end of the letter was a demand.

'Get a mobile phone if you want to speak to Alfie.'

This statement was so out of keeping with the friendly tone of the letter that Sid wasn't sure he understood it properly. What did that mean? What did a mobile phone have to do with Alfie? He chewed absently on his thumbnail. For the first time, Sid began to have doubts about the whole thing. Maybe Alfie didn't exist; maybe this was some cruel joke by that Curtis guy. But then he had spoken to Alfie on the phone. He had giggled, talked about Googers. He would have to ask him about Googers. Maybe it was a made up game he played with his friends. He had to be real, that voice had been real. And now the drawing, no adult would draw like that, and even if they tried, Sid didn't think it would look quite like this. The doubts still hung like sleeping bats in his head. Waiting for a beam of light to send them scattering in panic.

At his desk he took out a fresh sheet of paper and attempted to copy the drawing using his pencils. He couldn't, wasn't that proof enough? His version was obviously so contrived and careful, nothing like Alfie's careless hand and unusual choice of colour. Sid convinced himself that Alfie did exist, that it was normal these days for kids to be busy. There were so many clubs for them to go to. Not like in his day when there had been barely anything. Scouts was what he'd wanted to join. His mother agreed.

'It would be good for him Henry. Get him out of the house, teach him some useful skills.'

'No! I'm not having him playing with a bunch of poofters. Besides, it costs money. We're not made of money.' It was one of his standard phrases. George made himself small in the corner, willing his mother to fight back, to argue for him but Henry had that look about him that neither of them liked and so the subject was dropped.

'Stop looking so morbid. Get up to your room and quit bothering your mother and me,' Henry yelled. The picture of the horses chattered back against the wall. George slunk from the room and ran upstairs. There were kids that played football after school and that didn't cost anything, but George wasn't any good. Somehow his feet and the ball just never seemed to match up very well. It was better to stay away from the game than to be ridiculed. Sometimes his mother let him go down to the park on his own but only when Uncle Henry was out. He never did understand why, if Uncle Henry hated him so much, he didn't want him out of the house.

Alfie went to Cub scouts; he knew that much, and maybe swimming, or gym club. He'd seen them advertised in the newsagent's window. Alfie didn't have an Uncle Henry and if there was any bother about not enough money to go to Cub scouts, Sid would be happy to help out.

On Wednesday, Sid worked a half-day and went to the mobile phone shop in town. He spent half an hour looking at all the models and ignoring the sales assistants. Finally he told one of them which he liked the look of.

'What will you be using it for?' The girl with 'Jenny' on her badge inquired.

'That's my business.' Sid was almost ready to leave the shop but that statement at the end of the letter kept his feet rooted to the carpet.

'Sorry, I meant if you'll be texting, using it for business, if you want it to take pictures, that kind of thing. What time of day will most of your usage be?'

Sid didn't have a clue what the woman was asking him. 'Social,' he said. 'My family, friends.'

'Right so after six then?'

After six? When would he call Alfie? He would be at school until three fifteen, and then maybe one of his clubs. What time would he be eating his tea?

'Yes.' Sid decided.

'Ok then. And how many calls do you think you'll make a month?'

'I just want to buy this phone. What does it matter how many calls I make?' Sid was getting agitated. This girl's smile was like those awful American girls on the TV ads that are all white teeth and false good humour. At last the smile faded and she looked a little nervous excusing herself and going to talk quietly with one of her colleagues. Sid left the shop.

Back at home, Sid paced up and down his small room. The letter lay on his desk accusing him. Of course he wanted to talk to Alfie but why did he need a goddamn mobile phone to do it with? Wasn't his friend supposed to be helping him? Not putting obstacles in his way. Sid ate a late lunch and watched a stupid talk show on channel four. At five he decided to ring Alfie. In the phone box, Sid dialled the number he had used the week before. There was a pause after the musical notes of the digits and then a female voice told him the number was not available. What the hell did that mean? It surely didn't mean that Alfie was having his tea. Not available? But he'd spoken to him last week, on this number.

Back in his flat once again, Sid checked the yellow pages, there were two other mobile phone shops in town. On Saturday he would try again.

It was good wine; a gorgeous deep ruby colour glinting in his glass. The taste was full, 'blood-thick' Margret would have said but Joanie liked it. Was glad he'd ordered a bottle of it. He was sitting at the bar twisting his glass enjoying the feel of his full stomach.

'Mind if I join you?' she was foreign, Portuguese he supposed.

'Sure.' Joanie shifted his stool a little so she could squeeze onto the spare one by his knee.

'Drinking alone?' her English was excellent, only the hint of a Mediterranean accent.

Joanie nodded slowly and smiled into the jewelled glass. Deliciously alone, he thought, enjoying the kind of meal that Margret hated. Thick rare steak with fine chips. Nobody had complained about his choice. Nobody had said his stomach was getting too large for pudding, despite it touching the edge of the table.

Her knee touched his as she made herself comfy on the stool.

'Tania.' She held out a slender hand. A single silver ring on her right hand. Long red fingernails and delicate lines. Joanie took it.

'Brian. Not sure you should be drinking with a man who drinks alone?' There was a certain charm to her face, not overly made-up but enough to give her dark eyes emphasis and her lips a glossy red.

She shrugged and drew out a cigarette. Joanie didn't have a lighter, hadn't smoked for years but decided to accept when she offered him the packet. There was a brick on the bar with matches in the hollow dip. He lit both and watched her inhale deeply.

'Something's gonna kill us in the end. Why not this?' she turned the cigarette round to look at the glowing tip. 'You only live once right?' Below her long neck, the flesh continued to a deep cleavage with what looked like black lacy curtains either side. The blouse was sheer allowing glimpses of more black lace beneath.

Joanie drew in the smoke and for a moment thought he was going to cough but the feeling passed. The second breath was easier and he realised how easy it would be to pick up the habit again.

'Haven't seen you here before. On holiday?'

'I haven't been here before.' The wine slid smoothly down his throat, warm and syrupy. 'Do you live here?'

'Kind of,' she shrugged as if it was of no consequence. 'This is my favourite bar.'

Joanie looked around. He wasn't sure what had made him come in. Maybe the promise of steak on the blackboard outside or the dull anonymous lighting that hid wooden alcoves. The beery smell wafting onto the street or maybe he'd had enough of wandering through the old town. Glasses hung above the bar behind which two smartly dressed bar tenders whistled and served in a bustling manner, their eyes bright, sharing jokes with the locals, lapsing in and out of English and Portuguese. There didn't seem to be anything particular that made this bar stand out from the handful of others in the vicinity.

Joanie nodded; there was an atmosphere though. A warmth and easiness that made him feel a part of the general hubbub. She was still staring at him, her lips puckered around the end of the cigarette; she released it and blew a perfect smoke ring at him.

'What do you do?'

Joanie smiled to himself. 'Try to save the world, or my small corner of it.'

A quirky smile made funny wrinkles by her nose, she didn't look surprised. Instead she tapped the ash into a glass dish. 'Big job for a big man.'

'I'm a policeman actually.' Joanie drew his last on the cigarette and promised himself he wouldn't have another.

'Ahh! You do the walking the heat?'

'Walk the beat, no not any more, I solve crimes.'

'Of course, a detective,' she grinned knowingly, 'I'd say you were pretty good at it. You're a thinker, I can see that, and you're observant. If someone blindfolded you now, I bet you would give an accurate description of me and yet you've barely looked me straight in the eye. You notice things don't you?'

It was Joanie's turn to smile. This was a strange woman indeed. 'You don't miss much.' He closed his eyes as he continued. 'I've noticed, when you stood beside me, that the heel on your right shoe isn't quite even, and there's a ladder in your tights just above your knee.' Joanie peeked and saw looking down surprised, her skirt now covered her knee but when she'd sat, it had ridden up slightly. 'Your earrings don't quite match. But they're very pretty all the same.'

She laughed aloud then and Joanie chuckled offering her some of his wine. She accepted and they began to talk about Portugal, about sunshine and the easy pace of life. How sometimes you could reach a place and it was like there was thick mud on your shoes and you couldn't go any further and before you knew it, your whole life had been spent in one small town.

'There's a sadness in you,' she said abruptly after a pause.

Joanie knew exactly what she meant. It centred somewhere deep in his chest. For a while yesterday it had disappeared. A family had arranged themselves beside him at the beach. Cascades of towels, spades and beach balls spilling onto the sand. Two children bright and noisy. They had fallen into conversation, Joanie and the parents. They were from Nottingham, an area that Joanie used to know. The children were building a sandcastle and Joanie offered advice and eventually ended up helping, kneeling in the sand becoming absorbed in the simple activity. The sandcastle grew; they made a moat, found shells to decorate it and then dug a channel all the way to the sea. Once the water began to flow the children started splashing and Joanie got wet.

'Cass, Joshua, stop being cheeky.' The mother shouted when a particularly large splash soaked Joanie's shorts.

'It's fine.' Joanie responded and sat back onto his towel. The children continued to splash and shriek, salty spray blowing across the beach. Joanie grinned.

Shortly after, he waved goodbye as the family made their laden way back up the beach. Smiling to himself Joanie lay back and fell asleep for over an hour. When he awoke, his skin was red and a headache bloomed across the back of his eyes.

Today had been different though. He hadn't spoken to

anyone, other than a couple of waiters and the girl in the ice-cream kiosk. He knew what the feeling was in his chest, but it was scary to put a name to it. Made the hurt ache even more if he tried to think about it.

'I could make it better.' She had lit another cigarette, her brown eyes assessing his reaction.

He knew what she meant, he should have known from the start, what with the black lace and stilettos. It might be nice; a comfort of sorts but it wasn't what Joanie needed.

'Not tonight.' Joanie waved to the bar tender and pushed back his stool.

'Hey, wait, I never meant to frighten you away. We were talking; it was nice. I can see you're a decent man, stay awhile, I won't charge you for the talk.'

Joanie's instinct was to call it a night, go back to his hotel room that would thrum gently until the nightclub across the road kicked out at three. But there was something gentle about her eyes, a kindness that wasn't asking to be repaid. Just two lonely people in a bar, that was all.

15

The same questions came up again. When would Sid use it, what for, how often? At least he felt a little more prepared this time. A young man calling himself Rick showed him three phones and talked about different contracts. Sid tried to listen carefully but after a while the strange phrases and gobbledygook was too much.

'This one,' Sid stabbed the piece of paper with his finger. 'That one will suit me.'

'Are you sure? I thought most of your usage would be in the evening. This other deal might be more in line with your current needs.'

'Fine, that one then. Can I buy it now?'

'Er sure, I'll just get the paperwork.'

Sid later thought it was probably the most difficult purchase he had ever had to make. Short of asking him how much milk he drank each day, he felt there was nothing Rick didn't know about him. Apart from Alfie of course. Nobody knew about Alfie. A smile of satisfaction lit Sid's face as he rounded the corner near home. A plastic bag swinging by his legs; inside an oversized cardboard box containing a small mobile phone.

He unwrapped it and laid the phone on his desk. There was an instruction booklet, which Sid flicked through but couldn't be bothered to read. It was only after half an hour of punching buttons that he finally had a closer look. It didn't work. Three times he attempted to push the buttons in the order that it said and each time he got an error. The fourth time he used the end of a pencil on the keys to ensure he was hitting the right ones. When it still failed, he threw the phone down and swore loudly. It banged onto the desk, slid to the edge but not over it.

'Fucking people giving me a dud fucking phone.'

The pencil was blunt and by morning there would be half a dozen purple round spots on his arm where it had bruised but not pierced the skin. Sid eventually calmed down enough to find the shop number and trudged out to the phone box. The shop was now shut and wouldn't be open until Monday at 9 o'clock.

Sid banged the receiver against the glass before thrusting it back in the cradle. The woman from no. 33 with that stupid little prissy dog looked across at him. If she'd been close enough, he would have leapt out of the phone box and taken a swipe at her, or at least attempted to stamp on that moron of a dog. Its ears were pointing up, and its evil little black eyes were looking across the road at Sid.

'Fuck off!' Sid shouted through the glass. The woman dragged her dog quickly away and hurried back down the road.

Sid put the radio on, twiddling the dial until he found some classical music. He needed to calm down, lately he seemed to be either euphoric with love for Alfie or two steps away from killing somebody. This friend had better come up with the goods soon or there was going to be hell to pay. Sid stared at the curtains, drumming his fingers on the desk in time to the music. For a moment, his mind cleared like wiping a window after a heavy storm. The clear glass so clean it was almost invisible. There was no Alfie, it was all an illusion and the friend wasn't a friend at all. The thought was like a crystal, perfect and complete. Sid switched off the music and turned the television on instead. He couldn't be doing with thoughts like that. Alfie did exist, and Sid was going to be his grandfather. That was the truth. It was his mission, bestowed on him by Dr Casey. He was going to create his own happy ending.

When Joanie finally emerged the following morning, it was almost midday. The room was stifling hot despite the fan whirring lazily above his head. His skin was slick with sweat. Rolling out of bed, his head took up the beat of last night's club throbbing in his skull. A long cool shower and a shave made Joanie feel slightly better. A coffee and a pastry would help; somewhere that was air-conditioned and quiet. Lacing up his shoes, Joanie could see a nasty white stain across the toe; the brown leather caked with gunk. Taking out his foot, Joanie lifted the shoe to his nose. Gross, it was sick. And judging by how he felt, it was probably his own. Why hadn't he left earlier? Joanie rubbed his temples and took the shoe into the bathroom, he scrubbed it clean with a corner of a towel but it still smelled.

He put on his sunglasses and picked up the straw hat he'd bought himself two days before. Beneath it was his phone. Shoving it in his pocket, Joanie went down to the street and the nearest cafe he could find. His throat felt raw and wasn't helped by the scalding coffee. At least it calmed his queasy stomach along with a large raisin bun.

He'd brought his papers with him, the first time he'd actually looked at them. So far he'd spent his days wandering the old town, an excursion to a nearby castle with a good lunch, and a coach trip to the next port. But today he hadn't planned anything. Just as well considering how his head felt. He opened the files and started to read. An hour later he ordered another coffee and wished he'd brought some blank paper with him. Instead he had to make do with a couple of sheets from the waiter's pad and his bitten pencil.

Every which way he looked at it, Sidney White, Ross Thorpe and Mr Evans continued to pop up from the evidence. And then a new thought struck him, could they be connected? Was he actually looking at a paedophile ring, one that had progressed to murder? Joanie tapped his nails on the table. In his experience, a paedophile ring was unlikely to commit murder; it was taking things a step too far. Wouldn't it overstretch a possibly already strained friendship between the abusers? Which one of them would commit the murder, and if their aim was to abuse, it meant they had 'lost' one of their victims. Joanie shook his head and pushed the pieces of paper away from him, pulling the now cooling coffee closer.

Outside the sun was glaring on the cracked plaza, two old women all in black with sensible shoes were muttering to each other as they walked arm in arm. A couple waltzed past, their arms wrapped around each other. A man on a bicycle with an incredibly large box balanced on the back, free-wheeled out of sight.

Under the table, his phone vibrated against his thigh. An older woman on the table next to his looked at him disdainfully. There were three missed calls. It was currently ringing from a number he didn't recognise.

'Jeezus Dad. I thought you'd left the planet or something. Don't you listen to your messages anymore? Where the hell are you?'

'Sammy, I, what's the matter?' Joanie tried to think clearly, the fog of red lipstick and deep brown eyes kept swimming in his coffee.

'Oh shit Dad,' he could hear her voice quavering on the line. 'Is Mum with you?'

'No, she isn't.'

'That's good, look Dad I need to come home. I need to talk to you about something but I don't want Mum to know. How long will she be?'

'Umm, about two days.' The waiter came to collect his cup and Joanie nodded that he'd like another. Preferably with a brandy in it, but you couldn't tell a Portuguese waiter that with just a nod of the head.

'Two days! What do you mean? Is she in hospital or something? I thought you guys were in Portugal. What have you done with her Dad?' her voice was rising in panic.

This didn't seem the time to explain about painting in Italy. His daughter was obviously in trouble and he wanted to know what had happened.

'Sammy, now listen to me. Your mother and me are fine. We'll both be home by Sunday evening. Now tell me what's wrong. I love you pumpkin.'

She dissolved into tears on the other end of the phone and Joanie had to put his sunglasses back on before the waiter came back. He gave her time to collect herself making shushing sounds down the phone.

'I'm sorry Dad, it's such a mess, I don't know what to do. Matt's gone ballistic; I haven't seen him since last night. It wasn't deliberate, we've always been careful. But now he's gone off and I don't know how to find him.'

Joanie was trying to make sense of what she was saying. It reminded him of interviewing victims at the station. The weeping and illogical statements never quite telling you what had actually occurred.

'Sammy. Tell me why Matt went off.'

'I'm pregnant Dad.'

After three coffees, Joanie thought he might as well stay and have some lunch too. The woman next to him had long since left and the table had hosted a family of three and now a young couple. What a stupid arse he'd been. While Sammy had been wandering the streets of Prague until all hours looking for Matt, he'd been getting drunk in a bar with the local prostitute. What an utterly sad individual he had become. Was this what they called a mid-life crisis, or maybe, considering he was fifty-four, a latter-life crisis. What a fool he must look, playing on the beach with someone else's kids and fooling around with a whore. No wonder Margret hadn't wanted to go on holiday with him. Joanie looked down at his oversized stomach. A fat, balding idiot.

The sun was a little cooler when he stepped back into the street. His feet took him down to the beach and he walked along the promenade. At least he hadn't done anything with Tania. It was rather sad to think that even if he'd wanted to, he probably couldn't. The second bottle of wine had been to blame. He remembered kissing her, briefly, his hand between her shoulder blades, her breasts pressing into his chest. He had felt the band of her bra strap under the sheer blouse. Sure he'd been tempted, but alcohol and sex rarely went together, at least not for Joanie. He didn't remember at what point she left him, but he did remember standing outside the hotel alone trying to fit his key into the lock. Eventually someone had let him in. He was too old to be acting like that. What would Margret think? He hadn't kissed another woman in years. Not since that passionate embrace in Karen Quinton's kitchen one Christmas when they'd both been rather tipsy. This was different, a world away. What the hell was he doing in Portugal anyway?

'Being a sad fuckwit, that's what,' he said aloud watching some nubile bodies play volleyball. His headache had receded but he still felt like shit. It was a long time since he'd had a hangover and he didn't like it. The taste of smoke clung to his tongue despite brushing his teeth three times when he got back to his room. That evening, Joanie had his phone with him. There was nothing much he could do to help Sammy at this point. He had told her to ring him as soon as Matt turned up and if he didn't, to get herself the next flight home. He'd pay.

Joanie settled in a small seafood restaurant by the beach, well away from the smoky bar where Tania had found him. He ordered shellfish and water to drink. She rang at half past eight, just as Joanie was wiping the edge of his plate with a piece of bread.

'He's back,' she sounded tired. 'We've talked and we're coming home. I think it will take a couple of days, we'll take it in turns to drive. Prague's really nice, you should come.' But her voice held no enthusiasm.

'Are you sure? I'm still happy to get you a flight home. Matt hasn't,' Joanie paused wondering quite how to phrase it and decided there was no delicate way. 'He hasn't hit you has he?'

'Dad! He's not like that, just cos we've had a huge bust up doesn't mean he's turned into a monster. Why do you always think my boyfriends are going to end up in one of your cells?'

'Sorry love, just a protective father that's all. Make sure you drive carefully. What do you want me to tell your mother?'

'Nothing. Please Dad, don't tell her anything.'

For some strange reason this hurt Joanie more than anything else she'd said. There was no way he could tell Margret about his own episode but why Sammy should want to keep secrets from her too he didn't know. For a moment he felt terribly guilty that he should be protecting Margret, that both he and Sammy had failed her in some major way.

It wasn't until Joanie was on the plane that the reality of Sammy's problem really came home. Two rows away, a mother held a screaming infant. Its face red and troubled, screwed up into so many wrinkles. It bawled across the back of her seat, the high pitch penetrating every ear, even as far as club class. Sammy was pregnant. Sammy had a baby growing inside her. Crikey. Joanie might be a grandfather. The thought stunned him for a moment. Sometimes age caught up with you, not gradually in the way your hair turned grey but all of a sudden like a bang on the head. A grandfather at fifty-four. Confusion and fear rippled through Joanie's mind but then he thought about Cass and Joshua playing on the beach. How he hadn't laughed like that in what seemed like years. Sammy was only twenty-one though; she wasn't even married. There it was again, the morals of his parents coming out. What would

Margret say? Sammy would have to tell her, Joanie didn't want to keep this secret for long.

From beneath his seat, he pulled out his briefcase; he had more space this time. He was next to a window, the seat beside him empty and a young man probably no older than Sammy, or Matt, in the aisle seat. Joanie couldn't imagine the young man, in his jeans and headphones, being a father; he was too young for Christ's sake. To block out his troubling thoughts, Joanie took out the sheets he had photocopied from work. And the tiny sheets he'd scribbled on in the cafe.

Sid had to wait three more days for his phone to work. Apparently it was to do with the network setting up his account. He thought the modern age was supposed to make things simpler not more complicated. On Tuesday he received another letter from his friend, this instructed him to text a particular message to a certain number. It also told him exactly when to do it. Sid wasn't in a position to argue, it had been almost two weeks since he'd spoken to Alfie. He was ready to do whatever it took. That evening he read the instruction booklet fully and carefully typed in the message, deleting it again when he'd finished. That didn't seem too hard. He set the alarm on his watch just to make sure. Tomorrow he would do everything right. And then he would get to see Alfie.

While Sid was stacking up the cold meat store, Mr Jennings the stockroom manager appeared at his elbow. Sid jumped; he'd been lost in his thoughts of Alfie.

'You're to go up and see Mr Foster when you're finished here.'

Sid nodded and picked up three packets of mince. Mr Foster. What now? He hadn't done anything wrong. Nobody had complained to him about his work. Were the police back again? Sid began to sweat despite the chill of the cabinet. His mobile phone was tucked safely away in his locker. It wasn't illegal for him to buy a mobile phone, and he'd yet to make any proper calls. Neither had anyone rung him so what was the problem? Sid's hands slowed down, he didn't want to go and see Mr Foster. Sid moved ever slower but despite this, the pallet inevitably emptied until Sid stood beside the full cabinet, wondering if maybe he should say he was sick and go home. If he went home, the police might follow him there and then they might want to come in. With reluctance Sid climbed the stairs to the offices.

Mr Foster didn't look up when Sid knocked and walked in.

'Take a seat,' he muttered fiddling with the clasp on a binder. When he did notice Sid, the smile pasted to his face disappeared and he frowned, he leaned forwards a little and then recognition spread across his face.

'Sidney. Well, I must say I like the beard, makes you look,' there was a pause and a fleeting worried expression, 'quite different.'

Sid said nothing; he wasn't interested in pleasantries or the weather.

'Ahem,' Mr Foster cleared his throat. 'You seem to have settled into the stockroom well, but I've got a staff problem and I wondered if you'd mind moving back onto trolleys just for a couple of weeks. I don't think there'll be a problem like before. We've advertised so it won't be long, and if there's the slightest issue we'll bring you back into the store.'

Sid could feel the sweat cooling all over his body. It made him shiver involuntarily Thank god, he thought. This couldn't be a better day, what with contacting Alfie later at five and now this.

'OK,' Sid acknowledged. He didn't want to sound too keen.

'Great, the only thing is, we're a bit tight this evening and I wondered if you'd be willing to do a couple of hours overtime after your shift in the stock room?'

Sid normally finished at four, two more hours would make it six and he was supposed to text Alfie at five.

'No.' Sid felt suddenly panicky. 'No way.'

'Oh, I see. If you'd rather stay in the stock room, that's fine, I just thought as you've done the trolleys before. I'm sure I can find someone else.'

Sid's eyes grew very large. To be back on the trolleys would be bliss, working alone in the car park without the likes of Trevor giving him a hard time. And he'd be back with David. Tea breaks with his simple friend, no awkward questions, no funny looks. But he had to be free at five to call Alfie. Nothing could stop that.

'No I'd like to do it, really. Tonight is fine. I can rearrange.' Like hell he could, but somehow he would make damn sure he made that call at five. Trolleys or no trolleys.

'Well that's wonderful, that certainly helps me out. Make sure you fill in a claim form for the overtime and I'll put a new schedule up for you by this afternoon.'

As Sid took packets of pasta out of their boxes he thought about how he would slip quietly to the back of the car park and use his phone from there. It wouldn't be difficult, David wouldn't notice. Everything would be just fine.

David wasn't on the trolleys though; it was that ugly youth that Sid despised. At four as Sid put on the thick jacket to go out into the rain, he was coming in for a break.

'Not you is it?' The youth sneered. 'Get rid of the retard and I get the queer instead.'

Sid could feel his fists clenching at his sides. Where the hell was David? This wasn't how it was supposed to be. While Sid struggled with what to do, the youth disappeared inside the store. Sid followed him, heading straight up to Mr Foster's office.

'Mr Foster's gone already,' a young woman was putting some papers on his desk. 'He left a couple of minutes ago.'

Sid spun around and walked back down the stairs. It didn't change anything, he tried to tell himself, he would stay away from that awful kid and there would be no one to stop him making his call at five.

The rain drizzled, not enough to warrant an umbrella unless you were going to be out in it for a while, unless you would be spending two hours going to and fro across a car park. Sid looked miserably at the grey damp. The stack of trolleys by the front doors was disgusting and he spent the first ten minutes sorting through it before heading out across the wet tarmac. At ten minutes to five Sid's watch alarm went off. He was crossing the car park with a long metal snake heading for the entrance. He quickened his pace. An old woman with one of those trolley bags suddenly appeared in front of him walking slowly. She stopped to check in her purse and Sid almost ran her over. He swore under his breath, and then shouted.

'Excuse me!'

She dug deeper in her bag completely oblivious.

'Excuse me!' Sid could feel that throb behind his eyeballs. Get out of the fucking way, he wanted to add but instead he bit his tongue until he could taste blood. The woman looked up, raised a hand and closed her purse. Sid thrust the line of trolleys into the stand, clanging against the others.

'Not damaging them are you? Wouldn't want management to know you were chucking their trolleys around.' The youth wiped a hand under his snotty nose. He had a pathetic group of five trolleys; they weren't even the same type. Sid sucked furiously at his cut lip. He turned around and headed back across the car park. He wanted to run but knew he mustn't. Near the recycling bins he pulled out the mobile phone. Hastily he punched in the message.

'Alfie this is my new mobile', Sid paused and checked his watch, one minute to five. He decided to add a bit on, it wasn't in the script but he wanted there to be no mistake. 'Love Sid.' The number he knew by heart, not surprising considering how often he'd read the instructions. He pressed the send button and waited with the phone to his ear. It beeped, and when he looked, it triumphantly told him his message had been sent. Good. Sid breathed a sigh of relief. Now what? He stared at the glowing face until it went dark. Sid put it back in his pocket and looked around. Nobody was staring at him and he couldn't see the youth anywhere. Bright musical notes trilled from his pocket. In his haste, Sid dropped the phone onto the ground. He hit the receive button and put it to his ear. Nothing. Looking at the face it told him he had a message. These things weren't that easy to use, Sid decided, after he'd spent another five minutes working out how to get at the message. Eventually the words popped up on the screen.

'Thanx Uncle Sid sys Alfie.'

'Wehey!' Sid clasped the phone with both hands. Then his face dropped and a dark shadow shivered across his body. Uncle Sid. He wasn't an uncle. No, no, definitely not an uncle. Nothing like an uncle. Tears sprang from his eyes. He had to tell him he wasn't Uncle Sid at all, no. The trembling started somewhere deep inside rather like an earthquake bubbling out from the centre in waves. It shivered down his legs and along his arms so that the phone shook in his hands. Uncles were bad people. Sid couldn't stop the tears. He had to tell him he wasn't Uncle Sid, he was a grandfather. Grandpa Sid. Oblivious to a customer emptying their glass bottles into the containers, Sid punched in another message.

'Grandpa Sid loves you', Alfie had to understand. He wasn't some dirty cock-sucking bastard of an uncle. Sid wiped the moisture from his face and pressed the send button again. This time it didn't trill back at him. He waited until another car stopped and a woman got out.

'Can I put cardboard as well as paper in here?' she indicated the big blue metal container.

Sid looked up thrusting the mobile back into his pocket. He looked at the container and then at the woman. 'I don't know. Yes, yes, I think so.'

Sid left her looking undecided and headed for the nearest abandoned trolley.

It would be about half an hour before Margret picked him up. Joanie had phoned her from the airport knowing that she was due home the day before. She sounded bright on the phone. Joanie was feeling rather mixed, she hadn't mentioned Sammy so he assumed they hadn't spoken. Half of him was desperate to see her, lay his weary head on her bosom, but he was forbidden from telling her what he needed to discuss. He wanted to talk about Sammy and there were details in the case he'd come across too. But neither would be good choices for their first meeting. Why did he feel so nervous? This was his wife coming to meet him. Is that what a week apart did, made you frightened to meet the other. Joanie sipped his cappuccino. No he wasn't frightened of Margret, he was worried that this separate holiday thing might happen again if she'd had a good time. Although Joanie felt oddly refreshed, he certainly didn't want a repeat next summer, drinking with local whores and pretending he was young and handsome on a beach didn't work. He'd felt lonely and out of place. Gazing at historic churches and buildings without her familiar chatter, eating food he would never normally choose, drinking late in bars. None of this would have happened if she'd been around. Joanie sighed. He felt nervous too, he'd missed her, but had she missed him? Joanie sipped at the cappuccino. The investigation reports had absorbed his attention on the plane and now he had some further research he wanted to do on those three. As for the Hempstead case, a great deal of circumstantial evidence appeared to be pointing at the father, but Joanie didn't have anything to show they had interviewed the father as a suspect. That paperwork may still be in the file. If it wasn't he wanted to know why not. Killing your own child didn't make any sense but he knew it happened. How could someone ever contemplate killing their own flesh and blood? Sammy as a baby sprang to mind. Her perfect little body, pink skinned and crying in the hospital. Joanie was overwhelmed by feelings of love and the desire to protect and nurture this little miracle.

They had waited a long time for Sammy, thought that perhaps they would be childless. Margret was against going for tests taking the fatalistic view that if it was meant to be then it would happen. Two miscarriages and seven years later and they had both agreed that they would cope with being childless together. The third pregnancy didn't thrill them like the other two had; in fact it was fraught with worry. As the pregnancy progressed, they became ever more nervous that this miscarriage would be even more traumatic. Neither of them expected it to go full term. By the fifth month, Joanie had started to hope again. He bought Margret flowers, took over some of the domestic tasks like the hoovering and shopping. By the seventh month Margret actually believed it was going to happen and Joanie came home to find her in floods of tears. Not an unusual occurrence in itself but these were tears of joy, and that had been the turning point. From then on, they rejoiced every day, never more so than when he finally held his tiny daughter in his arms.

'I'm by the taxi stand, opposite the Avis car rental.' It was Margret on the mobile.

'I'll be right out.' Joanie gathered his bags and hurried over to the escalator.

Margret stood uncertainly by the car; it was difficult to read her face. Joanie swallowed and put his bags in the boot. They hugged, Joanie worried that it might feel different. It didn't. In fact they stood holding each other for almost a minute. He could feel himself relaxing in her arms, the smell of her hair; the feel of her warmth. Joanie smiled to himself and then they let go and Margret kissed him. A deep, long kiss, one that made his loins tingle, which was annoying because then a picture of Tania came into his mind.

'Let's go before you get a ticket.'

'Right, well the keys are in the ignition.' Margret moved aside and pulled open the passenger door, climbed in and waited.

'Have you heard from Sammy?' he couldn't help himself. She

was on his mind.

'No, there weren't any messages on the answer phone, only the Quintons. Have you?' Margret pulled down the mirror and checked her hair.

'Just a brief call.' Joanie swallowed the lie. 'She and Matt were thinking of heading home shortly. I think they're all travelled out.' He pulled into the moving traffic and headed towards the dual carriageway.

'Already? I thought they'd be gone till the end of September. Perhaps they've run out of money.'

Joanie stared out of the window watching the traffic shoot past in the opposite direction. An ambulance went by, no flashing lights. Just flowing along with the other vehicles. No need to hurry just yet, she wouldn't be fully dilated for another couple of hours. Joanie's imagination took him into the back of the ambulance. It was Sammy on the stretcher, her face grimacing in pain, her stomach swollen making a big hump under the blanket.

'What did she say?' Margret asked, looking across at him.

She's pregnant. He wanted to say it so badly, wanted to share his thoughts with her. Find out what she felt. They'd never talked about becoming grandparents. Would she like the idea? Not that it was their choice but he'd like to talk about it anyway. Instead he muttered something about Prague being nice.

'How was the painting in Spain?'

'It was lovely, the weather was magnificent. So warm but not too hot you know. There was one spot we went to down by a river with all these dragonflies and birds by the water. We sat under the shade of a huge tree with our easels and everyone was so quiet, just the swish of paintbrushes and the birds singing.' She paused; Joanie glanced across and saw a wistful look. 'That was a magical afternoon, and everyone painted something really good and yet everyone's was different. It's funny isn't it, you're all looking at the same scene and yet out of ten paintings, none were the same.' Joanie could see the white lines at the edges of her eyes where she must have squinted in the sun.

'We went to this gorgeous old church in the next village along, St Augustine's built in thirteen something. The stonework and these little gargoyle faces made it really strange but you could feel the centuries in it. I mean it's amazing to think a building has been used for prayer and worship for hundreds of years. It makes me wonder what all those prayers were for; the harvest, a son in the wars, rain, sunshine.'

Joanie smiled to himself and let her words soothe his thoughts. Her voice waxed and waned telling him about an old cart and horse they'd seen as if they'd stepped back in time, the buildings, and their eccentric Spanish teacher. Joanie wanted to close his eyes and lean his head on the glass, but the traffic needed his concentration.

Margret had prepared a delicious fish pie that was warming in the oven when they got back. The smell was so strong when he opened the front door that he was immediately transported back ten years. Sammy loved fish pie. Aged eleven she had learned to make it with Margret and it was a dark evening just like this when he'd come home to his beaming daughter wearing an oversized apron. She was spattered with bits of potato and stank of fish but Joanie couldn't have cared less. Margret smiled from the kitchen doorway and together they had sat around the table. Sammy bent down to the oven, giant gloves on her hands and brought forth the pie.

'Tah-dah' she announced putting the heavy dish carefully on the table. 'Look,' she pointed with the wooden spoon. Joanie stared at the crispy potato topping. 'It says Dad.' He could just make out the forked impressions on the surface. Grabbing her to him he'd bitten into her neck hungrily.

'Careful, don't knock the dish,' but even Margret was laughing.

They hung their coats in the cupboard and Joanie left his bags in the hall. The kitchen was warm, the table already laid.

When she put the dish on the table, he half hoped she might have written something on it, but there were just the regular criss-cross marks of the fork.

'That smells lovely, thanks Margret.' The kitchen seemed empty though, his words echoing in the stillness. Something had been lost, some joie de vivre. They ate in silence, and Joanie wondered where the sparkle in his life had gone.

Sammy phoned again that evening, on his mobile. Fortunately Margret was upstairs in the toilet.

'We're getting the eleven o'clock ferry tomorrow. Matt's going to go home and he'll drop me at the station. I'll give you a ring just before I get on.' Her voice sounded small and far away.

'Mum or I will come and pick you up. Everything will be fine pumpkin.'

He heard her sigh and then the money ran out.

Joanie was consumed by paperwork when Kelly knocked at the door. He stood up, shifting a large pile of papers to the side, motioning for her to come in.

'I've got a lead on the Hempstead father.' Joanie sat down and continued flicking deftly through a pile.

'The father's dead. Here.' Kelly plopped a white sheet onto the smothered desk. Joanie grabbed it and scanned the coroner's report.

'Suicide? That's a bit convenient isn't it?' Joanie leaned back in his chair.

'That's what I thought, but there doesn't seem to be any doubt about the cause of death.'

Joanie steepled his fingers together and brought them under his chin. He nodded at Kelly, she had more and he wanted to hear it.

'From what I can tell, a lot of the evidence appeared to point at Mr Hempstead but there's nothing really solid there. A couple of the transcripts show they interviewed him as a suspect but he doesn't admit anything useful. A couple of spots of blood were found on a pair of Mr Hempstead's jeans that matched his son but he couldn't say how they got there. For all we know it might be something perfectly innocent. Kids are always hurting themselves with minor cuts and bruises.'

Joanie nodded. 'I think it's time I spoke to Morgan. What's Curtis been up to?'

'I'm sure he'd prefer to tell you himself but maybe it's better coming from me.' He could see her reluctance. 'The lollypop woman remembered both boys but not any unusual adults with them. It would appear that Kieren often cycled to school and Martin normally walked. However, Curtis showed her Sidney White's picture and she said she remembered seeing him hanging around on several occasions.'

'What?' Joanie leaned forwards. 'What the hell is Curtis doing brandishing that about?'

'I know.' Kelly had her hand up. 'Anyway she couldn't give any specific date or tell us what he was wearing, just a vague description.'

'What did she say when Curtis took out the photo?'

'She said she'd read all about him in the papers, and then went on about him hanging around in the mornings when the kids were on their way to school.'

'Then why didn't she come forward when it was in the papers?' Joanie thought the woman must have been lying. Too often suspects had their faces splashed around and people who'd never seen them in their life before claimed familiarity.

'She said she didn't really think about it. Thought it wasn't important.'

'What crap is that? A kid dies and she thinks it's not important to tell the police the man everyone thinks did it, was hanging around the schools. Rubbish, either she's lying or she's one dumb fuck.'

Kelly's eyebrows rose and Joanie knew he must be overreacting again. He pulled out his penknife and, in silence, cleaned out his thumbnail.

'Well, what did you think? Was she lying or am I totally off the mark?' Joanie demanded.

Kelly shrugged, 'Possibly. I have a feeling if we'd shown her any photo, she'd have jumped on it.'

'Exactly.' Joanie flicked his penknife closed.

'Exactly what? We don't know that Sidney is innocent; neither do we know if he's guilty. Furthermore, if I discount the father in the Hempstead case, I think they're linked. Did Sidney kill both of them and if not, who the hell are we looking for?' Kelly slapped her hands on the desk. 'You know this case is beginning to piss me off, how about we go and get a bite to eat and you tell me about Portugal.'

Joanie nodded. 'Best idea I've heard all morning.'

16

Instead of the canteen, Kelly and Joanie went out to a small cafe on the high street that sold hot paninis and soup. It was busy, orders shouted behind the counter, people at every table, a queue along the counter. They squeezed into a tiny round table at the back by the kitchen door.

'You've caught the sun at least, makes you look healthier. How about Margret, did she have a good time?'

'Yes.' He frowned. 'Too much of a good time. This new hobby is all very well, but I don't like the idea of more of these separate holidays.'

'Well, you know what they say, if you can't beat them, join them.' Kelly was grinning. 'I can just picture you, with one of those blue smock things on, painting palette in hand standing on a hillside with your easel.' She was laughing openly now.

'Alright, give it a rest. It's not funny.'

Joanie stared into his carrot and coriander soup. It was hot and thick. 'Do you think I'm a sad old man Kelly? Look at me, fat, balding, nothing but work to talk about.'

'Oh dear, having a bit of a crisis are you?'

'Maybe I am. Margret's changed. We don't seem the same any more. Maybe I've changed.' Joanie looked out of the large plate glass windows, a young woman with a pram walked past. He was tempted to tell Kelly about Sammy but decided against it. 'Seriously Kelly, have I changed?'

Kelly took her time, chewing slowly on the warm bread. 'Everybody changes as they get older, you've put on a bit of weight that's true. Perhaps you need to do something fun. Something to contrast with work, especially at the moment. For God's sake don't let work get between you and Margret; you know how it messed things up for me and Mark.'

Guilt tugged at his chest, the late nights over the past few months, his lack of understanding with her retirement. They hadn't really talked much about it. Such a change in her life, Joanie couldn't imagine what he would feel like stranded at home every day. And then there were the red fingernails he'd allowed to caress his face. What a self-centred creep.

'How are things between you and Mark? I'm sorry I haven't asked.'

Now it was Kelly's turn to look away. 'So, so, we're still trying. Things are better than they were. It all depends whether it's worth saving. Your relationship with Margret is twenty years or more. And you've got Sammy. That's a hell of a lot more than me and Mark.'

He knew what she was saying. They'd come too far to give up now. But it takes two to build and maintain a relationship.

'She was on about me calling her sweetheart, sweeping her off her feet, buying her flowers. But that's not us.'

'Sounds lovely, wish Mark would do that for me, add in a cosy meal and a romantic film at the restaurant, yep, that would do just nicely.'

Joanie studied Kelly's face to see if she was joking, but no she looked quite serious.

'It's not a lot to ask, maybe it doesn't seem like you two, but you could try, especially if that's what she actually asked for, you can't get clearer than that. What were you hoping for a post-it list on the fridge? Heading: How to love me, number one, buy flowers every Friday, two, take me out to dinner once a month, three...'

'Ok, Ok, enough. You're embarrassing.' Joanie checked around him to see who was listening, but the nearby diners all seemed far more interested in their own food and conversations.

'I gather she's not having an affair then?' Kelly gently inquired.

'No,' Joanie sighed, 'No I don't think so.'

'Then for you own sake, do those little things, from a woman's perspective, they mean a lot.'

Joanie munched on the end crunchy part of his panini. Kelly was right; there was a time when they often went to the cinema, shortly after Sammy had left for her first year at University. And Margret had been right about those little love gestures, he simply hadn't been doing them, but then neither had she. Margret had this incredibly sexy way of breathing in his ear when his back was turned. How did these things slip away so easily?

The following morning, after Sid had eaten two bowls of sugar puffs and dropped his bowl into the sink, he rang Alfie. He tried the number he'd used previously for the text message.

'The number you called is unavailable, if you'd like to leave a message...' Sid listened to the clipped female voice, frowned and pressed the end button. Perhaps Alfie was busy getting ready for school. Sid tucked the mobile into his trouser pocket and went off to work. He was looking forward to seeing David again. Yesterday's rain had cleared and it looked like a bright warm day ahead. Sid arrived in plenty of time but by nine when David still hadn't appeared, Sid went to check the rota. Somebody called Luke was on the board, not just for today either. He went down the stairs and out into the sunshine. At ten past nine the sullen youth appeared in his car park jacket and Sid stared at what must be Luke. Perhaps he could speak to Mr Foster and get put back in the stock room. Make up something about the customers giving him abuse. But Sid didn't want to say something like that. The fact was nobody had even given him a funny look so far. It must be the shorter hair and his beard. It was a relief not to be recognised and seemed somehow shameful to say otherwise to Mr Foster. Two weeks. He could manage that out here. The good part was: if Alfie phoned him, it would be easy to speak to him without alerting suspicion from his colleagues. So long as he avoided Luke, he would pretty much be on his own. Having his phone in the stock room would be quite different. Any number of people might hear it ring, and then listen in on his conversation. No, he would stick to the trolleys.

At break time, Sid locked himself in the disabled toilet and tried to ring Alfie again. This time he left a message. If only he could speak to him again, they could arrange another meeting.

His phone remained silent all day. Sid contained his disappointment until he got home. There might be another letter. There wasn't. He rang Alfie again and left another message and then he wrote a text. He kept his phone close at hand all evening, placing it carefully on the bedside table before he went to sleep. For two more days he left messages to no avail. On the third day his phone buzzed. He was by the entrance having just brought a line of trolleys back to the stand. An electric thrill ran right through him. He ripped the phone out of his pocket and checked the display. A message.

'Got a girlfriend have you?' it was Luke leering at him.

'Fuck off.' Sid hissed under his breath.

'Charmed I'm sure.' Luke came close; Sid had nowhere to back away, the trolleys pushing into his backside. 'You fucking little weirdo,' Luke breathed into his ear. Not loud enough for the gentleman with the basket to hear, but enough to give Sid a shiver. He pushed past him and out into the car park. The phone gripped in his hand, he hurried over to the fullest stand. Tapping urgently on the phone, he read the message.

3pm Fri. Betsy

Sid read it twice before he understood. It was another meeting. It was from his friend. The swirling excitement inside him was tempered by the fact that it hadn't been from Alfie. Did that mean the number he'd been phoning belonged to the friend? He had assumed it was Alfie's personal phone but thinking about it logically, Alfie was rather young to have his own mobile phone. What Sid really wanted was direct access to Alfie, this friend of his felt like an obstacle. Still, if a meeting meant he would get to see Alfie then that was fine by him. Sid put the phone away and handed out a trolley to a young woman with two children. She smiled at him and said thanks. He was going to be a grandfather after all, Sid couldn't help grinning. Unfortunately Friday was another two days away. He would need to be patient; he would also need an excuse to get out of work. This thought occupied him until he left at four. The following morning he would explain that he had to leave early on Friday for a dentist's appointment. It seemed more realistic than the doctors who offered late surgery whereas dentists were notoriously difficult to get into.

Sid cooked himself some sausages and baked beans when he got home. He watched television for an hour or so and then started playing with his phone. He felt rather embarrassed about the messages he'd left. His friend would have picked them up. Sid took out the picture Alfie had drawn and laid it on the desk. It would be so lovely to meet him. Maybe he should do a drawing for him, something personal to give to him on Friday. Pulling out his pencils, Sid chewed on one end and then began to draw a house. It looked like no.10 Compton Drive. He added a face at the window with a dark beard and then a small figure in front of the door. In his mind, Alfie had just rung the doorbell. Sid put down his pencil and brought his hands to his face. They smelled of soap, clean and fresh. They smelled of Alfie.

Joanie stood outside the dark green door. Dusk was falling making the door appear almost black. The street was quiet, smart town houses lined up with minimal front gardens. The houses themselves weren't minimal. In fact it looked like most of them extended up to a third floor. A selection of nice cars lined the curb, Audis, BMWs, a few of the over-sized Chelsea tractors. He hadn't rung ahead, feeling it might be better not to let Morgan prepare in any way. Of course he may choose not to speak to Joanie.

There was a gold coloured knocker with the face of a lion but no bell. Joanie used it and a satisfying 'thonk' reverberated from the door. A boy with dark hair and large eyes pulled open the heavy door and looked questioningly at Joanie.

'Hi, I'm here to speak to Mr Morgan.' Joanie watched the silent teenager recede down the hall, white boxer shorts all too clear above his jeans which seemed to hang more under his bottom than round his hips or waist.

Ex-inspector Morgan had lost weight. When Joanie knew him, he'd always been chunky heading towards fat; a good rugby player for the police team. Now as he watched the man come down the hall he looked taller, slim lines stretching him upwards.

Morgan's eyes widened as he reached the doorway and the hall light fell on Joanie's face. He nodded once but his face was guarded.

'I take it this isn't pleasure Inspector Johansen.'

Joanie stuck out his hand and they shook once. 'Morgan. No, I'm afraid not.'

Morgan stood silently and Joanie could see him weighing him up. Eventually he stood back and let Joanie through the door. They went through to the kitchen where a woman was busy at the stove; she looked up briefly and smiled. The teenager who'd opened the door was sitting at a breakfast counter, his chin on his hands with his nose inches away from a small TV screen. At the table was another boy, younger, doing his homework. Joanie wasn't introduced to the woman; he assumed she was Mrs Morgan. They continued through a conservatory and Morgan grabbed a heavy coat from a peg.

'We'll be in the shed.' He spoke over his shoulder. Joanie watched Morgan's wife bite her bottom lip, her eyes darting to Joanie. He tried to smile reassuringly.

They set off across the lawn to a large wooden shed near the end. There was a light, a desk, a couple of lawn chairs with foam padding and a small electric heater in the corner.

'This is my hideaway,' Morgan said as if in explanation. He sat down and pointed at the other seat for Joanie.

'Cosy.' Joanie nodded at the wooden interior, a couple of photos above the desk of his wife and the boys.

Morgan nodded and then leaned forwards towards Joanie, 'I won't pretend to know why you've come here and neither will I pretend that I'm happy to see you. An Inspector at my door unannounced can only mean bad news in my book.'

Joanie spread open his hands and explained. 'I've come about the Martin Hempstead case. We've had a child murdered since then, and I want to know if they're linked.'

'I know, I followed it in the news. Kieren Matthews. But they're not linked I can tell you that much.'

Joanie pulled out the penknife from his pocket and began to clean his nails. 'What makes you say that?'

'The killer's dead. Dead and buried and it's over with now. There's no link. Martin's case is closed.' Morgan folded his arms checking his watch as he did so.

'But it isn't closed, that's just it and I wondered why. It looks like the evidence pointed to Martin's father but there's no conclusion.' Something flitted past the single window, probably a bat.

'The father's dead, isn't that conclusion enough? For Christ's sake, what do you want to dig up? Haven't the family suffered enough?' Not only did Morgan raise his voice but it trembled slightly at the end. Joanie looked at him, studied the receding hairline and the cheekbones prominent in what used to be a round face.

'Committing suicide is not an admission of guilt.'

'It is in this case.' Morgan replied firmly.

'If Mr Hempstead killed his son, why wasn't the case brought to that conclusion and closed?'

The electric light gave Morgan an unhealthy pallor, 'Because, because, there had been enough death and hurt already. The family didn't want the other two sons to know their father was a killer. How do you think that would've affected them? And what about the repercussions in the community? Roger Hempstead was a well-known public figure, people respected him, his family.'

Joanie clicked his penknife shut, he didn't like this at all. 'So you're telling me, it was better to hush things up and let the boys think there was still a killer out there? So if that was the game, for what reason did they think their father committed suicide?'

'Come on Johansen, a family with a dead son. Don't you think it's believable that the devoted father might kill himself?'

'No. Neither do I think if he was the murderer that he'd kill himself.'

Morgan looked whiter than ever; he stood up. 'It's stupid talking to you.' A sheen of sweat covered his top lip. 'Roger knew we were on to him, it was only a matter of time before we had enough to know for sure. That's why he topped himself, there was no way out.'

'Motive?' Joanie refused to give in.

'Look, I've had about enough of this. The case is as good as closed and I don't want you round here stirring things up. I've told you what you wanted to know. Roger Hempstead killed his son and now he's dead. End of story.' Morgan yanked open the shed door. 'Get out.'

Joanie stood slowly and stepped out onto the wet grass. They walked back across the lawn; a bat swooped low under the trees. The lights from the conservatory beckoned them in.

'Are you staying to supper?' she opened the door as Joanie's face appeared.

'No, he's leaving.' Morgan stated.

'But thank you Mrs Morgan.' Joanie held out his hand and the woman shook it automatically although her face showed confusion. She gave Morgan a quizzical look. The boy at the table took his eyes off the TV long enough to give Joanie a frosty glare. Down the hall and out into the street, Joanie could feel Morgan at his back. He walked down the few steps and through the gate but the light on the pavement showed the front door was still open.

'There is nothing else.' Morgan said behind him. Joanie turned to see the shadowy slim figure framed in the doorway. They stood that way for a few seconds and then Morgan shut the door firmly. Orange street lamps glowed across the road leading him back to his car. There were two things that bothered him, Mr Hempstead's suicide, and Morgan's conviction that he was guilty.

'Where are you off to?' moaned Luke as Sid strode past. It was only two thirty. Sid ignored Luke's complaint and continued across the car park. It didn't matter if Luke thought he was skiving, he'd cleared it with the boss. In fact if he walked down Charles Street and round the back of the fire station, that would take him past a dentist on his way to the park. Sid smiled to himself, what an excellent idea. Fifteen minutes later Sid stepped through the park gates and headed for Betsy's bench. There were two women sitting on it with buggies. Sid stood for a moment biting his thumbnail wondering what to do. He would have to keep close, try to make eye contact with people as they came past to be sure he didn't miss his friend. Sid went to sit on the bench in front of the tennis court, there was no one playing but he sat sort of sideways so he could glance across at the two women. From what he could tell, they were getting out something to eat. Damn, why did they have to sit there. Benches were meant for old people, for grandfathers like him not young women. Every few seconds, he had to twist the other way to see who was coming up the path. At five to three he saw what might be a man with a small child turn into the park. Sid's stomach somersaulted. Sweat broke out across his body as he stared at the apparition.

He was smaller than he'd expected, perhaps about six. His hair was ginger, virtually orange in the afternoon sun. They walked slowly up the path, Alfie's steps sometimes skipping. They stopped as he bent down to pick something up off the path and showed it to his friend. He could hear him laugh, a deep throaty laugh. The man scooped him off the floor and up above his head. Sid grinned; Alfie was laughing too, a high-pitched shriek. Sid got up from the bench and went to stand on the path ready to meet them. His friend put Alfie back down and they continued their way towards him. Sid found himself grasping his hands tightly together, he could barely breathe. He tapped his breast pocket feeling the stiffness of the picture beneath; his present for Alfie. The man was tall, a dark mass of hair crowned his sturdy frame. Their voices got closer and Sid could hear what they were saying.

'And how many steps to the top?'

'Fwee.'

'One, two, three.' With that the man picked up Alfie and swung him around once more. Sid would be able to do that, pick him up, and make him laugh. A wide smile pasted across his face.

Sid stepped forwards uncertainly. 'Hi,' he managed.

'Hello.' The man nodded his head briefly and then ignored him.

'Um,' Sid didn't know what to say, the friend didn't seem to recognise him. But then of course they'd never met, and Sid was by the wrong bench. He looked ahead to see the women had moved off but now there was a man sitting there. Alfie and his father carried on along the path. Sid stood rooted to the spot. He had to get to the bench. He darted behind them and hurried ahead, there was room for him to sit down. He didn't want Alfie to mistake the other man for his grandfather. Again Sid waited for them to approach meandering up the path, now singing a nursery rhyme. At last, when they were level, Sid leapt up. He thrust out his hand.

The man looked startled and took a step back. 'Do I know you?'

'Yes, it's me. Sid, Sidney White,' he hurried on, 'Grandpa Sid. This must be Alfie.' Sid knelt down but Alfie hid behind his father's legs.

'This is Charlie,' the man said. 'I think perhaps you have us confused with someone else.' Sid stood up as if burnt, falling back onto the bench. The man looked concerned and picked up Alfie. Only it wasn't Alfie, it was Charlie. He put him on his shoulders and continued past. Sid looked horrified at the man's retreating back. What had he done? Pain and shame came crashing down on his head. How could he be so stupid? Sid looked cautiously at his watch; it was two minutes past three. He wiped a trembling hand across his forehead and realised he was alone on the bench. But not quite alone. Beside him sat a brown envelope. Although upside down, the printed name was obvious. Sidney White. Sid picked it up with trembling hands. A jogger ran past and Sid clenched the envelope tightly.

There had been a man; a man sitting on the bench. Sid stood up and searched up and down the path. He could still see the boy that wasn't Alfie with his father, and the jogger disappearing into the trees, but not the man that had been on the bench. Sid went back the way he'd come and hurried straight home. He felt sick, stupid, as if he'd laid himself open and now only bad things would come. He kept the envelope clutched in his hands.

Once inside his flat, he ripped it open feverishly. There was a photograph and on the back was written the word Alfie. Sid turned the photograph around the right way and studied the boy. His hair was blond, deliciously blond, pale and lovely just as it should be. Sid sighed with satisfaction. He was wearing his school uniform, the one from Priory. Alfie was smiling showing the hole where one of his front teeth was missing. A few freckles dotted across the bridge of his nose and there was a dark mole under his left eye. Sid could feel his heart beating. He was lovely Sid realised. A perfect substitute for Tommy and the real story. As Dr Casey had said, it was only perception after all that mattered and Sid could see his perfect film beginning to unfold. The happy ending was getting closer all the time. This was the boy that played googers, who laughed down the phone at him. This was his grandson. Sid struggled to put the feelings that had been so strong before into the picture of this boy. He wasn't exactly how he had imagined but then you didn't choose your grandchildren. He liked the freckles, they looked kind of cute. He would be much better in real life. Sid put the photograph to one side and checked inside the envelope, there was nothing else, no letter.

Sid now had two treasured things, Alfie's drawing and the photograph of Alfie. Two was better than one. But still he hadn't met Alfie. Frustration made his skin feel prickly. Who was his friend? Sid tried to remember what the man on the bench had looked like but he'd been so concerned about getting to the bench that he hadn't really looked. He closed his eyes and replayed the scene in his head. Blond hair, the man definitely had blond hair. He'd been wearing a light coloured jacket and dark trousers. He drew out some paper and one of his soft pencils and began to sketch feverishly. The face had been pale, fixed, Sid struggled to try and capture the image in his head. Finally he put down the pencil and leaned back in his chair.

What was difficult was working out exactly when the man had disappeared. He was there when Sid sat down but after he'd spoken to the tall man, he'd disappeared. His friend must have stood up almost as soon as Sid had sat down. Why hadn't his friend simply posted the envelope to him? That was something else that bothered Sid. At first they were hand delivered, then posted and now it was a peculiar meeting on a bench. Suspicion and fear crawled across his skin. He got up and washed his hands in the kitchen sink. Then he went back to the desk, holding Alfie's photograph close to his face, he touched it to his lips, and closed his eyes. Everything would be all right, he soothed, one hand reaching down to his crotch.

Later as he ate his shepherd's pie for one, he thought again about the elusive friend. Somehow he needed to find a way to bypass his friend to get to Alfie. A small light flickered in the back of Sid's brain, and as he continued to stare at Alfie's photo, it gradually filtered through the darkness and into his conscious mind. Priory School. The uniform he was wearing was from Priory School.

Of course it was too late now, the school kicked out at three fifteen. But tomorrow, it was a perfect way to see Alfie; he could wait at the school gates. Tomorrow was Saturday though; he would have to wait until next week. Then there was the problem of work; he couldn't have another dentist appointment. Perhaps he could go before work, watch Alfie arrive at school instead. It would make him slightly late but he could claim his alarm hadn't woken him. That he'd been feeling ill all weekend after the anaesthetic the dentist had given him.

As Joanie pulled into the driveway he noticed a light on upstairs. It was Sammy's room. He hadn't had a call on the mobile so he assumed she must have rung home and Margret must have collected her from the station.

The house was quiet, he found Margret in the lounge reading

her book.

'Where is she?' Joanie asked.

'Shh, she's gone to bed. She was very tired. I think she must be coming down with something, she looked ever so pale.'

Joanie nodded, Sammy obviously hadn't confessed anything then. 'I'll pop up and see if she's still awake.'

He padded up the stairs and knocked gently on the door. The light was on but there was no sound. Joanie pushed the door open and Sammy turned towards him blinking.

'Hello pumpkin.' He stood in the doorway wondering if he should go all the way in.

She smiled and patted the edge of the bed. It had been years since Joanie had sat on the bed with her and kissed her good night but right now it seemed the right thing to do. He sat down and stroked her hair.

'How are you feeling?' Her skin felt hot under his fingers and her eyes red as if she'd been crying.

'Tired. You're late.'

'I had to go and see someone. Sorry I wasn't here when you arrived.'

'It doesn't matter, Mum's been sweet, feeding me up with chicken curry. I'm so full I don't think I'll be able to sleep now.'

Suddenly she looked so child-like tucked up under the quilt, her pink eyes looking up at his. This poor child who now had her own child hidden inside. He shouldn't think like that, he didn't know what she wanted to do yet.

'We'll talk tomorrow. I have to leave at eight if you're up, otherwise I'll be home at six, I promise.'

She crooked herself up on one arm and kissed his cheek.

'Thanks Dad.' It wasn't thanks for coming in to see her, or promising to come home early, he knew it was thanks for keeping a secret. A secret he would rather not have.

Downstairs Joanie helped himself to the leftover curry, heating it in the microwave and then joined Margret. She had put her legs up along the settee with the cushions propped behind her head on the armrest. Joanie sat in the armchair and began to pick at his food.

'Gone off curry? Or have you already eaten a take away?'

'No, I was just thinking. Do you remember Inspector Morgan?'

'Morgan? Was he the rugby chap with the huge laugh? Yes, not exactly charming but likeable enough. Didn't he retire a while ago? We went to his do.'

'That's the one. I wondered if we'd met his wife.' Joanie watched Margret thinking. She was good at faces, usually remembered who was married to whom and so forth at the police dinners. Joanie was good at faces too, and names, but Mrs Morgan was one he couldn't remember having met before tonight.

'Was she at the retirement do? I thought he had Gary's wife on one side and your boss on the other. In fact wasn't he on his own that night?'

A picture of the table spread with dirty plates and glasses sprang to Joanie's mind. A raucous speech by the inebriated Morgan followed by more shouts from the audience. Some of the younger lot had gone off to a nightclub afterwards, he was pretty sure Morgan had gone with them. Margret was right; Mrs Morgan hadn't been there.

When Sid opened his front door, early that morning, he was surprised to find a brisk wind. Leaves chased down the street and ruffled his hair. Going back into the hallway, Sid grabbed his coat and headed across town. Priory School was situated near the Harding estate. It was a large sprawling building with a long fence bordering Bainbridge Road. Sid had been here several times before, usually on a day off. The playground was easily visible through the chain-link fence and there was a good spot by an old oak tree to watch. However, the main entrance was round the corner and this was where Sid needed to be if he was going to spot Alfie. A few kids were already kicking their feet along the pavement. Despite being there at half past eight, he could see some were already inside the building. He hoped he hadn't missed Alfie. Sid walked past the entrance to the corner. He couldn't just stand there, that would be foolish, and people might get the wrong idea. It was annoying he couldn't be there at the end of the day when it was normal for parents and grandparents to be hanging about. Instead Sid spotted the bus stop back past the entrance on the other side of the road. What a genius. He would wait at the bus stop; no one would think that was odd.

With his hands thrust into his pockets, Sid stood hunched against the wind. It felt funny against his beard, almost as if someone was gently tugging it. Two children on bikes zipped in through the gate. Then a boy on his own with dark hair. He was very tall though, far too tall for a primary school, Sid thought. Then a group of six or seven jostling each other. It was difficult to get a good look at all of them. The uniform helped, all the girls were in skirts so if he got confused he could look at their legs then their hair colour. This enabled him to be more selective but even then a couple of boys went through the gates that he hadn't really been able to see properly. Then the cars started arriving. One parked right in front of him in the bus stop. A particularly large woman got out and fiddled with a buggy. She kept standing then crouching right in the way. Sid felt like he was playing dodgems, he had to keep shifting his feet so he could see across the road. Of course there were more cars now by the gate despite the yellow paint on the road asking drivers not to.

'Excuse me.' It was the large woman having finally loaded up the baby in the buggy. A sullen looking girl in uniform stood beside her. The woman was trying to get past him and across the road. Sid clenched his fists in his pockets and moved back. There was so much activity now at the gate that Sid's eyes had to move frantically to and fro trying to get a glimpse of every child. Suddenly his view was blocked completely by a huge bus.

Sid stood on his tiptoes to see if he could see straight through the windows to the other side. There was a loud honk from the traffic.

'Are you getting on or what?' It was the driver, the door stood open and he was scowling at Sid.

'Er, no.'

'The number 57's the only one that comes along here. You're at the wrong stop if you were expecting anything else.' The driver raised his eyebrows; several of the people on the bus were now looking out of the window at him.

'I'm waiting for a lift,' Sid blurted, 'from a friend.'

'Typical, damn drivers blocking up my lay by.' The doors hissed shut and the bus heaved its way between the parked cars. The children were beginning to thin out and Sid was sure he hadn't seen Alfie yet. He hoped he hadn't missed him. Damn the bloody bus. The fat woman returned wheeling her baby up onto the pavement.

'Wasn't that your bus?' she stood assessing him.

'What?' Sid had to pull his attention away from the school gate. 'No, I'm waiting for my lift.' She was still looking at him, 'to get to work.' This seemed to satisfy her and she went about dismantling the buggy. Sid stepped back and to the side so he could still see the gate. The school bell clanged causing a sudden rush for the door from those children that had been milling in the playground. A couple more cars stopped and a small passenger leapt out and through the gate. Sid checked his watch. He had to go; it would take him another twenty minutes to get to the supermarket. Maybe he should try earlier tomorrow. What would be even better would be to swap his shift to Saturday giving him a day off in the week. That would mean he could be here at three fifteen when he could stand close to the gate like the other parents. Sid turned into the wind and strode away from the school.

'Sid? You look different. You're late.' It was David by the

disabled parking.

Sid did a double take. When he'd first seen the jacketed man, he'd assumed it must be Luke and had kept his head down ignoring him on his way into the store.

'David.' Sid couldn't help his grin. 'David,' and then he gripped David's hand and pumped it hard. If they'd been alone Sid might have hugged him but there were people around and David was giving him a funny look. 'I'll be right back.' Sid virtually skipped into the store and up to his locker. He didn't see Mr Foster or the other managers and was shortly back in the car park. David was helping an old lady disentangle two trolleys.

'We'll talk at break time OK?' Sid nodded encouragingly.

'Er, alright.' An uncertain smile crossed David's face and then he frowned at the trolleys. With a big yank he pulled them apart.

'Ooh my, you are a strong young man, thank you dear.'

Sid sighed contentedly and made his way over to the nearest half empty stand. Life was definitely on the up. He was bound to see Alfie soon and now he was back with David things couldn't be better.

They went up for their break at eleven, Sid got David a coffee and they sat together at the table. It was just like old times.

'Why were you late Sid?' David looked annoyed over his mug.

'Well,' Sid glanced across at the sink. They were alone. 'I had to take my grandson to school.'

'Your grandson? I didn't know you had a grandson. Gosh. What school does he go to?'

'Priory, he has a very smart uniform.' Sid explained.

'I went to Priory. It was good there especially Mrs Burton, she was my teacher, she said I could go far.' David nodded emphatically. 'And I have, me and Mum went to Majorca last week. We stayed in a hotel with stars on the door. And we swam, and I drank wine. Mum gave me some and I liked it.

Have you ever had wine Sid?'

'Yes.' Sid loved this; here they were having a normal chat like normal people. Sid was a grandfather and David was, well, just David. Sid's chest swelled with satisfaction. The staff room door swung open and David twisted in his seat.

'I'm glad it's not Luke,' it was one of the girls from the checkouts. 'I hate Luke. He's always late and he doesn't do the trolleys properly. He gets them all mixy and then they don't all fit in the stand. Not like you Sid. You do it properly. Are you going away again?' David gulped at his coffee and pulled out a squashed mars bar from his pocket.

'No. I don't think so.' Sid should try and get himself back on trolleys permanently. 'I'll speak to Mr Foster,' he added.

'I hate him too. He said I couldn't swear at Luke in front of the customers but Luke does. And he smokes. And he's got long hair.'

Sid could see that David was working himself up into a strop.

'What are you having for lunch today? Shall I get us a cake to celebrate?' Sid wanted to prolong the good feelings.

'Why? It's not my birthday, is it yours?'

'No, but we'll have one anyway, a Monday cake.'

'That sounds silly.' David stood up still finishing the mars bar. 'I'll help you eat it. Let's go,' he mumbled through his mouthful.

17

Joanie was at his desk poring over the latest set of paperwork his team had put together. They'd been working hard while he'd been away sunning himself and fooling with Tania. He gritted his teeth; it was time to get this whole mess moving. Inspector Johansen wasn't going to be beaten. On separate sheets of paper he wrote down sketch notes of the different scenarios. The first he forced himself to do was for Sidney White, as the killer of Kieren Matthews and possibly Martin Hempstead. It would be nice to leave it to the end but he'd decided it was his own prejudice holding him back. A poor abused kid named George Boswell at school was in the past. Sidney White was a suspect that may have committed a horrific crime in the present.

Next came Roger Hempstead and his son. No matter how much of the circumstantial evidence Joanie read, he still couldn't believe he'd murdered his son. Still, he noted down the facts as they currently stood or at least had been reported at the time. He did the same for Mr Evans the swimming instructor, and finally Ross Thorpe. The last sheet was for an unidentified man who brought the two murders together. If an unknown person was responsible then both Sidney and the late Roger were innocent. This last sheet was divided in half with two further unidentified men, one for each boy murdered but completely independent of each other. Again Joanie added notes of evidence, witnesses etc. that fitted with each scenario. By the end of the morning he had thrown the unknown killer sheet away, and Sidney White's sheet was looking decidedly full. Perhaps he would need to speak to Curtis.

'I've known it was him all along.' He sat opposite Joanie, a harsh almost triumphant look on his face.

'These are the things I want to know,' Joanie began, 'Where did Sidney White live after he left Shellbrook Road as a kid. What jobs has he had and where. See if you can find out his past addresses. Any girlfriends, boyfriends, anybody who had a relationship with him.' Joanie paused; Curtis was looking at him with a queer smile. 'What is it? How much of this do you have already?' Joanie tapped his pencil on the desk.

'Quite a bit, do you want to hear it?' Curtis' smile slid across his mouth like a wet eel.

Joanie counted very slowly in his head to five and then he said, 'Yes.'

'Well, George Boswell was taken into care at aged twelve into a children's home in Blackheath, after his uncle was arrested and his mother turned to drink. He left there when he was fifteen and worked for three years in a newsagent just round the corner, living in a room above the shop. I managed to track down the old owner Mr Parks who still lives in a nursing home in Blackheath and he remembered George. Let's see.' Curtis stopped for a moment with a finger on his temple.

Joanie didn't like the affectation but he let it pass.

'A quiet lad kept himself to himself; found him stealing sweets to give to the Droxy twins.'

'Who were?'

'Two little boys that lived on the same street, 'cute little buggers' were Mr Parks' words. Anyway he sacked him and then it would appear that George Boswell became Sidney White and the next thing I could find was him working in a shoe factory in Leeds about ten years later.'

Joanie put up a hand to stop the biography. He leaned forwards across the desk, 'Exactly when were you intending to tell me all this stuff?'

For the first time Curtis looked unsure of himself. 'You said to find out about him, his profile and not to come back until I had enough evidence.'

'So is this life story leading anywhere?'

Curtis looked deflated. 'From what I can gather he seems to move on every five or so years. Something happens, I don't know; in one place he hit somebody and was sacked. Other times there doesn't appear to be a reason, he just ups and leaves. He doesn't have any family left, and as for friends, there was no address book found when the flat was searched. Nothing at all to indicate he likes anyone, not even a phone.'

Joanie nodded. 'He's certainly a loner. Leave your notes with me and I'll take a look.'

Curtis reluctantly passed over two files. 'I'm going to get him sir. There may not be enough there yet, but I'm working on it.'

Joanie could see that flash in his eyes as if they were made of solid marble, unbreakable. 'You were the one who leaked Sidney White to the press, weren't you.'

Curtis looked back at Joanie, his gaze unwavering. 'I want to catch the killer, sir.'

He had a self-righteousness about him, standing there like some great statue of justice. How could he be so positive about this goddamned case? Maybe he'd been right all along; maybe he was justified in his position. Joanie could see that Curtis was not going to answer the question. But he knew.

'Don't ever do that again.' Joanie commanded.

Curtis continued to stare defiantly, 'You're still trying to protect him.'

'What?' Joanie had to clamp his mouth shut, he wasn't about to let his emotions run away this time, not after that stupid outburst at Kelly. Instead he stood up and closed the door. When he turned back again, Curtis continued to stand but no longer looked statuesque.

'Now listen to me Curtis. I'm not protecting anyone, least of all Sidney White. And you have still yet to produce enough evidence to lock him away.'

Joanie had gradually moved closer to Curtis, his voice low and threatening.

'What I want to know is why Sidney is so important to you?'

Now that they were only inches apart, Joanie could see a few dots of perspiration on Curtis' top lip.

'He's not.'

Joanie waited, the answer was lame.

'Spit it out Curtis, because if you don't I will make sure that I find out exactly who, in the press, you tipped off. And you know perfectly well what that will do to your career.'

Joanie watched the possibilities flitting across Curtis' face; he was weighing up the consequences. At last Curtis dropped his gaze and looked away towards the window. Joanie backed off, moving back behind his desk and leaning in his chair. He waited, steepling his fingers on his chest.

'It's not what you think,' Curtis paused and sat down. Again he looked down at his hands. 'It's like what you said a while ago, about not all victims being able to come forward in a case, that sometimes they couldn't for whatever reason.'

Joanie watched him picking at the edge of his fingers. Suddenly Curtis' hand flew up to his face wiping angrily at his eyes. These were tears, Joanie stayed still.

'Fuck, I don't have to tell you anything.' Curtis stood up angrily. 'You sit there like Mr Know It All, but you don't know what it's like, you have no idea what men like Sidney White do, how it affects people.'

Joanie opened his top drawer and pulled out a box of tissues.

He placed it on the desk and then got up and turned away towards the window.

'No I don't,' he conceded quietly. He could hear Curtis rip a tissue from the box. 'But was it Sidney White?' he spoke quietly, looking out onto the street, the leaves on the tree opposite blowing gently to the ground.

'No, of course not, but they're all alike those fucking bastards. They go around fucking up people's lives and get away with it.'

Joanie turned around, Curtis was still standing, a damp tissue clamped in his fist. He nodded silently and went back to his desk.

'I don't want to hear your story Curtis; I'm not here for your pain or pleasure. I'm sorry you've been a victim, but that isn't why you're here. You're here to be a good copper, and from what I've seen of your recent work, you are. Curtis, I need people like you on my team, people who understand the stakes. Use your passion, your sorrow, make it work for you. Find the evidence to get the right man, or you might be letting a killer go free, and how many more lives will be fucked up if we get the wrong man?'

The room was silent. Joanie could feel his words leaching into the walls. He only hoped they would get through Curtis' thick skin. If not, his career was doomed to failure. He thought back to their first meeting, the charming smile that could so quickly be turned to a devilish glint. If Curtis could use that, and his developing powers of research, he might do very well.

Left alone, Joanie thoughtfully considered his next move. Well he now had a large amount of background information on Sidney White, thanks to Curtis. He should do due diligence on Mr Evans and Ross Thorpe too. Joanie tapped his pencil on the desk and remembered purple-eye or rather Ross Thorpe brush past him and down the stairs. The man had been punched by Mr Charles but dropped the charges. Joanie thought about what Mr Charles had said back then, it didn't really make any sense.

Why did he punch him? It was completely out of character, and why would Ross Thorpe let him off? Joanie rolled this thought around his head and wondered if another visit to Mr Charles might shine a light on the incident.

Joanie remembered his promise to Sammy and managed to be home by six fifteen. As soon as he walked into the hall, he knew something was wrong. Everything was quiet, too quiet, yet the air was thick. Sammy must have told Margret he assumed. With soft steps he ventured into the lounge. Nothing. A couple of magazines on the table, an old coffee cup and one of Margret's paintings leaning against the wall.

Upstairs he found both bedroom doors shut. So this was where they were hiding, each to her own. Joanie stood for a moment wondering which to tackle first. The guilt he felt towards Margret was the overriding factor so he went into their bedroom. She was kneeling on the floor by the chest of drawers. The bottom drawer wide open. She spun her head round when she heard him enter. Her face was pinched, accusing, but then it relaxed seeing Joanie standing there. Her hands quickly folded and replaced something white and lacy.

'What's that?' Joanie asked.

'Nothing.' She continued to bundle it back into the drawer and heaved it closed. Joanie knew perfectly well it was Sammy's christening outfit. She stood up and faced him squarely, her eyes red, and a strange pink blotch on one cheek.

'And I understand you already know.' She stated. 'And I thought we had a marriage.'

Joanie didn't quite follow. 'We do.'

'Don't you think that something like this should be discussed with your wife, with Sammy's mother? How could you keep something like that from me? Why,' she paused, he could see her fighting back the tears. 'Why didn't you trust me enough to tell me? Why am I the last to know when she's my daughter?' Her voice was rising, not simply in anger but there was a tremor of panic in it too.

'Margret.' Joanie stepped around the bed. 'It wasn't like that.'

'Don't come near me.' She swiped at him like an annoying fly. 'Did you think I wouldn't be strong enough, that this little secret might not affect me?' She was shouting now. Joanie stood and allowed her to vent her frustration on him. It was venomous, bringing up things from the past that Joanie had all but forgotten about, right up to the present day and his lack of understanding over her retirement. 'And I bet you haven't a clue that I've been going through the menopause. No, too wrapped up in your own little world to notice anything but yourself and your damn work.'

Joanie suddenly noticed their bedroom door had opened. Standing there in her jacket was Sammy looking pale and washed out. Silence descended, Margret turned her back on them and ripped a tissue out of the box on the night table.

'For your information Mum, I asked Dad not to tell you, because I knew you'd get all worked up. I'm going to go and stay with Annabelle for a few days.' Then Joanie noticed the bag behind her in the hallway.

'Look, I'm sure we can work something out. We just need to calm down. I know it's a shock for everybody. We'll go downstairs, have some tea and look at this logically and carefully.'

'Logically! Wonderful, as if this is one of your cases, that's right. We'll just look at the facts, note them down and magically we'll have an answer. This isn't about the law, it's about life,' Margret fumed at him. Joanie turned to his daughter for help but she had already left the room. He heard the front door shut and crossed to the window. She carried the holdall, the one she used to use for her hockey kit when she'd been in the school team. Joanie wanted to call after her, bring her back but he knew that for now, it was probably the best thing, even if it did make his heart ache.

Joanie swung around and fixed his wife with a hard glare.

'Happy now, you've driven our daughter away?' He stormed out slamming the bedroom door behind him.

In the kitchen he boiled the kettle, switched it off half way through and found a beer in the fridge instead. He couldn't see any evidence of dinner so he picked up the phone and ordered Chinese takeaway for two. When it arrived he called up the stairs for Margret but there was no reply. After he'd unwrapped the dishes he went upstairs to get her. He was feeling calmer, and the smell of the food had lifted his spirits somewhat.

'Are you coming down? I've got some Chinese, beef in black bean sauce if you'd like it.' It was Margret's favourite dish chosen deliberately. She was lying on the bed facing the window. Slowly she turned her face towards him. It looked like she'd been battered, her eyes all puffy, her hair damp and pressed flat against her cheek.

'Come on love,' he held out his hand and she took it, swinging her legs off the bed.

'Give me a few minutes,' she said.

Joanie left her in the bathroom and went back downstairs to make a start on his sweet and sour. About five minutes later Margret appeared looking slightly better, she'd brushed her hair and washed her face. Her eyes were still puffy though and there was a roundness to her shoulders. It reminded Joanie of defeat. She ate about half her meal and Joanie finished it off with the last of the prawn crackers and then made coffee for them both.

'I thought you'd be excited about becoming a grandparent.'

Margret slurped the coffee and started a coughing fit as it went down the wrong way. When she'd recovered she said, 'A grandparent? Well, I certainly won't be a grandparent to this child. You know she's not intending to keep it.'

Joanie hadn't. Of course, a part of him had known that it was Sammy's decision and she may choose to abort it, but he'd assumed she wouldn't or hoped so at least. He certainly hadn't entertained the thought of an abortion. No wonder Margret was so upset. There were fresh tears running down her face.

'Sometimes I ask myself why, when there are so many people desperate to have children and so many unwanted babies are just flushed away. It's so cruel.' Joanie remembered this argument from years ago. It had been something they had both felt at the time. Their wish to have a child was so strong and yet it seemed it would be impossible, and all around them were teenage girls having abortions. Young women choosing careers over children. And yet there they were, childless too, but not out of choice. It seemed that those who had the choice were making the wrong decision. But then like some miracle, Sammy had come into their lives and they hadn't looked back. Now it was like a slap in the face. How did he feel about it? Did it matter that he wouldn't be a grandfather, at least not yet? It was Sammy's life; he could see how difficult it would be for her if she had the baby. What about Matt? He didn't even know if he would support her. The authorities would see to the practicalities but that wasn't the point.

Margret was still crying, silent tears rolling down her cheeks.

'It's not our baby love. We have to support Sammy; we need to find out how she and Matt really feel. It's all we can do. They're adults and must make their own decisions.' It felt like the right thing to say but it didn't feel quite right deep in his gut.

Margret snuffled into a new tissue. 'But it's not fair,' she wailed.

Joanie was tempted to ring Sammy at Annabelle's house but he thought he'd leave it until the morning. Perhaps he and Margret should speak to Mrs Jenkins, Annabelle's mother, but what could they say? Sammy wasn't a child that they had the right to check up on at her friend's house. She was an adult, one in trouble it was true, but Joanie was cautious. He was frightened if they did the wrong thing they would lose her. There was no way he could risk that.

They talked a little more. Neither of them apologised for the argument earlier. Joanie was feeling sore from the things she'd said, would defend himself if she said anything more and yet he knew she was right. No wonder Margret had been having disturbed nights and seemed rather moody these last couple of months. He hadn't given the menopause any thought. Now that she'd mentioned it, as Kelly had, so much seemed to fall into place. It also made him realise how much of an ostrich he'd been. Instead of sand, he had used his work to bury himself.

At eight thirty the following morning, Sid was at his desk. It had been quite a battle to stay in the flat. He desperately wanted to go to the school again and watch but he reminded himself that he was too conspicuous. Yesterday afternoon, he had rearranged his day off and next Monday he could go to the school at three. That would be his best opportunity and it would be safe. Not only that, but Mr Foster said he would consider allowing Sid back on trolleys permanently.

At twenty to nine, Sid left the flat and headed straight for the supermarket. David was waiting in the staff room.

'Do you want the front today Sid?' David waited patiently while Sid put his jacket in the locker. The mobile phone he slipped into his trouser pocket.

'Yes. I'll work the front and we'll swap at lunch.' Sid smiled at David and they went down to the main store. Sid had barely touched the first abandoned trolley when his phone buzzed. It was another meeting. This one read:

7am Betsy tomorrow

Sid put the phone back in his pocket with a frown. Seven in the morning was earlier than he normally got up. He assumed it would be light by then but even so, wasn't it rather strange to meet in the park at seven? He knew now that Alfie wouldn't be there, but maybe this time he would get to see who this friend was. Despite the gnawing doubt in Sid's stomach, he had to admit that these meetings had brought him closer to Alfie. He knew what he looked like and which school he went to. Another meeting would surely be a positive thing.

Sid enjoyed the day, some of the warmth of summer had come back into the air and he found himself sweating in the afternoon. The beech trees that surrounded the car park had begun to turn and the afternoon sun burnished them a golden brown. Sid didn't often notice this kind of thing but he took it as a good sign. Enjoying nature was part of being happy and healthy. To Sid, this meant he was becoming like normal people. A normal grandfather that noticed the trees changing colour. He could feel a smile spread across his face, he'd been smiling more and more recently and it felt good.

Sid was careful to set his alarm for six fifteen; that would give him time to wash his face and have a cup of coffee before heading out to the park. He wasn't sure if he would come home again afterwards or carry on straight to work. Either way he would need some breakfast. He could always stop at that new cafe in town and get a bacon roll. Visions of Alfie smiling at him from a park swing ran through his mind. His freckles standing out in the early sun, his blond hair all shiny and clean.

When Sid thumped the alarm clock, it was still dark. His mind felt fuggy as he tried to read the digital display. He hadn't expected it to be dark. His eyes wavered and he thought he would wait another five minutes before leaving the bed. He turned his face towards the pillow and let his eyes close.

Sitting up with a start, the first thing Sid realised was that it was lighter. Grabbing the alarm clock he thrust it in front of his face. It felt like he'd closed his eyes for two minutes but the clock showed it had been half an hour. Frantically Sid threw the quilt off and wrestled into his trousers. He didn't bother to wash his face or boil the kettle. In fact he even forgot his wallet in his rush to get out the door. Half running down the street, Sid could feel his vest cutting uncomfortably at his neck; he must have put it on back to front. No matter, if he hurried, he might make it. There were a few cars heading into town and a couple of dog walkers as he neared the park. He tried to run although it was more like a fast stumbling walk. It certainly warmed him up and he was panting by the time he turned into the park gates. Up along the path, he could see the bench, it was empty. Further along there appeared to be a figure but as Sid staggered up the hill, it turned out to be a jogger. Sid slowed so he could catch his breath, there didn't appear to be anyone else about. The jogger nodded at him, a peculiar high squeaking leaked from his headphones as he padded past. Sid had to stop for a minute, he was breathing hard and his chest hurt. Sliding up the cuff of his jacket, he could see he'd forgotten his watch too. Sid gave one final look across the park before slumping onto the bench and then he saw it, sitting there waiting for him. One brown envelope. This one was unmarked but there was no mistaking it. Sid knew it was for him. Did the jogger leave it? But he'd watched the man running towards him from much further back and he hadn't approached the bench. No, someone had been here earlier. Sid shoved the envelope into his inside pocket and leaned forwards on his knees. His breathing was ragged and Sid wished he had that hot coffee now to soothe his throat. The air was cool this morning and it burned his throat. For several minutes he sat until his damp vest began to feel chilly.

At home, Sid undressed as far as his vest, and then twisted it round the right way. He put on a fresh T-shirt and picked up his watch from the bedside table. It was quarter past seven. With a mug of steaming coffee and a bowl of cornflakes ready, Sid slid one of his pencils under the flap of the envelope. Out fell a newspaper clipping. Sid studied the washing machine advert and half a 9% loan. Turning it over, Sid's eyes widened. It was a photo of a group of boys in Cub scout uniforms. They were holding up an oversized cheque. Beneath the picture it read: The 2nd Churchill Cub scouts raised £3544.67 for the St Nicholas Hospice. Sid held the flimsy paper closer to his face. There he was, second in from the end. His Alfie. Darling, lovely Alfie in his Cub scout uniform. Lowering the cutting, Sid thought back to that first meeting when the Cub scouts had walked past. He must have been with them but he hadn't known then which one. Now he did. Again he stared at the photo. There was a certain thrill about seeing Alfie in a newspaper. It meant he really did exist, that it was all true and that he would meet him soon. He was sure of it. He picked up his mug and took a sip and for the first time noticed a small slip of white paper. It must have slid out of the envelope when he pulled the newspaper cutting out.

The white paper was no bigger than his first two fingers. He turned it over and read:

Meet Me

Nothing else. Sid sat motionless. It had to be a message for him surely. It was the same typeface but meet him where? When?

All through work, Sid kept taking a secret peek at the clipping in his pocket. He almost showed David at break time but at the last moment thought maybe he wouldn't after all. Sid now had the key to another part of Alfie's life. But when and where was he supposed to meet Alfie, had his friend forgotten to put the rest of the message? Sid looked around him and then slipped the cutting out of his pocket, maybe there was something in the writing under the photo. But then Sid had a brainwave. Somehow he needed to find out where and when the 2nd Churchill Cub scouts met. He remembered seeing that kind of thing advertised in the newsagent window. He would try there first. Unfortunately the clipping hadn't come with its accompanying article, neither was there a date to see when the paper had come out. Surely it wouldn't be that hard to find. Maybe it was on the street map he had at home. He racked his brain trying to remember if he had ever seen a Scout or Guide hut in town.

After work, Sid walked through the centre, he stopped at every newsagent window he could find but none of them had anything about Cub scouts. He did find a mention of the Brownies with a phone number to contact. Disappointed he continued home, he was hungry and tired. As he entered Compton Drive, a thought struck him. That time he'd seen the Cub scouts come past; they must have walked from their building. Unless they had a minibus but he didn't remember seeing one. They walked into the park and therefore their place couldn't be far from the park. He could simply walk down all the roads radiating out from the park until he found it. If he limited himself to within a mile in any direction he was bound to come across it.

Sid made himself a quick dinner and then headed back again to the park. It wasn't easy trying to follow the roads. They kept changing direction and he wasn't sure if he was heading away from the park or parallel to it. One time he walked a complete loop and just when he thought he must be at the limit of a mile, he saw the huge hedge of the back of the park up ahead. There were streets and houses he'd never seen before, but no Scout place. It was dark when Sid gave up, his left foot had started to hurt and he was sure a blister had formed. He could try again tomorrow; he was bound to find it eventually.

At the door to his office, Joanie looked across the open plan room. Kelly and Curtis were at their desks. Curtis tapping into the computer and Kelly was on the phone. He'd get them a coffee too. Bypassing the machine, Joanie went upstairs to the second floor. Here they had a proper percolator, the only one in the building. Not surprisingly the jug was empty but Joanie didn't mind. He had time to wait. He filled it up and turned it on, adding more ground coffee to the overused filter. As it burbled away, he leaned against the nearest desk and slid his penknife out of his back pocket. He would make sure he left on time today; get some flowers on his way home for Margret. Twice he had been tempted to pick up the phone to Sammy this morning but had decided he should wait until this evening when they would be free to talk for as long as needed. Margret was due an apology; it was time he brought his family back to normality. This feeling of things being out of kilter had to stop. Now he felt he was getting a handle on the case, he knew he also needed to get a handle on his family. Staring at the dark brown liquid filling up the jug, Joanie realised he hadn't brought any mugs with him. There was a small kitchen in the corner, more of a cupboard with a sink and a fridge. He searched until he found two old mugs and pulled a plastic cup out of the bin. He rinsed them under the hot tap and poured a little milk into each one.

'Thanks boss,' Curtis helped himself to the nicest mug. Kelly took the other, leaving Joanie to scowl at the plastic cup.

'You could have taken ours.' Kelly raised her stained Santa mug. She put it back on the table next to several newspapers.

'What are those?' the papers had worn slightly yellow.

'Oh, just the press from when the Hempstead kid was found. I've been doing some research, trying to find if there's anything hinted at by the journalists. Something that isn't in the files basically.'

Joanie picked up the nearest paper and stared at the photograph. 'Good god!'

'What is it?' Kelly stood up to try and see over his shoulder.

'There.' He jabbed a finger at the paper. 'That woman, it's Mrs Morgan.'

'Who?' Kelly twisted the paper so she could see. 'No. That's Mrs Hempstead with her other two boys, after her husband killed himself.'

'Exactly!' Joanie couldn't believe it. 'Give me a minute.'

Joanie left Kelly and Curtis staring after him and shut the door behind him. He laid the paper on the table and tapped the desk with his pencil. The woman in the paper was definitely the woman he had met at Inspector Morgan's house. The boys too, although considerably changed in the last 3 years, they were obviously the Hempsteads. Joanie's thoughts turned back to the suicide of Roger Hempstead. Could it be possible that Roger was under so much pressure, firstly the trauma of his son's death, then the accusations of the police and the last straw was discovering that his wife was having an affair with the case inspector. The more Joanie played with this scenario in his mind, the more likely and real it became.

Joanie re-read the circumstantial evidence that pointed at Roger Hempstead. They were like hints, laid here and there. Did they really amount to a murderer? In fact, now as he read the reports with a belief that Roger wasn't the murderer, it began to look like a set-up. Surely Morgan wasn't as corrupt as all that? He looked at the papers on his desk, so if Roger Hempstead didn't kill his own son, the other suspects were pushed to the top of the pile. Joanie made a plan. Today he would concentrate all his efforts on Mr Evans, which reminded him that he'd asked Curtis to find all about the swimming teacher's personal life. Tomorrow he would tackle Ross Thorpe.

Joanie bought some chrysanthemums at the Shell garage on his way home. The house was dark and quiet when he walked in. For a moment Joanie thought it must be painting night but then that wasn't till seven and on a Thursday not a Wednesday.

'Margret?' he walked through to the kitchen and put the flowers on the table next to a folded piece of paper. In her pleasant curly script, Margret had written him a note.

'Damn.' Sighing, he put the flowers in a bucket of water and made himself some bacon and eggs. Sitting alone at the table, Joanie felt crushed. The day's work on Mr Evans including everything that Curtis had found amounted to very little. He was no further forwards. Perhaps tomorrow might be better. It would be Ross Thorpe's turn.

Joanie mopped up the last of the egg with his bread. The silence of the kitchen pressed in on him. Some happy family this was, what on earth had happened? Margret was at her mother's. Only a hundred and twenty miles away, he reminded himself. It wasn't like she'd gone to the moon or anything. Sammy was even closer, almost round the corner at Annabelle's.

But it felt like they'd deserted the sinking ship. He felt at odds with both of them. Joanie dropped his plate in the sink, made himself a tea and went through to the lounge.

The television droned at him until he switched it off. If things couldn't get worse, then he should damn well start making them better. He needed a strategy to get the two women he loved back home.

'Sammy, how are you? It's Dad here, just wanted to see how you're doing, if there's anything I can do.'

'I know it's you Dad, your number comes up on my mobile. Annabelle came with me to see the doctor today. I have to get a second opinion apparently and then it's all a matter of procedure.' She sounded distant, her voice clipped and factual.

'So you're,' Joanie paused wondering what the PC was for abortion, 'going through with it. Have you spoken to your mother today?'

'No, and I don't intend to. She can only see it from her point of view; she doesn't understand that I don't want to give up my life just yet. Matt's the same, we're too young. We haven't even started our careers yet and a baby isn't going to help our relationship. I've barely got to know him, how do I know if we're going to stay together or not with a baby in the way.' She sounded convincing but Joanie didn't believe it.

'You were never in the way.'

'But you and Mum wanted me, you'd been trying for ages, you told me so yourself. I never asked for this baby.'

Joanie wondered if anybody ever really did ask for a baby. Of course people wanted them, prayed for them, made choices, but in the end it wasn't up to the people. Either it happened or it didn't. If he believed in god, he would say that it was an act from heaven. He didn't say that to Sammy, neither did he share his disappointment that he wouldn't be a grandfather. If she hadn't spoken to Margret today, then she wouldn't know that she'd gone to Granny G's. Joanie didn't mention it.

'If you'd like me or your mother to come with you, or if you just want to talk, we're here for you OK?' It seemed an empty promise. 'Why don't you come round for supper tomorrow, I'll cook.'

'You cooking?' That certainly added a cheery note to her voice. 'Really?'

'Sure, why not? How about seven then?'

'Alright Dad, but I don't want Mum having a go at me.'

Joanie grinned to himself, part one completed. Next he phoned Grace, it was Margret who picked up.

'Hi, thought it might be you.'

'Just checking in, see how you are. Have you told Grace?'

'No, I thought I might, but she loves Sammy so much, I was worried it might... hang on' Joanie could hear Margret shut a door. 'That's better, I didn't want to worry her.'

'No, I guess not. How is she?'

'She's fine, surprised to see me of course. Not sure the home help is doing everything they should; found some mouldy cheese cake in the fridge.'

'I don't expect that will kill her.'

'That's not the point Brian, and you know it, she pays good money for their service and I'm not sure they do enough.' Margret was annoyed.

'I'm sure she'll be fine, she always seems to muddle through. Are you coming home? We need to talk about Sammy, she needs us.'

'Oh and Mum doesn't?' Now she was definitely angry. 'So it's only Samantha's problems that are important then? Of course me and Mum can take a back seat, I seem to be doing that quite a lot lately. Don't worry about Margret, she'll be there, ready to pick up the pieces, cook a few dinners, tidy the house, sweep a dead baby under the carpet.'

'Margret!' He was shocked. 'Stop getting carried away. I just meant that it might be easier for Sammy if we acted, well united. I know it's not easy for any of us.' This conversation wasn't going quite the way he'd hoped.

'So you agree with what she's doing do you? I thought you might feel the same as me after all we went through together. That you might support me in trying to talk about other options with her.'

'I would, I do. But…' Joanie didn't know how to explain his mixed up feelings. He hadn't told her about the kids on the beach in Portugal or his disappointment. But he understood it had to be Sammy's decision, that he must support her in whatever she decided. 'Look Sammy's coming round for supper tomorrow night, she'd like to see the both of us, I'm cooking.'

'What a pizza?' she added harshly.

'No, a proper meal. My treat.'

'I don't remember you cooking for me, not since I had that flu thing back in March.'

Eventually Margret agreed she'd be home by tomorrow evening, after Joanie agreed to at least try and talk to Sammy about changing her mind. He wasn't looking forward to it but at least he'd persuaded his women to come home. God he missed them. Taking his cup into the kitchen, Joanie started flicking through the cookery books. He'd have to buy some ingredients on his way home tomorrow.

It felt strange to lie in bed alone. Joanie stretched out diagonally just to see what it felt like. It was OK, nothing special, more space to fling out his arms but he'd rather have Margret's body in the way, her hand gently nudging him, encouraging him to turn over and stop snoring. Often he lay here listening to her breathe. But now there was just the incessant ticking of the clock and occasionally a car purring along the road. This wasn't something he wanted to get used to. He missed her warmth, the way she curled into a ball and ended up nudging his leg with her toes. She was coming home tomorrow, and Joanie promised himself he would start doing all those little things that Kelly had reminded him of. Pity the flowers he'd brought home were still in a bucket downstairs.

18

The afternoon drifted on, Sid's watch barely moved. The supermarket was quiet and so he and David had time on their hands. They spent it talking about football. David now played at the High School playing fields after the Kieren fiasco. The kids were bigger but they liked him playing in goal.

'Jason said I saved a cracker last night. He said if I can save Tonky's goals then that means I can play with them on Saturday.'

Sid was only half listening; his mind was still wandering the streets around the park looking for the Cub scouts. 'Uh-huh. David you don't have any brothers do you?'

'No. No sisters either, Mum said I was so special that she didn't want any other kids.' David smiled brightly.

'Do you know what a Cub is?' Sid tried to sound offhand.

'Sure, they're cute baby animals, like lion cubs and puppy cubs and stuff, my Nan used to take me to the zoo to see the bear cubs. She liked bears, said they were nicer than people. I don't like bears. What about you?'

Sid shook his head, 'I meant Cub scouts, do you know what

Cub scouts are?'

'Silly, why didn't you say so, I used to go with Michael from down our road. It was fun and I got lots of badges, I had the swimming badge, the gardening badge, and, and lots of other badges too. One time we had to go to the Guide hut because ours was being mended. Akela said that there'd been a fire set by some naughty boys and nobody was allowed to have any matches.' David spotted a lady leaving her trolley by a car.

Sid didn't want him to go just yet. 'Where was it?' he followed David striding purposefully across the car park. 'Your scout hut, do you remember where it was?'

'It was behind the park by the red post box.' They had reached the trolley, ''Scuse me Sid.'

He got out of the way and watched David take the trolley back to the stand. There couldn't be too many post boxes around the park. He intended to have another look this evening anyway and the post box would be a further clue as to the clubhouse's whereabouts.

At home Sid took out a new envelope and wrote his own address on it. Unfortunately he didn't have a stamp so instead he used his colour pencils in the top corner. It would make a passable prop just in case someone got suspicious. Sid set off back to the park. He'd changed his shoes and put a plaster on his left heel. Even so, it was still uncomfortable. When he arrived, he asked the first person he saw, a middle-aged woman loaded down with bags. He waved the envelope at her in a vague way.

'Let me see,' she put the bags down and turned around. 'The post office is a bit far from here, but I think if you take a left here, then go along and on the second or third road on your right, I think there's a box on the corner. That's your closest one.'

Sid thanked her and headed off, she was almost right; it was actually the fourth turning. Houses surrounded him with not a hint of anything else and certainly no Cub scouts. Sid continued into the maze of streets until he found a teenager on a skateboard. The boy just shrugged and continued flipping the skateboard off the edge of the curb. Further on was an elderly gentleman walking his terrier. While the dog sniffed at Sid's trousers, the man tried to explain where there was a post box. Sid did his best to follow the directions but ended up at the park gates without finding it. He was about to turn into the park when he saw one a hundred yards further on. He'd definitely been along this road before but it wouldn't hurt to check it again. Just before he reached the post box, a long driveway disappeared over a stream on his right. Sid stopped and stared. Then he noticed the tiny sign on one side. It was half covered with ivy. '2nd Churchill Scouts', he knew this must be it. He followed the driveway down to a small car park with just three cars. There was a lot of noise coming from a brick building. Excitement fluttered inside him. Drawing close to one of the windows, Sid had to balance on a rock to peek in. A lot of big boys in green sweatshirts were playing some kind of running around game. They were scouts, he knew that much, but didn't Cubs come here too? He walked over to what appeared to be the main entrance. A small poster detailed a Halloween party at the community centre. Next to it was a list of groups and their meeting times. The 2nd Churchill Cubs met on a Thursday at 6pm. That was tomorrow. Sid rubbed his hands together in delight. Just then a car came towards him and swung into the car park. In front of him the wooden door flung open. A teenager in a bright red jacket faced him.

'Excuse me.' He jumped down the step and ran over to the waiting vehicle. The door was left open and he could hear a woman shouting instructions, two mothers were now walking down the driveway chatting to each other.

'Rover,' Sid said bending over. 'Here Rover.'

'Have you lost your dog mister?' another boy had appeared, this one carrying a plastic bag out of which blue feathers were sprouting.

'Er yes. Rover's his name.'

'Ah, poor doggy, what's he look like? I'm good with dogs,' he started to call out 'Rover' looking under the cars. Sid turned and walked off down the driveway, as he neared the women he looked back and called for Rover again, then hurried into the street.

Joanie stood in a darkened corridor one flight up the huge block of flats. He peered at the numbers above the doors. Behind him the balcony railings looked out onto the road where two abandoned cars sat brooding. Number eighteen didn't actually have a number but number twenty did, and so did seventeen, although the seven had swung on its remaining nail and hung upside down like a sloping L. He couldn't see a bell or a doorknocker so instead he banged his fist against the wood. He banged twice more before he was sure he could hear movement and a light had sprung on further down the corridor.

'Who is it?' Mr Charles drew back the door letting it snag on the chain. 'Joanie?'

Joanie smiled, 'Can I come in?'

'Sure, sure. Just a minute.' He closed the door to remove the chain then ushered Joanie in. 'Your wife thrown you out? You're always welcome Joanie; I've got a sofa, a couple of blankets. You're not drunk are you? Difficult time, I know, I know. Here have a drink.' He thrust a half-finished bottle of whiskey at Joanie, and then grabbed a smeared glass from the coffee table.

'Er no I won't thanks.' Joanie perched himself onto the grubby sofa, sinking down further than he'd expected until it felt like he was virtually on the floor looking up at Mr Charles' white beard.

'I'm not in trouble am I? Haven't been out all week you know, in fact not since the swimming pool. Got away with that one, I'm getting smarter Joanie,' he tapped his nose with the glass then poured himself a generous measure. 'Thought I was a silly old fool and forgotten my swimming trunks. Get away with murder when you're my age, you should try it. In the grocer's the other week they actually believed I'd forgotten to put my trousers on. Can you believe how naive people can be?'

'Alright, alright,' Joanie raised his hand to prevent any more dastardly tales of indecent exposure. 'I came to ask you about a few months back, when you were in the church.'

'Church, I don't go to church Joanie, I'm a Buddhist I've decided, it's more relaxing. You just sit quietly in a chair and think nice things and then eventually you get to a person called Nirvana, whom I assume is like an angel or something and she makes everything perfect.'

'Just listen, will you.' Joanie tried to lean forwards but found it impossible in the sunken sofa, instead he used a firm look to try and pin Mr Charles to the armchair.

'A few months back you were down at the station after exposing yourself in the church. You gave someone a nasty black eye.'

Mr Charles looked down at his threadbare slippers. 'Oh dear, dear me. That's not nice Joanie. Friends aren't meant to rub salt into old wounds. I told you then it was a mistake, I didn't mean it.' He looked up, his eyes all pink.

'I know, it's OK you're not in trouble. The man you hit. What was it that made you strike out? What was he doing when you hit him? Think carefully, tell me exactly what happened.'

Mr Charles frowned and stroked his beard. 'He was standing at the end of a pew, just about there,' he motioned to a position just to his left, 'and then he leaned back and I saw this little girl all done up in her Sunday best, and she saw me, saw everything but I didn't mean her to see it. I didn't know she was there until he leaned back and then it was too late.'

'And?' Joanie was beginning to think he might have wasted his time.

'The girl screamed, a really loud scream, an awful scream. I didn't mean to frighten her and I was sorry, really sorry. The man looked at me and smiled. It was like he was happy that she was screaming. Not just that but he seemed to be happy that she was screaming at me so I hit him. It was like it was him making her scream as if he was pointing me out to her by leaning backwards. It was awful Joanie.' He shook his head and took a deep swig from the glass in his hand. 'When I went to the pool, I made sure it was an adult session Joanie. I don't do kids, you know that. It's not the same, much better to see Mrs Jones in the grocers with her eyes popping.' He gave Joanie a cheeky grin before draining the glass.

Joanie stood up, or at least he tried and Mr Charles apologised and offered to haul him out of the soggy mess of cushions. Finally upright Joanie shook hands.

'You've been a great help Mr Charles, look after yourself.'

'Is that it, you could have tea, I think I have tea, no milk though.' He swayed slightly towards the kitchen.

'No, no, it's fine; you've given me exactly what I needed.'

Joanie hurried along the walkway and down the stairs avoiding the stink of urine that lay in puddles in the corners. This was important, he knew it, behaviour like that spelled trouble. He wanted to go through a list of all the children that Ross Thorpe had ever taught. Joanie's mind ticked fast, his feet slapping on the wet pavement as he neared his car. This morning Ross Thorpe had still looked pretty rosy, but now. He opened the door and sat behind the wheel. The first thing he wanted to do was to speak to the boy who was Ross Thorpe's alibi. Supposedly having a lesson at the time that Kieren disappeared. Joanie pulled into the road and headed back to the station, it was growing dark so he switched on his lights. The dashboard sprung to life and so did the clock, coming into sharp focus. It was almost five o'clock.

'Damn.' Joanie swore. He was supposed to be cooking for Sammy and Margret tonight. Ordinarily he would head back to the office and try and do as much through the evening as possible. But not tonight. Joanie changed direction and headed towards the supermarket.

He'd spent too many evenings in the office ignoring his wife, last night lying in bed on his own. It wasn't something he wanted to get accustomed to. Kelly's words came back to him: 'Don't let work get between you and Margret, you know how it messed things up for me.'

Kelly was right, now that he'd started to make amends with Margret, he couldn't let it fail now, and especially with Sammy in such a delicate situation. Besides, if Ross Thorpe was truly a threat, would he really uncover anything so important tonight that couldn't be done tomorrow? Probably not. For once Joanie decided home and family would have to come first. He buried his worries about Ross Thorpe with thoughts on what he intended to cook tonight. Imagining a delicious feast, Margret holding his hand across the table and smiling warmly at him, Sammy laughing at a joke. Joanie was determined the evening would be a good one.

Sidney was sure this evening was going to be one of the best of his life. He shut the locker, turned the key and headed out of the store. Just by the entrance, a man stopped and stared at him. Automatically Sid lowered his eyes to the floor, hoping the man wouldn't be aggressive. A hand touched his jacket and Sid shrank back.

'Mr White?'

Sid looked up and realised it was one of the policemen who'd interviewed him, the older, thoughtful one. What did he want? He had the newspaper clipping of Alfie in his pocket, his hand wrapped around it, scrunching it up tight.

The inspector paused, and Sid automatically put a hand up to his beard. He felt under scrutiny. Now what? But the man's face softened a little.

'Been working?' he asked.

Sid nodded.

'Busy day?'

Sid looked at him and shrugged. There was something about the Inspector's face, the shadows out here hid the wrinkles and the dark marks under his eyes, made him look younger. Sid continued to look at him; it was like someone far away was calling him. The inspector responded by tilting his head slightly as if questioning Sid's stare. The face of a boy. A face with longer hair, dark hair that almost touched his shoulders and despite the other boys mocking, was actually quite cool. George had wanted to grow his hair too but Uncle Henry wouldn't allow it.

Joanie, the kid they'd nicknamed with a girl's name cos of his long hair. The one that cycled along his street most nights; the orange glow reflecting from the spokes. But there'd been one night when he'd seen him, Joanie had been walking, not cycling. He could tell there was something wrong with the bike. The front wheel looked slightly flattened where it touched the ground. As George stared the boy looked up and they held each other's gaze. How he'd wished with all his heart to swap with the boy and his flat tyre. Take the bike to whichever home he was destined, to a warm home with hot food on the table. He didn't care how far it was, he would walk all night with the lame bike if it meant he could get away from Uncle Henry.

Joanie removed his hand from Sid's jacket; there was a look of sadness in his eyes. 'I'm sorry,' he said and then turned away and continued into the store. Sid watched him walk away. His mind was still whirring, trying to catch up with the now, with the recent past when Joanie had been at his front door with the pictures. He'd told him then, 'They call me Joanie.' Now Sid understood; it was that kid in school. They'd only known each other a year or two before George was forced to change schools and homes yet again.

People were giving Sid funny looks; he forced his legs to move. He didn't have time to hang about, not tonight, not with Cub scouts starting in less than an hour. The thought sent a little thrill down his legs and galvanized him into action.

Sid decided not to go home, but to go straight to the clubhouse. Oddly enough the policeman hadn't frightened him as much as he expected, in fact, it had seemed oddly comforting. But it certainly wasn't going to prevent him from finding Alfie. As he neared the post box he could see cars turning in and out, and a few mothers and sons on foot. What if he was wrong about the meeting, it would be foolish to walk right in, instead he continued into the park forcing himself to walk casually as if enjoying the autumn evening. Inside he was anything but casual; this would be his first real meeting with Alfie. Checking his watch, Sid doubled back and paused by the ivy-covered sign. The car park looked dark, just the lights from the clubhouse shining through the windows. Cautiously Sid started down the driveway, he found the rock he'd used before and stood up on it to look through the nearest window. They were all standing in a ring, some of the boys with their backs to him. There was a woman at the front, also in uniform who seemed to be telling them something. Every couple of minutes one of the boys stepped forward and said something and then moved back into the ring. A car went by on the street at the end of the drive and Sid automatically ducked. He would be lit up like a stage performer if a car pulled in to the driveway. Stepping off the rock, Sid tried to see the ground. It was almost fully dark and although the windows were bright, the light didn't reach the ground along the side of the building, instead they lit the leaves on the surrounding trees. Slowly Sid walked down towards the rear of the building, rubbish and rotting wood attempted to trip him up and a particularly vicious bramble ripped at his trousers. At the last window, Sid stood on tiptoes but couldn't quite see. Searching amongst the undergrowth at his feet, he found a small log, stinging his hand on some nettles in the process. Up again, he found he had a clear view and from this angle could see some more faces. Almost immediately he recognised Alfie and thought he would faint. He had to step off the log and take some deep breaths fearing he would topple if he wasn't careful.

The boy's hair was tousled, a big grin on his face as he stepped into the circle and spoke. The other boys clapped when he'd finished and then the woman signalled the start of a game. Boys ran in every direction, when the whistle was blown they all shrieked and ran to a corner. Sid was careful to keep his face just back from the glass despite his desire to reach through and pluck Alfie up into his arms. He watched how he ran, his smile with the gap between his two front teeth. One of his green socks had wrinkled down and the bottom of his trousers was caught in it at the back.

Sid wasn't sure which he was aware of first, the buzzing in his pocket or the throbbing of his penis. They were one and the same until his brain managed to disentangle the sensations and Sid slipped off the log thrusting his hand into his pocket. The screen glowed blue and told him there was a message:

Cubs for tea

For a moment all Sid could think of was feeding time for the bear cubs that David's Nan took him to see at the zoo. But then the reality of the boys shouting inside the building caused Sid to suck in his breath. Was he watching? Sid stared into the trees, slowly turning his head 180 degrees with his back to the building. He couldn't see anyone. The blue screen winked off leaving Sid alone in the dark. A part of him wanted to switch it off but he didn't quite dare. Maybe it had been a mistake; maybe the message wasn't for him at all. He thrust the phone back into his pocket and stepped up again onto the log.

Now they were in groups spread around the room. Various bits of coloured paper, scissors and selotape were being put to use. Whatever they were making, the boys were completely absorbed. Alfie was sitting with another boy; he held an orange piece of paper flat while his friend cut out a large circle. Running across the room to retrieve something, he returned and they started to draw two large eyes and a jaggedy mouth.

Sid was getting uncomfortable, despite the log; he was still stretching on his toes to get the best view. His left foot was getting pins and needles. He decided to come down for a rest and then his phone rang. Grabbing it from his pocket, he had to answer it to make it shut up. There was a pause on the other end and then a man's voice spoke.

'Sid. Tonight is the night. You will have all you've desired but you must follow my instructions. Be ready.' And then the phone went dead. Sid flicked through the options and eventually found the number that had called him; it wasn't one he recognised. He bit at his thumbnail wondering what to do. His stomach hurt and he felt slightly sick. It hadn't been a wrong number; it had to be his friend, who else would know he was here? Who else would ring him and talk about Alfie? Sid wanted to know what being ready meant. He returned the call but it wasn't answered.

A car with bright beams pulled into the driveway. Sid pressed himself into the brick wall of the clubhouse. Nobody got out, and he waited until the lights went out. Here amongst the trees and bushes, he couldn't be seen from the car park. Up again on the log the children were still busy making things, a few had already been put on the walls and he recognised the familiar Halloween shapes that he'd put out on the shelves at the supermarket. Another two cars arrived. Each time Sid ducked back against the wall, waiting for them to park up before peering up again through the window. The boys were now packing up, a great scurry of activity as unused paper was rolled up. Someone went dashing about with a broom which caused mostly laughing and hitting and very little sweeping. There were now voices coming down the driveway and Sid began to panic. He was quite well hidden from the car park, but pedestrians crossing the bridge over the stream might spot him. Carefully Sid brushed through the nettles to the furthest corner of the building. There were no windows here, just a fire escape leading down a few steps. There was a bad smell of something rotting and although Sid wanted to sit down, he didn't want the smell to stick to his clothes.

Listening to the sounds, he heard the boys shouting, then they quieted and a strong female voice commanded their attention for a couple of minutes before the boys erupted once more. He heard the front door bang open and footsteps as they ran into the car park to go home. Car doors slammed; there were a few beeps and the sound of engines pulling away. He was ready, but for what? Where was Alfie, had he missed his chance? Sid waited for a few minutes until he couldn't hear anything. Peering around the side of the building, he could see the lights were still on so not everybody had left yet. There didn't appear to be anyone on the bridge, and it was difficult to tell from here if there were cars left in the car park. Sid found his original log with his feet and stood up to look inside. By a table at the front, the leader was shuffling some papers and gathering her bags together. Dancing across the centre of the room was Alfie. Sid couldn't believe his eyes, he was still here, his blessed Alfie, smiling and racing about the room. For a moment he stopped as the woman asked him something looking at her watch as she did so. Alfie shrugged in response and ran over towards the front door. The phone call echoed in his head. He had to be ready. Nerves tingled along his spine as Sid softly approached the entrance. With his hands on the brick, he began to lean around the corner. He could hear Alfie humming to himself on the steps. Another car swung off the main road and Sid felt himself lit up. A voice called from the doorway of the hut, strong and purposeful.

'Alfie! Stay inside until your mother comes. God knows why she's late this time.'

'It's not Mum, it's Callum's Dad. I'm having a sleep over.'

Sid lurched back along the side of the building, orange and blue spots blooming in front of his eyes from the headlights. The phone in his pocket rang again before he'd reached the safety of the bushes; he crouched down and yanked it out.

'Hurry, it's the police, go down the stream.' The voice was urgent, commanding.

Sid could feel his heart thumping hard, he looked behind him and saw the car stop on the bridge, its lights still full on. He panicked and charged headlong into the trees, he only managed a few yards before he barrelled into a tree trunk and fell to his knees. Scrambling upright he staggered on, almost losing his shoe in a particularly muddy spot. A pale wash of moonlight occasionally lit the ground but mostly it was dark shapes and twigs that caught him in the face. He felt his sleeve catch and rip on something as he blundered on.

Finally he reached another bridge with a large street lamp on it. It was a footbridge linking up two sides of the housing estate. Sid crawled underneath and sat down breathing heavily.

19

It took much longer to find all the ingredients than Joanie expected. He had to keep asking the staff and then he wasn't sure which kind to get. He'd never realised how many types of tinned tomatoes were available: plum, chopped, chopped with garlic and herbs, whole, sieved. Eventually he took the ones on special offer, chopped with Italian herbs. Perusing the wines took a while too; he wanted a nice red but couldn't remember the label of the ones Margret bought. She was good at that sort of thing.

By the time he got home, it was already after six. Following the recipe carefully he soon had a pan of bubbling mince and tomatoes, a pan of lumpy cheese sauce and some raw mushrooms he'd forgotten to add sitting on the draining board. He decided they could do without the mushrooms, slung them in the fridge and proceeded to layer up the dish. While he was trying to smooth out the remaining cheese sauce across the top, the doorbell rang and then a key turned in the lock.

'Helloo.' It was Sammy. Joanie wiped his hands on the dishcloth and went to meet her.

She looked better than the last time he'd seen her but it seemed strange to take her coat and usher her into the kitchen as if she was a guest in her own home.

'Looks pretty good Dad, although I thought we were eating at seven.'

'Hmm, took a little longer than I expected.' He put it in the cold oven, switched it on and set the alarm clock.

'I bought some wine if you fancy,' he offered, showing her the bottle for approval.

He watched her frown, 'Erm no, actually I'll just have some juice.' She got up and went to the fridge finishing the carton and reaching in the cupboard for some more.

'You've run out. Doesn't matter, I'll add some water.'

Another small reminder that Margret had been away for two days. Joanie felt his shoulders tense. This meal felt like a test. They went through to the lounge and Sammy told him what Annabelle was up to in her new job and that she herself would be starting in a couple of weeks. He'd forgotten all about it, what with her zooming off to Europe and the baby.

'Annabelle and I are thinking of getting a flat together in Southampton.'

'You can stay here,' Joanie offered. 'It's still your home, and as you'll be working so close it seems silly to spend all that money on somewhere else.'

'I'm not sure I can live here Dad, no offence to you and Mum but since being at university, I kind of got used to having my own space.'

'You've got your own room, you can come and go as you please, we're not that strict are we?'

Sammy smiled for the first time. 'It's called independence Dad. You should be pleased; loads of people I know are still living with their parents at twenty-five. Hey, you wanted me to go to University and get a career, it's all part and parcel.'

Joanie knew she was speaking sense but he couldn't help feeling rejected.

'Your mother should be here soon.'

'Oh? I thought she was visiting Granny G.' He could hear the disappointment in her voice. It saddened him, at what point did a daughter reject her own mother he thought. At the point when she's about to kill her unborn child came the unbidden answer. Sammy was looking at him quizzically.

'She was, but we'd both like to see you, you've barely told us a thing about your travels.'

It was the best thing he could have said, she immediately jumped up and ran to get some photos from her bag. As they were looking through the third packet Margret arrived.

Joanie saw Sammy's face change, the smile slid away and was replaced by a guarded look. He got up to greet his wife in the hall. She was hanging her coat in the cupboard, her overnight bag at the bottom of the stairs. They kissed briefly and then Joanie nodded towards the kitchen.

'Is everything alright?' Margret whispered.

Joanie shrugged and nodded and then pointed at the wine.

'Ummm, you have been busy.' She smiled and accepted the glass.

Sammy was busy putting the photos away when they went back into the lounge but Margret persuaded her to keep them out, and while Joanie went to see to the lasagne he could hear their voices and even a couple of laughs. At least talking about Europe was neutral ground although it occurred to Joanie that in one of those Eastern cities, the baby must have been conceived. Or maybe it was earlier, he didn't actually know how far gone she was. Perhaps Margret knew. The lasagne looked passable and he put it on the table. He emptied a bag of salad into a bowl and shouted that it was ready.

Margret asked him why there were no mushrooms, but they all agreed it tasted fine although he saw Sammy remove a particularly large creamy looking lump and push it to the side of her plate.

'Have you noticed the leaves in the park since you've been

back? Gorgeous colours this year, I really ought to take my easel and try and capture it.' Margret chatted.

'I used to love the leaves in the park, when the council swept them into those massive piles and we'd jump straight into the middle.' Sammy laughed.

'I hope you don't still do that.' Joanie interrupted.

'Oh Dad, don't be such a stickler. Where's your sense of fun?'

Joanie wondered if he had any. When was the last time he'd really laughed or even just enjoyed himself? Tania arose unbidden with her red fingernails gripping his hand. Fun? It was what Kelly had been trying to explain was important to keep in a marriage. There certainly wouldn't be any fun for Joanie for a while. Not with the case still hanging over him.

'You remember when Sammy was small and we used to swing her through the leaves in the woods on Bishop's Hill. I seem to remember you had as much fun as Sammy. You were only about this high.' Margret turned to Sammy and put her hand slightly below the height of the table, and then her face fell and she let her hand drop. She bit her lip and looked across at Joanie. There was a tense pause.

'Look, I'm sure I'll have children one day, just not now OK?' he could see tears welling in Sammy's eyes. Margret was staring fixedly at him.

'Your father and I just want you to know that there are other options. Lots of couples out there can't have children of their own. You could always put it up for adoption.' Margret tried to lay her hand on top of Sammy's but she yanked it away.

'Adoption? Are you crazy? Do you think I could go through nine months of pregnancy and then just give it away? That's worse than an abortion. It's not a baby yet Mum, it's just a bundle of cells that's all. I think it would be horrible to bring an unwanted child into the world. That's just plain irresponsible.' The tears were running freely now.

Margret threw a desperate look at Joanie.

He cleared his throat, 'I don't think any of the options are easy love. But you need to be absolutely sure you're choosing the right one.'

'I am! God why did I come here? You only wanted to pin me down and make me change my mind.'

Joanie gave Margret an accusing look before turning back to his daughter.

'I'll support you in your decision. Whatever that is, I'll be there Sammy.' And he meant it, life was different now, he couldn't assume he, or Margret, knew what was best. Their youth seemed an eternity away, the norms of their day bore little resemblance to what Sammy faced. He was damned if he'd lose the love and respect of his only child.

'Whatever you need pumpkin, just say the word.'

Awkwardly he hugged his daughter in a sideways hug as Margret looked on furiously. He could see she was trying to maintain her control by scraping at the lasagne dish and offering them seconds. A placatory silence descended while Sammy blew her nose and dabbed at her eyes. Joanie was watching his wife; he could see her face twitching. She refused to meet his gaze; instead she concentrated on their daughter. Finally Sammy raised her blotchy face.

'What?' she asked her mother.

Carefully, quietly, Margret spoke. Joanie could see it was taking all her effort to remain steady. 'There is a child living inside you and I'm afraid I find it very difficult to accept that you want to get rid of it. I don't think I can agree with your choice.'

'Stop!' Sammy shouted clamping her hands over her ears.

'Oh Sammy,' Margret sighed, 'I don't hate you. It's just very difficult for me and what I believe.' Margret attempted a smile. 'OK, that's it, I've stopped. Shall we have some pudding?'

Joanie was caught off guard, he hadn't bought any pudding.

'Sure. I'll clear these away first.' Fortunately he found some ice cream in the freezer and Margret made some coffee. While the kettle boiled she went upstairs to the loo leaving Joanie and Sammy to make a start on the washing up.

'I've got an appointment Dad.' She sounded almost guilty. 'It's tomorrow at two o'clock. I'd ask Annabelle, only she's got her new job and she can't really take the time off. I thought maybe you might be able to get away for an hour or so.'

It took a minute for it to sink in. Initially Joanie thought she meant an appointment to talk to the doctor. Last time she'd talked about getting a second opinion. But no, she meant the actual abortion.

'What about Matt? Where is he hiding?'

'Oh Dad, he's not hiding, this is hard on him too. It's like he's too close to it, I don't know. If he comes, I think it will be even harder.'

'I see.' Joanie didn't, not at all. Surely the father to be, or not to be, should be the one with Sammy. He put another plate on the drying rack. 'Where will it be?'

'At the hospital, D wing.' They could hear the toilet flushing upstairs.

'Of course I'll come,' he passed her a glass to dry.

They couldn't persuade Sammy to stay the night but at least she and Margret were talking even if it was a bit stilted. Joanie closed the front door behind Sammy and went into the lounge. Margret followed.

'You didn't try very hard did you?' she accused.

What could he say? It was true, he hadn't but he hadn't wanted to either. How could he tell Margret that he was frightened of losing his own child?

'I can tell from your eyes that you're finding this as hurtful as I am,' she shook her head. 'If she goes through with this, it will leave a lasting scar mark my words. Maybe not physically but she won't forget it.'

When Joanie came out of the bathroom in his pyjamas, he found Margret sitting on Sammy's bed, her eyes wet and a tissue clamped in her hand.

'Why doesn't she come home?'

'Oh Margret.' He sat down beside her and put his arm around her shoulders. She laid her head against him.

'I saw the flowers,' Margret turned and smiled at him. 'Thank you.'

'Long overdue I believe.' Joanie squeezed her a little tighter. 'Let's go to bed.'

'No, not yet, I'll just stay here a little longer.' She smoothed her fingers along the edge of the pillow. 'I'm fine, really. You go on.'

Sid continued to crouch until his breathing felt more normal. His left leg jigged underneath him until he shifted his position ending up half sitting against a rough block of stone. Just as he started to rise, a man walked onto the bridge with a small dog on a lead. Sid shrank back against the undergrowth and held his breath; he listened to the man's footsteps and the dog tapping above him. Again he waited. Sid felt like a wild animal, his ears pricked up listening for the slightest sound. It was his phone that broke the silence. He was amazed it had remained in his pocket through the jungle. He pressed it to his ear and listened.

'Has anyone seen you?'

'N..no. Who are you?' It was that same voice again, the commanding urgent one.

'Don't worry, here's Alfie.' There was a pause and then a different voice came on the line. Sid knew exactly who it was.

'Er, hello Grandpa Sid.' There was a sniff and just when Sid was about to breathe a deep sigh of relief the friend was back on.

'Down the stream there's a bridge, ignore this one and stay in the culvert till the next one. Turn right into Joiners Lane and you'll see a blue Ford parked on the left hand side. We'll meet you there.'

Sid stared at the phone in his hand, he hadn't been given a chance to respond, let alone chat with Alfie. And yes, he was sure that had been Alfie, it had sounded like the boy at the door of the scout hut. Sid could feel his spirits rise, his friend really did have Alfie, and they were going to meet him at the next bridge. He shook his jacket, and with it his doubts fell away along with some leaves. The street was quiet, and Sid looked ahead down the culvert, the streetlight lit the first ten or twenty yards but after that it looked deeply dark. He scrambled down the opposite bank and slowly made his way into the blackness. In fact this stretch was easier. The houses backing onto the stream were closer, their fences just at the top of the rise on either side which left little room for bushes and trees, thus the vegetation was thinner and a pale moon helped to reflect back where the water lay. Not really a stream at all, just a series of muddy puddles.

His left foot was already soaked, but it didn't matter now, nothing mattered except getting to Alfie. As he approached the next bridge, he slowed down; he could hear voices, an occasional shout and a laugh. Sounded like teenagers. Sid waited trying to work out where they were located. Cautiously he climbed the bank and peered up and down the bridge to the streets beyond. He couldn't see anyone, another shout and he realised it must be coming from a garden very close. The fence was high so he pushed himself up onto the bridge, dusted himself off and turned right. There were several cars parked, but only one on the left hand side, Sid found himself hurrying, almost running towards the car.

Alfie was waiting for him inside. Sid peered through the side window, no one. He stood up and looked at the cars on the other side. There was a street lamp a short way back and the last two cars looked empty but he wasn't sure about the other one. Perhaps he'd misunderstood; Sid crossed the road and checked each car carefully. As he stood up and looked across the road again he was startled to see a man walking on the opposite pavement, a large dog padded silently alongside. He was watching Sid.

'Evening.'

Sid nodded, thrust his hands in his pockets and continued along the pavement back towards the bridge. His heart hammered. What the hell was going on? Where was Alfie, and what would that man think of him staring into all the cars?

At the bridge, Sid kept going a little way beyond and then sneaked a look behind him. The man was just disappearing from view. He turned round again and came back to the original car he had first thought was Alfie's. It was a Ford, that was for sure, and it was on the left hand side. Perhaps they'd gone into the house opposite. Sid stared at a dark doorway; there were no lights on in the house. His feet refused to move and Sid stood rooted to the spot unsure of what to do. Finally he checked that no one else was about to startle him and tried the doors of the car. The driver's door opened and Sid slid into the seat behind the wheel. Perhaps they'd left a message for him inside. He felt with his hand along the dashboard for a piece of paper and tried to see if there was anything on the passenger seat. There wasn't.

Sid began scratching at his arm, the movement becoming faster and the nails digging deeper. Where were they? This wasn't how it was supposed to be, not at all, he was wet, tired. A throb had started in his ankle and now he realised it felt hot and sore. He wished he had his knife with him; he clawed at his arm more vigorously until the pain began to help him see sense. What a fool, believing in happy endings, believing in films you could write yourself. Dr Casey had been wrong, it was impossible to re-enact his past, not when the players kept being so elusive. Was this what his dream had led to, sitting in a strange car, covered in mud, a twisted ankle with no clue as to where he was. Bastard. Fucking bastard. What kind of friend did that? Sid swung open the door and leaned to the side swinging his legs out. A hard bulge in his pocket poked awkwardly into his thigh. It was his phone. Sid paused.

Inside the car with the door shut again, Sid was studying his phone. He had to make a decision. Give up on his dream and go home, or give it one last try? Sid steeled himself, he would return the previous call, if it was answered, then he would do whatever it took to bring Alfie into his arms. If not. If not he'd rip up those pictures of Alfie. Burn every last thing he could find about his so-called friend. And then, and then, he didn't really know what he'd do, could only think about the knife in the drawer of his desk.

He thumbed the button and put the phone to his ear. For the last time he used the mobile to return the previous call.

'Where are you?'

Sid was startled; he'd barely heard it ring before the voice demanded a response.

'I..in...at the car.'

'Well you're too late now, we couldn't wait for ever. Never mind we've left you a key in the glove compartment. We have to visit his granny tonight but we'll meet you in Bournemouth tomorrow.'

Sid could feel the relief wash over him, so the dream would continue. And tomorrow he would perform the final act, the climax to all he'd dreamed. He reached into the glove compartment and his fingers curled around a cold piece of metal. He drew it out and put it to his lips, the key to Alfie.

Joanie had the file open on his desk, Ross Thorpe. Those neatly tied laces. Mr Charles' reaction in the church. An over-neat house, his open dislike of children. He'd added the papers Curtis had given him too. Quickly he thumbed through the papers and pulled out the statement that Ross Thorpe had signed. He'd been teaching at the time of Kieren's disappearance, teaching a boy named Max. Joanie tapped his finger on the paper, they had obviously followed up and the lesson checked out. But, but what if Max was also a victim? What if Ross Thorpe had a hold on several of the children he saw regularly, couldn't he use that power to manipulate an alibi for himself? He didn't get a chance to pursue such thoughts as his phone rang loudly.

'Inspector Johansen.'

'Sir, Officer Short here. We're on our way to a 999. Boy been missing since last night.'

Joanie shot up out of his seat; the curly phone wire caught and then pinged a pencil across the desk and onto the floor.

'What? How old? When was he last seen?'

'Last night, about seven at his Cub scout group. His name's Alfie Rainham, aged seven. His family live at number seven Railway Avenue.' There was a pause, 'Funny that, all sevens.'

'Time of call?' Joanie barked looking at the clock on his wall.

'Twelve minutes past nine sir.' It was now twenty-five minutes past.

'Right, carry on, I'll meet you there.'

Joanie threw open his office door.

'Meeting room NOW.' He boomed across the open-plan office. For a second there was a stunned silence, and then chairs moved, fingers grabbed paper, pen and they herded into the room opposite.

Before the door was even shut, Joanie was sketching the simple details, Officer Short had relayed over the phone, onto the whiteboard. He also scrawled the names of his 'hot' three. Ross Thorpe, Sidney White and Mr Evans. He flung the dry marker back into its cradle where it bounced hard and dropped onto the floor.

'I want 4 teams of two. I want these three men found now.' Joanie looked quickly at the faces round the room. 'Where the hell is Gary?'

'Day off sir.' Kelly replied.

'Call him in, I want everyone on this.' Joanie paired them up and gave each pair one of the names on the board, the last two officers he sent to do some preliminary checking around the scout hut. Joanie followed the men and women out of the room and went to fetch his coat. The Chief was standing in the corridor as Joanie rounded the corner.

'I need to know one thing.' The Chief stepped back against the wall to let two of Joanie's team go past.

'I have to go.' Joanie replied gruffly.

'I know, I heard.' He sized Joanie up and then he said, 'Do you think the Hempstead and Matthews cases are linked?'

Joanie had been ready to brush him off, to hurry outside; time wasn't on his side. But the question made him stop. Roger Hempstead's suicide, as Joanie saw it, was not the result of a guilty father but of a deeply troubled man who felt he'd failed his family. Failed to protect his son from some unknown beast and failed to keep his wife in a loving marriage. He couldn't believe he was the murderer of his son. And with that premise, the cases were very likely linked.

Joanie looked the chief in the eye. 'Yes.'

He watched the chief stoop ever so slightly, as if a heavy weight had just been placed onto his shoulders. He lifted his arm to Joanie and nodded at the door. Joanie needed no further encouragement.

Behind the wheel of his car, Joanie could feel his heart beat. The thrill of the chase, he mocked himself. He was also driving too fast. As the traffic lights neared, he slowed down and stopped. There was no need for flashing lights; it wasn't as if the boy had been seen bundled into a car ten minutes ago. How on earth could a boy of seven be missing for fourteen hours before someone thought it a bit odd?

The piano, it was the first thing that Joanie noticed walking into the Rainham's lounge. It stood in the corner by a standard lamp. If Officer Short hadn't already been in the middle of his questions, Joanie would have dived in. Instead he bided his time and listened. He didn't want to alarm the parents any more than they were already.

'He'd planned it earlier in the week. To sleep over at Callum's house. Callum's Dad was going to fetch him from Cubs, it was all arranged. I spoke to his mother.' Mrs Rainham talked rapidly as if convincing herself that she had done everything right.

'And how did you discover he was missing?'

'We'd arranged for them to drop Alfie home at nine this morning because he has his soccer practice at half past.' Her lip began to tremble and fresh tears bloomed in her eyes.

Joanie nodded for her to continue but it was the father who spoke next. His voice gravelly.

'It was after nine, and we didn't want him to be late, so we rang Callum's house. They said Alfie hadn't stayed over; that I'd rang and told them Alfie had been in trouble and wasn't allowed to come. They said I rang them, told them it was off.' He looked angrily pointing at his chest.

'I didn't ring anybody.'

'That's right, he didn't. We didn't use the phone last night.'

'What's Callum's surname, address and telephone number, we'll obviously need to speak to them too.' Joanie nodded at Officer Short to take notes. As he did so, Joanie stood up and walked over to the piano. He ran his hand over the smooth dark wood.

'Do you play Inspector?' it was the father who asked.

'No, but I wish I did. You?'

'Yes a little.'

'How about Alfie, does he play?' Joanie tried to sound a little offhand, as if this was of no consequence, belying the tension singing across his shoulders and down his arm onto the white keys.'

'Yes, he's just learning.' Mr Rainham looked proud for a second and then troubled.

'Are you teaching him yourself?' Joanie pushed a little further, steeling himself for the answer.

'Oh no, he goes to a proper piano teacher.'

Joanie wished he could stop it there, stop the words from forming, wishing he could back track fourteen hours, could he have prevented Alfie being taken? Joanie clamped down on his thoughts and turned around to smile at Mr Rainham.

'And who is that?'

'Mr Thorpe,' came the damning reply.

The air was still and cool outside; Joanie had excused himself from the family and stood in their front garden. The sun was hidden by grey clouds; he breathed in deeply and watched a golden leaf float gently downwards from the tree in the front garden. There were still some pink roses along the front border, the edges of the petals turning brown.

All his nerve endings were shouting for Ross Thorpe. If only they'd had one more day, or maybe only yesterday evening. Joanie thought about what he'd been doing at seven o'clock yesterday when Alfie disappeared. Why was life so unfair? Had he really made the wrong choice, chosen his family over a murderer?

He rang Kelly. She should be at Thorpe's house, but it was engaged. Cursing he phoned Curtis who was following up on Mr Evans, 'Well?'

'He's here sir, with a hangover and his girlfriend. Looks like they've got a reasonable alibi for last night.'

'Fine. Get a statement, then get back to the office, it's Ross Thorpe we need.'

'We're almost done, what about Sidney White?'

Curtis was right, it was his next call, but it wasn't Sidney he wanted to find.

Joanie tapped the phone against his cheek; he could feel his shoulders tensing. Next he checked in with Barry.

'We're on the Woodlands road sir.'

'What are you doing there?' Joanie was getting irritated fast. They should have been at Sidney White's flat.

'We've broken down sir.'

'What? For Jesus' sake!' Joanie shouted at the tree in the front garden and then swung round. Inside the lounge window, heads were still bowed, thank goodness for double-glazing.

Finally he rang Kelly again, she answered on the third ring.

'Hi Joanie.' He could already tell by the disappointment in

her voice that she hadn't found him.

'He's not there?' Joanie confirmed.

'No. House looks empty although there's a car in the drive. We're knocking on a couple of doors to ask the neighbours.' Kelly tried to sound encouraging.

Joanie thought hard about what they knew of Ross Thorpe, could he justify a forced entry? Probably not, at least not yet.

'Keep me posted.'

Joanie decided to leave and visit Sidney White himself. He needed to prove his conviction that Sidney wasn't their man, and Ross definitely was. He looked back over his shoulder through the lounge window; Officer Short and WPC Bradley were quite capable of taking the detailed statements from the family.

On Compton Drive, everything looked rather peaceful, someone was out washing their car, and a lady with a tiny dog on a pink lead was tottering along the pavement. Joanie looked up at the side window of Sidney's flat. There was nothing to see. He climbed out of the car but before he could shut the door, a police car came swinging into the road, zoomed up to Joanie and parked just behind him.

Curtis got out and stared at Joanie.

'What are you doing here?' Joanie couldn't keep the annoyance out of his voice.

'Barry called us, said they'd got stuck.' Curtis shrugged his shoulders. 'We thought you were with the family,' he added as way of further explanation.

Joanie couldn't very well tell them to go away, it was only right that they should follow up where the other team couldn't.

'Right come on then,' he nodded at Curtis. A small smile flickered across his face; he could prove to Curtis too, that Sidney White was innocent. They stepped away from the cars and another policeman got out, Joanie turned and acknowledged the other officer, 'Wait by the car, you'll know if we need help.'

The front door was locked; Curtis knocked and rang the bell several times.

'Go and phone the station and get the supermarket number, maybe he's at work.'

Curtis nodded and went back to the police car.

Joanie turned his back and looked up at the sky as if for inspiration. It had been odd bumping into Sidney only yesterday evening. He'd looked different, and now that Joanie concentrated on it, he realised that Sidney had looked kind of happy. But about what? He could see Curtis by the car talking on the phone, he caught Joanie's eye and shook his head frowning. Good grief, Joanie squeezed his hand around the penknife in his pocket, was he, even now, not facing the possible truth about Sidney White? Time to stop he decided, no more excuses. Looking at the door, he noted the cheap new-looking lock. He pulled out his penknife and a small paperclip and got to work.

'He's not there, and not due in until twelve today.' Curtis was back at his shoulder. 'Hey, it's open.' For a second he looked startled and then stared hard at Joanie.

'Yes, funny, I thought it was locked too,' Joanie watched Curtis face.

'You..' Curtis began but Joanie raised his hand.

'I guess we didn't turn the handle far enough.' Joanie added innocently. The cold blue eyes in front of him took on an icy glare. 'Perhaps I won't need to follow up on that press leak.' Joanie met Curtis' accusing look with his own. Stalemate. Joanie waited for Curtis to acknowledge the deal with a slight nod of his head before stepping through the doorway.

The flat was empty, of people at least. But Joanie noted the things, the details that spoke of recent activity, the thrown back sheets on the bed, the mud in the hall and up the stairs. A half-finished bowl of cornflakes on the desk next to a sheet of paper with three numbers on it:

7:36

8:08

8:36

'Train times?' Joanie wondered.

Curtis looked too, 'Or bus times.'

'Note them down.'

They were careful not to accidentally touch or move things; Joanie used his hanky on the kitchen door to push it open wider. Back in the main room, he used it again to pull open the desk drawer. It was the pictures. Joanie could feel himself drawn to them again, the fine lines, the careful sketches that somehow seemed at odds with a murderer. The detail, the softness. He picked up a few at random wondering if he could read more into them. Nothing. He was about to put them back when the one on top, left in the drawer stared up at him. It was a face he knew. Carefully Joanie laid the first pictures aside and pulled out the new sketch. Different to all the other drawings in only one respect. This was the face of a man. A man Joanie had met before.

20

The waves rumbled across the pebbles. Sid watched the foam dance over the smooth boulders. The sea looked grey, matching a lead sky. Sid has his hands thrust deep into his pockets. A cool breeze chilled his neck and circled around his legs making his trousers flap. He looked down the beach; a man was throwing stones into the water for a Labrador to fetch. The dog leaping into the waves and splashing back eager to do the same again.

Sid turned and walked back up the beach towards the promenade, more people were around now, the sea front coming to life. His ankle throbbed, the swelling had gone down in the night, but now he noticed his sock looked stretched and again it felt hot. A couple of the cafes were opening up, a woman, wearing an apron was placing a blackboard by the walkway; another was carrying a stack of chairs from inside. Ahead of him was the pier, where most of the noise and people seemed to be. He fancied a warmer place to stop than these open fronted cafes. So he trudged along keeping his hand tight around the key. In fact he'd been holding it tight ever since he'd left the car yesterday evening. Held it under his pillow last night, clenched in his fist all through the train journey early this morning. It was the one concrete item he had that held his mind steadfastly on his dream. It was a real key and would unlock a real door, to a real boy. Sid couldn't help smiling to himself, and his steps quickened slightly.

It was while he was eating a bacon sandwich and sipping a coffee that the doubts reappeared. He was opposite an amusement arcade; the flashing lights and noises clear even through the glass of the cafe. It reminded him of the one he'd frequented as a boy, never to spend money, just to watch, to look, to pretend. The owner was a forbidding woman, tall with what looked like a steel bosom. They were all scared of her, she didn't like kids. But if you stayed out of her way, which of course George did, then it was a nice place to go. The noises, the fascination with winning, he was always drawn to that delicious sound of coins tumbling and sometimes overflowing. He'd round a corner and there would be someone, smiling, their hands cupping round the machine that chinked and spat the winnings too fast. He dreamed of winning enough money to run away, to buy his own house in Blackpool, and have all the ice cream he could ever eat. Occasionally he'd find a coin that someone had dropped, or had rolled underneath one of the machines, it would take him a long time to decide which machine to use it in, and every time he did, the coin disappeared. Swallowed whole. No winnings. No exciting chink and drop. Always a disappointment. Like his life really. He didn't run away, there was nowhere to go, and no money to run with. Good luck didn't shine on Sid. And that's when his thoughts moved to Alfie, and could he really believe that he would see and hold the boy of his dreams? Surely not, when had Sid ever been lucky? When had he ever had what he wanted?

A face pressed itself to the glass right in front of Sid's nose. He threw himself back in his chair.

'Sid' a voice yelled through the glass and the unmistakeable face broke into a huge grin. David. What on earth was David doing here?

'Hey Sid, what are doing?' David had thrust open the cafe door and marched across to his table. He dropped into a seat and bared all his teeth.

'Er, Hi.' Sid wasn't sure he knew why he was here. But his hand quickly found the key in his pocket and he gripped it tighter. 'I'm here to see a friend.'

'Me too,' replied David, 'Only Roddy's not coming today, his Dad's sick so he's not going to the meeting, but Mum's going so I'll have to be on my own, but that's OK. Still got my ten pounds.' David opened his sweaty palm to reveal a ten-pound note.

'What meeting?' Sid could feel his own hands beginning to sweat, of all people why did it have to be David?

'It's Mum's support group, I used to go, but me and Roddy think it's boring, so we always come here instead. Then we all have lunch together, I have to meet Mum at twelve thirty.'

'What are you going to do with that?' Sid nodded at the money in David's hand.

'Spend it,' he grinned again and nodded out of the window, 'in there.'

Sid followed his gaze to the flashing lights across the road. Of course, he should have remembered, this was a monthly outing for David; he'd often talked about it, coming to Bournemouth to play the arcade games.

'Why don't you come with me? Maybe you'll win.' David was standing again.

Sid looked up and wondered at David's enthusiasm. He looked back at the table, his coffee was almost finished and there were only crumbs on his plate. The key was warm in his pocket, there was time. Maybe the key would bring him luck.

'Alright then.'

They crossed the road and entered a barrage of jingling

machines, each flashing for their attention. Sid followed David to the centre where change machines were placed. The ten-pound note was sucked in and out spat a bunch of coins. Maybe David would be his lucky charm, maybe David could win for them, provide enough money for Sid to take Alfie somewhere special. Maybe forever. Sid let his mind wander as he followed David from one machine to the next. Coins dropped, lights flashed, lemons and oranges spun round, fighting figures turned red as David fired a mock gun at a screen. Sid barely registered the activity; his mind was with Alfie, soft warm Alfie. And suddenly Sid panicked and checked his watch, it was only ten thirty. His appointment wasn't until three. Plenty of time, although he didn't know yet where the house was, needed a map to look up the address his friend had told him on the phone.

Sid turned away from the screens and stumbled out of the exit. The noises made it difficult to think, a map, he needed a map. And there as if put just for Sid's benefit was a large cabinet by the road offering maps for a pound. He fished around in his pocket and pulled out the correct coin. Out flopped a foldout map with an index of street names. Sid unfolded it and began to study the list.

A hand gripped his shoulder. 'What are you doing Sid?' It was David staring at the map.

Sid could feel himself getting annoyed; the amusement arcade had been a distraction, a silly distraction reminding him of dreams gone by. But today was about another dream altogether, and he didn't want David messing it up for him.

'Nothing, I have to go and meet my friend.'

'What, now?'

'No, well, yes actually.' Sid jumped on a reason to lose David.

'OK, well I've spent my ten pounds so we can go, which way is it?' David ran his finger in a haphazard way over the map.

'Get your finger off, I'm trying to see.' Sid found the street and checked the scale; it looked to be about a mile and a half away. He could walk it in half an hour or so. Perhaps he should go there now to check it out, just to be sure.

Sid looked across the street to check he was oriented correctly and then set off left.

'What's the name of your friend?' David was trotting by Sid's left heel like a dog. Sid had a huge urge to kick him out of the way.

Sid stopped and turned to David. 'You can't come with me.'

The smile disappeared from David's face, it seemed like all his features took a downward turn, the eyes slanted down, the corners of his mouth, even his cheeks seemed to droop.

'He's not expecting you, only me.' Sid tried to explain, a small knot tying itself deep in his stomach.

David looked down at his feet and scuffed his foot on the ground. Sid looked down too. David was wearing worn trainers, the end of one almost threadbare, the other deeply scored. One of his laces lay splayed across the shoe and on the pavement.

'Your shoe lace is undone.' Sid pointed.

David stuck out his bottom lip but didn't move.

Sid sighed, crouched down and tied it, securing it with a double bow. For a moment he paused, thinking back, when he'd been lying on the ground in the supermarket car park, seeing the shoes of his attackers. David wrestling with the security guard and finally breaking free to thump one of Sid's attackers. He stood up and looked at David thoughtfully. He had protected him, David was a true friend. Their times together working the trolleys, their breaks, lunches, chocolate cake, all those times when David had made Sid feel safe, feel normal. That's what a true friend was, and maybe that was exactly who Sid needed with him today. A true friend. It was his dream after all, and he got to choose the actors.

'Alright, then.'

'Really?' David's face bloomed immediately.

'Come on then.'

David slid his arm through Sid's and marched on.

Joanie stood outside Sid's flat; he'd already sent Curtis back to follow up on the numbers from Sidney's desk. The phone pressed against Joanie's ear, this time Kelly answered immediately.

'Hold on, I'm with the people who live next door,' Kelly paused and Joanie could hear a door open, then close. 'OK, this is what we have: Ross Thorpe has apparently gone to visit his mother, he'll be away for the whole weekend.'

Joanie could feel the throb behind his eyeballs. Could Ross Thorpe and Sidney White really be working together? If only he'd gone back to work last night, if only he'd gone to see Mr Charles before... but enough, he could go on all day with that kind of thing, what mattered was finding the boy before it was too late.

'Where did they say his mother lived?'

'Bournemouth, and there's something else, we found out he has two cars, the one out front and another he normally keeps in the garage, apparently he went in that one. Seems strange to me.'

'You're right, why would a bachelor have two cars, it's not a classic car or something special is it?'

'Nope, not according to the Phillips's.'

'OK, get on to the DVLC and get a fix on the other car. Kelly.'

'Yes sir?'

Joanie paused, 'We can't find Sidney White either.' There was silence at the other end of the phone. 'We HAVE to find Ross Thorpe. Sidney White drew a picture of him.'

'What? A picture of Ross Thorpe?' Kelly exclaimed loudly in Joanie's ear. 'Oh Christ.'

'Do what you can Kelly, I'm heading back to base.'

Joanie was glad to find the office was alive with activity. Nobody was taking a back seat on this one. Barry waved a sheet at him as he walked through.

'So you got towed back then?' Joanie frowned.

'Yep, sorry sir.'

'Not your fault, what have you got there?'

'The DVLC came back and said there's only one car registered for Ross Thorpe at that address.' Barry gave him the fax.

Joanie raised his eyebrows. That meant the second car was illegal, or possibly, a car registered somewhere else, perhaps registered at his mother's?

'Barry, get back to them and find out all the cars registered to any Thorpes in Bournemouth.' Joanie dismissed him and went into his office leaving the door open.

The report came back with twenty possible matches. Joanie scanned the list, nothing jumped out. Five of the addresses were linked to Mrs, Ms or Miss Thorpes, only 2 of which were of a likely age to be Ross Thorpe's mother. Joanie didn't consider his options for long, this time he acted, knowing that for once he was right about this case. Ross Thorpe had taken the boy to his mother's in Bournemouth.

He spoke to Kelly on his way out, gave her a photocopy of the list of addresses with the two likely ones highlighted.

'Get the local police to these two addresses immediately. Warn them what we're looking for; we don't want to scare our Mr Thorpe to do anything drastic.' Like killing the boy, Joanie thought. He could only hope that Ross Thorpe would follow the previous pattern, keep the boy alive for a while before killing and dumping the body.

Joanie shoved open the door to the stairwell and almost collided with Curtis who was on his way in.

'Sorry Sir.'

'Curtis.' They faced each other. 'Kelly will fill you in.' He strode down the stairs.

'Wait,' Curtis had caught him up. 'I checked up on those numbers, the ones from Sidney White's flat.' his eyes were shining. Joanie paused with his hand on the door to the car park. He nodded for Curtis to continue.

'They're train times, all bound for Weymouth, although two are slow trains and the other fast. I checked what stations they all stopped at; there are only three in common, Southampton, Bournemouth and Weymouth.'

Joanie couldn't help but smile, Curtis was doing well, but then he frowned. So Sidney White was also on his way to Bournemouth. It couldn't be a coincidence, not when he'd drawn a sketch of Ross Thorpe; it hadn't been an exact likeness, but the classic nose, strong features. What could have possibly drawn those two together?

'That's where I'm headed, to Bournemouth.' Joanie put a hand on Curtis' shoulder, 'Good work.' Joanie opened the door and went outside.

As he opened the car door, he realised Curtis was just a few steps behind.

'Is there more?'

'No, only, don't you want a colleague with you?' Curtis' mouth twitched. 'Sir?'

Joanie looked at the young man, the charming smile growing across his face, he also thought about the icy glare at Sidney's front door when Joanie had broken the rules. Perhaps they'd both been right, Curtis so sure Sidney was the perpetrator, and Joanie sure it must be someone else. Now it seemed that Sidney White was working in collaboration with Ross Thorpe. Curtis deserved to come.

'Let's go, you can choose the music, so long as it's classical.'

Sidney found it difficult to concentrate on the map with David's incessant chat, however, they only went wrong twice, turning up a road too soon because there was no street sign, and then going too far along another because the layout was confusing with what looked like a forked road leading off that turned out to be two roads.

'So that's how I got my new football boots.' David paused

and sighed, 'Are we nearly there yet?'

'Yes, yes.' Sid was limping now; his ankle throb had changed into a piercing pain. And then there it was, Marley Street. Sid could feel his heart fluttering nervously, this was the street, and along here was the house. He held the key tightly as they moved down the row of terraced houses. Number thirty-two had a chipped green door. The front window was distorted by a net curtain. Sid checked his watch, it was quarter to twelve. He was almost three hours early. Suddenly he felt frightened, he wasn't supposed to be here yet, his friend had said very precisely. David reached for the doorbell.

'No!' Sid smacked his hand away.

'Ow''

'Wait.' What should they do? Go and sit and wait somewhere? His ankle wasn't going to last much longer and the key was burning a hole in his hand. He drew it out and looked at it carefully. He smiled; this was his dream, his choice, Dr Casey had said that you make it like a film, change some of the facts. He could make this film just as he wanted. And if he wanted to go in the house early, then he would. He slid the key into the lock, shut his eyes tight and turned it. The lock slid back and the door swung inwards soundlessly.

They stepped straight into what must be the lounge. White sheets covered a chair and a sofa; nothing else was in the room, not even pictures on the walls.

'Where's your friend?' said David.

'Sshhhh.' Sid put his finger to his lips; he could feel his heart thumping madly. There didn't seem to be any sound.

'Oh!' David giggled. 'Are you going to boo him?'

Sid stepped through the only other doorway, a small space with steep stairs disappearing up to his left. Ahead lay a kitchen, it was bare, cupboard doors, an empty sink. It certainly didn't look lived in.

Sid turned around and faced a grinning David who was pointing up the stairs and keeping a finger to his lips.

'Wait here.' Sid whispered. Holding the handrail, he climbed cautiously up. He couldn't deny the fear pounding in his chest, despite the empty appearance of the house. It was the control. He felt he'd lost control of his dream, of the film he was trying to create. There was a key actor, not of his making, not following the script. At least not the script in Sid's head.

At the top of the stairs, another flight disappeared even higher; on this floor lay a bathroom and a bare room at the front. Sid stared at the green carpet; a dark stain bruised the floor by the netted window. Back in the stairwell, he peered upwards. David's back was disappearing through a doorway at the top.

'Wait!' And that was when Sid heard a noise. It sounded like a squeak, not of a mouse, louder, more metallic. Sid grabbed the rail and hauled his sore ankle up the last stairs, chasing David into the room above.

'Who the fuck are you?' the voice was loud. Sid pushed David out of the way so he could get through the doorway into the bedroom at the top.

'You're three hours early you imbecile, and what the hell are you doing bringing him with you?' The voice belonged to a man, tall, blond, a classic long nose that added authority to his face. The man on the bench. For a moment Sid cringed from his wrath but then he saw the boy. Alfie lay on the bed, his blond curls spread across the white pillow. His clear skin pale in the wan light from the dormer window. His lips were red, full, painted onto his perfect face. Sid felt lighter, felt as if he was rising into the air, a joyous feeling flooding his body. He took a step closer to the bed and smiled at Tommy, beautiful, gorgeous innocent Tommy. An arm grabbed his shoulder.

'Sid!' He shook the arm away angrily and touched Tommy's hand. It was warm and deliciously soft. He was in time, in time to complete the dream.

'Sid Please!' an urgent cry that only fuelled Sid's annoyance. He looked up. The room swayed somewhat, white walls becoming tinged with yellow, the curtains patterned with the flowers of his childhood. And there in front of him was what must be Uncle Henry. Evil, hurtful Uncle Henry. Now was the time to act, now was the time to bring this dream to its rightful conclusion. Sid lunged, the figure twisted and broke free leaving Sid to collapse against the wall. He turned round to see a huge figure looming over him, a glint of something in his hand. Sid would not fail this time. That soft hand had been warm, he wouldn't let Tommy die, he wouldn't let that hand go cool, not ever again. With a scream Sid grabbed his attacker; the noise rang in his ears, and was joined by a higher pitch from the bed. Sid pulled, pushed, grabbed at something that stung his hand, clawed at the man's face and all the while the scream echoed around his skull. It was all around him, inside him, outside him like water flowing into all the spaces. A noise so consuming there wasn't room to think. Sid clung on, even when his head connected with the door, he thrust himself forwards, his head slamming against Uncle Henry. And still he screamed. They stumbled, as one. There were too many arms, had Uncle Henry turned in to a four-armed monster? Locked together, they were falling. Sid felt the air breeze through his hair and then he landed on a body and felt it crunch beneath him. They slid and tumbled and this time Sid's head hit the wall. He sat dazed staring at something between his legs. It was hairy and matted with blood. The screaming in his head was dying away. A distant sound of feet on carpet thundered away like the rain on the roof. The hairy thing moved and a distinct grunt came from beneath Sid's leg. His hand was roaring with pain, and when he looked, there appeared to be something stuck in it. He pulled the knife out and marvelled at its fine blade and then he looked down at Uncle Henry's head and smiling, raised the knife over and over and over.

His arm trembled with tiredness by the time he finished, and he sat regaining his breath before looking up at the long dark stairs above him. A mountain that had to be climbed, the last mountain to the prize of his life. Using his one good hand, Sid grabbed the handrail and hauled himself into an upright position, his ankle gave way and he thumped to his knees almost falling again on the uneven body beneath him. Awkwardly with a kind of sideways shuffle, Sid stayed on his knees, one elbow and his hand on the rail; gradually he made his way to the top. As Sid crawled into the room, he noted Tommy's foot first of all. It moved quickly, shooting out of sight under the bed. Sid sighed, this truly was his dream come true. Slowly Sid wrestled his body underneath the springs, catching his hair as he moved towards the trembling boy. Tommy whimpered and tucked his head in, shutting his eyes tight.

The roads were relatively clear and Joanie found he was coasting along at a steady eighty. It would only take an hour at this rate. His mind wandered across the fields, the horses grazing, the trees almost bare leaving brown and yellow patches on the grass. Would Alfie get to play in those leaves again like Sammy used to? The local police were on their way, and Joanie would just have to trust, and hope of course. Hope that the boy was at least alive. Joanie glanced across at Curtis, and wondered what damage he'd received as a boy and the legacy it had given him. And what of Sidney White, what legacy did he have from a convicted uncle?

'Sir?'

'Nothing, I was just thinking.' Joanie concentrated back on the road.

'They'll get him, I'm sure of it. And Sidney White, I think your hunch is correct, about the house in Bournemouth. How long do you think they've been working together?'

But that was it; Joanie still didn't think they were; yet with so much now stacked against the two of them, how could he deny the connection?

'I don't know.'

They drove on in silence until Joanie's phone went. He hit the hands-free and listened, it was Kelly.

'They've got him. The first address of the two on your list. Both Thorpe and the boy. They're keeping them at the house until you arrive.'

'Great. And the boy is OK?'

'Seems completely fine from what they've said.' Kelly answered, surprise in her voice.

Joanie felt a slight nervousness tick at the corner of his eye. That was easy. Too easy. And where was Sidney? They were coming towards the exit and Curtis would have to map read them to the address.

As they pulled into the street it was obvious which house by the police car parked up outside. Joanie and Curtis leapt out and went straight to the door. Joanie pushed hard on the tiny bell and heard it tinkle gently within the house. The door was opened in seconds by a tall uniformed officer. Joanie showed his badge and walked straight in.

'They're in the kitchen.' The officer pointed towards the rear of the hallway.

Joanie marched through and stopped in the doorway. A blond man was sitting at the table, a young boy to his left, striking in the way his face mirrored that of his father at the table. They stared at Joanie, the father baffled, the son nervous. Curtis leaned over his shoulder, giving a surprised gasp.

'Shit.' Joanie muttered, spun on his heel and stormed back towards the front door. 'You. With me. Outside now!' he yelled at the officer that had let him in.

Out in the street, Joanie and Curtis stood facing the confused policeman.

'Who's checked the other address?' Joanie demanded.

'But, but, we've got them, they match the description we were given, and he is Mr Thorpe.'

'Answer the bloody question, who's checked the other address?' Joanie could feel the heat rising up his head. The headache that had bloomed earlier that morning came back with a vengeance.

'Well no one sir. Once we'd found them here, there wasn't any point.' The man looked worried, and well he might thought Joanie.

'Get your personnel to the other address right now! And leave that poor kid and his father alone.'

Turning to Curtis he said. 'Let's go, see if we can beat these bloody numbskulls.'

They jumped into the car and Joanie shot forwards, pausing at the junction only long enough to shout at Curtis.

'Come on. Fastest route.'

Curtis was struggling with the map across his knee, his face hunched over the street names.

'Got it. Head northwards.' Curtis stabbed the map with his finger.

Joanie stared at him.

'Right, go right.'

They could hear the siren behind them but Joanie refused to let it pass, instead concentrating hard on the traffic, ducking and cutting as best he could. The traffic opened for them as the siren kept pace behind. Curtis concentrated, firing out directions and street names.

'This is it, left here, number thirty two.'

Joanie squealed the tyres round the corner and braked hard to try and read the numbers, then sped up quickly again coming to a stop further along opposite a green door. They jumped out. The police car had stopped back at the corner, and they watched one of the officers get out and disappear round the back of the houses.

'At least they're not completely stupid.' Joanie said.

The car screeched in behind Joanie's and a tall officer joined them at the door. They waited until his colleague radioed from the back of the house before doing anything further.

'What's your name?' Joanie questioned the officer as he put

his radio away.

'MacKenzie sir.'

'Well MacKenzie, there could be two men in there. We don't know for sure.' Joanie knocked hard. 'Get the door open, then take it careful, we'll be right behind you.' If there was going to be a tussle, Joanie was wise enough to know that age and fitness were not on his side, far better to let the young blood go first.

MacKenzie nodded, pulled out his baton and then put his shoulder to the door. It took two shoves before the lock gave, splintering the doorjamb in the process.

The officer darted in, and disappeared into a room beyond. Joanie and Curtis followed. White sheets draped the two pieces of furniture, sheets that made Joanie think of the piano teacher's front room. The house felt still. Curtis went and stood at the bottom of the stairs and looked up, he raised his eyebrows at Joanie who nodded. Cautiously Curtis disappeared upwards closely followed by MacKenzie. Joanie ignored the stairs and walked through into the kitchen. The white cupboard units stared blankly back. Joanie wiped his finger along the marbled worktop and then held it up to his face. Smooth and clean. Joanie nodded to himself; Ross Thorpe had been here. But then he noticed a mark on the edge by the back door. He looked carefully, it was a dark smear, Joanie leant closer so that the grey light from the window made the smudge a little clearer. It looked like dark rust, like blood. Joanie paused, his eyes like that of cat switching to and fro across everything in the room and there it was, a bright red spot on the floor. Joanie knelt down, it was clearly wet and fresh, and this time he was sure it was blood. Through the back door he could see the other policeman looking up at the windows on the first floor.

There was a shout from above; Joanie braced himself in the kitchen doorway, looked around for a weapon but saw nothing but the smooth surfaces. Someone was running down the stairs, Joanie leaned back against the nearest cupboard, keeping himself out of view until the last second.

Curtis burst into the front room.

'Sir?'

'Behind you.' Joanie stepped forwards and put a hand on his shoulder.

'Fuck!' Curtis leapt from under his hand. His eyes wide. 'There's a body sir. A man.'

'Where?' Joanie could feel an icy hand clutching at his chest.

'Blocking the stairs.'

'There's another floor?' it had seemed just a tiny terrace, two up, and two down.

'Yes sir, into an attic room I presume.' Curtis was breathless, Joanie could see his chest rising and falling too fast.

'Go outside and get an ambulance and back up.' Joanie went back to the stairway and shouted up. 'MacKenzie?'

'Yes sir.' His face appeared at the top of the stairs. 'He's dead sir.'

'Have you been to the top?' The icy hand was clutching Joanie tightly now, where was the boy?

'No sir.'

Joanie used the handrail and climbed the narrow stairs. The smell got to him first, that distinct tang that reminded Joanie of the butcher's shop his mother used to go to. At the top, an empty room and a bathroom and the start of more stairs going up, but sprawled across these stairs was a misshapen man. At least that was how he appeared; the angles were all wrong and it made Joanie shudder. The light was poor and the man's face was buried against the bottom step. Joanie crouched down and touched the neck, it felt cool, certainly no pulse.

'Do you want me to go up?' MacKenzie asked.

Joanie stared up towards a doorway that shed some light onto the top stairs. As he stood there, he thought he heard something faint, perhaps it had been from outside. But there it was again, a lilting sound. MacKenzie had heard it too, his head tilted to one side.

'They're on their way sir.' Curtis appeared beside Joanie. 'He's been hacked pretty bad,' he commented pointing to the pool of blood and the smears down the wall.

'Shh.' Joanie cautioned him and the three of them stood still, their ears pricked to the sound that was beginning to gain clarity, it was singing. Soft, a little croaky, but definitely singing, and it was coming from the open doorway at the top of the stairs.

Joanie touched Curtis' arm and pointed for him to proceed up the stairs. Curtis attempted to step over the body, but it was too large, too sprawled for Curtis to get any kind of footing up the stairs.

'Step on it.' Joanie whispered.

Curtis looked back surprised, grabbed the handrail and trod on the body, quickly gaining the first visible stair. Joanie followed suit, stepping where Curtis had, on the dead man's bottom. The room was tiny; Curtis stepped cautiously to the end of the bed and pointed downwards. He was right; the singing was coming from under the bed. Curtis made as if to crouch but Joanie shook his head forcefully, he didn't want one of his officers to get kicked or worse in the face. Instead he pointed at the mattress and mimed lifting it. From what Joanie could see, it was an old-fashioned metal sprung bed. Joanie silently counted to three, mouthing the words at Curtis and then they heaved the bottom of the mattress upwards leaning it back against the wall.

One eye stared up through the metalwork. A wild frightened eye. Alive, thank god, Alfie was alive. It was difficult to make out the big lump of clothing beneath the criss-cross of springs. Joanie leaned down trying to make sense in the gloom. The boy was curled up tight and bound to a large mound, it was this lump that was singing.

'....down will come baby, cradle and all.' There was a pause and then the familiar rhyme started again. 'Hush a bye baby,..'

Curtis looked at Joanie, incomprehension clear in his eyes. Joanie put his mind to the body on the stairs, despite the gloom, the matted head had looked blond, and the man beneath the bed that was gripping Alfie so tightly was dark.

Joanie cleared his throat. 'Sidney White.' His voice was loud in the little room.

The singing paused only briefly, and then continued on. '..When the bough breaks..'

He might have a knife, could strangle the boy, anything. The space was so limited, Joanie wasn't even sure they could get the bed out. He went back to the stairs.

'MacKenzie.' Outside he could hear a siren approaching. 'Give us a hand.' Between them they managed to shift the mattress towards and out of the doorway, it slipped out of MacKenzie's grasp and slid down to lie on top of the body at the bottom.

'Get it off him and into the spare room.' Joanie hissed.

Back in the bedroom, the wild eye continued to watch them through the springs.

'Are you alright?' Joanie whispered to the boy.

There was the slightest movement, and then the boy shut his eye quite deliberately and opened it wide again. Joanie smiled down at him, tried to send him the most encouraging vibes that he could, given the situation. 'We're going to get you out Alfie.'

'...on the tree tops, when the wind blows,..' the singing continued, sometimes the voice cracked and a word got lost.

'What now?' MacKenzie was back, sweating. 'Shit, who's that?' He hadn't seen into the room before, he'd been stuck in the doorway as they'd pushed the mattress out.

'I think we should try and get the frame out. Get some more help, I don't want that metal frame landing on the body.' Joanie sent MacKenzie away again.

Curtis was staring at the couple under the bed frame, Joanie could see high colour on his cheeks.

'It's alright, we'll get him out. He's not being hurt Curtis.' Joanie could see that Curtis was near breaking point, that it wouldn't take much for him to leap at the figure beneath. There was talking from the stairway and then MacKenzie reappeared.

'Ready, we can make a chain to get it down.'

'Right.' Joanie nodded at Curtis and they began to lift the frame.

Joanie noticed the sweat under his arms for the first time. The bed clanged against the wall and then scraped as they tried to turn it on its side without knocking the ceiling or the figures on the floor.

'...the cradle will rock...' So long as the singing didn't stop, at least not yet. Joanie had seen this kind of behaviour before. A woman by the name of Tina Baker in a high security hospital. Hers hadn't been singing, it had been talking, the same phrase over and over. They'd been trying to interview her, trying to find out a key piece of information. She had ignored them completely, talking over and over until another patient had slammed a door in the next room. That had made her stop, look around her and then leap at the nearest orderly. She'd taken a deep gouge out of his cheek before anyone could react.

Joanie knew the bed frame would be heavy, but this was ridiculous, he could feel his left arm straining and beginning to shake with the effort, it was clear of the two on the floor, but not at an angle that would get it through the door. They tilted it upwards, banging the light, and then Joanie shuffled round the end so they could get it through the doorway. It hit the doorjamb as they leant it down again, and Joanie tensed staring at the bundled shapes.

'....breaks, the cradle will fall,..'

As soon as the bed frame had left their hands Joanie had to grab Curtis before he pounced on Sidney White.

'I'll pull him back, you can grab the boy.' Curtis had his baton in his hand.

'Wait.' Joanie wiped a hand across his forehead and took a deep breath. He could hear the frame banging against walls and ceilings as it made its way down the stairs and into the room below. Sidney's face was buried in Alfie's hair; it was amazing he could sing with his face so muffled. Alfie's open eye regarded them hopefully.

MacKenzie returned once more.

'Stand over there,' Joanie spoke quietly and pointed for MacKenzie to stand by the boy. 'If he jumps, you get the boy, Curtis will go for Sidney, and I'll go for the weapon, if he has one.'

'...down will come baby, cradle and all.'

'Sidney!' Joanie shouted this time, the singing stopped for longer but after a few seconds it continued as before. Maybe he should call in a professional, but the boy's eye was pleading now, staring at Joanie without blinking. A professional like Dr Casey. Joanie thought hard about what she'd told him. A past trauma that he still hadn't dealt with, something from his childhood most likely.

Joanie took a breath and this time he spoke firmly but didn't shout. 'George. George Boswell!'

Sidney White stopped singing. The men in the room tensed. Joanie locked onto the boy's eye watching for even the slightest flinch. The boy watched him back. Sidney let out a shuddering sigh and then he rolled away from the boy and towards Curtis.

In less than a second Curtis sat astride Sidney's back, his arms yanked back hard making him cry out in pain. Alfie was off the floor, ducked under MacKenzie's arms and flew straight into Joanie's leg. He had to stagger backwards to keep his balance. Gently, Joanie reached his hands under Alfie's armpits and lifted him up; the boy wrapped his hands around Joanie's neck and burrowed his head into Joanie's shoulder. Alfie's legs wrapped around his waist and, like a monkey, hung on tight. Joanie was startled by the physical strength of the boy, he had to pull his arm slightly from his neck so he could breathe and look down at his own feet. Slowly, Joanie carried the boy out of the room.

21

Joanie leaned against the roof of the car. It was wet but he didn't mind, he'd been standing in the drizzle for a while, could feel the cold drops seeping into his scalp.

'Can I get you anything?' It was Curtis; 'One of the guys is going to fetch some sandwiches from the corner shop.'

Joanie shook his head, staring across the road at a small patch of green hemmed in by black railings.

'Are you alright?' Curtis was still hovering.

'Fine.' Joanie dismissed him with a wave of his hand. He knew his eyes must look red. He wasn't ashamed, just tired. The tears had sprung the moment the boy was safe in his arms. He'd carried him down the stairs ignoring the undulations of the dead body under his feet, keeping Alfie's head pressed against his shoulder. The sensible thing would have been to pass the boy between them to avoid excessive disturbance to the dead body but Joanie knew the boy had been through enough, didn't need to see a dead man sprawled on the stairs or be handed like some random parcel from person to person. No, he kept a gentle but firm hold of Alfie all the way down to the street, and had only given him up in the safety of the back of the ambulance. There he had sat down on one of the beds with the boy.

'You're going to be safe now.' Joanie looked at Alfie's bright eyes. Alfie reached up and touched Joanie's wet cheek. It was the lack of tears on Alfie's face that stopped Joanie's own. He smiled at Alfie and left the van without looking back.

Joanie watched the drops gather together on the car roof and run down towards the rear window. Perhaps a sandwich would be a good idea after all, break him out of his black mood. He couldn't stop thinking that if only he'd followed up on Ross Thorpe last night; he wouldn't be standing here now knowing that Alfie had been to hell and back. Maybe he could have prevented this bizarre couple from whatever they'd had in mind, which had so obviously gone wrong.

Joanie's phone beeped, it was Kelly.

'I've got some strange news, thought you should know.'

'Oh?' Joanie pulled open the passenger door and slipped into the car. 'What is it?'

'There's been a missing person report sent in, only been missing a couple of hours, but the mother was very distraught. In fact I wouldn't have known if it hadn't been Gary who answered the call. He recognised the name.'

'Get to the point Kelly.' Joanie was feeling tired.

'It's David, Sidney White's colleague from the supermarket.'

'David?' a picture of the Down's syndrome young man eating Joanie's maltesers sprang to mind.

'And,' Kelly continued, 'he went missing in Bournemouth.'

Joanie's eyes widened, he watched out of the side window as three boiler-suited men carried a stretcher out of the house.

'Wait!' Joanie fumbled with the door handle, scrabbled out of the car and halted the men before they put the zipped body bag into the back of the ambulance. David had blond hair too, was tall like Ross Thorpe but heavier. Joanie noted a slight tremble in his hand as he unzipped the bag. He stared at the bruised face, matted with hair and blood.

'Oh shit!'

'Kelly, get back to Ross Thorpe's house, and wait for him.'

'I thought he was there with you guys?' Kelly sounded concerned.

'So did I, so did I.' Joanie sighed.

'Hey, I know it probably doesn't matter now, but I found out that Mrs Thorpe's dead.'

'What? When?'

'Three years ago.'

Joanie watched the rain dribble down the back of the ambulance. They had shut the doors and it moved off, splashing water across the pavement. The threads in Joanie's brain rearranged themselves and he looked up at the grey sky.

'When exactly?'

'January 23rd.' Three months before the Hempstead boy was killed. It felt important; Ross Thorpe had slipped through their fingers. Joanie switched off the phone and turned to Curtis. He was munching on a sandwich.

Joanie nodded at the departing ambulance. 'It wasn't Ross Thorpe.'

'What?' Curtis coughed tuna onto the pavement.

'Let's go. We can't learn any more here, the SOCO's will do the rest.'

Sidney White had already been driven away, had remained silent throughout, although Joanie knew he was compos mentis, because he'd given Joanie a nod of recognition when he'd walked out of the house.

A huge sadness weighed on Joanie. How could David have been caught in this mess? Surely Sidney White wouldn't abuse David, and surely David wasn't an abuser. Judging by the state of Sidney White's hand, and the blood all over his clothes, he'd been in a serious fight, and had most likely killed David. Did that mean that Ross Thorpe had just been a wild goose chase?

Joanie's head ached. Of course it wasn't, this was Ross's mother's house, and Sidney White had a sketch of Ross Thorpe in his desk drawer.

As they drove homewards and entered the outskirts, Joanie veered off towards the nicer end of town.

'Aren't we going to the station?'

'No, there's someone else I need to see first.' Joanie had been in deep thought, about Mr Charles' reaction in the church that day to Ross Thorpe's apparent amusement at a poor girl's fright. Kieren Matthews' neatly tied trainers. Martin Hempstead's 'clean' murder.

'Whose is this house?' They'd stopped by the curb.

'If I'm right, Ross Thorpe is implicated in three murders not two.' Joanie looked up at the heavy door with its lion knocker.

'But it was Sidney White who had Alfie, and he killed David.'

'Possibly true. But why did Sidney draw a picture of Ross Thorpe?' Joanie turned to study Curtis.

There was no answer, neither of them knew, but Joanie would discover the truth, he knew that much.

'I won't be long.'

The drizzle had turned into a persistent rain, but Joanie didn't care. The Morgan household appeared quiet. Leaves lay flattened on the ground around his feet. Joanie wondered if Morgan would let him in, after their last conversation he hadn't expected to confront him again, although it wasn't him he'd come to see. He stared up at the darkened windows, curtains were closed upstairs but the lounge ones were open.

There was a spy hole in the front door and Joanie assumed it was this she had used before opening the heavy green door.

'Inspector Johansen, he's not here I'm afraid.' She stood in the light of the hall, her hair glowing from behind. 'He's on a job in Kent for a few days.'

'Actually it was you I came to see Mrs Hempstead.'

'I see.' She pulled the door open wider. 'You'd better come in. I'll put some coffee on.'

Joanie was surprised by her kindness. It was almost as if she felt sorry for him standing in the wet on her doorstep. They went through to the kitchen where he'd first seen her at the stove. She wore a silky pink top, a pale pink that brought out the shine in her hair. He could see why Morgan might have fallen for her.

'Instant OK?'

'Sure whatever you're having, I don't mean to take up much of your time.' Her eyes had a piercing quality, one that could be misconstrued as sexual intensity.

'Mike told me, you think my husband was innocent.' She poured water into the kettle and set it on the electric base. Her movements were calm, unhurried.

'I'm not certain who killed your son Mrs Hempstead. I'm not here to give you any hope.'

'Hope? Of course you can't give me hope. My life has been changed forever. You know it doesn't really matter to me any more whether my husband or someone else killed Martin. In some ways thinking that it was Roger's fault made it easy for me to lay blame. To get through the pain by hating him. But now I'm past all that, I've lost two of the most important people in my life and I've moved on.' She filled the cups and passed one to Joanie.

'It would matter to Mike though. I think he doubts himself, I don't know what he told you Inspector.'

Joanie wasn't about to share his own thoughts on Morgan's behaviour, he cleared his throat, 'I'm sorry to rake all this up again, but I wanted to ask you about Martin, about whether he ever played an instrument.'

She raised her eyebrows, 'Interesting angle, is it relevant?'

'It's relevant to me, I can assure you.'

A worried look crossed her face and for a second Joanie caught a glimpse of the deep well of grief she had climbed out of. Cautiously she sipped her coffee.

'He played the guitar, had only been going to lessons for a

few months, but he loved it. We had to get him a three quarter size so he could get a better grip. He used to sit on the sofa strumming away despite his brother's teasing.' She shook her head, the memory adding a brief smile to her lined face.

'No other instrument?'

She shook her head, 'One's enough don't you think?'

'Of course.' Joanie felt guilty yet again, not only had he arrived unannounced, but he had booted his way into her memories, igniting her sadness. And for what? Perhaps the kid had never even set eyes on Ross Thorpe.

'My daughter Sammy learnt to play the flute, but she gave it up after a couple of years.' Joanie shrugged and gulped at his coffee.

'I think Martin would have kept going, it suited him somehow you know?'

'Sure, I didn't mean-'

'It's fine, really. He tried the piano once but not for long.'

Joanie gripped his cup tighter forcing himself to remain glued to the kitchen stool. 'I see,' he tried not to let her see his excitement. 'Privately or through school?'

'Oh privately, I don't think music is much good in schools any more, too many other subjects hogging the curriculum. Is something wrong?'

'Who was his teacher Mrs Hempstead?'

She let out a small laugh, 'God, I don't know, he only went to about three lessons. The chap was very good, by all accounts, he certainly came recommended. Martin didn't take to it, the piano nor the teacher.'

'Do you remember what he looked like?'

She frowned at him drawing her second hand around the cup, cradling it as if to protect herself. 'This is important isn't it?'

'Yes.'

'He had blond hair, I remember that, sort of classic features, and his house was so tidy. Really neat and clean, I remember thinking it was odd for a bachelor.'

Joanie put his cup back on the counter half finished. 'You've been a great help Mrs Hempstead, I'm sorry to be so rude and for disturbing you.'

As he walked down the steps, she stood in the doorframe watching him leave.

'Good luck Inspector.'

He raised a hand in reply. Luck wouldn't come into it, not now. Joanie knew he would be able to unravel this case, that Ross Thorpe was the man involved in three deaths, how Sidney White fitted into it, and the death of David was something he would find out. But for now, Ross Thorpe was wanted for murder.

Walking down the steps, Joanie glanced at his watch. Shit! Time! It was quarter to four. He was supposed to meet Sammy at the hospital.

'Get what you wanted?' Curtis questioned as Joanie slid into the driver's seat.

'Absolutely. Has Kelly called back?'

'Yes, Ross Thorpe walked into his house about five minutes ago.'

'Call her, tell her that they can arrest him on the charge of murder, Kieren Matthews' murder, we'll get him on the others later.' Joanie thrust the car into gear and shot down to the end of the street.

'How do you know?'

'Coincidences Curtis, too many coincidences, he's a slippery eel but he's well and truly slipped up this time.' Joanie thought about Sidney, his blank refusal to answer any questions, just a beatific smile, as if he was some place else, somewhere akin to heaven. Even without his help, Joanie was certain they'd discover the truth about all three crimes.

'What's the hurry?'

'I have an important appointment.' Joanie refused to elaborate further. At the hospital, he jumped out and told

Curtis to drive the car back to the station.

He found Sammy at the entrance to 'D' block. She looked red-eyed and fretful.

'I'm sorry love. I'm not too late am I?'

'Dad, where have you been? I've been trying to ring but your phone's always engaged.'

'Busy day love.' He tried to smile and took her hand giving it a squeeze. A woman and a young boy came past them through the door. The boy had freckles like Alfie. Joanie stopped and stared as the two walked across the car park.

Taking a deep breath he turned back to his daughter, 'Right, where do we go then?'

But Sammy didn't move. She was studying him thoughtfully. 'You don't want me to get rid of it do you?'

'Sammy, this isn't about me, it's you, your life, and Matt's.' Joanie could feel Alfie's arms wrapped tight around his neck. His strong little body, warm and trusting.

Sammy squeezed Joanie's hand and led him along the pavement.

'I made you miss the appointment!' Joanie felt terrible, he stopped and forced his daughter to face him. Tears were running down her face, snot dribbled onto her top lip.

'No Dad,' she sniffed loudly, 'We didn't miss it,' and then she kind of laughed or was it a cough. It took Joanie a minute to understand and then he hugged her, hugged her so tight. He knew exactly how Alfie had felt, released from a nightmare.

THE END

Acknowledgements

Many people inspire, encourage and criticise in this long process of writing and I thank every one of you who has joined me in this project. Specific thanks go to the Forest Writers' Group, Medway Mermaids and my dear friends for their feedback and support.

To my biggest critic, my greatest friend, and the father of our gorgeous children - thank you for believing in me.

Cover designed by the talented Lois Webb of Lois Design & Photography.